Victoria ... . London
She used to work in publishing and is now the author of
six novels.

THE
Silent
FOUNTAIN

VICTORIA FOX

ONE PLACE. MANY STORIES

HQ
An imprint of HarperCollins*Publishers* Ltd.
1 London Bridge Street
London SE1 9GF

This paperback edition 2017

1

First published in Great Britain by
HQ, an imprint of HarperCollins*Publishers* Ltd. 2017

ISBN: 978-1-84845-500-9

Printed and bound by
CPI Group, Croydon CR0 4YY

For Joanna Croot

PROLOGUE

Italy, Summer 2016

It was always the same dream, and every time she saw it coming. She knew where it began. A bright light, gathering pace from a sheet of dark. A lucid thought, a picture more real than any she could fathom in waking hours. Afraid to look but more afraid to resist, she stepped towards the light, arms open, weak, and she knew it was a trick, but suddenly there she was, blissful, forgetting, her lips on his forehead, his soft skin and his smell; she could capture it now, so many years later and on the other side of consciousness. His hair, the warmth of his body, they were locked away in the deepest parts inside her, still intact despite the storms that place had weathered.

She knew where it ended. He shouldn't have spoken; he shouldn't have asked.

Don't leave me. Come with me. I'm waiting.

I'll catch you. We'll be together again.

The water, still and cool and silver and quiet. Inviting. *Come with me…*

I'm waiting.

*

The woman wakes with a jolt. Her bedclothes are bunched and damp with sweat. It takes a moment to surface, the weight of water all around, pressing down. The air is tight in her lungs.

Adalina, the maid, comes in, opens the shutters and welcomes the day.

'There, signora, that's better. How did you sleep?'

Quick, efficient, the maid sets down the breakfast tray, pillows plumped, sheets pulled tight. And then the rainbow of pills, a box of medicines laid out like sweets, as if the colours make it better, make her want to take them, willingly.

The woman coughs; it is like bringing something solid up, a ball of wire.

There is blood on her handkerchief: a spray of bright dots, the worst omen. It won't be long now. She folds it into her clenched palm. Adalina pretends not to see.

'I…' The woman's mind is empty. Her tongue is swollen, a stranger to her mouth, as if she is the one who has swallowed the swamp.

'Open the window,' she says.

A flick of the wrist; the sun spills in. She can see the tips of the cypress trees, twelve fingers pointing towards the sky. She used to think he was up there, believe in useless comforts, but she doesn't any more. He isn't in the sky. He isn't in the clouds. He isn't even in the ground. He is inside her. Calling her, needing her.

Air. Warmth. Birdsong. She receives the scent of her

budding gardens, can picture the roses on the arches beginning to bloom, pink and sweet, and the lavender and chives
clustered against their high chalk walls, bursting white and
lilac. How easily the outside creeps in. How easily it bridges
that line, as fast and fluid as rain. How easily she ought to
be able to do the same, one step, one foot in front of the
other, that was all it took, that was what the doctors said.
The same as trespassing into those rooms, those wings,
that have been locked in dust for decades: unbearable now.

'*Such a beautiful house,*' they whispered, in the village, in
the city, across the oceans for all she knew. '*How tragic that
she's the way she is… Still, I suppose one can understand
it, after…you know…*'

'The girl is due at midday,' says Adalina, rattling the pills
into a plastic receptacle at the same time as pouring the tea,
as if one were no more unusual a feast than the other. 'I've
checked the airport and there are no delays. Will you be
able to greet her? She'd like to meet you, I'm sure.'

The woman glances away. She watches her pale hands
resting like a corpse's on the sheet, the bloodstained handkerchief hidden there: a terrible key to a terrible secret.
Her wrists are brittle, her nails short, and she thinks how
old they look.

When did I grow old?

She shakes her head. 'I shall stay in bed,' she says. Just like
every other day. This house has too many corners, too many
secrets, crooked with shadows and silence. 'And I shouldn't
like any disturbances. You can settle her in, I've no doubt.'

'Very well, signora.'

She swallows the pills; Adalina retreats, her face a mask of discretion. The maid has no need to voice her feelings, but it is no matter. Let them be disappointed. Let them say, '*She should make the effort. The girl's come a long way.*' Let them think what they wish. Only she understands the impossibility of it.

Besides, she doesn't want the girl here. She has never wanted her. The help knows too much, asks too many questions; they make it their business to pry.

What choice does she have? Adalina cannot manage. The castillo is enormous. They cannot do it alone.

This time, the truth is hers to keep. No one is getting to it.

She closes her eyes, drowsy, her pills beginning to take effect. On the cusp of sleep, she hears his voice again. Calling her from the water, the orange sun setting.

Come with me. I'll catch you. I'm waiting.

She falls, her arms open wide.

PART ONE

CHAPTER ONE

London
One month earlier

They say you can never love again like you love the first time. Maybe it's the heart changing shape, unable to resume its original form. Maybe it's the highs made more acute for their novelty and strangeness. Or maybe it's the soul that grows wise. It learns that the risks aren't worth taking. It learns to hurt, and in doing so protect itself.

There is consolation in this, I think, as I thread through the crowds on the Underground – commuters in rush hour, plugged into their phones; tourists checking maps and getting stuck by the ticket machines; couples kissing on the escalators – the certainty that whatever happens, wherever I end up, I will never again go through what I have been through before. We are shepherded from the Northern Line up into fresh air, where the blare and hum of the city bleeds past in myriad lights and colour. I pass a group of girls heading out for the night; they must be my age, I suppose, late twenties, but the gulf between us is yawning. I look at them as if through a window, remembering when I was like them, frivolous, carefree, naïve – how it feels to stand on the brink of the world, no mistakes made, at least none so irrevocable as mine.

One thing I love about London is the anonymity. So many people and so many lives, and it's an irony that I came here to be noticed, to be someone, yet it was at the centre of everything that I achieved invisibility. I will miss the anonymity, when they find out. I will look back on it as a cherished prize, never to be regained once lost.

I catch the bus, staring out of the window at rapidly darkening streets. Across the aisle a guy in glasses reads the *Metro*, its front page belting the headline: MURDERER HELD: COPS CATCH CAR BOOT KILLER. I shiver. Will I earn my own headline, one day soon? What will they say about me? I see my name, plain old Lucy Whittaker, in the round, friendly handwriting that as a child adorned my homework, my thank you letters, the birthday cards I wrote to my friends, then latterly the typed headers on my job applications, become all at once horrid and threatening, a name to be appalled by. People I once knew will say, 'Not *that* Lucy Whittaker? But she's far too quiet, far too shy, she wouldn't do anything like that…'

But I did, I think. I did do something like that.

We come to my stop and I step out into the evening, wrapping my coat tight as the wind picks up. I keep my head down, the plastic box clamped under my arm.

My phone beeps. For a stupid moment I think it's him, and I despise myself for how swiftly I dive into my pocket, hand trembling and hope sinking as I realise it's not. It's Bill, my flatmate. Belinda's her name, but she never liked it.

When are you home? I have wine ☺ Xxx

I'm almost there so it isn't worth replying. My walk slows. As ever when I open my messages I find my eyes drawn to his, our chains of all-night conversations, flirty, thrilling, the way my heart danced every time that screen lit up at two in the morning. I should delete them, but I can't. It's as if wiping them will erase any proof that it happened in the first place. That before the bad, there was good. There was, before. It was good. What happened, there was a reason for it…

Don't be an idiot. There is no reason. Nothing justifies what you did.

And of course he wouldn't be in touch. He'd never be in touch. It was over.

I turn on to our street. Unlocking the front door, I see Bill still hasn't got the hang of sorting through the post, so I scoop the scattered envelopes off the floor and divide them between the flats, before taking our own upstairs. Bill still hasn't got the hang of a lot of shared living, I've noticed, like replacing loo roll or putting out the recycling every once in a while. I don't mind, though. She's been my best friend since we could walk; she's been with me through it all and she's still with me now, the only one who knows the brutal truth and even then she didn't walk away, when she really could have. When she should have. That's why I don't care about the recycling.

'How was it?' She's waiting when I go in, drink poured, TV on, some rehash of a talent show, and she drains the volume when I lift my shoulders.

'As expected.' I set the box down and consider, as I had back at the office, how five years can be compressed into five minutes' packing. Some old notecards, my desk calendar, a sangria-bottle fridge magnet from Portugal sent to me by a client.

'No fanfare, then?' Bill gives me a hug and a squeeze. The squeeze brings up tears but I blink them away. '*It's your own fault*,' Natasha, his deputy, had hissed, as I'd slunk towards the exit of Calloway & Cooper, trying to ignore the stares that followed, fascinated and horrified, like traffic crawling past a pile-up.

Natasha has had it in for me from day one. My theory? She's in love with him. As his Commercial Director she was widely regarded as his second in command – but then I came along, usurping her as the closest person to him, his PA, and I know she tried to get someone else into the role because Holly in Accounts told me. Only, Natasha didn't win. I did. And I think she couldn't handle the fact that, for a second there, towards the end, before it all went wrong, it looked as if he might have loved me back. When it blew up, all her Christmases came at once. Natasha was delighted to see me go, and couldn't believe her luck at the circumstances that drove me to it.

I try a laugh but it dies in my throat. 'No fanfare,' I agree, and grab the wine and sink it in one. Bill refills me. I want to smoke a cigarette, but I'm trying to give up. *Great timing, Lucy*, I think. *Who cares now, if you live or die?* But that is melodrama, and I annoy myself for thinking it. Instead, I keep focused on the alcohol. If I keep drinking, I'll get numb, and if I get numb, I won't feel anything. I won't feel his touch on my cheek, his kiss on my mouth, my neck...

'Come on,' says Bill, with an uncertain smile. 'It's finished.'

'Is it?'

'You never have to see those people again. You never have to see *him* again.'

One thing Bill doesn't understand, and I can't find the words to explain: I *have* to see him again. Even after everything, how I should want to run as far away from him as I can, I'm as addicted to him as I was the first day. Inappropriate isn't the half of it. I read that the funeral happened this morning, in a cemetery south of the river, and I can't stop thinking of him, rigid with grief, those grey, beautiful eyes set hard on the ground, the cool drizzle settling on the shoulders of his coat, a coat I'd once warmed my hands in on a cold night on Tower Bridge, and he'd kissed the tip of my nose. How I long to put my arms around him now, tell him I am sorry and that I miss him. When what I should be feeling is guilt, burning guilt, shame and disgrace and all those things, and I do feel them, every day I do, but at the same time I can't forget the power of us. We don't belong with any of that confusion or chaos or sadness.

'...You could consider it, you know, if that's what you want.'

Bill is looking at me gently, waiting for a response.

'What? I was miles away.'

'Freddy's sister's boyfriend,' she says, presumably for the second time. 'He's just come back from Italy – that language course he went on in Florence?' Bill prompts me and to placate her I nod, even though I have no memory of this (so much over the last twelve months has dissolved to insignificance; I can't even remember who Freddy is – someone Bill works with?). 'While he was out there,' she goes on, 'he made friends with this girl who was looking after a house on weekends. Well, I say house, but it's more like a mansion. In fact Freddy said it was this giant pile, and someone famous lives there but the friend never met her, and anyway, this woman's a recluse and never goes out.' Bill slumps down on the sofa. 'Sounds intriguing, right? Like the start of a novel.' There's something behind the cushion and she reaches to retrieve it. 'Hey,' her face lights up, 'I found 50p!'

I frown. 'What's this got to do with me?'

Bill crosses her legs. 'The girl got fired and they're looking for someone to replace her. All very hush-hush… apparently they'd never advertise. The woman sounds a bit weird, sure, but how hard could it be? Dusting a few shelves, sweeping the floor…' She makes a face and I wonder if her knowledge of looking after a house extends beyond *Cinderella*. 'Then getting to sunbathe all day with some sexy Italian you've met in the city? I'd do it myself if I didn't have to go to work on Monday.'

I'm wary. 'What are you suggesting?'

'Think about it, Lucy.' Her voice softens. 'Since this thing happened, you've been desperate to get away. You haven't stopped talking about it, how you can't stay here. Look,' she says, standing, 'I want to show you something.' She steers me to the mirror in the hall. 'Tell me what you see,' she says. 'Honestly.'

It doesn't help that strewn across the wall are pictures from the days before. Nights out with Bill, holidays with friends, a bungee jump I did on my twenty-fifth birthday, after I finally broke free from home and started building a future for myself. That's how I see it, this looming punctuation mark in the story of my life, isolating the years preceding him and the lonely days after, creeping into weeks, and I was a different girl then: bright, hopeful, lucky, alive. What do I see now? A dull ache in my eyes, my skin wan with nights spent thinking and wondering and turning over what ifs, hollowness in my cheeks, and sadness, mostly sadness.

'I don't want to do this,' I say, shrugging free.

'You're not you, Lucy. This isn't you.'

'What do you expect?' I round on her, not keen on starting a fight but unable to help it. I need to shout at someone, to be angry, because I'm sick of being angry with myself. 'Her funeral was today – did you know that? And I'm supposed to leave everything behind, the mess I've made, and swan off to Italy for a holiday?'

'It's not a holiday,' says Bill, 'it's a job. And, let's face it, you need one.'

'I'll manage.'

'What about the press?' She's silenced me now. 'What about when they're blowing up your phone, or when they're smashing down the door and you're afraid to go outside? Do you think he's going to defend you, then? He doesn't care, Lucy – he doesn't give a crap about you. He'll put it all on you and then how's it going to look?'

'Don't say those things about him.'

'Fine, we won't go there. You know how I feel. My point is: this is your chance. I mean, talk about timing! You could leave it all, come back once it's settled.'

'How's it getting settled?'

'It will. Everything fades eventually.'

I snort. But my back is to her, so she can't see my face.

'What's the alternative?' Bill asks.

I think about the alternative. Fronting the world, my family, my face splashed across the nation's papers, quotes taken out of context, painted to be someone I'm not.

Would he break his silence then? Would he reach to help me; would he stand at my side? Bill's words sting: *He doesn't care. He doesn't give a crap about you.*

Her question hangs unanswered. It's all I can do to turn to my friend, the fight gone out of me. 'I'm sorry,' I say, meaning it, and she shakes her head like it doesn't matter. 'I just…' A well swims up my chest, threatening to spill over, and my voice goes funny. 'I'm just not coping.'

'I know.' Bill hugs me. 'Please promise me you'll consider it?'

In bed that night, I do. Lying awake, pretending to myself that I'm not waiting for my phone to light up, I listen to the passing hum of traffic that gradually dwindles to quiet, before, at around two, I finally fall asleep. The last thing I think of, for the first time in months, isn't him. It's a house, surrounded by cypress trees, deep in the middle of the

Italian hills. As I walk towards dreams, I'm in a tangled rose garden. Something unseen beckons me, a shadow slipping in and out of sunlight.

I come to a fountain, quiet and glittering silver.

I look in the pool at my reflection.

It takes a moment to recognise myself. For a heartbeat, it's not me I see.

CHAPTER TWO

Italy

My train arrives in Florence three weeks later. It's happened quickly – the best way, Bill tells me, to counter my usual inclination to overthink everything – and back in London I barely had time to make my decision, take a short phone interview with the owner of the house, renew my passport and get my papers sorted before Bill was yanking my suitcase from the top of the wardrobe and encouraging me to fill it.

I suspect she's right. Without getting caught up in momentum, there would have been too many opportunities to stall, to opt out, to say that something this reckless and ill thought through really wasn't me. Then again, what was? What made Lucy Whittaker? I had forgotten. I had lost her – and I wasn't going to find her hanging around in our Camden flat, jobless and trapped in the past.

'Go.' Bill held me by the shoulders when she said goodbye. 'Don't think about anything here. Be happy, Lucy. Let go. Fall in love with Italy.'

My first impressions of the city aren't great. Santa Maria Novella station is hot and crowded; I'm on the receiving end of a wave of distrustful glances when I kneel to sort through my bag because a bottle of shampoo leaked over my clothes on the flight to Pisa, and, as I'm trying to fathom the bus timetable to get me into the centre, a guy falls into me from behind, apologises – '*Mi scusi*, signora…' – and seconds later I realise fifty euros are missing from the back pocket of my jeans. But when we enter the streets that I recognise, see the bronzed, proud hood of the Duomo with its decorative Campanile, all that marble shimmering pink and white in the sunshine, I forget my plight for a moment and succumb to Florence's spell. Locals speed past on mopeds, exploding dust on cobbled streets; pizzerias open their shutters for lunch, red and white checked tablecloths being laid on a baking-hot terrace while waiters smoke idly, breaking before service; tourists wander past in sunhats, licking pink gelato from cornets; a dog drinks from a pipe on the Via del Corso. We said we'd come together, once, he and I. He wanted to bring me, promised we'd take a boat out on the Arno, eat spaghetti and drink wine; we'd stroll around the Uffizi, fall asleep in the afternoon in the Boboli Gardens. '*Forget Paris – Florence is the most romantic city in the world.*'

The bus stops and I have to move, as if physical distance might stow the memories away, as if I can leave him here in the empty seat next to mine.

It's a quick change to take the bus to Fiesole. I'm ready to get there now, see the house and meet its proprietor, fill my hours with tasks that have nothing to do with him or my life at home. My dad wanted to know what on earth I was doing. 'Italy?' he interrogated. 'Why? What about work? You left your job, Lucy? What happened?'

My sisters were the same. Sophie called from a fashion shoot to tell me I was walking away from the best role I'd ever have. Helen emailed from the luxury of her Thames-side apartment to brag about her lawyer fiancé being made partner at his firm, then saying as an afterthought that my 'mini-break' in Florence should be fun, but why wasn't I going with a boyfriend? As for Tilda, I haven't heard from her in weeks. She's scuba diving in Barbados, with a surfer named Marc. Unlike the others, Tilda didn't go to university. That was probably my biggest battle, as the eldest, trying to run my own life while taking the place of our mum: the endless months of Tilda stalemate, attempting to convince her that I knew better when maybe I didn't.

The years between us are nothing significant, the kind of gap an ordinary family wouldn't think twice about. But, for us, they were everything. They marked me as an adult before my time, and my sisters as children when really they could have been more. Helping to raise them was just what hap-pened, a natural choice – no, not a choice, a given, but never one I resented. My dad couldn't do it alone, and my sisters were too young to understand what it meant to be without their mother. It broke my heart that she would never see them pass their first exams, meet their first boyfriends, make and break those intense alliances exclusive to teenage girls, ever see them engaged or married or with children of their own – and of course much of this applied to me, although I never dwelled on that. I'm proud of the role I took on, but sometimes I wonder what might have been if I'd had the chance to have normal teenage years, be a normal girl. Then, maybe, my first love and first mistakes would have been less devastating than the ones that brought me here.

As the Tuscan countryside rolls past, winding and winding up from Florence through flame-shaped cypress trees and golden fields dotted with heat-drenched villas, I consider if what I'm doing here is exactly what I did after Mum died. Running without moving. Building a wall of practical tasks, tangible end goals, things I can get my hands dirty with, to avoid feeling… Feeling what? Just feeling.

None of my sisters knows about what happened. It's not their fault – I haven't told them. I've never told my family anything about my life, and the more personal it is, the more precious and the less willing I am to share it. Because I've always been the reliable, responsible one, and I've always looked after myself. I've never needed them for comfort or reassurance, not like they've needed me.

They'll find out soon. Everyone will.

And then what?

The question echoes in my mind, unanswered and unanswerable.

'Piazza Mino,' the driver calls, as the bus jolts to a stop. I haul my bag. There's no GPS signal so I consult the map I printed before I left, and begin walking.

The path is scorching. My muscles burn as I travel uphill, bright sun drenching the backs of my legs. I enjoy the air in my lungs, the sheen of sweat that gathers on my lip. These things make me feel alive, remind me I'm still breathing.

Thirty minutes later, I'm hot and thirsty. I've long since left the village behind and entered an ochre landscape, fields of maize and barley rolling wide on both sides, as I climb dusty lanes and take refuge in the occasional dapple of the olive groves. Silver-backed leaves offer flickering shade and I rest a while beneath them, drinking from my bottle and starting to feel faintly worried that I shall never find this place.

Then, beneath the smell of almonds and the sweet hint of blue-black grapes, a brighter scent: I spy a crop of lemon trees over the hill, running as far as the eye can see, each richly laden with yellow fruit. Squinting against the sun, I step up to the wall. On the horizon, melting to a blur in the fragrant heat, there is a building. It is enormous, its façade the colour of overripe peaches and with a sprawling, age-damaged terracotta roof. There are turrets, and the dark outline of arched windows.

I look at the map. This is it. The Castillo Barbarossa.

The road winds in a great loop around the estate and, making a decision, I topple my bag over the wall and opt for the shortcut. If the size of the castillo is anything to go by, it owns this grove and several other hectares beyond. I pick my way among the fruit trees. The lemons make me want to drink. I picture the owner of the house welcoming me with a refreshing glass, but then I remember what Bill told me. I remember what the woman was like on the phone – that strange, stilted interview, disconcertingly brief and undetailed, as if she hadn't wanted to speak to me at all and was doing so under duress. I was relieved to know she wasn't Italian, as I was planning to learn the language on the job; instead, I met a hint of an American accent, blunted by years in Europe and carrying with it the sharp plumminess of wealth and power. Afterwards, I told myself the connection had been bad. It would be better when we met in person. The follow-up message I received to tell me I'd been successful was testament that I had passed muster. There was nothing to doubt.

As I come closer to the house, dwarfed now by its massive proportions, the sun slips behind a cloud. The place looks ancient, and curiously un-lived-in, its wooden shutters bolted, its creamy walls more cracked and dilapidated than they had appeared from a distance. A sprawl of dark green creepers climbs like a skin rash up one side. I frown, checking the map again, then fold it and put it in my pocket.

Wide stone steps descend from the entrance, spilling on to a gravel shelf that rolls on to a second, then a third, then a fourth, at one time grand and verdant but now left to decades of neglect, their oval planters crumbling and full of dead, twisted things. At the helm is a fountain, long defunct, a stone shape rising from its basin that I cannot decipher from here. I feel as if I have seen the fountain before, though of course that is impossible. I emerge on to the drive and when I pass the fountain I do not want to look at it. Instead, I stop at the door and raise my hand.

CHAPTER THREE

The woman hears the door go. They have so few visitors that it shakes her with a jolt. She hasn't been sleeping but she hasn't been awake: somewhere in between.

Distant voices. One is Adalina's; the other belongs to a stranger.

The woman sits, unease racing from her toes to her stomach, where it settles. She watches the walls, listens for the telltale creaks of a board, wonders how long it will be before Adalina explains her absence. What will the maid say? How much will she elaborate? The woman has been clear about the story she wishes to tell, but whether that story gets translated, behind locked doors, in hidden corridors, in hushed voices in the old servants' quarters, is another thing. She is no fool.

It is an effort to bring her legs out of bed, but the floor feels welcome on her naked soles. Sometimes she pictures the materials of this house, the solid wood and hard marble, the cool stone, absorbing every thought and feeling her body has expelled. If she squeezes the drapes, tears will seep out, like the wringing of a cloth; if she scratches the stairways, secrets will plume and curl in a thin ribbon: grey smoke.

She goes to the door and checks it is locked. At the window, she parts the shutters and checks the approach for some clue of the girl who has entered her home. There is none. Just the distant spread of olive groves and a wide, empty sky.

Her reflection is transparent in the glass, a see-through woman. It is forgiving, this trick: it makes her appear young, no shadows, no creases – no evidence of the painful years that have scarred her face. She can seldom recall the person she was; it is like peering into someone else's life, a life that bears no relation whatsoever to one's own. It is peculiar to think of that other self. She sees the photographs and watches the movies; she reads the items they printed about her in magazines, that bright white smile, the lacquered waves of blonde hair, that slick of raspberry lipstick… She'd been beautiful. There was no denying it. She'd been charming. She'd been witty. She'd been scintillating. Everybody had wanted to know her.

How quickly the world forgot. How efficiently tragedy brought leprosy on whomever it inflicted. She ought to be grateful for her obscurity. Most days she was, but on others she thought about the woman she had given up, or who had given up on her, and the difference between her life then and her life now was so staggering, so acute and painful that it stole her breath away. That vanished her would have flung the door wide and gone to greet their guest. She would have intimidated her with beauty and standing, and enjoyed the effect those assets had. No female would have got the better of her. But that was another world. She has learned a lot since then.

The shutters close, blink-quick. One glimpse of the fountain is enough. Adalina cannot understand why she doesn't switch rooms. It might make her sleep better, chase the nightmares away. But she cannot. Instead she rests her forehead against the wall, a shiver of cold rinsing her body. She fights the bleeding cough that rattles in her throat, fights with all her might but still it breaks free, a warning, a candle slowly licking itself to extinction. A thread of sunlight filters through the shutters and on to the floor, where it pools, and at its centre a black beetle circles pointlessly, round and round, round and round, intent on its journey, going nowhere.

She'd been going somewhere, once. Years ago, in another life, a young girl with her toe on the brink... She'd had it all ahead of her, the map undrawn.

CHAPTER FOUR

Vivien, America, 1972

It was April, the hottest on record. In the little chapel in Claremont, South Carolina, Vivien Lockhart and her mother stood side by side, Vivien careful not to slouch or round her shoulders because her father told her off for that, and when he told her off she'd be better off dead. Her white cotton dress stuck uncomfortably to her waist and she longed to tear it off, run in her petticoats down the aisle and out into the fresh air where the other teenagers were leaping into rivers and sunbathing on the grass, climbing trees and kissing boys. But instead she stayed where she was, every part of her yearning for more, pretending to pray and not to be having any of these thoughts.

Eventually, the silence was broken. Both Vivien and her mother straightened, just as they did at home, where, when the man of the house opened his mouth, all else ceased to exist. He demanded to be heard, and never more than when he was talking about God. His congregation clung to his every word. Vivien thought of him at the breakfast table that morning, wiping dots of fatty milk from his moustache, flipping out the newspaper and telling them that the blacks were getting away with murder.

'And what did the Lord say when the blind man came to Him, and asked to see again?' Gilbert Lockhart paused, forehead beaded with sweat and excitement. He leaned forward, extending one talon-like finger, like a vulture peering off a tree branch. 'He said, in all His Glory and Almighty Power, *I grant you eternal sight*!'

The crowd exploded in applause. Even the prim Mrs Brigham, in her neatly pressed frock and a hat that resembled a bowl of fruit, shook with elation.

'And what did the Lord say when the deaf man came to Him?'

This time, the minister's beady eyes landed on his wife.

'*I grant you eternal hearing*,' replied Millicent obediently. The crowd went up, their shouts at fever pitch. Gilbert forced his wife and daughter to rehearse their script before every sermon. He would hit them when they slipped a word or forgot a line – stupid women, dumb women, good-for-nothing women without a sensible thought in their head. Vivien wondered if he trusted these lies. She didn't know which was worse – that he was mad enough to, or that he knew he spun a wicked fiction.

Vivien knew what was coming, though every time she wished it weren't so.

'Indeed,' cried Gilbert, '*ye shall hear for ever*!'

Vivien joined in with the appreciation, hoping that might be enough for him today, her mouth already drying at the thought of having to speak. But then he turned on her, and so too did the attention of his flock, for, in her lily-white dress with her neatly ringleted blonde curls, sixteen-year-old Vivien was the only child of the most beloved man in their community. Every word that spilled from her lips was nectar.

'And what,' said Gilbert slowly, 'did the Lord, in all his wisdom and mercy, bestow upon the man who feared for his life?'

She knew the answer. The trouble was, she didn't believe it. How could she say something she didn't believe in? Millicent jabbed an elbow into her side.

'I don't know, Daddy,' said Vivien meekly.

Gilbert was making an effort to remain calm. She could tell by the lightly throbbing vein in his temple. *Just say it. Say what he wants to hear.*

Above her father's head, Jesus stared down at her from the cross, feet nailed with a bolt, a bloody crown of thorns around his head. The crimson slash in his side grinned horrendously. His chest was concave, his ribs visible. *He died for your sins.* Words Vivien heard every day of her life, and she didn't understand them now any more than she had when they were first uttered. Vivien had never sinned – at least not in any way so serious as to condemn a man to death. Telling Mother that next door's dog had eaten the vanilla-cream muffins when in fact it had been her didn't count.

'Yes, you do,' said her father.

Say it. Or you know what will happen. Her mother did, too. Millicent was stiff as a board at her side, her head bowed. Why did she never stand up for herself – or for her daughter? Like when Vivien asked to play with the Chauncey kids one evening on their lake swing, or she was invited to Bridget Morrow's birthday party and had the idea of going dressed as her favourite movie star, or she wanted to run barefoot across the prairie after lunch and chase the wild ponies who grazed there, her mother would fold her arms and say brittly: 'Your father won't like it.' And that was the end of that.

What *did* her father like? Apart from God, she didn't know.

Did he even like her?

'He said,' Gilbert capitulated in a strained voice, its menace perceptible only to his family, '*I shall take your Fear away, and grant you everlasting Peace*!'

The pews exploded once more in adulation.

But there would be no peace for them tonight.

*

Gilbert Lockhart was a supreme minister. His disciples exalted him. Vivien watched him outside church every Sunday, shaking hands, issuing blessings, and wondered where this kind, caring man went the instant they arrived home on their porch.

Today, she didn't wait to find out. No sooner were they inside than she ran upstairs to her bedroom. Her father was mad. Crazy mad. She'd seen it in his eyes on the drive back, their pearl-grey Cadillac bouncing along the dirt track, how he glanced at her every so often in the rear-view, cold, threatening, a *Just you wait* kind of glance.

She wished she had a lock on her door. Instead, Vivien hauled a chair to lever against the knob. She pressed her ear against the wood. No footsteps yet. She focused on slowing her racing heart, safe now in her room, where no one could get her.

Downstairs, she could hear his booming voice, and her mother's answering one, frail and meek, conciliatory. The weak attempt Millicent would make at dissuading him from his wrath, but as soon as he struck her the fight would go out of her. Vivien balled her fists. She had known at church that it would end this way, but even if she could go back and do it differently, she wouldn't.

I don't believe what he says, she thought. And it wasn't that she didn't believe in God – she didn't know what she believed in, it was too early to say – but she didn't for one moment accept any kind of creed whereby a man could be a saint to his congregation, could spout about good and evil and fairness and forgiveness, then beat his wife and daughter black and blue the second they were out of sight. That wasn't a religion Vivien was interested in. She couldn't lie for him. She couldn't lie to herself.

Opening her closet, she stared at the bag inside. *Take it. Go.*

It was everything she needed, enough to get started. Over the past year, sitting cross-legged on her bed, deep in the deep, dark night, when the house was quiet and the only light left on in the town was the light of the moon, it had given Vivien solace to choose these belongings, fingering the hem of a blouse or the edge of a pin. *I will leave this place. I will get away. I will, I will…* She had almost been able to forget the stinging welts across her back, like paint slashed on a canvas, slowly drying.

Vivien knelt to the bag. In the front pocket was a crumple of bills, money she had collected from girls at school for completing their homework. What else had she to do with her time? While girls like Felicity and Bridget were taken dancing or to the pictures, Vivien was made to study every hour she wasn't in class. Once, she had completed her Math prep early and asked to be excused; Gilbert branded her a liar, smacking her and telling her she would never be clever enough to finish so quick, and she could forget about leaving the house until she had. From then on, Vivien resolved to take her classmates' work home, too. Gilbert told her she wasn't allowed a job, wasn't allowed to earn, because money gave women 'ideas'. Ironically, it was he who facilitated her first transactions, and he who had set her in the direction of escape.

From downstairs came the sound of china smashing… followed by silence. Vivien slammed the closet shut, diving to the security of her bed.

Something crackled beneath her head. Carefully, she slid her hand beneath her pillow to withdraw the folded paper, before with reverence she flattened it out. It was like looking through a window into another universe. Someone's sister in the top grade had had the poster pasted up inside her locker. Vivien envied it, seeing it in the corridor; she had never clapped eyes on anything so glamorous and stylish, a beautiful woman in a mini-skirt, and a man gazing on with a look in his eye she was too young to pinpoint but that promised something sweet and strange. Vivien had paid the girl a week's earnings, and the girl, about to chuck the wrinkled old thing away, accepted. Audrey Hepburn in *How to Steal a Million* – that impish beehive, a thousand miles from Vivien's own constructed ponytail, promised fun and naughtiness and freedom; and her daringly exposed knees, never to be seen in Claremont Town, at least not without a slap on the thigh that bloomed humiliated-red. The poster had fed her appetite for Hollywood, as had a cherished photo she'd found in last month's paper of Marlon Brando (was it possible that people that handsome existed? They certainly didn't in Claremont) and a glossy print of Sophia Loren, so exotic and dangerous.

The impulse to conceal them had been instant. There was no place in her father's world for such things. Vivien could hear Gilbert's words without needing to provoke them: Hollywood was a filthy breeding ground of vanity and wickedness. Money and fame were for sinners; they held no value in the eyes of the Lord. Anyone who followed that road was heading for disaster – that way the Devil's arms opened.

Every night before sleep, Vivien would look at her pictures, these faraway people, and remind herself that they were real, that this life *did* exist, many miles from here and who knew how many risks beyond, but it did. It did.

And maybe, one day, she would find the courage to follow.

In the meantime, it gave Vivien pleasure to keep a secret from her parents. They fundamentally outnumbered her. How she yearned for a brother or a sister! Once, she had thought there was a chance. Vivien had prayed for an ally, a friend, and her father always told her that God answered prayers – but He hadn't answered this one. There had been a time, years ago, hazy now in her memory, when Millicent had brightened, blossomed – then one night, when the stars were silver-bright, she and Gilbert had driven in a rush to the hospital. At dawn, her mother had returned pale and ruined, and Vivien had found a pair of bloody knickers in the laundry basket. Later, when she finally plucked up the mettle to ask after a possible sibling, she had been slapped hard round the cheek and the subject had never been raised again.

Thump, thump, thump... The footsteps made her wait longer than usual, but when they came they were unmistakeable. A slur to his gait: he'd been drinking, hence the delay. What was it the Bible said about abstinence? Gilbert Lockhart chose which orders to obey. More often, he made up his own. The belt was one of them.

Quickly, Vivien bundled the poster back under her pillow. She watched the door until, sure enough, the brass knob began to rattle. There was a brief quiet, then a shove, and the chair began to shake. Then there her father was, a glorious rageful vision, red-blotched and a fire in his eyes, his hands like rocks at his sides.

'You stupid girl,' he spat. 'You know what happens when you disobey and yet still you do it. You got your mother into trouble as well. Are you happy now?'

I'm not happy. I can never be happy here – with you.

But still Vivien could not bring herself to say sorry, when there was nothing to be sorry for. She sat completely still, taking her mind away to a place he couldn't touch, a place that was hers alone. She imagined she was Audrey Hepburn or Sophia Loren. Like a golden light, fantasies of a glittering Hollywood encircled her, a life in the sunshine, by the sea, with a man who loved her. The bag in the closet shone in her heart like a beacon, its promise mere feet from where her father stood but utterly invisible to him. He was the stupid one, the blind one. He always had been.

'Showing me up like that,' he seethed. 'You deserve to be punished.'

As Gilbert drew his belt from its buckle, Vivien knew what she had to do – kneel on the floor, lean over the bed, just like she was begging – and it was easier not to fight. Physically, she would always lose. She had to be cleverer than that. And as the first stroke stung the backs of her thighs, that hot, searing pain she knew so well, she prayed. Not to God, or any god her father recognised. She prayed to herself – to be strong, and to do what she must. *I will get out of here*, she vowed.

Tomorrow, I'm running away.

CHAPTER FIVE

Italy, Summer 2016

'You must be Lucy.'

I am greeted at the door by a woman, her hair scraped back in a bun, not unfriendly looking but at the same time I'm hesitant to call it a greeting because it's distinctly lacking in warmth. She introduces herself as Adalina, 'personal maid to Signora'. As she ushers me over the threshold, her manner is one of a hostess at a dinner party, obliged to show guests around but with her mind perpetually on some other distracting matter: if everyone's glasses are filled, who is mingling with whom, if the canapés are running low. I smile, deciding friendliness is the best approach.

It's impossible to hide my surprise as I step into the hall. Adalina glances at me with satisfaction. Working here every day, she must forget the impact the place has on new arrivals. For a moment, I'm stunned.

'It isn't what you expected,' says Adalina.

I gather myself. 'I'm not sure what I expected.'

There is one word for the atrium in which we are standing – *enormous* – and the word echoes in my head, those round, open vowels, just as it might around the ceiling's frescoed vaults. A shaft of sunshine spills from a circular window in the cupola, warming the flagstone floor. It's church-like, and breathtakingly beautiful – but at the same time somehow tragic, and I stare up at the painted figures on the arched ceiling, angels and terrors, weeping and clasping, a maelstrom of human experience. In an alcove by the door, a finely painted Madonna in Prayer kneels, her hands together and head lowered, in blessing or mourning for visitors, perhaps both.

Adalina rings a large, heavy bell, one that brings to mind wake-up calls in boarding school dormitories, and an old man appears at the foot of the stairs. He wears a faded blue cap and frayed dungarees, and has the weathered features of someone who spends all day outdoors. 'Take these to the east wing,' instructs Adalina. 'The Lilac Room.' She motions to my bags and dutifully the man nods. His age suggests he's less equipped to take the cases than I am, but, as I reach to help, he hauls the load on to his shoulder and I can picture him working the surrounding land, carrying hay bales or injured calves across his back as lightly as a satchel.

'That's Salvatore,' Adalina says, when he's gone. 'Don't waste your time with him.' She taps the side of her head with her finger. 'He's not right. Hasn't been for thirty years. Signora keeps him on out of pity.'

My interest must be visible, because Adalina assesses me for a moment before saying quite mildly: 'Remember, Lucy, you are here to keep this house in order. Any questions you have about the building, the village, the city, you may ask me. Any questions you have about the people who live here, keep them to yourself. Do you understand?' There's no threat in this, just curiosity, as if Adalina is getting the measure of me, as if this is an extension of that bizarre interview.

'Of course.'

'Discretion is everything,' says Adalina. 'Now, come, I will show you the rest of the house, but be aware it will take time to familiarise yourself. We have just two rules. One,' she says, gesturing to a closed door, leading, I surmise, to that part of the mansion I saw was covered in strangling vines, 'the west wing is out of bounds. Two, so is the top floor. I will show you when we get there. It will not be hard for you to obey these rules – those parts are always locked so you will know if you trespass.'

Trespass. The word conjures Biblical transgression. Sin. Forbidden fruit.

I think of him.

'This way, Lucy.'

Adalina leads me through the hall.

We embark up a grand staircase, burned-amber sandstone with an ornate banister, where we pass a series of portraits. 'Who's that?' I ask, forgetting Adalina's warning, transfixed as I am by the image of a man wearing a red blazer. One of his eyes is black and the other is green. He is standing against an emerald forest and the light of mischief dances in his stare, a light so convincingly caught on the canvas that I'm certain in the real world he is dead. Adalina watches me sideways.

'We are in the process of covering these up,' she says

carefully, and beyond I spy several further frames draped in dustsheets. Reluctant, I follow her. Off the first landing, she shows me a series of bedrooms, unused but all the same needing care. One houses two rows of wooden sleigh beds, hospital-like, intended for children.

'It was a sanatorium, last century,' explains Adalina, a little too quickly.

The first thing I'll do is air the rooms, I think, making a note of tasks I can begin in the morning. I've decided quickly that this is not a place in which I can allow myself to grow idle – partly because that road leads to him, and partly because I'm already resisting temptation to tease open drawers, to explore inside cabinets, to force rusted locks… to fling pale shrouds off portraits and read the names beneath.

The upper three floors are the same. There's an old library, books caked in powder with spines cracked, and a mezzanine looking out over the garden. I want to climb up but Adalina tells me the steps are dangerous. 'They haven't been used in years.' There are dressing rooms, reading rooms, water closets; pantries, larders and butteries; boudoirs and cabinets, storerooms, undercrofts and cellars; spaces left empty and who knows what they were once used for. The whole impression is one of a labyrinth, winding and never-ending, deliberately confusing where one space resonates almost exactly another. If I were alone, I'd already be lost.

We come to a door at the end of a corridor, and stop.

'This leads to the attic,' I say, and take the wooden handle in my palm, as if I'm testing it, as if Adalina might be wrong and it will swing open unaided. It doesn't.

'Nobody goes,' confirms Adalina, and I understand this is the out-of-bounds top floor. 'Your work extends to this point,' she says, 'and not beyond.'

I take my hand away.

'I tell you this because of the girl we let go before you,' says Adalina. 'She did not heed my advice and Signora had no choice but to dismiss her.'

'Will I meet her?' I ask, and it hits me then that no one has told me her name. *She. Her. Signora. The woman of the house...*

'Soon.' Adalina's gaze flits away. 'For now I will show you your quarters.'

*

The Lilac Room, as it turns out, isn't lilac at all. It is painted cream, with high, corniced ceilings and a four-poster bed swathed in thick red fabric. Crudely painted olive trees adorn one wall, just above the skirting, drawn, I'd wager, by a child.

Adalina wasn't lying when she described this as my quarters, for, like the rest of the Barbarossa, it's extensive. There is an adjoining bathroom, a little rundown but I'm not about to complain (I don't relish the thought of getting lost out there in the middle of the night in pursuit of the loo), a writing desk, a couple of armchairs by a handsome fireplace (a peep up the flue tells me it's long been blocked) and a mahogany wardrobe several times the size of the one Bill and I share back in London. Below the window, whose panes reach to twice my height, is an embroidered chaise.

Alone now, I can appreciate the full spread of the estate. Once upon a time the lawns would have been neatly land-scaped, descending in tiers separated by stone to a pink- and peach-strewn rose garden, but the steps now leak into each other, the walls peeling and draped in vines, the grass overgrown. Beyond the roses, light catches on glass, where an old greenhouse is bursting with plants, and etched into a screen of brick I detect the subtle outline of a door. It reminds me of a book I read as a child, or maybe Mum read it to me, because the memory is accompanied by the mellow tang of cloves, but then I realise the window is ajar and it could just as easily be the cluster of herbs whose scent swims in on the breeze. I want to step outside and go towards that door and turn the rusted key. *You will know if you trespass.*

Further still, the lemon groves and the track I came in on, and, to the west, where the sun is gently setting and flooding the sky with orange and gold, there is a pergola, majestic on its mound of grass, as perfect as the curve on a paperweight. Against the bloodshot sky, twin swifts dip and dive their dusk-hour acrobatics.

There is one thing I'm omitting from this view, the thing I came past earlier and that I'm reluctant even now to acknowledge. The fountain by the entrance, set amid a dozen cypress trees, appears gloomier now the sun has fallen. I don't know why it's such a horrible thing. The protruding shape I detected earlier is an ugly stone fish, eyes bloated, scales crusted, its open mouth gasping air, fossilised mid-leap as if cast under a terrible spell. The trees don't help either, standing guard, their spears raised – and perhaps that's all it is, the notion that there is something cosseted within that requires protection, something beyond the decaying stone and stagnant water...

I turn away and fumble in my bag for my phone. There is a message from Bill, asking if I got here OK, but I must have picked it up in the city and then gone out of signal, for there's no reception here at all. The thought of asking after Wi-Fi is anachronistic. Back at home, I'd have panicked at being off radar, but here it seems natural. Nobody except Bill knows where I am. Nobody can find me. I think of the bomb waiting to detonate in London – Natasha triumphantly handing my name to whoever's interested, whoever wants to destroy it – and it seems impossibly far away.

Only when I lie on the bed and close my eyes does it occur to me that no contact means no him. What if he needs me? What if he has to get in touch, and can't? I reassure myself with a plan to get connected in the city: soon, soon.

In the meantime, there is a pinch of pleasure in the thought, however unlikely, that he might be trying to reach me, that he might be the one seeking me out, instead of my repeatedly glimpsing a screen that gives me nothing. For once, I'm unavailable.

I'm gone. Nobody can catch me.

In minutes, I'm asleep.

CHAPTER SIX

'Vivien?'

The maid knocks gently then steps inside. It's rare that Adalina addresses her by her name, and Vivien knows it is because they are about to share a confidence.

'What is she like?' Vivien asks. It isn't what she really wants to ask, but she cannot ask that yet. It will seem too desperate, too close to the bone.

'As we expected,' says Adalina. 'She'll be fine.'

'You told her…?' Vivien glances away. 'How much did you tell her?'

'I told her nothing.'

Vivien exhales. Adalina lays down a supper tray, soup and crackers, a bunch of grapes the colour of bruises, but she has no appetite.

'Are you all right, signora?'

'I saw her from the window,' Vivien says, daring to meet Adalina's eye, wanting to know if the maid has seen it too. But Adalina gives nothing away.

'Do you think she looks like…?' Vivien swallows. She cannot say the name. 'I saw her and I thought what a remarkable resemblance she has to—'

'She's dark. That is where it ends,' says Adalina.

'But her height, her build, everything – it's everything.'

'Not at all.' Adalina protests, unwilling to give her charge any scope for indulgence. Vivien notices this, and seizes it as proof of her agreement.

'You can't deny it.'

'I can. Up close she is entirely different.'

'It was like seeing *her* again.' The 'her' is spat like venom. It's been years – *years* – but the poison remains. She cannot get her mouth around it, the taste bitter, too horrible, too immediate, all that hate multiplying inside her with nowhere to go.

'Then you must meet the girl,' says Adalina. 'I will arrange it.'

'I cannot have her living here if you are wrong.' Vivien is trembling, her voice skittish, her heart leaden. *Get control of yourself*, she thinks, aware the resemblance the girl has is impossible, a trick of her mind, but the uncanny is all around, in the windows, in the water, in shadows and reflections, and she would not put it past the house to test her in this way. Vivien has heard the noises late at night, the creak of a floorboard, the slam of a door, the howl of the wind so like a woman's scream…

'You must eat,' says Adalina. The pills come out, the tray set down.

Without warning, Vivien takes her hand. Adalina is surprised.

'It isn't her, is it?' she asks in a strange, disembodied voice.

'Of course not, signora.'

'That would be impossible.'

'Absolutely.'

'She wouldn't come back for me, would she?'

Adalina is frightened now.

'Never,' she rasps.

'She wouldn't dare.'

'No, she wouldn't dare.'

Vivien releases her grasp. Adalina fills a water glass, as if nothing has happened. Sometimes, the maid stays to help with supper. Tonight, she leaves.

CHAPTER SEVEN

Vivien, Los Angeles, 1976

In years to come, Vivien Lockhart would look back on the night that her world began: on the point at which her journey was set. Four years since she had run from home, four years of surviving on luck and a dime – until the stars joined up their fatal alignment and the wide, brave future gathered her to its beating chest.

In a velvet-swathed dressing room at Boudoir Lalique, Vivien perfected a final swipe of mascara before sitting back to appraise her reflection. Wide blue eyes lined with dashing kohl; full, crimson lips; and her sleek blonde hair tied beneath a majestic scarlet turban, studded with rubies. Each time the vision was surprising – this person was a girl and a woman, herself and a stranger. Jewels glimmered at her forehead, and the neck of her opulent Biba robe, reminiscent of the one Farrah Fawcett wore to that premiere on Broadway at the weekend, made her appear like the head of a powerful sphinx. At Boudoir Lalique, she was no longer Vivien. She was Cleopatra.

'You're up, hon,' said one of the girls, wafting into the

dressing room in a mist of knockoff Chanel. 'There's a new guy out there tonight – he's smokin'.'

Vivien stood, swallowed a knot of fear that she would be assigned this fresh patron. It made no difference if he was handsome or not: she was still at his mercy.

'Thanks,' she answered, watching as the girl grabbed her bag and hooked up with the others at the door, giggling and shrugging their coats on. Vivien had this idea of friendship among women, a caramel-hued roller-skate ride through buttered popcorn and candyfloss and hairspray, and they had asked her before to join them, tried to include her, but she always said no. She was scared of them, their breezy confidence and happy conversation, their cola bubblegum and easy swear words, so far removed from the dark, punitive annals of her own past. She'd love to have a friendship like that but she didn't know how. She didn't know how to dismantle the fortress she'd built, knowing its every limit and parameter, instructing herself to stay inside.

Vivien took a breath and stepped through the swathe of fabric on to the dance floor. The heat hit her instantly: of bodies, of liquor, of thick, glowing cigars… of wealth. All eyes were on her as she moved across the room, as lithe as a panther.

The Lalique wasn't any old discotheque. Whereas others in town were as light as Cinzano, this was as syrupy and dark as the throat-searing brandy it served in diamond-cut tumblers behind the bar. Lavish, smoky, sexy, and strictly private, it oozed decadence. Men clustered in leather booths, some lone wolves, some prowling in packs. Vivien could smell the dollar bills that came through the doors, and wished each night that the cash would whisk her away, an ocean of it on which to cast her sailboat, taking her to the life she'd always longed for. Until then, she would close her heart and soul to the men who took her backstage, just as she had closed her heart and soul to her father. What choice did she have? She was never going back.

'Hey, baby...'

'Lookin' good, honey...'

'You wanna come sit with me for a while?'

Murmurs of approval and invitation followed her through the sultry space. Chin up, smile on, Vivien poured cognac and champagne and absinthe, prepared perfect squares of glass with their neat lines of cocaine, and sat with her company for the night, a group of Japanese business-men. Quickly she ascertained the one in charge, the one who would have paid, and made sure to compliment him on his suit, his tie, his expensive cologne. The drunker the group became, the more freely their hands roamed. Vivien remembered the first time a client had touched her leg: the feel of his thumbs, pressing, pressing, first on her knee and then on her thigh, higher and higher still, hot and dry. She had frozen, but the club kept turning, the drinks kept flowing, and this was how it was.

'Is there somewhere we can go?' the chief asked now, his eyes red-rimmed. Vivien judged he had twenty minutes before he passed out.

When she had arrived at the Lalique two years ago, wide-eyed and hopeful, she had taken the job of hostess, welcoming parties, pouring drinks, looking pretty, draped against the glass-topped bar smoking one of her impossibly long silver-tipped cigarettes while David Bowie's 'Fame' twanged its bass – at least that was how Mickey, the owner, had sold it. For a while she had enjoyed being Cleopatra, her alter ego, relishing the chance to run from the child she'd been in Claremont, spritzing perfumes, donning costumes, collecting her tips in a plush satin pouch at the end of the night. But then her job description changed. It started with the odd grope, the occasional leer, and then it was no longer enough to laugh at their jokes or let them squeeze her hand. 'You gotta do what you gotta do,' said Mickey, which was less advice than instruction. Each time one of her clients led her into the back, she drove out her dread and did her duty. She blocked out the rest.

'Sure,' Vivien told him. 'Another drink first?'

'You're gonna lead me astray…' he slurred.

She was about to respond when a figure caught her eye. A man was standing in her peripheral, alone and all the more brazen for that solitude.

His appearance threw her. Conversation dried on her lips – but luckily her companion was too trashed to notice. The stranger was handsome, fair, tall, but it was the way he was looking at her that stole her breath. *There's a new guy out there tonight – he's smokin'*. This man radiated power. He radiated money.

Vivien tried to look away, but each time she was pulled back. He was magnetic. She grappled for words, offered liquor to her clients and realised as she did that her hands were shaking, and still the man neither moved nor averted his gaze. He had to be the only sober one in the room. She felt his scrutiny scorch into her, but not in the usual lecherous way. He was admiring her; he was assessing her. Vivien sensed his interest penetrate every part, making her skin prickle, not unpleasurably.

Finally, she forced out, 'Please excuse me. I'm not feeling well.'

She stood, and nearly brought the table down with her. A flurry of sloshed jeering; a hand reached out to steady her, or grab her, she wasn't sure which, and she turned and fled. She had never bailed on a client before: it was forbidden. But she could sit beneath the burn of this stranger's sun no longer. It made her vulnerable, as if he knew her; as if he could see right through her to the broken girl beneath…

Back in the dressing room, Vivien caught her breath. Moments passed.

Mickey yanked open the curtain.

'What's goin' on?' he demanded. 'You've got a five-grand table tonight.'

'I know, I'm sorry. I – I came over funny. Thought I was going to faint.'

'Well, get yourself together.' Mickey clamped down on a bitter-smelling cigar. He checked behind him. 'Anyhow, don't worry, I got Sandy on it.'

'Sandy's taken my table?' This was unheard of.

'Yeah.'

'Why?'

Mickey drew the cigar out of his mouth.

'Someone wants to meet you,' he said.

Vivien knew whom he meant.

'Who is he?' she whispered.

'You mean you don't know?'

She shook her head.

Mickey watched her a moment, then said: 'Come with me.'

He took her elbow and steered her through the dimly lit passage to his office. Of course the stranger and Mickey had spoken: Mickey took the measure of every man who stepped into the Lalique. But what did he want with her? For some reason, she felt sure it wasn't the usual request. The man had been too... expensive looking, to just want a roll in the back without so much as knowing her name.

'Tell me who he is,' urged Vivien. Mickey said nothing, just gestured for her to keep up. 'Aren't you going to answer me?' she pressed.

'Here.' Mickey stopped. Gently, he lifted the fabric from her head and let her golden hair tumble free. He drew a strand of it from in front of her blue eyes.

'Always knew you were too good for this place,' he said.

Vivien parted her lips to respond, and then, suddenly, there the man was.

He was standing outside Mickey's door.

'You wanna know who he is?' said Mickey. 'Why'n't you ask him yourself?'

CHAPTER EIGHT

Italy, Summer 2016

I'm up early on my first morning. The house is quiet and for a moment I forget where I am, before I see my bags heaped at the end of the bed, still full. I'd meant to unpack before falling asleep, but supper must have finished me off – a glance at my panda eyes reminds me I forgot to wash my face. I think of my predecessor, Bill's friend's friend, the student whose inquisitiveness got the better of her, and decide that if I'm going to avoid the same fate I'll need to start as I mean to go on. Ten minutes later, I've sorted the shampoo explosion I'd noticed at Pisa, the rest of my clothes are neatly hung and folded, and my belongings are arranged in the Lilac Room.

I shower before heading downstairs. The shrouded portraits, though blinded, watch me as I pass. I remember the man I saw, covered now. Who is he?

The hall is empty. I cannot hear a thing, no voices and no movement, just birdsong. In the scullery, breakfast is left out like a still life: a loaf of bread, a pat of butter, a jug of orange juice and a bunch of grapes. Adalina told me that she alone prepares the meals – 'Signora prefers it that way' – and that I must never interfere with cooking. This seems unusual, given that Adalina's description of my job extends to tending every other aspect of the Barbarossa, from sweeping fire grates to dusting shelves to going to the foot of the drive each morning to collect fresh milk. Perhaps the woman of the house is fussy. Perhaps she can eat only certain things.

I mull this over while I devour the food, not half so picky myself. The grapes burst on my tongue and the butter soaks into the bread crusts, warmed by the morning heat. From a narrow window I can see out to the courtyard, and, as I take my first sip of coffee, I'm surprised to catch a figure resting a bucket on the lip of that ugly fountain. I can only assume it to be the maid. The figure appears to steady herself, before lifting the vessel and emptying it into the well. For a moment the scullery feels weirdly hostile, as if I'm witnessing something I shouldn't, something clandestine, and am myself being witnessed doing it. The bucket goes to the ground and another comes up in its place, is emptied and then replaced by a third, then a fourth, then a fifth. I consider the heat of the Tuscan sun and how the pool would dry up otherwise – but why sustain it when its function is long gone? The fish hasn't sung in decades.

If I listen hard I can hear the slosh of the water as it meets the stone, an urgent, vital connection, as if the liquid keeps the fountain alive, heart beating and lungs filled – like feeding something feral in a dark pit. The coffee tastes suddenly sour.

I look away, my appetite diminished. When I glance up again, the courtyard is empty.

*

Afterwards, I begin my commission for the morning – the ballroom. It hasn't been used in decades and I have to force the door, which swings on rusted hinges. Peach drapery adorns the high windows, whose panes are adrift with cobwebs. I climb the stepladder and watch a thin spider pick its way across gossamer threads, before casting it away with a cloth. I sneeze, the dust in my nostrils.

The fireplace, a once-majestic stone cavern occupying the length of one wall, is equally clogged. Soon the dust is in my hair, and when I wipe my sleeve across my brow it comes away caked in grainy damp. Sunlight fires the room, its huge windows acting like a hothouse, making me sweat. I'm feeling light-headed when:

'Lucy.'

I turn. There is nobody there.

I daren't move for a moment, the room charged with some still, waiting entity. Silence comes back at me, no longer calm but malevolent, the empty room, the patient shafts of sunshine climbing across the floor, and the door, firmly closed, daring me to believe in the impossible. There is nobody there. Nobody here.

But I can hear her voice as clear as a bell. She'd said my name, then, too.

Lucy...

And I had turned to face her on that train platform, at once a stranger and a woman I knew better than my own reflection, for I had thought of her so many times and been told so much about her. Commuters, clueless on their slogs to work, had surrounded our tragic island, plugged into their tablets, swigging coffee to get through a hangover. It was different for us. We were separate. And I will never forget the look in her eyes, right before she did it. It wasn't anger, though it should have been. It was resignation. Disappointment. As if in saying my name she might have proved herself wrong: I wasn't Lucy, I hadn't done those things; it had been in her head all along.

Lucy.

A kind voice, soft, inquisitive – not what I had expected.

I return to the fire grate, sinister now, its black hood as hard and cool as the rail tracks beneath our feet… *Stand behind the yellow line.* I had been conscious of a stupid thing, not what I should have been paying attention to at all: the fact I had just been with him. We had spent all night together, all morning, and his smell was on me.

The worst part was that I didn't stay. In the turmoil that followed, I'd fled the scene, breathless, the world truncated to a series of shuddering camera frames, galloping at me, disorienting, fundamentally changed. I'd emerged into the day and thrown up on the pavement. Then I'd run. Like the coward I was, I'd run…

The sound of the castillo's bell pulls me from my thoughts. Scrambling up, desperate to get out of the stifling room, I cross the floor. I didn't really hear her voice. It was my imagination. I don't believe in ghosts. Mum has never come back to me, so why should anyone else?

At the door, a man is holding two large boxes. He gets me to sign for them and then seems in a hurry to leave, rushing back to his van and disappearing down the drive in a cloud of chalk. I frown, examining the weight in my hands, and nudge the door shut with my foot. The boxes are plastic, sealed tight with lots of brown tape, and the contents labels are written in Italian. I see numbers and percentages, a warning in bold red type, and when I gently shake them, a force of habit born of a little girl's fascination with her mother's belongings (those delicately wrapped gifts my dad presented her with each Valentine's Day; the soft leather purses she kept in her wardrobe, filled with mysterious things; the make-up bags she chided me gently not to play with, heavy with bottles and tubes that knocked against each other like boiled sweets), I hear a metallic rattle. The address is headed:

Sig.ra V Lockhart

I'm trying to figure out from where I know that name – some dim recess tosses it up as recognisable, Vanessa, Virginia, it's on the tip of my tongue – when Adalina materialises behind me, relieves me of the boxes and says, 'You must never answer the door. Only I answer.'

I'm about to reply, to object that I hadn't known this because nobody told me, when, armed with the shadowy delivery, Adalina turns on her heel and vanishes upstairs to return to her charge, and I am left alone once more.

*

I don't mean to go near the attic that afternoon, but I'm
on such a roll come five o'clock that I decide to venture
to that furthest corridor before calling it a day. From the
windows, I can see right across to Florence. The Duomo
shimmers against a golden sky, and the blue-green Arno
snakes like a ribbon through the city. I can't wait to be
there: it'll be like re-entering the world after weeks orbiting
outer space.

I'll start by getting online.

I tell myself it's to contact Bill, to let my family know I'm
well, but really I'm thinking of him, each hour that passes
another hour in which he might have decided it's been long
enough, that we need each other, that he does still want
me in his life. Then, buoyed by hope, I'll have a sorbet in
the Piazza della Signoria before strolling across the Ponte
Vecchio and browsing the stalls. I'll buy Bill a present, and
my dad too, and then only when it's late will I get the bus
back to Fiesole and find my way up to the Barbarossa. Every
day off will be like this, and, for the first time in a while,
I feel as if I'm in the right place. As if maybe, just maybe,
things might turn out OK.

The first thump takes me by surprise. But I'm not quite
describing it right – it's less a thump than a… *drag*. Like a
heavy chair moving across floorboards.

It startles me and I sit back on my heels, listening, alert
as a cat, my ears pricked to the slightest sound. The castillo
is full of weird snaps and creaks, a maze of emptiness and

silence compounding the effect, and I remind myself that just hours before, in the ballroom, I tricked myself into believing someone had said my name.

But then I hear it again. The same noise, louder this time. It is coming from above, and when I look to the ceiling, a patina of cracked, mottled stone, I hear it for a third time and am able to position it exactly. There is somebody in the attic.

I check behind, half expecting Adalina to haul me up and away, accusing me of breaking another law, but the corridor is deserted. I hear a bee outside the window, the pitch of its buzz lowering each time its body rushes against the pane. Slowly, I turn to the door at the end of the hall. *Nobody goes. Your work extends to this point and not beyond.* But Adalina didn't say anything about other people being up there. If someone already is, won't I be doing a service in exposing the contravention?

I advance. The door sits low, with a tapered hood, like those odd little accesses you see in churches. It strikes me that whoever once used this must have been short in stature, and I remember the abandoned sleigh beds. I press my ear to it, and listen.

No more thumps, no more drags, but I know what I heard. I push the handle, a coarse, rusted loop that leaves an orange stain on my palm. Puzzled at how something so feeble looking can be so robust, I resolve to apply my whole weight to the door, turning the lever as I do. It gives not an inch – except for a sensation of absolute cold on the shoulder touching the wood. I shake the lock, afraid to make too much noise, but I know that it won't surrender. Never mind Adalina: this is its own gatekeeper.

Crouching, I notice a coppery tear-shaped flap. With some persuasion it shifts, exposing the keyhole. I press my eye to it. The cool hits me like a fan, and an old, musty smell emerges. The darkness is absolute. Whoever is up there is in the dark.

In the dark. In the quiet. Waiting.

I wait, too.

I'm reluctant to call out, because I don't want Adalina to hear. It isn't anything to do with the whistling anxiety that I might get a response, an anxiety that gathers pace by the second like a breeze on a moonlit lake; it's that, contrary to all my logical sense, I'd be summoning someone or something I really don't want anything to do with. I know that dragging sound was not friendly.

I replace the flap and return down the hall.

By the time I reach the stairs, I am running.

CHAPTER NINE

Vivien, Los Angeles, 1976

His name was Jonny Laing, the man with the Midas touch. He introduced himself as if she ought to recognise the name, and Vivien was embarrassed that she didn't.

'It's OK,' Jonny said, with a cagey sort of delight, like a fox eyeing a chicken coop. 'I wouldn't expect you to. It's one of the many things I like about you, Vivien. You're... how should I put it? Uninitiated. Innocent. Unspoiled.'

Vivien had never considered herself to be unspoiled; her father had done a pretty good job of putting paid to that. But she liked that Jonny imagined her to be so, because he was smart and successful, and if he thought there was a scrap of purity left in her then maybe he was right. As she listened to him explain what he did for a living – 'I'm in the movie business, and I know a star when I see one' – all she could think was: *I'm dreaming. This is a dream.* Here was the answer to her desperate prayers, bam! Straight into her life, just like that. It couldn't be happening, but it was.

He took her for supper at a restaurant downtown, and told her his plans: this project, that project, she would be perfect for them all. Was it really so easy? Or would she wake in a few hours' time and realise she had imagined the whole thing? Vivien found herself confiding in him about where she had come from, about Gilbert, the thrashings, the escape, all the demons from her past and the parts that made her vulnerable, ugly. She braced herself for his criticism, to be told to pack up and go back to Claremont like a good girl. But Jonny didn't treat her like a girl, he treated her like a queen. He was kind and generous and exciting. And, contrary to Vivien's expectations as she stumbled home on a cloud, he was true to his word.

The next morning, a sleek motorcar arrived outside her crummy apartment. For the second time in her life, Vivien bundled her belongings into a canvas shell and prepared to embark into the wild unknown. Hollywood: the ultimate prize.

The following weeks and months were a storm. Vivien barely had time to think. If Jonny hadn't reminded her to eat and sleep, if for nothing else than to preserve her 'extraordinary' beauty, she would have forgotten that too. Every day was a hurricane of photo shoots, magazine interviews, power brunches, castings and read-throughs. Jonny didn't allow her a moment's rest. The beachside condo he set up for her was exquisite, but she never spent any time there. She dined in the finest bistros, she had a wardrobe from the most exclusive stores, she was thrown in with the most influential movers and shakers in the business and she drank it up like nectar from heaven. Not any heaven Gilbert Lockhart would recognise, of course. If her father could see her now – his chaste, belt-lashed little girl – if he could see the things she had done to get here… *To hell with you, Daddy*, she thought. *I'm through*.

It wasn't long before Vivien Lockhart's name was on the lips of every major player in Hollywood. Her days at Boudoir Lalique seemed another world, the long, high dive board from which she feared she would never spring. Jonny was her saviour: he had flung her into the blue. She couldn't thank him enough, not just for the promise of her career but also for restoring her faith in friendship. She had all but given up trusting anyone and then he came along, the friend she had yearned for, showing her that good could affect a life as tangibly and irreversibly as bad. There didn't have to be a catch. Jonny had seen a light in her and fanned the flame. Over time, her soul began to lighten and heal. She reached out, full of hope.

Vivien savoured every moment of her rebirth with a grateful and open heart. She passed through LA awe-struck at her luck, marvelling at the glass buildings where Jonny and his partners forged fortunes on a lunch break. LAING FAIRMOUNT PICTURES, his sign read. She thanked every star in the galaxy for its existence.

And then Jonny had news.

'Burt Sanderson's asked to see you,' he told her, arriving at her condo unannounced one evening. It was unlike Jonny to be flustered – but Burt was major league. If Vivien worked with the famous director, she was going stellar. Jonny knew it; she knew it. They had worked hard for this, getting all the pieces into place. Jonny likened it to engineering a racing car: you built it, you honed it, you polished it – then you just needed the track on which to see it fly. Burt Sanderson was that track.

'Tomorrow,' he said, taking her hand. 'I'll see you there.'

*

Despite her nerves running off the scale, in the end it wasn't so different to her gigs at the Lalique. Fixing her smile, saying the right thing, working to elicit this reaction or that. Burt and his panel were inscrutable to begin with, but then, as Vivien warmed to the part, channelling her character, a girl from the slums who makes it big, it occurred to her that she wasn't acting at all. She didn't need to. She *was* this person.

When Burt called the next day, Vivien was beside herself. Sitting in Jonny's office in a sun-drenched window, she watched him replace the receiver.

Jonny met her eye. He looked at her strangely, his expression indecipherable.

She didn't move from her chair. 'I didn't get it, did I?' she said in a small voice. Never mind, it had been a long shot. It would probably go to Ava, or Faye. They deserved it. She was just the new kid on the block; she couldn't expect to just—

'He wants you,' said Jonny.

'What?'

Jonny's face broke into a grin.

'Honey, he wants you. We got it. You got it.'

Vivien blinked. A buzzing sound galloped through her ears.

'Do you hear me, Vivien?' Jonny held his arms out. 'The part's yours! Burt frickin' Sanderson – do you understand what this means?'

Rapture struck. Vivien's hands flew to her face. She leaped up and ran into his waiting embrace. 'Oh, Jonny!' she cried. 'Oh, thank you, thank you!'

He held her, kissing her hair over and over. 'You did it, Viv,' he murmured.

'I can't believe it!' Tears swam to her eyes, happy tears, elated tears, but she contained them because she was an actress now and she had to start as she meant to go on. Besides, she had nothing to cry about any longer. Jonny had rescued her: she need never cry again. He had transformed her life, this wonderful, brilliant man. She could kiss him! For a crazy second she thought she would.

Then, without warning, Jonny beat her to it. Before Vivien could protest, his lips were on hers. But instead of playful brevity, that impulsive kiss she had considered bestowing on him a moment ago, he lingered. His mouth pressed too hard.

She pulled away, laughing uneasily.

'It's swell, Jonny,' she said. 'I'm thrilled.'

He grabbed her again; his breath was hot in her face.

'How thrilled?' he rasped.

Vivien put her hands on his chest and pushed. He was as excited as she was, that was all. This was a huge deal for both of them.

He kissed her again. This time she did break free.

'I have to go,' she said, spots of confusion bursting

behind her eyes. The balance that had sustained their companionship was suddenly off. She felt indebted to Jonny, his advance an open palm waiting for payment – and her pockets were empty.

'Where?' Jonny demanded.

'I have a lunch date,' she said meekly. It was a lie, the quickest one she could come up with. It occurred to her that she had never lied to Jonny before.

'With who?'

'A friend.'

'Can't you call it off?' For the first time, a glint of menace appeared in Jonny's eye, a petulance. She took a step back. 'We did this together, Vivien,' he said. 'We secured Burt Sanderson together. We should celebrate… together. You and me.'

'Like I said, I have plans.'

The next part happened too quickly to know what came first. Vivien opened the door, but in the same movement it was slammed shut. Jonny came at her, turned her against the wall, and then his hands were hitching up her skirt.

All at once Vivien realised she'd been fooled. This had always been the price – just like at Boudoir Lalique. There was no such thing as a no-strings contract.

'C'mon, baby,' he murmured, 'you know you owe me.'

Vivien fought back with all her might but it was impossible; he was too strong. 'Get off me!' she screamed. 'Get your hands off me!'

'You want it too. You've wanted it from day one.'

'Jonny, please—'

'This is what you're good at, isn't it, baby?' His greedy hands crept round to her breasts. *No*, she prayed, *no, no, no. This can't happen. I won't let it.*

'All those men you went with at the club...' Oh, God, she had told him too much, trusted him with her darkest secrets. *How could I have been so stupid?* 'Just a sweet whore at heart, aren't you? So, come on, it's my turn now; I've earned my right. I've waited long enough. I've paid you more than any of those jocks...'

It took all Vivien's might to free her arms, but once she had, the rest followed. Throwing her weight against him, she scraped her heel down his shin, at the same time digging her elbow high into his diaphragm, winding him. Jonny staggered back. Vivien grabbed his shoulders and brought her knee into his groin, making him howl.

Every part of her shook – with fear, with adrenalin, with victory. She didn't know where her strength came from. Perhaps it had always been there, buried inside.

'Never touch me again,' she said, her voice quavering. She wanted to weep – with shock, with disappointment, with sadness at the innocence she had lost, the friendship she had watched blow to ash before her eyes. Would she ever meet a man who would care for her and put her first? Would she ever know love without pain, without expectation, without betrayal? Would she ever be able to trust a living soul without that nagging voice telling her: *You're safer on your own*? Would she always be frightened, lonely, damaged... the eternal outsider? Something hardened within Vivien in that moment: something liquid turned to stone. 'I owe you nothing, Jonny,' she said, 'do you get it? You found me. You offered me this. It never came at a price.'

She straightened her clothes and willed her trembling legs to carry her into the corridor. As she stepped out, she heard his voice ring out from behind.

'I'll get you for this,' Jonny choked. 'You're nothing without me, Vivien. I've given you everything – and rest assured I can take it away just as fast.'

I'd like to see you try, Vivien thought, lifting her chin.

I'm stronger by myself. I'm stronger than you know.

CHAPTER TEN

Italy, Summer 2016

We speak, finally, on the Friday. Adalina tells me: 'Signora isn't able to see visitors; she's unwell. But if you go to her room at midday she will talk with you.'

I'm curious as to how this encounter will unfold, and when I reach Signora's room at the appointed time it's all I can do not to laugh, because Adalina wasn't joking. There is a chair parked outside the woman's door, and the door itself has been left ajar. A shaft of light seeps from the mysterious bedroom, but nothing else is visible. Gingerly, I sit. Nothing happens. Finally, I venture: 'Hello?'

The space is so quiet that to move the chair would be startling. Instead I adjust my position, so that another inch of the room creeps into view. Rugs. Drapes. Heavy furnishings, gold and black... There is the edge of a mirror, in which I think I glimpse a fraction of the woman's reflection. The back of her head, her shoulders, perhaps. It's like turning an abstract picture, trying to make sense and finding none. I realise I am desperate to see her. I imagine her as tall, her pale hair secured at the nape of the neck with a velvet clasp, her shoulders broad and her jaw firm, still crisply defined despite her years, her lips full and wide… I draw her not as pretty but as handsome: someone whose face, having seen it once, you will not forget.

When she speaks, I recognise immediately the person I talked to on the phone.

'Lucy.' Her voice is distinctive, deeply mellow, like plums in autumn on the verge of rot. It comes from a place much closer to me than the mirror would imply, and a chill skitters down my spine at the prospect that she is closer to me than I think, and that she isn't the person in the bed, if indeed that is a person.

She says my name as if it tastes bad, her tongue splicing it in two.

'Yes,' I answer.

'You've settled in?' It isn't a polite enquiry; there is no warmth or friendliness, more an impatience. I hold my hands together in my lap.

'Yes,' I say again, feeling like a schoolgirl outside the headmistress's office, waiting for punishment. Only in this case, I have no idea what I've done wrong.

'We wished to avoid hiring,' the voice says shortly, rudely. 'But the house won't look after itself – and I can't very well expect Adalina to do it.'

I'm unsure how to react. 'I'm glad you decided to,' I say, and before I can stop myself I'm babbling, eager to please and it emerges as over-share. 'It came at the right time for me. I was looking to get out of London. This was too good to pass up.'

Stop talking. She doesn't need to know.

'Oh?' comes the voice.

'Family stuff,' I say quickly. It sounds weak, a quick step back – and, though it's impossible, the silence that follows is so loaded that I start to wonder if by some miracle she knows my story. What would she think of the crime I committed?

'As you're aware, I rarely take company,' she says, and I'm relieved to move off subject. 'You might view this job as an escape clause, or a frivolous holiday, but this house is my home and I will protect it with all that I have. If it's equal to you, I would ask that we stay out of each other's way wherever possible.'

My mouth is dry. Relief turns to surprise, then shock. 'Of course,' I say.

'You may go now.'

The end of the meeting, if it can be called that. I'm debating the correctness of saying goodbye, surely too formal but then it's hardly as if she's set any other tone, before the door in front of me closes abruptly, a swift sharp snap then silence.

*

That evening I take the bus into town. Florence is coming to life on the cusp of night as only a city can: twinkling lights dance on the river, couples stroll through cobbled piazzas, the scent of burned-crust pizza fills the air along with a heady tang of wine.

I turn on my phone. It seems to take an age for it to switch network, find a signal and connect to 3G. I wait. The moments pass. Each time a message beeps in from my new server, my heart leaps then dives. There's one from Bill, another from our landlord. Tilda WhatsApps from a Barbadian beach, wishing me luck, lots of smiling emojis. To my shame I'm not waiting for them. I wait for anything from him, an email, a text, a missed call, anything. I blink back tears: of course there's none. What would Tilda think of her reliable big sister, the person who put her to bed and cooked her tea and waited up each night she went out, being responsible for…?

I can't say it. I can't think it.

Shoving my phone back in my bag, I head to the library, so focused on the distraction it will give me that I almost trip up the steps to the entrance.

It's open late, quiet, studious, deliciously private. As I settle into a booth with a stack of archives, I turn my phone to vibrate, and read Bill's message again:

Spill, then – who is she? What's she like? Xxx

Today's encounter with Signora has set me on edge. *Horrible*, I start to write back, *horrible and rude and weird. Why did I come here? Why did I let you convince me?* But I delete the draft. I don't want to admit the truth to Bill – that the woman I spoke to is hard and cold, cruel and dismissive, but that for some insane reason I'm drawn to her, fascinated by her, and I feel connected to her in a way I can't express. I need to know who she is. I need to know why she's cut herself off.

Just like me.

I've become protective of my quarantine. Connecting to the outside world makes me panic that I'm about to learn drastic news. It'll be Bill, or one of my sisters, or my dad, or some random on Facebook I haven't spoken to in years, emailing me about the exposure at home. I can see it now; rehearsed the way it might unfold so many times. *Lucy, what the hell? Is it true?* Or perhaps, simply: *It's started.*

As ever, temptation lingers to check the websites, Google his name, his wife's name, see if anything new has cropped up, but I have to trust that Bill would tell me first. She doesn't reference it, doesn't even mention it, and I know she's being kind. She's trying to help me forget. How could I forget? I can't. I decide to click the phone off altogether, instructing myself instead to the task at hand. In this, at least, I can distance myself from my plight. However challenging I've found the Barbarossa so far, it's at least proved a change of scene – and however obstructive its owner, she's given me a diversion. Something happened at that house. I sense it in the walls, the shadows and the dark. From Adalina's secrecy and Salvatore's madness. From the voice behind the door; from the noises in the attic, the cold and the quiet…

Something happened.

I begin by looking up the castillo on the library's bank of computers. A quick search reveals nothing of its possessor, but the local records surrender more. It's all in Italian so I run a quick translate – the rendition isn't perfect, but it's enough, and soon the story is forming. I scan the text, tracing reports back to the earliest point I can find: 1980, when she moved here from America. Her arrival had caused a stir.

Tuscany welcomes home its son, renowned doctor Giovanni 'Gio' Moretti, and his wife, Hollywood actress Vivien Lockhart, to the Castillo Barbarossa in Fiesole. The pair married last month in a romantic ceremony in Los Angeles and now return to Italy, according to their spokesperson, 'to begin family life in a more peaceful setting'. Moretti will be engaged in a top-secret research project, for which he was privately selected, while Lockhart is said to be taking a break from her movie career...

So that was she. Of course it was. *Vivien.* Seeing the name in front of me, it seems obvious. Her fame was before my time, a bright brief spark in the seventies, but I'm sure Mum had her films on video when I was growing up, and in my mind's eye I catch a flash of what she used to look like. Even the sound of her voice, lilting, seductive, embroidered with heavenly promise. It doesn't match the voice I heard today. That voice was coarse with suffering. As if a demon had got inside her...

Moretti's younger sister, about whom little is known, accompanies the couple; the trio are said to be close, and are 'looking forward to facing a new start together'. Signor Giacomo Dinapoli, the siblings' uncle, owned

*the fifteenth-century Castillo Barbarossa for many
years before his death...*

I read on, but the relevance to Vivien thins out and it
becomes more about the house. I flip to the next article relat-
ing to her name, then the next and the next. I'm spoiled for
information about the Barbarossa but there is little about its
inhabitants. Was Giovanni Moretti the man whose portrait I
saw on the staircase? I recall his unusual eyes, the insistence
in his glare, and how quickly Adalina steered me on. And
who was the sister? Why was she with them? There are
items about parties thrown at the mansion, lavish, colourful
affairs, a masked ball at Halloween, an annual occasion for
which the Barbarossa is, or was, famous, but I'm unable to
scratch beneath the surface and uncover what I'm hungry
for. What *am* I hungry for – a scandal to put my own in
the shade? Some act that Vivien committed, or was committed to her, that makes mine seem incidental, or not so
bad? I try another search, marvel at her glamorous black
and white headshots, magazine covers, Vivien laughing at
parties where the vintage glitterati sip from teardrops of
champagne and smoke Cuban cigars; screen grabs from
her movies where she resembles a cross between Marilyn
Monroe and Katharine Hepburn, and there is something
familiar about her, a face I feel I met in another life, long-
lost now. I Wikipedia her, but the material on her personal
life is scarce. She was born in South Carolina, a religious
upbringing then the move to LA, the swift soar to fame,

leading to her marriage to Giovanni and the relocation to Europe.

After that, nothing… the trail ends.

Only, it doesn't. I know it doesn't.

Abandoning the web, there is one more thing I unearth in the district papers. It's an account dated from November 1989.

… Furthermore to our report on last year's tragedy at the Castillo Barbarossa, La Gazzetta *can reveal that one-time actress Vivien Lockhart is now living alone at the mansion, having been abandoned by her husband. Signora Lockhart has not been seen in weeks and has become confined. One wonders what effect, both mental and physical, she suffered after the events that took place last winter. We send her our well wishes for recovery – as well as for her reconciliation with Signor Moretti.*

I check back in the documents for *La Gazzetta*'s write-up from the previous year – but I find nothing. No other files under Vivien Lockhart.

I've reached a dead end.

'*Mi scusi,* signora, *ma stiamo chiudendo.*'

The librarian distracts me from my thoughts. I look at the time. It's gone ten. How have I spent three hours looking at this stuff, and not even noticed?

'*Grazie,*' I reply, gathering my things.

The library is deserted, the wooden booths empty. At the

front desk, a woman is checking books back in, and smiles at me as I pass. I'm heading down the stairs to the street when I hear footsteps behind me, matching mine perfectly. I slow. So do the footsteps. I start again, quickening my pace. Whoever is behind me follows suit.

My pulse speeds up.

I'm relieved to reach the normality of the real world, but don't stop until I am safely across the road and swept up in the crowd. A carnival is unfolding, the beat of a deep drum surging the revellers forward through the streets, flags held aloft, faces painted, and I duck into a doorway to catch myself. Only then do I look behind.

I'm in time to see a man watching me. My eyes go straight to him, though he is surrounded, as if I always knew I'd find him there. Perhaps it is because he is standing totally still, like a rock in furiously churning water. His face is obscured, I cannot make him out, but I would put him at a little older than me; he's broad, dark, and staring right back. Immediately, I know who he is. I've always known.

They found me. It was only a matter of time before they did.

I turn and rush through the bleeding, blinding streets, weaving flames and hollering voices, desperate now to get back to the Barbarossa, frightened of what lies behind me but frightened, too, of what waits for me there.

CHAPTER ELEVEN

Vivien, Los Angeles, 1978

Vivien Lockhart rolled over in the warm glow of Californian sunshine, and stretched inside satin sheets. Outside, the green ocean sighed, waves lapping against a golden shore. What day was it? Ah, yes, an important one. Tonight, she would accept her first Leading Lady Award at the annual Actors Alliance. Everyone knew it was in the bag – her recent turn in the mega-hit *Angels at War* was unrivalled: she was a tour de force, a masterclass, a vision to behold, and the only way was up. Vivien was the brightest star in Hollywood. She had it all, everything she had fantasised about and more. Every studio wanted to work with her, every designer wanted to dress her, every rising starlet wanted to be her. Oh, and every man wanted to bed her.

'Hey, baby...'

The model-slash-actor she'd brought back last night reached for her: bronzed arms, a mane of jet hair like John Travolta in *Saturday Night Fever*. She couldn't remember his name. No doubt this was, for him, the start of some grand love affair.

'Screw, is that the time?' Vivien swung out of bed and

headed for the shower; she had brunch with her agent at ten. 'I gotta get ready. Dandy'll kill me if I'm late.'

'You don't want breakfast?' The model-slash-actor was disappointed.

'No.' She smiled sweetly at him. 'By the time I'm done, I want you out.'

*

She bagged the award, of course. It had never belonged to anyone else. As Vivien went to collect her gong and deliver her speech, she reflected on the glittering crowds gazing up at her from the ranks. Envy on the women's faces; lust on the men's. Vivien's crown was untoppleable: her beauty and talent were second to none.

'Don't you think you oughtta slow down a little?' Dandy asked as they took a car to the after party off Broadway. Vivien unscrewed the cap off a Chambord miniature – her third. But that wasn't counting the brandy.

She drained it. 'Say what?'

'You'll be drunk.'

'Haven't I earned it?'

'The night's not over yet. You're still on the clock.'

'And I'm still fine.'

Dandy knew better than to press the issue. As Vivien applied lipstick, she decided that if it was a choice between the warm burn of alcohol in her throat and any approval Dandy could offer, she would choose the alcohol every time. For many years, she'd been dead against it – her father had been enough to put her off. But these days, it was all that would do. It kept her moving and stopped her thinking; it sped the days and nights along like a leaf in a rushing stream, never pausing or getting caught.

That was her motto: Keep going, keep striving. Looking back never did anyone any favours. *Learn your lessons and wear them like armour.*

Their car pulled up outside the warehouse venue. Owned by Warhol, inside it was a tropical, decadent paradise of exquisite creatures. Vivien was regaled on entering, the Halston jersey dress she had changed into after the ceremony admired and revered, her shimmering trophy marvelled at as if she held the sun in her hands.

'Congratulations, Vivien,' 'Darling, well done,' 'Oh, you look ravishing!'

Compliments fell about her like rain. Dandy steered her through as best he could but everyone wanted to stop and take her hand, tell her how much they adored her and what a stunning performance she had achieved, hoping to delay her long enough that a paparazzo would pass and take their picture together and it would appear in the glossies in the morning. Fame was contagious, or so they hoped. Vivien was the golden lamp: touch her arm and she might just make their wish come true.

Her own wishes, of course, had come bountifully to fruition. Perhaps that was why, amid the clamour of appreciation, Vivien could only see the hollow truth beneath. These people had got her wrong. They imagined her to be the girl Dandy sold to the press – a butter-wouldn't-melt ingénue who had walked into a Burt Sanderson audition one balmy afternoon and claimed the part she was born to play.

Nobody knew about her sordid beginnings, her violent father or her shameful work-for-tips at Boudoir Lalique. She was determined it would stay that way.

The hours passed in a haze of booze, drugs and dance. Vivien moved across the spotlit floor, disco balls shattering kaleidoscopic light and she was in one man's arms and then another's and then another's, each of them faceless, nameless. She thought about the girls she had known in Claremont and at the Lalique – what did they make of her celebrity? Did they respect her, or pity her? Did they wish for the studs in her bed or did they have husbands of their own, children, families?

Vivien wondered if she herself would ever have a family. The one she'd left behind had injured her so badly that she vowed never to be beholden to one again. Besides, she was too sullied. These men thought they wanted her, and they did for a night, a week, a month – but for always? No. Not once they saw the hidden scars.

She was drifting to the bar when a voice pierced her from behind.

'Hello, Vivien.'

It was like being stabbed in the back by a thin, sharp blade.

Not you. Please, not you.

'Jonny Laing,' she forced herself to answer. 'What a surprise.'

She should have been more careful. She had checked

tonight's list and he hadn't been on it, but clearly he'd managed to slide his way in, insidious, horrible, Jonny all over. She'd got sloppy; she had to be smarter. Vivien avoided her adversary at all costs, for the mere sight of him chilled her. Jonny relished the cards he held: even after all this time, he still believed he could have her. He believed that one day she would capitulate and he would get a return on his investment. The higher her star climbed, the more of a payout it would deliver. Tonight, she was stratospheric.

'It seemed a shame not to congratulate you,' said Jonny acidly. 'You're a hard woman to get hold of these days. To think of the partnership we once had…'

Vivien was desperate to shake him off, scrub herself down and erase any trace of him. Her heart galloped and her lungs strained. Everywhere she turned, her fellow luminaries appeared grotesque, made up like circus clowns, laughing and roaring.

Jonny held the key to her downfall. Imagine if they found out…

'Leave me alone,' she forced out. 'Please. I'll do anything.'

'Anything?' He grinned. 'You know what I want.'

Vivien shook. Even if she did sleep with him, he would never leave her alone.

'Never,' she croaked. 'Not that.'

'Then we're stuck.'

'I've got money. You can have it. I'll pay back every cent—'

He laughed, horribly. 'Come on, Vivien, listen to yourself.'

'I won't sleep with you, Jonny.'

He licked his lips, slow, tantalising.

'Come along, sweetheart, you never know – you might even enjoy it.'

'Go to hell.'

'Remember I know about you,' he said. 'I know everything.'

It took all her will not to spit in his face. She was trapped – as trapped as she'd been back in Claremont, hiding in her bedroom awaiting the sting of her father's belt.

'Jump off a cliff, you bastard,' she said.

Vivien stepped away but he seized her arm, just as he had that day in his office. She couldn't see, couldn't hear, the world spiralling out of control. Twisting from him, she lost her balance and stumbled, fell, was caught—

'Oops!' Suddenly Dandy was with them, holding her up. 'Let's get out of here, shall we, darling?' Casual smiles for their observers; it was nothing, a long day and an exciting night; he'd spin it right in the morning. 'Come along, Viv.'

Grateful, she allowed herself to be led. And she heard Jonny's parting hiss:

'I'll tell the world, Vivien… if you don't give it to me.'

*

Over the coming weeks, Vivien lay low. She became a recluse in her apartment, too paranoid to go out but at the same time afraid to stay in: afraid of the bell ringing or the phone going, and Jonny reiterating his menace. She ignored calls from Dandy.

How had it come to this? All the glitter and fortune she had longed for, and yet at its heart a whistling void. She felt invisible, a ghost girl, not really here.

She drank to escape the pain. And one Friday night, things came to a head.

She had started with one gin, the alcohol rushing to her head, making her eyes sting. Next time she looked, the bottle was empty. That was the way of it, great blackouts, time losses she couldn't account for. Just as she was nodding off on the couch, the telephone rang, startling her. Bleary-eyed, forgetting, she reached for it.

'Hullo?'

'Vivien, it's your aunt, Celia.'

Vivien sat, rubbing her eyes, her blotted brain struggling to kick into gear. She hadn't heard from Celia since… well, since she'd left. Since the last Sunday service they had both attended in Claremont. The woman's voice severed her.

'I'm afraid I have bad news,' Celia went on. 'Your mother is dead. The funeral is on Sunday. Your father told me not to bother but I thought you'd want to know.'

The conversation must have continued after that, but Vivien played no conscious part in it. When Celia hung up, she dropped the phone. She drank more. She stared her image down in the mirror and when she could stand it no longer she punched the glass, cracking it like a beautiful mosaic. Alcohol – she needed it. She needed to be numb. But there was none left, the cupboards empty, her secret stash under the bed depleted. Only one thing for it: she grabbed the keys to the Mustang.

It was kamikaze to go driving. Directionless, delirious, drunk, Vivien was the last person who should have got behind a wheel. It was a wonder she hadn't been killed, the newspapers said afterwards, or that she hadn't killed anyone else.

Vaguely she was aware of heading downtown. Once she had a drink she could work out what she was going to do. Saying farewell to her mother would mean seeing her father again. She couldn't. She just couldn't. Her father had been right. God only did look after the virtuous. She had always been destined for the gates of hell.

The car spun off the road and, after that, only black.

CHAPTER TWELVE

Italy, Summer 2016

It rains all weekend, a damp, flat, rolling sky bursting with pent-up heat.

I'm inside when the Barbarossa's phone rings. Having been chastised for answering the front door, I don't go for it myself, and instead continue my work cleaning and sorting the old study. This morning I discovered a photograph in one of the desk drawers, of Vivien as a young woman. Without question, she had been fabulous, gazing into the camera, her blonde hair curled round her ears and a smile on her face. I'd wondered who had taken the picture – from the way she was posing, it was someone she had been in love with. In the background, I could make out the castillo. The note on the back, scribbled in pencil, read: *V, 1981*. And it wasn't so much Vivien's appearance that had arrested me, how young and vibrant she looked; it was the *hope* in her. The optimism. All that was gone now.

Forget it, I tell myself. *Don't go there*. After my scare at the library, I've resolved to put a lid on my curiosity. The man was a journalist, I know it. By now he will have reported back to London, to some ravenous editor in an office on Southwark Street, a woman not unlike Natasha, polished and cutthroat, with the toothpaste-white smile of an angel but with a dagger concealed in her silk blouse. The woman will be celebrating, kicking off her heels, opening a chilled bottle of wine… But she won't tell anyone, not yet, this story is too hot and too precious. Just for tonight, it's hers alone. The story of the year: a tale of seduction, betrayal and murder.

And love…

I can't risk meeting the same fate as my predecessor. I can't risk being sent home. Right now, the Barbarossa is the only protection I have.

Yesterday, I overheard Vivien in conversation, presumably with Adalina. I was outside, clearing the rain-clogged gutters of leaves, head bent against the downpour, when from an open window I detected her voice. '*You mean you really can't see it?*' I fought to catch Adalina's response over the spit of drops bouncing off the veranda roof, but what followed from Vivien filled the blanks. '*God, woman, it's unmistakeable. It's like looking at a photograph. She's too like her; I can't bear it…*'

Too like whom? Who was Vivien talking about?

I had to get Vivien on side. For as long as I was here, secluded in these hills, I was safe. She had succeeded for years in hiding from the world. Why couldn't I do the same? I'm used to hiding, after all. Those years I spent at home caring for my broken family – maybe they were as much for me as for them. I needed to be closeted away. I needed to be forgotten.

Adalina appears at the study door.

'It was for you,' she says.

'What was?'

'The telephone.'

I'm startled. I haven't given this number to anyone, not even Bill.

'Who was it?'

'They did not say. They only asked for Lucy. I told them to leave a message.' She frowns. 'And they hung up.' Adalina is clearly annoyed, though at the distraction to her busy day or by her suspicion that I'm spreading Vivien Lockhart's personal contact details all over Europe it's hard to know. 'They sounded... impatient.'

Fear scatters through me, and I ask: 'Was it a man or a woman?'

'A woman.'

The slice of hope that it might have been him (never mind the fact he has no clue that I'm in Italy and, even if he did, wouldn't be able to track me down: love makes us believe in the impossible) is pinched out. 'A woman?' I repeat.

'Please tell your friends not to call the house in future.'

'It can't have been a friend. Nobody knows this number.'

Adalina doesn't buy it. *Just tell them*, her expression says, before she leaves.

I listen to my breath for a moment, fast and short.

I've been found.

*

I return to the library that evening, only this time I'm not chasing Vivien's story. I'm chasing my own – and I have to reach it before someone else does.

I have to make contact with him. Now the time is here, now it's happening, I feel strangely calm. All the things I've rehearsed to say go out of the window.

I take a breath and begin. *Compose message.*

> So, here I am. It's been a while. I never thought it would be so long, and longer still when every moment hurts. I'm sorry. That's the first thing to say. I'm sorry for what happened.

The cursor blinks. I delete what I've written and start again.

> I have a question, and it's this. Am I bad? Am I evil? Tell me, because I don't know. My crime is that I fell in love with a man who told me he was single. You told me you were single. I fell in love with your laugh and your hands and the gentle frown you wear when you are concentrating. I fell in love with adventure, with excitement. I fell in love with the girl you promised me I was: the girl I'd always wanted to be.

My fingers hover over the keys. When words aren't enough, what then?

I remember the day we met. He interviewed me for the role, and all I could think of right the way through was a line from the job description: *The position of PA requires you to work intimately with the director.* Here he was. *Intimately.*

He'd been cool, calm, everything I wasn't. Steel-grey eyes, burning in some lights, thawed in others; a sharp, square jaw; messy gold hair. I kept seeing those eyes. I see them now. Where absence forces other details to fail, that one never does. I've looked into them too many times. They've looked into me.

I was shocked by the revelation he was married, ready to walk. *Don't*, he said. They were estranged. There were children but he barely saw them; his wife was with someone new, a man they called Daddy. It broke his heart. I loved him more.

Had I really been that stereotype?

Had I really been the mistress who waits, hands wringing, for a break-up?

Divorce was impossible, he promised. He was an important man, and his wife was Grace Calloway, a well-known TV personality. I was taken in by the glamour – my life had been anything but glamour up to that point. How beautiful she was, how celebrated, and yet he chose to spend his nights with me. *It's fake*, he told me, *none of it's real.* I clung to that. He needed me. I kept him going. Kept him sane.

The nights without him were the worst. I'd lie in bed, picturing him in a home that didn't welcome him, his wife away with her lover, his children refusing to let him close. It was easier to imagine than the alternative. That maybe they had made up; maybe she had cooked him a meal (saltimbocca, his favourite) and they'd shared a bottle of

Chianti (like the one we had in that cosy Italian under London Bridge on my birthday, where the bottles came in cork baskets with molten wax down their sides), and then she'd told him she wanted to try again. The children were what got him. He could never turn his back on them, nor should he even think of it.

I erase what I've written. This is what I mean to say:

Right in that moment before she died, James, she looked at me and I knew. I knew that she loved you. I knew that you were never estranged and that you were happy – at least as far as she was concerned. She was a fragile, injured woman, a wife and a mother, and I had done a terrible, terrible thing.

I wish you would talk to me. I wish you would call. I wish you would tell me that I'm wrong about all this. You loved me then and you love me now and you didn't lie to me.

Where are you? I cannot do this alone.

Someone is watching. Someone is here.

What should I tell them? What should I say? How can I know, if you won't talk to me?

Bill's words fly back at me. *Do you think he's going to defend you? He doesn't care. He'll put it all on you and then how's it going to look?*

I can't believe that – but what, then, am I supposed to draw from his silence? I have no idea how he's coping. The funeral is over, the daytime-TV world moving on from their mourning, her *Chic Chef*'s corner deserted, soon to be replaced with some other voluptuous, cocoa-fondant-loving beauty, and now the questions are being asked. Grace Calloway committed suicide? Why? What possible reason could she have had to take her own life? Grace had everything: the perfect job, the perfect family and the perfect husband. There's nothing like perfection to whet the appetite of the press. Scratch the surface, just a scratch; see what's lurking beneath…

It wouldn't have taken much. A bit of digging, the media turning up at his workplace, a snake-like Natasha disclosing everything to a reporter over a number of cocktails, realising next morning she'd perhaps said too much but not really caring.

I close my account, without sending the message. Tears prick my eyes, the uselessness of the whole thing; my utter lack of clarity as to what to do next. For a second, I consider ringing one of my sisters, but the thought of explaining it makes me weary. They wouldn't understand. They couldn't compute an impulsive Lucy. All their lives I've been the one who imposed rules and told off and packed lunches and burned toast, while they pushed boundaries and rebelled against an anger and sadness they couldn't articulate. It was always their personalities that were entertained, their quirks and mischief and instincts, not mine. I was functional; I just got on with it.

Looking back, it might not be that my sisters overrode a more complex me; it might be that a more complex me simply had not existed. I buried her when I was fifteen and Mum was carried out of our house in the middle of the night, the life pinched out of her like a candle between two fingers. It was only when I met James that I set her free, the girl who had been caught and put in a jar, the lid screwed tight.

But I kept that girl to myself. She was my secret. And to my family I remained the trustworthy person they had always known.

They'll find out soon enough.

I leave the booth, sling my bag over my shoulder and take the steps two at a time. Out on the street, the warm evening hits me like a fan. Suddenly, I'm dizzy. I cling to the wall, tiny pinpricks of light shimmering behind my eyes.

There is a café next door. I stumble in, ask for water, and sit in the cool of the air-conditioning, beneath an age-stained photograph of Michelangelo's *David*.

I'm beginning to calm when I notice something. There is a man at the table opposite mine, a little older than me, watching me intently. It's him.

The same man I saw outside the library last time.

Get up. Get out. Move.

The man stands. He approaches slowly, tucking his phone into his jeans, casually finishing his drink, and for an optimistic moment I expect him to walk right out of there, proving me wrong, but then his eyes are on me again and like a bad dream he closes the distance, stopping at my table, his hands in his pockets.

I pretend he isn't there. When he pulls out a chair and sits down, I am forced to acknowledge him. He leans forward, his voice barely more than a whisper.

'My name is Max,' he says. 'We need to talk.'

CHAPTER THIRTEEN

Vivien swallows the pills with relish. The green ones are her favourite; they can knock her out for hours. All she wants right now is to be knocked out.

Every time she closes her eyes, she can see the girl's face. Up close, the resemblance is uncanny, and what she hoped was a mistaken similitude, a trick of distance or light, is exposed as fact. They could be sisters. The girl is the spitting image. *I thought you were gone from my life*, she thinks. *I thought we were through.*

Adalina closes the curtains. 'You will sleep now, signora?'

Vivien can sense the pills start to take effect, a drowsy, rocking motion like being on the swell of the sea. In the early days she would fight it, begrudging how it robbed her of control. Now, she surrenders, lets it claim her, oblivion.

'Find him, Adalina...' she whispers, as she tumbles towards sleep.

'Shh...' The maid sponges her forehead.

'I have to see him again,' murmurs Vivien. 'Let him know I'm...'

'Quiet now, signora, go to sleep.'

'Find him for me, Adalina. Before it's too late.'

'Calm now, signora, that's it, there now, calm...'

'You must find him... Promise me you'll find him...'

Against her delirium, Adalina's face morphs and swells and at points ceases to be there at all. Vivien is aware of a sponge crossing her brow, or is it her own hand, her own skin, hot and damp and cloying? She hears the maid exhale, or perhaps it is herself, on the cusp of sleep, falling, dreaming... Quietly, Adalina leaves the room.

CHAPTER FOURTEEN

Vivien, Los Angeles, 1978

'Ms Lockhart?'

The voice came at her from the sky.

'Vivien…?'

It was closer now. Warm. Kind. It seemed to hold a hand out to her, and in the darkness behind her closed eyes she travelled towards it, her senses awakening one by one. *Where am I?* White walls, a smell of disinfectant and the low hum of conversation – then the sound of a curtain being pulled. The voice, where had it gone? She needed to hear it again. It was like water, quenching an ancient thirst.

'Ms Lockhart, my name is Dr Moretti…'

She blinked, drawing the vision into focus. A man. His voice was deep and rich, with a gentle European accent. He was handsome beyond measure. Dark hair, wild and dangerous, falling to the collar of his doctor's coat; the glimpse of an earring, a single dark cross. One of his eyes was black and the other was green.

He was a different breed to the men she was used to. He looked like a prince who had lived for a thousand years and never aged a day. His skin was marble, lightly tanned by the LA sun but harbouring the deep, permanent colour of foreign blood. She imagined him living in a forest, surrounded by sky and leaves.

It wasn't the first thing patients typically thought when (as Vivien later learned) they first emerged from a week-long coma. But she couldn't help it.

'You might feel confused for a while,' said Dr Moretti, slipping his board into the slot at the end of her bed. 'Your memory will take a while to come back. You've been through a trauma, Vivien – you must be good to yourself.' He spoke this last part with affection, and while Vivien's pride told her not to fall for it, to keep her walls as strong and high as they had ever been, she wanted dreadfully to trust him.

Her memory, though, seemed fine. While the exact circumstances that had brought her here were misty – the strained call with Aunt Celia, the empty bottles of gin scattered over her dresser, that blind stumble to the car and the gunning of the engine – she was remembering acutely the pain and heartache she'd felt that night, the utter despair. Except all that seemed a distant shadow now, now that he was standing in front of her, this beautiful man with the strange-coloured eyes and the earring that made him look like a pirate. Her pain alleviated, as if she wasn't only waking from a deep sleep but also from her old, outdated life. Gilbert Lockhart had used to talk about rebirth. Baptism. Emerging from the water and into fresh air, beginning again.

'I'll leave you to rest,' said Dr Moretti, drawing the curtain back. Vivien wanted to speak but no words came, though whether this was a physical non-starter or a state of being tongue-tied she didn't know. 'Forgive the nurses if they get excited,' he said before leaving, with a sideways smile that thawed the hardest, furthest part inside her that no one on earth had touched before. 'It's not usual for us to care for somebody famous. But the good news is, Vivien, you're going to be absolutely fine.'

*

Over the next few days, she drifted in and out of sleep, torn between the urge to get up, get dressed, stalk out of there, and the pull of being tended to, cared for, looked after. The doctor came and went, a perfect vision, and as Vivien's strength slowly returned so did her voice. Until, one morning, she found the courage to speak to him.

'You must think me a terrible mess,' she said. Humiliation burned when she imagined being brought into hospital, a ruined starlet, selfish and spoiled, while Dr Moretti was a disciplined medic, concerned with saving lives, not wrecking them.

He was about to leave, but stopped at the door. 'Not at all,' he replied.

'I don't know what I was thinking,' Vivien stammered. 'I guess, I – I wasn't thinking at all. I was upset, that's all. Well, that's an understatement.' She laughed emptily but Dr Moretti's face gave nothing away. Those eyes took her in, those strong, stormy eyes, with barely restrained feeling, like a stallion roped to a gate.

'I'd had a telephone call and it threw me,' she went on, unable to stop and yet conscious she was spilling too much, spilling it all, but now she'd started there was no way back. 'I've been pretending for a long time,' she explained, somehow feeling that she *had* to explain, she had to make this man understand her just the tiniest bit because if she didn't then what was the point of anything in the world, anything at all? 'I've been surviving without joy,' she choked. 'I've forgotten how to feel joy, how to feel happy about anything. Did I ever know how? I seem to be better at knowing sadness, and destroying everything I touch. Oh, God, I'm sorry. I'm so sorry. I'm talking and talking and everyone thinks they know me but they don't know me at all. I'm not even sure that *I* know me. I thought it would be easier for everyone if I just…'

She trailed off, feeling as though she had bared her soul in a way she had never expected to again: she had trained herself to be wiser, instructed herself to know better and she *did* know better. But how strange was the human heart. It told itself to close and yet still it opened, time and time and time again, in faith, towards the light.

He was silent for a long time.

Then: 'Can I call someone for you?'

'I don't have anyone,' she said.

His expression shifted in surprise. Those eyes again: how could she not fall into them? 'No family?' he pressed softly. 'A mother, father… a friend?'

Vivien thought. 'You can call my agent,' she said. It sounded hopelessly sad, this brittle, proud star, with no one to call but her manager.

Dr Moretti came to her. He put a hand on her shoulder and it was the loveliest, tenderest touch she had ever received. A tear seeped down her cheek.

'You'll be all right,' he told her gently.

She blinked and another tear fell. 'Will I?'

He smiled. 'Without doubt,' he said. 'I know a fighter when I see one.'

*

It was with some regret that Vivien was discharged a fortnight later, for she feared she would never see him again. She tried to occupy herself with getting back to work, and in true agent style Dandy leaped back on the wagon, seeing dollar signs where she saw redemption – she was surely hotter now than ever, the diva who had cheated death.

But Vivien couldn't concentrate. It all seemed meaningless. The movie business no longer held her in thrall, the competition and rivalry that had charged her ambition dissipated like a whisper on the wind. Her life thus far had been about chasing the next prize, the next key, so that she could keep opening those doors and slamming the past shut behind her. But there were more important things than fame and money, things she had never contemplated before: things she hadn't been *able* to contemplate before, because she had never met anyone with whom to share them.

She couldn't stop thinking about Giovanni Moretti. She remembered how he had stirred emotions in her that she thought she had lost, his compassion, his patience, how he had drawn her honesty without even trying. Now she had uncovered that intimacy, she was frightened she would never find it again. In the short time she had spent with him, she'd felt a connection she had only read about in books. Had it been real? Had she been foolish to trust it, or had she been right this time? Was it still possible for her to know a good thing when she found it? Physically, too, he cast her under his spell. She woke in delicious sweats and ached to be kissed by him.

Months passed. Vivien had all but given up hope of ever renewing contact, when, out of the blue, he got in touch. She received the note through Dandy.

Vivien, I have to see you again. Meet me at Rococo's, Friday, 8 p.m.

She didn't need to be asked twice.

*

Their relationship began in earnest. Giovanni Moretti was, without doubt, the best thing that had ever happened to her. He was a strong, fine man in a reef full of sharks – intelligent, courageous and loyal, but with a mysterious, bruised soul that kept her guessing, kept her wanting, and she knew he would reveal it to her in time. She, after all, had revealed herself to him. Not since Jonny Laing had she been so truthful about her history – and she knew this time was different. She knew Gio Moretti wasn't like other men. She told him everything, from Gilbert's beatings through to her escape, from her nights at Boudoir Lalique to that sick advance in Jonny's office and everything in between: the fact she kept on running but could never outrun her past.

He didn't judge her, just took her in his arms when she had finished her story and stroked and kissed her hair. 'It's over now,' he said. 'I promise, it's over.'

She sensed that her vulnerability mattered to him, though she couldn't say why. He seemed to understand her in a way that no one else did, as if she reminded him of someone, as if they had perhaps known each other in another life.

Vivien's only white lie was that it wasn't just her mother who had died, but her father too. Both her parents were dead. She figured they might as well have been – Gilbert had ceased to exist for her that very same day she walked out of his house. Had her father been to visit her in hospital? Had he called? Had he cared? Had he sent even a card or a flaky bunch of flowers to wish her well? Had he hell. She owed him nothing. It was easier, cleaner, to cut all ties. To pretend there was zero left.

When she disclosed she was an orphan, Gio searched her eyes. There was something he ached to tell her, but he caught himself in time. Instead, he drew her to him and didn't let go. 'It's you and me now, Vivien,' he murmured. 'Always.'

Their courtship was magical. She had never felt such desire, such safety, never thought the two could go hand in hand. She had written herself off as too selfish and damaged for commitment, but here Gio was, her guardian angel. She could stare into his eyes all day long, one black, one green, and lose herself in his embrace.

Dandy called night and day, demanding she answer his

messages, asking why she'd let him down at a casting yet again. Why had she lost interest? What was going on? Speaking to Dandy was like yelling across tundra to a distant figure in the snow. He couldn't hear her. She spoke another language; one that said, *I'm through with this. It's a heartless world. I'm done with Hollywood and I'm done with you all…*

'I need a break,' she told her agent.

'Are you knocked up?'

Normally Vivien would have taken affront, but it was difficult to feel mad about much these days. 'Very funny, Dandy.' Privately, the promise of carrying Gio's baby was like a flurry of wings inside her. Now was too soon, but in a year or two… She couldn't believe how swiftly it had happened, how much had changed. Having survived her accident, she was in awe of her body, of the things it might achieve.

She clung to her renaissance like a ship in a storm. Her heart said it was because she was full to the brim of love for him. She ignored the alarm that wormed between her ears at night, telling her that she had sabotaged the life she'd built – both lives, her one in Claremont and her one here – and Gio was all she had to tether her. If she lost him… Well, it wouldn't happen, so there was no point thinking about it. So what if Gio was all she had? So what if she relied on him utterly? So what if, when you took him out of the equation, there was nothing left? Wasn't that what real relationships were about? Vivien wouldn't know; she'd never let herself find out.

Every day, Gio decorated her with roses, chocolates, perfumes and impromptu trips, to spas, cosy bistros, a boat on the lake. Vivien didn't know where he got the money – he was a fine doctor, but he couldn't earn enough to cover that kind of expense – but she wasn't about to question it. Since opting out of work, her funds had started to dwindle. She hadn't realised how much debt she'd stacked up, the compulsive sprees she'd undergone in an attempt to blot things out. She had spent foolishly on her high and was suffering for it on her low. Gio didn't seem to mind.

I've got him, she thought. *It doesn't matter. He's not going anywhere.*

And it felt good, for once, not to have to build her barriers. They were untouchable, the pair of them: a couple who could take on the world.

*

Life continued happily for a while. Vivien knew she was recreating everything she had lacked as a child: sanctuary, certainty and security. She only wished that Gio would agree to move in with her. She didn't pressure him, only suggested it once or twice, but he point-blank declared it a bad idea. 'Why?' she asked. But he wouldn't say. There was always some excuse – it wasn't the right time, he couldn't get a lease on his place, couldn't they wait just a bit longer? It didn't make sense, though. Gio spent most of his time at hers and he seemed more in love with her than ever.

It began to bother her that he never invited her back to

his house. It had crossed her mind as odd in the early days, sure, but Gio was too full of distractions, too clever at diverting questions, that with a kiss or a look her curiosity had been postponed. As time went on, Vivien's suspicions crept in, threading through her like weeds, making her doubt, making her question, terrified that the ground on which she had gambled to plant her feet was yet again about to shatter beneath her. She couldn't understand his secrecy. Her paranoia multiplied, niggling, tormenting, impossible to ignore. When he told her that he could no longer see her on Friday nights – Fridays had to be his – she drew the line. If Gio wanted space, fine. But he had to be truthful.

'I don't want space,' he said, his face clouding. 'I'm crazy about you, Viv.'

'Then what's going on?'

'Nothing,' he said, turning away. 'It's the hospital. My shifts have changed.'

She didn't buy it. But she was too afraid of the alternative, of pushing him into a confession. *Is he having an affair? Is there someone else?* The notion made the sky fall. *What will I do without him?* The thought of another woman chilled her.

She had to find out. The following Friday night, she drove to his house, parked opposite, and watched the windows. Her hands gripped the wheel.

Liar.

So much for the hospital. Why were his lights on? Why was there a gleaming Chrysler parked on the drive? Vivien knew. He wasn't at work at all. He was in there, with some other woman he deemed special enough to bring home. They'd be making love right now, on the sheets Vivien had never slept on. They'd eat a meal at the table she had never sat at. They'd shower in the bathroom she had never stepped into.

How could he? How could he do this to her?

Even with the evidence as plain as day, Vivien couldn't accept it. Gio was in love with her. He wasn't like the rest. They were lovers but they were also friends.

Friends didn't do this to each other – did they?

Minutes ticked by and turned into an hour, maybe two, she lost track.

Still, she continued to watch. Until eventually, at around ten, the payload appeared. In one of the upstairs windows, a woman could be glimpsed, a fleeting sight before she vanished in shadow. Vivien's knuckles whitened. Her tears turned to fury.

She swung open the car door.

I'm going to catch them together and then I'll punch his fucking lights out.

In a rage she stormed up the drive, past the gate, past his precious car, tempted to scratch it with her keys but there would be time for that on the way back, and pounded her fist on the door. In her mind, she rehearsed all she would say and do to the traitor. *Who is it? Who is she? Someone I know?*

But nothing could have prepared Vivien for the truth.

Nothing could have prepared her for who the woman was.

CHAPTER FIFTEEN

Italy, Summer 2016

Maximo Conti isn't a journalist. It takes me a while to figure this out, even though he's talking, and everything he's saying is about the Castillo Barbarossa and not at all about me. I keep waiting for him to get round to it, even while I'm noticing details like the fact that he's local but his English is fluent. I notice how his chestnut hair spills over his brow and there is a cleft in his chin that makes him appear younger than he probably is. I notice the softness of his T-shirt. I keep waiting for him to say: *So anyway, I know about you, and here's the deal…* But he doesn't.

'You're Lucy,' Max says. At my cautious expression he goes on, 'Nobody starts work at the Barbarossa without at least someone knowing their name.' He orders us drinks. His hands are broad and dark, roughened by labour. This isn't a man who toils behind a desk, or makes malicious phone calls to hacks in London.

'I expect that sounds…' He pauses.

'Creepy?' I supply.

Max tries an uncertain smile. 'I saw you at the library.'

'You were following me.'

'I wanted to speak to you.'

I process what he's already told me, try to get my head around the fact he isn't who I thought he was. Max is half English and half Italian. His aunt used to work at the Barbarossa – and he looked sad when he told me this, so I throw a guess out there.

'You want me to get her job back…?' I hazard. 'That's what this is about?'

His puzzlement is genuine. 'No,' he says after a moment. 'My aunt is dead.'

'Sorry.' I'm embarrassed. 'I assumed—'

He waves a hand. 'It's OK.'

I'm relieved when our drinks arrive. 'Limoncello.' Max touches his glass to mine. 'The lemons round here all come from the Barbarossa. You eat them straight from the trees. Just tear them open with your hands, eat the skin, everything.' The drink is sweet and sharp and alcoholic. It knocks me back to my senses.

'I have information you might be interested in,' he says.

'Information about what?'

Max lifts a sceptical eyebrow, and I consider how he must have witnessed me at the library scanning archives, digging for dirt, so engrossed that I didn't even notice I had company; that this handsome Italian was watching me the whole time. My prying shames me. Isn't Vivien entitled to her scandal, just as I'm entitled to mine?

'You won't find what you're looking for there,' Max says. He rakes a hand through his hair; his nails are blunt and square, cut short. I try to figure out who he reminds me of.

There's something wholesome about him, straightforward. He looks like someone's older brother you might have fancied when you were twelve.

'You read the piece in *La Gazzetta*?' he goes on. 'Someone, at some time, must have known what happened at that house… but it's impossible to come by now. My aunt was one of the only people who knew. She knew everything about Vivien, they were best friends, and she was there the whole time, since Vivien and Gio moved from America. But she never told me. When Gio left, she never said why.'

I try to keep up. 'Why are you telling me this?'

'Because it's important.' Max is serious; this matters to him. 'My aunt was important – to me, I mean.' There's a pause while he takes me in, decides if he can trust me. 'She raised me,' he says. 'My parents were young – they split soon after I was born and my mother turned to drugs, so my aunt took me in.' He delivers this perfunctorily, as if it's a tale he's used to recounting. It neither causes him pain nor demands sympathy; it's just what happened. 'She used to tell me stories about the Barbarossa,' he says. 'It sounded like a fairy tale, this big castle and the glamorous family who lived there. Sometimes it was frightening, imagining such a big place. I used to get scared that my aunt would become lost in there and be unable to come home. She'd be caught in a maze and couldn't find the way out… It terrified me. She was all I had. The Barbarossa has always been an enigma for me: the ultimate secret.' A pause. 'It was also the place that took my aunt away. She died there, with Vivien.'

I watch this stranger, bearing his truth to me, and wonder at what cost it comes. 'When?' I ask.

'Five years ago,' he says. 'It was a massive heart attack, right there in the castillo. Vivien found her; she called an ambulance but the damage was done, it was too late. The paramedics were able to stabilise my aunt enough to get to hospital – but there was nothing they could do. She died hours later.' Max leans forward, chooses his words. 'I rushed there as quickly as I could. Lucy, I was with my aunt when she died – and right before, she held my hand and said she had one wish, and she could not rest until it was done. She asked me to tell Vivien Lockhart that she was sorry.'

'What for?'

Max lifts his shoulders. 'That's it. I don't know.'

'And you want me to find out.'

Max traces the rim of the glass with his thumb. 'I didn't think much of what my aunt said at the time – I was too cut up. But since then… I can't get past it. I have to know what she meant. What did she have to apologise for?'

I consider it. 'Why haven't you done anything before?'

'I have. I've tried. The Barbarossa is a closed fortress, as you know. For a while I thought I could get in myself, that surely Vivien would give me work if she knew who I was. But no – the opposite happened. The connection made me unemployable. Then I spoke to the girl who took the job before you, but she got careless. Started asking questions. Getting confident. Vivien let her go before we got a break-through.' He sits forward. 'Lucy, the way my aunt begged me… I can't describe it. She was so desperate, her plea so urgent. I can't ignore it. I can't.'

'Why not pass the apology on and be done with it?'

Max shakes his head. 'And what, that's it? Leave it and walk away?' His voice grows passionate. 'The more I learn about the woman at that house, the more I dislike her. I'm not saying sorry for anything my aunt did until I know what it was. And if Vivien Lockhart refuses to see me or talk to me, why should I go to her and say something I don't mean? Who even knows if my aunt did anything wrong? She gave me everything. I have to do this properly. I owe her that much.'

He catches himself, realises he's perhaps given away more than he intended – but I see a man at the end of his ideas. He's reaching out to me and I believe him.

'Your aunt was there when there were three of them?' I ask.

Max nods. 'So you found out about the sister.'

The sister…

I think of the Barbarossa as Max would have heard about it as a boy, and, yes, it is a fearsome place. Some days I regard the castle as beautiful; on others, when the sun catches it wrong, it appears close to monstrous, a hulking blot against the landscape. *A closed fortress…* Except, I'm in. I crossed those walls.

'Look, Max,' I say, 'I want to help you. I do. But I can't get into this. I need that place for my own reasons. I'm sorry for what happened and I wish you luck, but I can't risk it like the girl before me. I can't be sent home. It's better this way, really. I've been hired to do a job and I should just do it.' I omit the end of this, which is surely to say that I got myself in enough trouble before leaving England that to compound it would be madness. I thank him for the drink then stand to leave.

'There's a skeleton key,' Max says, and to my surprise he takes my hand; there's determination in his eyes, a flame I can't put out. 'It's hidden behind the fireplace in the ball-room. My aunt used to tell me about the key, every night before bed, until I fell asleep. She took me all round the Barbarossa, every corridor, every corner, slipping it into every lock, until I was dreaming. I still dream about it. But the key's there – I know it is. All those doors? They open. Even the attic.'

I grab my bag. I want to repeat my refusal, but the words don't come.

*

That night, I can't stop thinking about what Max said. Midnight crawls to one, limps to two, and at three a.m. I'm wide awake and my mind is turning cartwheels.

The walls of the castillo seem to whisper, taunting me, teasing me, drawing me into their shadows and secrets. *Get up*, they call through my fever. *Look, look, look…* I can't stop picturing the key in the ballroom. *You're no part of this*, I tell myself. But the longer the night grows, the cooler and more constant the band of moonlight appears on the floor of the Lilac Room, the more restless I grow.

I remember the noises I heard up there, the dragging sounds and the darkness.

When I pressed my wide eye to the keyhole, the emptiness slammed back at me. I never before thought of emptiness as something solid, but up there, up there...

I look at the clock: 3:12 a.m.

I'm thirsty. At least that's the reason I give myself as I sit up in bed, pull off the sticky sheets and lower my feet to the cold floor. Then I'm in the corridor, down the staircase, into the glowing marble atrium, running the taps and filling a glass with water. Not wanting to return to bed, I open the door and greet the night, black and absolute, just the tips of those dozen cypress trees spearheaded towards the stars.

I slip on a pair of sandals and go out on to the gravel. As always, I keep my head turned from the stone fountain – it gives me the shivers, that bloated fish with its dried-up mouth, trapped in the eternal pursuit of thirst. I don't know where I'm going and it occurs to me I might be sleepwalking, but I feel awake. The house is reflected in the shallow pool and forces me to look. Why don't they demolish the thing?

At the trees, I turn to face the building, my eyes wandering up, up, up, and there's a cool breeze on the back of my neck, scented with lemons and silence.

Don't look. Look. Don't look. Look.

I see the attic window, and a black shape flits past the pane. A flame leaps in my chest. It's a bat, that's all. Nothing else – nothing solid, or living, or dead. Not a person. Not anything. I recall the voice saying my name inside the ballroom.

Lucy.

Afraid, I hurry back inside. Max's face fills my mind.

The way my aunt begged me... I can't describe it...

Barefoot, I mount the stairs, blindfolded portraits tracking my every step, and behind one of them is the man in the red blazer, lit like fire against the forest. He must be, or have been, Vivien's husband. *So you found out about the sister.*

I don't know what makes me change my mind and turn back down. Leading off the atrium, the ballroom door is ajar. I slip through, amazed at my soundless footsteps and how lightly I am able to tread. The house is slumbering deep.

If Adalina woke and found me here, it would be instant dismissal. But I'm not in my right mind. It's as if someone else is guiding me, forcing my hand to reach out, pale and strange, those fingers not mine but another woman's, a mad woman's, and I follow them towards the fireplace like a candle in the dark.

At least this way, I'll know. If there's nothing there, I can forget about Max.

Carefully, with stealth I never knew I possessed, I slip my fingers beneath the hood. I don't know what I'm hoping for. Then I feel it.

My grip tightens around an unmistakeable shape. The key.

So easy... It's cold in my palm, but carrying the weight and burning sensation of something significant. Out in the hall, my heart is beating fast and strong. I feel as if I could run a marathon. My senses are alert, my hearing fine-tuned, my eyes trained into the night, my muscles ready to spring. I know where I am going.

I take the steps, one flight, two, three, up towards the attic, padding quiet as a cat, my mind more focused than it's ever been. It is freezing up here, my bare soles padding on the stone but the chill doesn't bother me. The key seems alive in my hand, like a butterfly I caught on a buddleia in Mum's garden when I was eight. It's as if it wants to be taken, wants to be used; it wants to show me the power it has.

It fits in the lock as if it's waited its whole life to be returned there.

There's a rusty click and the key turns. I expect a creak, but there is nothing.

I am met by a gust of loneliness, an age-steeped draught of abandonment, and it smells of years and years of stillness. It is like walking on someone's grave, but still I walk. I feel as if there is a presence at my back, urging me forward, encouraging me to explore. As my eyes adjust to my surroundings, blooming shades of white where the moon peers in, I make out a candle on a shelf, half exhausted, its wax splurging over its brim. Beside it is a box of matches. I strike one.

The attic shivers to light. Here is the window I was moments ago looking up at from outside. I remember the black shape and a cool funnel scuttles up my spine; I expect to see Vivien in the doorway, or Adalina, but there is no one.

The floor is bare and coarse, splintered beneath my tender soles, like bruised apricots on a wooden board, about to be stoned. There is a single bed, right in the centre, and its position is intimidating, erect somehow, as if it is alert, animated.

The eaves slope sharply above my head, so it's only possible to stand in the highest point of the triangle. An old chest and a writing desk occupy one corner, on which a mottled glass lamp is covered in fly carcasses; on it is a stack of books, which I flick through, hardbacks written in Italian. Against the far wall leans a portrait of a young girl, its canvas thick with dust. She has blonde pigtails and wears a frilled white dress, and there is a man standing at her shoulder. Her bright blue eyes are sharp with fear and that fear is older than her years. Her eyes follow me around the room. I nudge the window, trying to force it open, but it's stuck fast. The atmosphere is cloying, saturated with heavy accusation. I'm being stared at, pointed at; the candle has disturbed something that has long been sleeping. All at once, I'm numb with cold. The wick flickers and spits.

The impulse to get out is so strong that I almost leave without seeing the chest. It is draped in a sheet and tucked in a nook, each end tied with rope like a barrel containing something dreadful that's about to be tossed into a deep sea never to be returned. I go to it, kneel, and begin to work on the ropes. I have no time to question it; I only know I have to get inside. The rope is frayed and comes apart easily.

It's a dark-wood box, its metal buckles rusted. I push hard, trying to snap them open, then place my hands either side of the crate and lift the lid. I spend a long time absorbing its contents: a cotton soldier wearing a blazer, cap and blank smile; a toy rocking horse, its leather rein split; a

musical carousel, which I wind up, tiny steeds limping round
a once lively circuit, the chimes ringing sickening slow. There
is a blanket, unbearably soft, and beneath it a folded piece
of paper. I open it.

Ht'll never be yours. Ht'll always be mine.

The words grin up at me, ink blotched and dark, desperately, raggedly scrawled, as if this has been written by
someone who has lost control of their mind.

Psychotic. Obsessive. Possessed.

The candle sputters a final time, before dying. Without
knowing why, I tuck the note into the sleeve of my nightdress, close the lid and replace the sheet and ties.

It isn't hard to return the key to where I found it. The
castillo is still sleeping soundly, as if nothing has happened,
as if I could step back and reclaim the last ten minutes and
still be safe in my bedroom, without that note knifing my
mind's eye.

Only when I'm back in bed do I realise that, in my haste,
I neglected to lock the attic door. I lie awake, fretting,
until at five in the morning, just as dawn cracks over the
surrounding fields, I drift towards sleep, finally letting go
of all I've seen and reassured by the fact that everything in
there is long dead anyway.

CHAPTER SIXTEEN

Vivien, Los Angeles, 1978

Gio chased her down the drive. She couldn't face him, couldn't bear to look at him; his treachery was too much, too shocking. The car shook in her vision. Somehow she managed to unlock the vehicle, before Gio's hand landed on the door, keeping it shut.

'Vivien, listen. Listen to me!'

'Nothing you say can make this better.'

'You don't understand—'

'Damn right I don't.'

'Look at me.'

The quiet command in his voice compelled her. Instantly, she wished she hadn't. She should have hated him in this moment, but couldn't. *What is wrong with me?* she thought wretchedly. *Why can't I be happy? Why does it turn to dust?*

'There is no other woman,' he said, so simply and plainly that she knew it was the truth. 'She's my sister.'

There was a long moment. Vivien stepped back. 'What?'

'I have a sister, Viv. She lives with me. Here. Her name is Isabella. I never told you because… it's complicated.'

'Tell me now.'

Gio exhaled. He looked about him, as if this wasn't the place, as if all this had caught up with him too fast, as if he didn't know where to start.

'I don't know where to start,' he said.

'Try the truth.'

Gio's head bowed, and for a time she thought he wouldn't speak. This was where it ended, then, this huge roadblock of a lie. But then he lifted his chin and those magical eyes met hers, and in them was a resolve she hadn't seen before. He took Vivien's hands in his. She ought to have snatched them away. She didn't.

'Our parents died when we were children,' said Gio, 'back in Sicily. I'm an orphan too, Vivien. It's part of the reason I fell in love with you. You know what that feels like. I've never met anyone else who understands. Only you.'

Vivien's mouth went dry. She remembered the mystery she had always seen in him: the part she couldn't reach.

'I was ten and Bella was seven. The boat she was on with my parents got caught in a storm and capsized. Our parents drowned. She was with them the whole time.' Gio's expression was grave, regretful, etched with pain. 'I'd been a brat that day, a sulky kid – said I wasn't going anywhere. Stayed home wasting time, and, you know, that's the worst part, I can't even remember what I was doing, what was so important that I couldn't go with them. But it should have been me, Viv – it shouldn't have been her. She shouldn't have gone through that. I thought I'd lost them all, my whole family wiped out. But Bella was found days later, half dead. She was clinging on to the hull of the boat with one arm, my father's body with the other.'

Vivien was stunned. A thousand comforts sprang to her lips but every one escaped her. It was awful. She couldn't imagine it – that poor girl. Poor Gio.

Gio looked up at the house, at the window where Vivien had glimpsed the woman's figure. No lover. Only his younger, damaged sister. *Isabella.*

'Two whole days,' he said, 'alone on the sea. Only God knows what she suffered. They brought her home, but she was never the same. How could she be?' His confession was like glass, easily shattered: prick it and you'd bleed. 'I vowed to look after her from that day on. But no matter what I do, I'll never forgive myself for not going. I could have changed things. I could have stopped it.'

Vivien moved to object, and he seemed to anticipate this because he took his hands from hers and held one of them up. It was what he had decided. The accident had been his fault. His parents had died, and Isabella had suffered, because of him.

'Bella didn't speak,' Gio said, 'from that point on. She hasn't spoken to this day. I know it's all in there, bottled up, but she won't share it. She stopped eating. Stopped reading. Every little thing she'd taken pleasure in, killed. A part of her died with them on the boat – it was only a ghost that was left. Bella lost years and years to the disaster, locked away in her room, neglecting her friends, opting out of life…'

Turmoil boiled in his eyes, flashing black and green as the raging sea. Emotions crashed in on Vivien – confusion at having had her assumptions reversed in a heartbeat; amazement at Gio's brutal, tragic story; guilt at having deceived him about her own situation, for to lie about her orphan status when his was searingly true was despicable; and some other, shapeless fear she could not pin down, a fear that the tide was ready to change and there was nothing she could do to stop it.

She scarcely recognised the man before her. This wasn't her Gio, the man who had saved her life; it was a stranger, eaten up by regret and guilt and a childhood destroyed by calamity, a ferociousness of feeling that bordered on possession.

'I didn't tell you because I was afraid it would be too much,' he said hollowly. 'It's why it took so long for me to find you, after you left hospital. I kept talking myself out of it. I thought I would lose you when you found out about my responsibilities – because Bella *is* my responsibility, Viv. I've tried everything to help her. My sister has gone to every psychiatrist going, every shrink, but nothing has made any difference, no drugs or medication or therapy.'

Vivien watched the door of his house. To find out so much about a person before meeting them, their darkest, most painful truths, was eerie. She wished that Gio had told her sooner. She wished he had been upfront about Isabella from the start.

'She's buried it so deep no one can find it,' he confessed, 'and if we can't find it, we can't help. That's why I went into medicine. I thought if I could rescue just one person it would make me feel better about letting Bella down. But it didn't. It still happened. It can never be undone. I have to live with that.'

'You rescued me,' Vivien said, touching his face.

He flinched from her. 'It isn't enough.'

She felt as if she'd been slapped. It wasn't enough… or she wasn't enough?

Don't be selfish, she chastised herself. *This isn't about you.*

It was about Isabella.

And so, Vivien was about to learn, was a great deal else.

*

It was months before Vivien got to meet her properly.

'It will take time,' Gio warned, holding her close and looking deep into her eyes. She could see his devotion, never doubted it for a second. It was such a relief to know that he hadn't been cheating that she went along with it, accepted Gio's word that his sister was a complex woman and that the campaign to introduce Vivien into their lives would have to be a careful one. 'Isabella isn't… normal,' he told her.

'I don't care what she is,' said Vivien. 'She's part of you, so she's important.'

Gio was grateful for her understanding. Vivien wished that her unselfishness came from a more genuine place. Instead, she had the impression she was pretending, just telling Gio what he needed to hear for fear of putting distance between them. To her, family belonged in the past – a burden and, ultimately, a necessary sacrifice. She longed to begin afresh with Gio, but instinct told her this would not be easy.

Then, one day, he called her. 'She's ready.'

Gio picked her up that evening; he wore an expectant, hopeful smile that flipped Vivien's stomach. It was vital that she got on with Isabella: her relationship hinged on it. She swallowed her nerves, pulling down the hem of her emerald halter gown. She had spent ages getting dressed, discarding outfit after outfit in search of something better, sexier, classier, more sophisticated, and she wondered why she felt there was some competition here, as if she had to look more beautiful and intriguing than Isabella, had to snag Gio's attention and always be the centre of it.

Gio's line was that Isabella was sensitive. It had been the two of them for so long now that introducing another woman could set her back. Another woman…

Vivien had to bite her tongue. How had she ended up being *another woman*?

'She's seen how happy you make me,' said Gio. 'We're as protective as each other. She'll want to meet the person who's stolen my heart.' It was a strange use of the word, as if Gio's heart had been Isabella's to begin with.

Indeed, over time, the sister had morphed in Vivien's mind into some terrifying empress, the couple of years in age she had over her a yawning gulf of presumed author-ity. No wonder Gio had shied from moving in together. No wonder he hadn't wanted to bring her back to the house. No wonder he'd resisted whenever she'd suggested going away for the weekend. Since Vivien had learned of

Isabella, these subjects had become taboo, too complicated to approach, let alone discuss. Vivien felt that by even asking him, she was being disrespectful, insulting a clear and defined arrangement that had been in evidence long before she arrived on the scene.

Vivien was a late arrival to her own relationship. But she loved Gio, and knew that Gio loved her back. He was a decent, honourable man – that was why he still cared for his sister. It was precisely why Vivien had fallen for him in the first place.

She focused on the positives. Isabella could be a companion to her: they could be like the girls at Boudoir Lalique, heading to the beach to eat cheeseburgers and laugh till their stomachs hurt. They could be like sisters: the sister Vivien had longed for all through her childhood. Isabella could be wonderful. Isabella could be perfect.

'You look gorgeous, *bellissima*,' said Gio, as they turned on to his street. 'She's going to love you as much as I do.'

It was the first time Vivien had been back to the house since the night of the discovery, in part Gio's reluctance to summon her and in part her own imagination of Isabella holding fort, peering from her upstairs aperture, ever watchful. Did she cook for Gio? Did she send him off to work with a kiss? Did she wash his clothes, hold his shirts up to her nostrils and inhale his scent? *Don't be absurd. She's his sister.*

Vivien took a breath as they stepped on to Gio's porch. Her palms felt clammy and her heart was racing. She had been through so much in her life, thought nothing could ever faze her again, but here, now, waiting for that door to open, on the other side of which she sensed a dark, malevolent force like thunderclouds rolling blackly across a winter's sky, she felt just as she had in her bedroom in Claremont, anticipating the swipe of her father's belt. More than trepidation. Inevitability.

Gio stood back to let her through. She had expected to see Isabella right away, but the sister was nowhere. It seemed like a snub before they had even met. Vivien wasn't important enough to greet; she was a guest to be abided.

Quickly, she took in her surroundings. It was a homely set-up, and not what she had anticipated. Gio was so powerful at work, she had envisaged some of the same masculine authority here: clean lines, maybe some expensive art. Instead, it was a family home. Photographs adorned the walls, black and white framed prints of a smiling pair she guessed to be his parents. The furniture was haphazard, mismatched. The fridge was covered in scraps of paper, on one of which Gio had scribbled something in Italian, ending in a series of kisses. Vivien had the impression she had been invited to dine with a couple. She had been wrong about Isabella cooking – it was Gio who'd had a Bolognese simmering on the stove all afternoon, filling the house with the scent of rich tomato and sharp green basil. The table was set for three.

Gio was apprehensive. Vivien recognised with affection his charged energy, trying to make it flawless, just as he had on their first date when he had taken her for dinner and dancing at Rococo's. Isabella's absence in helping him suggested she left much of the running of things to Gio. It was he who had forged the comforts of this house, the reassurances, the memorabilia; it was he who held down his duties here as well as at work. Vivien resented Isabella for this, though she knew that wasn't fair.

She sensed the sheer imminence of Isabella, somewhere upstairs, biding her time, and yet a very real presence here in the room, all around, everywhere.

It was impossible to pretend it was just the two of them. Vivien was the impostor. Isabella owned this place. She owned her brother.

'Bella!' Gio exclaimed, so loudly that Vivien thought he was calling his sister from afar, and it seemed uncanny, therefore, that Isabella had already appeared before them in the doorway. She stood perfectly still, and silent. She wore no shoes, hence the quiet ambush, just a plain cotton dress that pooled almost to the floor, revealing a pale frill of white toes, like coral. Her dark hair hung in a sheet, obscuring her face so that only one almond-shaped eye was visible. It was a gleaming, malignant eye, and it surveyed Vivien as if assessing something rotten in a fruit basket.

'Hello,' Vivien stepped forward, putting her hand out, 'Vivien Lockhart.'

She felt stupid, standing there with her hand suspended and wondering when was the right time to take it back. Isabella didn't move that eye, not a flicker.

'Bella doesn't speak,' Gio murmured, patting down her hand. She'd known that; she was only trying to be friendly. Vivien detected annoyance in his voice, as well as the flash of something mean in Isabella's eye. Amusement? Victory? Vindication? She sensed she had already put a foot wrong but she wasn't sure where.

'Shall we sit?' said Gio.

Vivien wondered how the evening could possibly progress if Isabella didn't utter a word, but Gio was clearly accustomed to it. It didn't seem to bother him that she didn't respond, just a nod here or a shake of the head there. Gio discussed a range of topics that included his sister, either referring to her role in a past anecdote or shooting a question her way that demanded a small movement to reply. He addressed her in both English and Italian; their parents, before they died, had raised them as bilingual. *I must learn Italian*, Vivien thought, squirming every time the siblings shared their secret code, the lilting fluency that excluded her. And she was excluded. Vivien noticed how Isabella's gaze fell so differently upon her brother than it did when its laser was trained her own way. Fondness didn't come close; love didn't either. There was hunger in that gaze: a relentless appetite, something… insatiable.

He began talking about how he and Vivien had met. Finally, something she could participate in. Reaching across the table, Vivien took his hand. She saw how Isabella recoiled, and couldn't suppress the prickle of enjoyment that invoked.

'It took ages to figure the best way of asking you out,' Gio was saying, that smile she adored playing on his lips. His wild hair met the dark collar of his shirt and she thought again how reckless and handsome he looked. 'There she was, a movie star, and me knocking off shift at two a.m. in the ER. Hardly what she was used to.'

'But of course I said yes,' said Vivien, 'after what you did for me. Anyway, don't belittle what you do. You're the finest physician in town.'

'You want me for my brains, is that it?' Gio teased.

Vivien squeezed his fingers. A moment of softness passed between them, the calmest he had been all night, but then abruptly he pulled back, returning to his sister.

'You're not hungry?' he asked, motioning to her untouched plate.

Isabella's expression didn't move. Just that black sheet of hair, hanging like oil, and her brittle shoulders so roundly hunched that the ends of it brushed the wood either side of the bowl. Vivien felt irritated – at Isabella's incompetence, at Gio's split attention, at his guilt, palpable in the air around them – and wanted to shake her until she reacted. *Look at the things he does for you! Look at the impact it has on his life! Aren't you grateful?* But she told herself off for having these thoughts. She had to give Isabella a shot, make concessions after what she'd been through.

'Never mind,' he said, 'we can keep it for after…'

After she's gone, thought Vivien, upset at the inference. *When we're alone.*

Without a trace of impatience, Gio cleared the meal from in front of his sister and went to the counter to cover it. Vivien tried to catch Isabella in a moment of quiet, offer a smile and see if it was reciprocated: sometimes when a man was removed from the equation, it made things simpler.

But Isabella's eye was still on hers. Vivien met it and didn't look away. The smile froze on her face and then, little by little, dissolved. Isabella had no need for words when her stare was so potent. Vivien had never been on the receiving end of such absolute, categorical wickedness; such a pure intention, a clear purpose, and that purpose was vitriol. She recalled what Isabella had been through, the sympathy she deserved. But none of it matched up with that eye. The eye carried intelligence – worse, cunning – and it seemed to say all that words could not.

He'll never be yours. He'll always be mine.

*

Isabella went straight to bed after supper. Gio seemed to think the evening had been a success – 'I know she can be challenging, darling, so thank you. You were wonderful…' – and Vivien assumed, given his mood, that she would be staying.

'Oh, no,' he said, when they had spent an hour on the couch, kissing and talking, 'I'm sorry. Bella won't like it.'

Vivien sat up. 'But I'm your girlfriend,' she said coldly.

'I know,' Gio was quick to placate her, 'and this is awkward, I see that. Only it was a big deal for Bella to meet you tonight and I don't want to throw too much her way too soon. In the long run, it'll be better for us. You do understand, don't you?'

Vivien searched his beautiful face and couldn't help but nod.

'Of course,' she said, running her fingers through his hair. 'But it's hard for me too, Gio, I can't lie to you.'

'I know, *bellissima*.' He kissed her forehead and pulled her close. 'But I'm thinking of our future. That's why I want to tread carefully.'

Vivien smiled into his chest, solid with warmth and safety. *My Gio…*

'I want to be friends with her,' said Vivien. 'Only I don't think she likes me.'

'That's just Bella. She'll come round.'

Vivien thought of the sister's doctors. Wondered if her dosage could be upped, make her into a more amenable person. 'Does she take anything? Pills, medication?'

Gio's voice changed. 'She has, in the past,' he said, waiting a moment before continuing. 'Last time we tried her on medication…' He trailed off.

'What?'

He shook his head, and Vivien saw the years of worry scratched into his forehead and around his eyes. 'Nothing,' he said. She resented Isabella for causing him such grief and concern. *He lost his parents, too.*

'Can we talk about something else?' he asked.

Vivien snuggled back into his shirt. She needed to cement her connection to him, to prove it, and for Isabella to see that she wouldn't be got rid of with a few dirty glares. She was here to stay, whether the sister liked it or not.

'I'd like to be with you tonight,' she said, and kissed him. For a moment Gio held back, and she worried that Isabella had put a kibosh on this too, but then she felt him stir beneath her. His mouth moved round to her neck, grazed her collarbone, her hairline, her earlobes, and he murmured into her ear what he wanted to do to her.

'Make love to me, Gio,' she groaned, clasping him tight.

His hand cupped the flesh of her calf and travelled up the back of her leg, finding the band of her knickers. 'Oh, Viv...'

Then suddenly, he pulled away.

'You should go,' Gio said abruptly, moving back. Vivien sat, confused, and pulled down her skirt. As she did so, she was certain she saw a shadow slip past the living room door, so quick as to barely be there.

A shiver crawled up her spine. Had she imagined it?

'I'm sorry.' Gio's expression was closed. The evening was over. 'I'll make it up to you, Viv, I promise. Tomorrow. We'll see each other tomorrow.'

They said goodbye at the door and she was shut out in the night.

CHAPTER SEVENTEEN

Italy, Summer 2016

There's a secret garden at the Barbarossa. I noticed it when I arrived, the outline of a door on russet brick, but it isn't until Adalina tells me to tend the roses in the Oval that I have reason to explore it. Adalina's impatient manner can make it hard to ask for clarification, so often I find myself nodding, accepting the task, with little clue to what she means and with the resolve that I'll figure it out on my own later.

The Oval is one such thing. It takes me nearly an hour to discover that there is nothing warranting that name in the castillo's immediate grounds, and it's only when I'm by the orangery wall that I spy the opening once more. The handle has chipped off, only a keyhole remains, and I push on the brick and with a good shove it gives.

Beyond the wall, it's a broken paradise. I can just about make out the shape of the once manicured gardens, a circle bearing overgrown beds of dead roses, camellia, jasmine, a starfish of long-ago-fruitful plots that are now swamped by wild flowers. There is a savage beauty to it; the peace of this secluded suntrap is its own vacuum, a pocket of time stopped and stilled and surrendering to the bounty of nature. The estate is quiet at the best of times, but this new quiet is profound, disturbed only by the occasional flutter of birds' wings as they dive into an old dovecote set between two benches. I wonder who sat on those benches, surveying this magical space. Now, the wood is cracked and bleached by years, but the benches continue to watch all the same, facing me, demanding who I am, the girl among the butterflies.

I remember gardening with Mum, and how I tried to keep things growing after she died. It seemed important to do that. I got my sisters interested in it for a while, picking out worms from the soil, clumping up and down in their oversized rubber boots and giggling as they tried to rig a swing from the old apple tree. Afterwards, I'd helped them brush the earth from their knees, and each morning we'd check on the seedlings in their tiny pots, starting to open up and reach towards the sky.

'You should go home.'

I jump, startled, my hand flying to my chest. Salvatore is behind me.

'You frightened me,' I say, turning to where he stands in the entrance, a pitchfork in his hand, its points skewered into the cracked ground.

'You should go home,' he says again. 'Before it's too late.'

He is bigger than I remember, and not so ancient. I remember him hauling my bags on to his shoulder, the strength of him. He is blocking my exit.

'Too late for what?' I'm curious that we are conversing

in English, before recalling that Salvatore has been here for decades, working to Vivien's instruction.

'The water will get you,' he says. 'The water gets everyone.'

His green eyes are milky, unfocused.

He's not right. Hasn't been for thirty years. Signora keeps him on out of pity.

My brain works to join the dots. Thirty years, or thereabouts – that would tie in with *La Gazzetta*'s report of whatever tragedy befell the castillo. Images flash, of Max, of the skeleton key, of the attic, of the scrawled note, of Vivien's door ajar...

'You can't stop it,' says Salvatore. 'I tried once. She screamed. She was a wolf, teeth and blood. She wanted to kill me. *Never touch it*, she said. And they call me crazy but I've seen crazy. She wanted to kill me. You should go home.'

Salvatore's fingers curl round the handle of the fork, sinking it deeper into the ground. 'Except you can't,' he says, with the shadow of a smile. 'They say I don't know top from bottom but I see things. I know things. And I know about you.'

My lips are dry. The air has turned to menace. A grey bank of cloud bulks towards us on the blue. 'What do you know?'

'I see it in your eyes. They are like hers. You cannot go home. You did something bad, as bad as her, and the water will find you.'

I try to move past him but he's in my way.

'I saw her,' he says. 'Washing herself in it, out in the dark, washing herself with the water still left in the stone, over her nightgown so it got soaked, and I could smell it, the water, a black smell, black on black, grass and earth, the deep parts of the ground. Washing herself as if she could ever be clean. I saw her. The dead one.'

I shove past him and dart through the hole in the wall, out on to the terrace, up to the castle, my knees about to collapse. The air hits my lungs; the sky yawns and the ground prepares to swallow me up. The sun clings to the gravel, and it's only the fountain that sits in a pool of accusing shade.

*

At the house, I meet Adalina coming downstairs. She is in a rush, and looks ill.

'Is everything all right?' I ask, catching my breath. Adalina regards me in that way she has: irritation, affront, endurance. I am like a child caught out, half expecting Salvatore to be at my back, pointing a gnarled finger, picking out my guilt.

But Adalina isn't concerned about me. 'Fine,' she says. Only I see that it isn't. The maid's skin is wan; there are shadows round her eyes. She looks as if she hasn't slept and I think about Vivien's pills, the ones that arrived at the door, and how Adalina must be up all night with her. She grabs a coat and bag from the hall.

'Where are you going?' I have no right to ask questions, and Adalina's expression confirms it, hardening as she grips the banister.

'Signora is waiting,' she says. 'We will be back shortly.'

The heavy door closes, and seconds later I hear the crunch of gravel as Vivien's car eases off down the drive. I follow them out. I can decipher Adalina's tight shoulders in the driver's seat, but can't see Vivien. I picture her lying frail across the back, in the throes of her mysterious ailment, forced to surmount her fear of the outside and show herself to the world – or, at least, to a doctor. I struggle to match this image of Vivien with the portraits taken of her years ago. She was a siren, a coveted actress with the world at her feet. What happened to change all that?

The fountain glares at me, seeming to pulse with an answer.

Come to me. Come. Come and see.

My legs carry me there. I splay my fingers on the rough, cold brim, and peer over to meet my reflection. Behind me, in the mirror, amorphous clouds drift across a sky so patient that I could have been looking at the real thing, not a replica, and for a moment it's not an echo I meet but something true, and *I* am the echo, the living me no longer living, the real and reverberated world exchanged, so I am gazing through from the other side. I plunge deeper into the impression, hypnotic in its eeriness. My heart accelerates as if something is about to happen. I hold my breath and in that same instant the suggestion of a face appears at my shoulder, shocking and grotesque and savagely, resplendently malignant, mad eyes wild and deranged—

I stand, gasping for breath, backing up against the stone.

There is nobody there. I think I hear a child laugh, but there is nobody there.

*

Inside, I'm filled with adrenalin, and before I can change my mind I go to the ballroom and reclaim the key. It takes me a few seconds to find it, panicking a moment that I've been found out and the key moved, a silent reprimand, before—

Got it.

Instead of returning to the attic to lock it, as I know is the only sensible thing, I head for Vivien's quarters. Her door, predictably, is bolted shut. For a second I doubt if the key will turn, but then, with a satisfying switch, it does.

I am inside.

Vivien's bedroom looks out on to the gravel and the pointing cypress trees, and is furnished in a way that brings to mind the woman herself: once opulent, perhaps excessive, but now a ghost of times gone by. The curtains, heavy and scarlet, I recognise from my brief glimpse that day we spoke; the rug is ornate (I place it in a Middle Eastern souk, surrounded by jewels) but worn, the gilt-edged landscapes of Italy no doubt painted by masters but now faded by the sun, their rims tarnished.

The bed is out of place. What should have been a four-poster celebration, something Vivien might have lounged on in her Hollywood days, swathed in furs and diamonds and sipping champagne, is a clinical single on a metal frame. There is a tray table, levered to allow access at mealtimes, and a drinking flask. It looks as if it belongs in a hospital. The mattress has been stripped. There is a smell like vinegar.

Several marble busts sit in a line by the long-neglected dressing table, bearing a variety of wigs. There is something disarmingly helpless about this array, the lost dignity of a woman once so beautiful. No wonder she doesn't want us to meet.

What strikes me about the room is the lack of reference to her past. There are no photographs, no books, nothing to give her away; no clue to her interests, her loves or her hopes. Does she still have hope? All art resolutely avoids people as its subject. I recall the veiled man on the staircase, dead but somehow living. Did he once belong here? Did he stand where I'm standing; did he love Vivien, did he hold her in bed?

Her ghosts are my ghosts – at least some of them are. I think about the love I've lost, about his voice when I called him, right after his wife did it... the silence, stark and absolute in its direction. *I cannot know you any more.*

But what if I still want to know you? What if I can't survive unless I do?

Gingerly, I open Vivien's wardrobe. It's musty, seldom used, and when I see the outfits inside it's clear why. Glorious robes of silk and satin spill on to my fingers, lace sleeves and collars soft as rabbits' ears; I can feel their expense, the sheer luxury Vivien would have draped herself in. What parties had they held at the Barbarossa? Had Vivien swept downstairs to greet her guests, a train liquid as caramel pooling behind her? Had the man been with her, ready to take her hand, the perfect couple?

At the foot of the closet is a shelf. I crouch, expecting to see rows of shoes concealed beneath the skirts, but instead I spot a leather-bound book. I reach in. The cover is oxblood and worn, its surface gently cracked like the icing on a day-old cake.

Opening it, I find the pages yellowed. There are no dates, just passages, some beneath a day header, others random. As I flip through, the writing becomes erratic and harder to interpret. I settle on one entry towards the end, a Sunday:

Help me. I do not know how much more I can take. I cannot live like this, a prisoner in my own home. Is this my home? Has it ever been? Or has it always been hers? Hers and his, together… Some days it is all I can do not to leave. Would he realise, then? Or would that mean she had won? That's the way she sees it, I know. A competition. From the first day she has loathed me, and I her. But I cannot walk away. Not now. There is too much at stake. I've seen the way she watches me. She wants what is mine. She cannot have it. I will kill her before that happens.

Heat prickles on the back of my neck, my fingers white as they grip the page.

Outside, I hear the sound of a car door.

I bundle the diary back where I found it, close the wardrobe, and check the room a final time before locking it behind me. I hurry back downstairs in the hope that I might catch them, run into the woman who is appearing to me in so many pieces, finally see her whole, but the car is parked and empty and the hall is quiet.

*

That night, I can't stop thinking about Vivien's diary. I want to have it in my hands, read it from start to finish. Fragments swim before my closed eyes, joining dots, pieces slotting together then coming apart. Briefly it occurs to me that, for once, I am not consumed by him. Instead I am consumed by the black shadow settling over us, of the fountain, of Vivien, of Salvatore, of this tragic, elusive secret…

I need to speak to Max.

Finally, I fall asleep, or at least I must do, because the next thing I know I'm suddenly awake, pulse racing, sweat pasted across my chest. Blood thrums in my ears, hectic and hot. I struggle to catch hold of the nightmare that possessed me.

We were there again, on the station platform. Early morning, just like any other morning, with his scent still on me, the back of my hair dishevelled because I didn't want to lose one splinter of his touch. That stupid, love-dumb smile on my face, and it was an intrusion to my reverie when a woman said my name. *Lucy.* I had known it was his wife: if my fellow commuters had been less absorbed by their own worlds they might have known too. Grace Calloway was a household name.

My dream conjured her smile in just the way I remembered it, better than I remembered it, for in the ensuing weeks I must have frozen it out. Strange how the mind locks these details away – things we think we've lost, things we've *tried* to lose, but they're all still there, filed away in a dark recess. Why the smile? It wasn't happy, neither was it sad. Resigned. Stoic. Grace had known what she had come to do.

And then she'd done it. Right there, in front of my eyes. The twin lights approaching down the tunnel, the expectant shuffle of feet as the crowd moved towards the rim of the platform. *Stand behind the yellow line.* The rattle of the Northern Line train as it entered the station. She had been like a swimmer on the blue rim of a pool, elegant and calm. Jump! Never once taking her eyes from mine.

Vanished.

Only not. The crunch of her body, that shocking crunch I will never forget until the day I die and even then it will haunt me beyond, as her bones met the wheels. The awful screams as it dawned what had happened, and one of them could have been mine but I can't promise it was. I was running, up and out, have to get out, fumbling in my bag for my phone because all I could think about was hearing his voice…

I swallow, hard, in the darkness, and hear my throat contract.

My pyjamas are stuck to my legs. I sit, attempting to throw off the flavour of the nightmare but it clings on with grisly fingers, all up my spine and crawling around my shoulders. *Oh, Grace*, I think. *I am so sorry. I am so very, very sorry.* I wish I could say sorry to her children. She was a wonderful mother, by all accounts. But that would be selfish, an act to alleviate my own grinding conscience. Not for them at all.

So many times I've tried to make sense of what I did. Even believing that his marriage was in crisis, I was still sleeping with a husband and a father. The temptation was too great, too new, for me to resist. I didn't want to be predictable Lucy any longer; I wanted to amaze not just other people but myself. I wanted to look in the mirror and not quite recognise the person looking back, because she had become more powerful and remarkable than I'd thought she could. Until I met him, I'd been living for other people – but when the time came to seize something that was mine, just for me, I went too far. Every rule and discipline was thrown into the fire. Everything I'd thought I was, gone. It was a reckless thrill, like flying. And if I'd remembered to look down, I might have seen his wife and kids far beneath me, and my dad, and my sisters, and I might have decided to stop. But I never looked down. I flew for the sun.

My window is shut. Turning to the clock at my bedside, I see the time:

3:12 a.m.

The house is dead. I need fresh air and stumble out of bed. I'm not really concentrating when I go to the window and release the catch, but then, with a rush that leaves me breathless, I'm back in the instant, my nightmare blown like leaves.

There is a woman by the fountain.

She is dressed in white. She is looking in. For a wild moment I am seeing my earlier self, looking as I had into the well today, standing in just that way, leaning, leaning, until I thought I saw what I know is impossible…

I want to call out but my lips don't work. Am I dreaming? The figure is there but not there; her outline is unfeasibly pale, flickering in the uncanny light, as if she is underwater herself. I squint to draw her into focus. Is it Vivien? It can't be, yet I cannot process the alternative. I see the woman's back tense, her head lift abruptly like an animal picking up sound, as if she senses she is being watched, and with a surge of unease I watch her straighten and I know, I just know that she is going to see me. The thought of this wordless encounter is too terrifying to articulate, too dreadful to consider, but I am unable to move. I see her dark hair, so like Grace, and her pale skin, so like Grace. The room swims and I put my hands in front of my eyes like a child afraid of the dark, and when I open them again she is gone.

CHAPTER EIGHTEEN

Vivien, Los Angeles, 1979

The proposal came on a summer's night, in a restaurant overlooking the bay. Vivien hadn't been expecting it. Tonight was her birthday and that was celebration enough. All through her childhood – indeed, until Gio – she had never marked her birthday. A limp hug from her mother and a brusque nod from her father was all she had become used to, not like the other kids who got sticky iced buns and candles to blow out. And later, when she'd hit the private clubs in LA, then the movie studios in Hollywood, she'd let her birthdays come and go without telling anyone. What was the point?

With Gio, it was different. He treated her as if she was worth something, showering her with gifts. 'It's too much,' Vivien said, as she opened a box with a delicate gold bracelet laid inside. 'You shouldn't have gone to such trouble…'

'Why not?' Gio watched her in the candlelight, the sound of waves lapping on the shore their only accompaniment. 'You're an amazing woman and I'm lucky to have you. The way you've been with Bella this past year, I can't thank you enough.'

Vivien bit her tongue. She didn't want to ruin the moment. But try as she might – and she had tried – she had still got nowhere with Isabella. She put a brave face on it, visiting the house, bringing the sister gifts, making an effort to talk to her and encourage her and bring out a smile or a laugh, saying she didn't mind when Gio had to cancel a date last-minute – but privately it had started to eat her up. She struggled with how Isabella dictated so much of his life, and consequently her own. She couldn't bear how Isabella gave her nothing, absolutely nothing, except evil glares and hidden scowls, none of which she could tell Gio about because it would drive a wedge between them. Would he even believe her? Whenever Gio asked, no, she didn't mind; no, nothing Isabella did was too much trouble; yes, she liked her. She hated deceiving the man she loved, but she had no choice.

'You don't need to thank me,' Vivien said, sipping her wine.

Gio's face shone back at her in the gloaming, those intense, heroic eyes, his angular jaw and the way his hair caught the collar of his jacket. It was sexy how proficient he was at work, yet with her he carried this streak of jeopardy, this dark thrill that rendered her like a teenager whenever she was with him; she still had butterflies and grew tongue-tied, even after so many months.

I adore you, she thought. *You're worth it.*

And in that same instant Gio was on his feet, suddenly down on the floor, then his hand was in his pocket and in a rush Vivien knew what was coming.

The ring was exquisite. Gio's expression was determined as he asked:

'Vivien Lockhart... will you marry me?'

*

The wedding was arranged for the fall. Vivien couldn't wait to make Gio her husband. She thought of the beauty of the day, the beach – their special place, the scene of their early dates – where it would happen, the dress and the decorations. But most of all she thought of the moment at which he would be hers and only hers. She had the diamond but she wanted the wedding band. It was proof of his commitment. Once that was on her finger, Isabella would be forced to take second place.

VIVIEN SET TO WED DOCTOR HERO, the newspapers announced. THE DOCTOR AND THE STARLET! It was a shock to see her name in the press again. Dandy got back in touch with a script but she turned it down. Even Jonny Laing made an attempt at contact, wishing her his best and at the same time inviting her out to his holiday home in Frisco for a weekend if she ever found 'married life too much'. While the advance was brazen, it interested her that Jonny had retreated from her life. Maybe he sensed she could no longer be touched: he could tell the world whatever the hell he wanted and it could never tarnish her happiness. Or maybe he wasn't going to risk crossing Gio, for while Gio didn't have the credentials of a Hollywood titan, his status – and appearance – possessed a quiet, lethal command, like a tiger lounging on a tree branch. Jonny, for all his foolishness, at least had the sense to see it.

In striking out the superficial circles she'd once moved in, Vivien's guest list made for sobering reading. Family was a no-go – she didn't even know if Gilbert Lockhart was still living, and even if he were she could scarcely invite a man whom her fiancé imagined to be dead, and the maiden aunts that had terrorised her childhood wouldn't be missed. She closed off the part of herself that witnessed other people's weddings and saw the tight bonds of brothers and sisters, cousins, moms and dads, grandparents, because there was no point in dwelling on what couldn't be changed.

Never mind, she thought, flipping her address book shut. *It'll be more intimate this way – just me and Gio and a close crowd. Isn't that the point of the day?* The thought gave her comfort. She had the love of her life. He was all she needed.

If only Isabella wasn't such a bad apple in the proceedings.

'Involve her,' Gio urged, taking Vivien's hand, 'please.' And Vivien smiled, swallowing her misgivings. Involving Isabella was impossible. On those occasions Vivien tried, sitting with her at the house and running through menu cards and dress ideas, Isabella was impenetrable. The sister just sat there, her face inscrutable.

'Is she happy about this wedding?' Vivien asked.

'She'll come round,' said Gio. 'It takes her a while to get used to new people.'

Vivien hardly thought she could be deemed a new person, but Isabella's way, of course, was the way to which they bowed. If Isabella was in a dark mood, it wasn't a good time to visit. If Isabella was sobbing in her room, Vivien ought to leave. The worst part was when Vivien could tell that Gio knew more than he was letting on. Did Isabella speak to him? The thought was heinous not just for its deception but also for its implication that he was keeping things from his soon-to-be-bride. Vivien was strict with herself. She had to trust him. She *did* trust him. It was Isabella she didn't trust.

She was certain that Isabella loathed her brother's engagement. Those coal-black eyes roamed over Vivien like a snake, slow and sinuous, its poison bite only ever a heartbeat away and the results would be fatal. When they were alone, Vivien began to poke her like a child with a stick. She knew it was mean, but she couldn't help it; she had to get *something* from Isabella, and besides, Isabella was more than capable of giving as good as she got, without ever saying a word. 'Do you like this?' Vivien would ask. 'How about this veil with these shoes? I don't know… it's so hard being a bride… I don't suppose you'd know, never having been one…'

One time, Vivien pushed it too far. She had spotted a magnificent brochure for a boat wedding, out on the glittering Pacific, champagne in hand with only the horizon for company. Actually she hadn't brought it up on purpose, the significance of open water momentarily slipping her mind, but once she saw Isabella's reaction she couldn't help but nudge a little further. 'Just imagine,' she mused, 'out there in the middle of the ocean, all that sky and water, and the man I love…' Isabella had fled in tears. Vivien had thought it safest to bring the episode up with Gio herself and apologise in advance for her thoughtlessness. If Isabella *was* communicating with him, she wasn't letting her reach him first. It was a game – and one Vivien had to win.

Vivien knew it was spiteful but she couldn't stop. Life had taught her to protect herself at all costs – it was hunt or be hunted – and whatever she had to do, however she had to get there, she would see salvation and she would claim it. She was by turns frustrated and angered by Isabella, and her sole consolation was the thought that, once she and Gio were married, they could begin their lives together, alone.

*

October arrived and with it the most important day of Vivien's life. As she prepared early morning at home, hair and make-up girls showering her with attention, she could hardly believe she was here. When she'd been a girl, tortured by dreams of an unknown future and nightmares of a wretched past, when she'd been a hostess, when she'd been a hollow, fame-hungry actress, when she'd slammed her car into a wall because she'd had too much to drink, never had she imagined finding peace with someone like Gio Moretti. He would never hurt her. He would never hit her or make her feel bad; he would never let her doubt his love. Today proved it once and for all.

'Is your dress here?' her stylist asked as she applied an airbrush foundation – not that Vivien needed it, she was already aglow with the promise of the day. Nothing could ruin it, not even the press who had threatened to camp out by the beach house.

'Not yet.'

Vivien pictured perfectly the gown she had lovingly chosen from all her bridal magazines, a floor-length lace number with exquisite full sleeves and a high collar. It was an impeccable choice, Italian in flavour and quintessentially elegant. She planned to wear it with a short lace veil and baby white roses in her hair.

She thought of old photos she'd been shown of Millicent Lockhart's wedding dress, a starched smock that had been approved of by Gilbert on account of its shapeless dreariness. Gilbert had commanded chastity, and with it the closure of any beauty or freedom Millicent might have known. Vivien felt sorry for her mother.

But she let him do it, Vivien told herself, refusing to tumble into the past. *You won't allow the world to beat you like that. You're tougher than she was.*

And the dress she'd picked proved it.

Just wait until Gio's family saw her; they would gasp in amazement. It was particularly delightful to imagine Isabella's reaction. Vivien had been compelled to ask the sister to be bridesmaid. In a last-ditch attempt to forge some bond with her, Vivien brought a gift, turned up at the house with a slate wiped clean and a smile to start over – but Isabella had received the news with her usual blank expression.

'She probably feels helpless,' Gio had encouraged. 'Give her something to do: she likes to feel included.' So Vivien had awarded Isabella the job of collecting the dress – or, rather, because Isabella was unable to venture into busy public spaces, taking delivery of it and bringing it to Vivien's house, carefully preserved in its box.

Then he'll see who's most beautiful.

As Vivien regarded her reflection in the make-up girl's mirror, she saw how absurd she was being. Isabella was his sister – of course there was no contest between them. And yet a warning thread needled, rooting away day and night in all her fragile places. She'd seen how Isabella looked at her brother, the naked worship and affection she bestowed upon him. Call it gratitude, dependence, need, or plain old sibling fondness – whatever it was, Isabella wanted her brother all to herself.

'It'll be here soon,' Vivien promised the girls, focusing again on the dress and on stepping into it, the feel of brittle lace around her shoulders. She couldn't wait.

On cue, the bell rang. 'That'll be it!' Vivien ducked from underneath the curling tongs and raced for the door. Instead of meeting Isabella, as expected, the box was waiting on the step, unaccompanied. *That's strange*, she thought, collecting it and slipping back inside, but thought no more about it because Isabella never did the expected thing. She'd delivered the gown: nothing more was required of her.

Vivien had to contain herself as the stylists finished. She was itching to peek in the box, let the material cross her fingers, but the wait would be worth it.

'There,' the girl said, 'all done.' She grinned. 'So... can we see it now?'

Vivien had imagined Gio being the first to witness the dress, but since she had an audience she couldn't resist sharing her excitement. 'OK!' she trilled. 'Wait here.'

Vivien tore open the box, not bothering to untie the dove-grey ribbon securing its lid, and rustled through layers of fragrant tissue paper.

My dress…

Only it wasn't her dress. Yes, it was. No, it wasn't. Confusion hit her in a hot blast. For an awful moment she thought the wrong one had been picked up – but, then, as she examined the mess that spooled miserably between her hands, she only wished that were true, because at least, despite the inconvenience, she could have arranged to return it and claim the proper one, the real one, the one she had paid for and fallen in love with. A horrid taste multiplied in her mouth.

'Ms Lockhart – is everything all right?'

She found she couldn't speak. There were no words.

'I, uh… This is…'

Vivien didn't need to turn to gauge their reaction – she heard their gasps just fine. The bundle in her arms could only be described as a monstrosity. No longer white, it was dyed an awful sludge brown-green, as mottled as a toad's back. The lace had been ripped, the sleeves slashed, so that holding it against the light revealed a shaggy atrocity that neither she, nor any other self-respecting human being, would ever be seen dead in. Vivien knew straight away who had done this. *Isabella.*

'What happened?' the hairdresser asked, stunned.

'Just leave,' Vivien croaked. 'Go.'

The women retreated. Alone, Vivien consulted the clock. Clever Isabella had left just an hour between delivery and the start of the ceremony. There was no way of unpicking it. All she had in the laundry was a pair of sweatpants and her jogging T-shirt – the rest of her clothes were at Gio's. Vivien couldn't help a flash of admiration at Isabella's cunning. Isabella had hated it when she'd moved her clothes into Gio's room; the sister had hovered at the door like a bad omen, watching Vivien unpack, casting sneer after sneer her way. She knew that Vivien had cleared out her own place. And, as punishment, had no choice but to wear this carbuncle.

How could you? she thought, biting back tears. *You horrible, horrible thing.*

There was no time to cry. She had to make it work.

And she tried. Boy, she tried. Vivien scrubbed the aggressive colour, which only made it worse; she endeavoured to stitch together the more tattered of the torn seams, to no avail; she hemmed the skirt to give it more form but instead it just ballooned around her knees. She looked dreadful. What was her alternative? Guests would be waiting; Gio would be wondering where she was. She had even managed to mess up her hair with all the pulling and tugging of the material over her head. If only she had another outfit to wear, but it was this or nothing. Isabella had won this time.

I hate you, she thought, as she swiped at her tears, but the more she swiped the more her mascara bled. *I'll get you for this, you evil, vengeful witch. Just you wait.*

*

Under ordinary circumstances, the setting would be paradise. Azure ocean, lilac sky, amber sand giving way to a pearl-white pagoda beneath which Gio stood, suited, impossibly handsome, awaiting his bride… But Vivien was walking into a disaster zone. *Maybe it isn't that bad*, she had told herself as she'd left the house, thinking that perhaps the light of day would be kind, make the green appear less slime and more emerald, but the caws of the waiting press had soon put paid to that illusion.

As she approached the aisle, she saw Gio's face fall. Vivien glowed scarlet; her tears were ready to drown her. She wished she could explain, tell him everything; tell all the assembled guests who exchanged looks as she passed, but she couldn't.

One face struck her with absolute clarity. Isabella, just a glance from where she stood alongside her brother at the altar, but that glance was triumphant with malice. Vivien had never seen her look so pleased – or so sinful. To Vivien's horror she registered that Isabella was wearing white; she had deliberately let the sister choose her outfit independently, and saw now how foolish she'd been. Of course Isabella would have taken the chance to upstage her. Vivien hadn't thought her capable of it: cold, yes; cruel, yes; toxic, yes – but this duplicity required guts and determination. Isabella had always appeared to her a passive aggressor, not someone qualified to make such a bold and barefaced attack. Together, brother and sister looked every inch the perfect couple, and she, Vivien, the slime-drenched pretender.

'What happened?' Gio whispered as she reached his side and their guests sat down. Briskly, she shook her head for fear that speaking would make her cry. At least he hadn't imagined that she had *chosen* this miscreation. Not that the paparazzi would care for excuses. She envisaged tomorrow's papers and wanted to weep afresh.

The ceremony passed in a blur. Vivien was aware the entire time of Isabella's presence at her back, her long dark hair hanging beautifully and a clutch of peonies clasped demurely at her waist. What must Vivien look like next to her?

Afterwards, she was congratulated a touch warily. Nobody commented on the gown: there was nothing to say. Any compliment would have been comical.

'I know what you did,' she hissed at Isabella as soon as she got the chance, grabbing her elbow and pinching it hard. 'Don't think I don't know it was you.' And Isabella gazed back at her with wide, innocent eyes, a mere flicker of mischief dancing at their centre, a flicker no one else but Vivien would see – not even Gio.

She was reminded, appallingly, of her father. The way that Gilbert would send a scare her way in a single glance – a terrible assurance of what was to come.

You're done for, he had told her, without saying a word. Isabella said the same.

'So, how are you sisters getting on?' Gio joined them, smiling.

'Fine,' said Vivien tightly. *I'll tell him later.* She didn't wish to make more of a scene than she already had – inciting an argument would be the final disgrace.

*

That night, they made love at the lavish hotel Gio had booked. Vivien had worried that the dress would render her forever besmirched in her new husband's eyes, but thankfully that wasn't the case. Gio took her to heaven and back, and afterwards she was loath to break the spell but she had to. She had to tell him the truth.

'There's something I need to talk to you about,' she said.

Gio propped himself up on one elbow. Her husband: the light of her life.

'That's funny,' he said, 'I do, too. You first.'

Vivien opened her mouth to speak but the words dried up.

'No.' She lost her nerve, pulling the sheet up to cover herself. 'You go.'

Gio's smile widened. His eyelashes were soft and long, and she wished she had known him as a boy, in Sicily, far away from Claremont... He'd been an orphan.

Like you told him you were. What right did she have to throw accusations Isabella's way when she had deceived him so terribly?

'How would you feel about moving to Italy?' Gio tucked a lock of hair behind her ear. 'I've been offered a research placement in Tuscany.'

Vivien's eyes widened. 'You have?'

'It's a great opportunity,' he said, 'and we'd have a place ready-made. I've thought a lot about this, Viv, and it could work for us, really. When my uncle died a few years ago, he left me his mansion in the hills – it's been empty ever since. I thought I'd end up selling one day but I couldn't quite bring myself to let it go.' A faraway look overcame him. 'It's the house where Bella and I grew up. My uncle took us in when we lost our parents. It's a big place, and… unusual. But it's special to me, and I always hoped I'd go back but the timing was never right – until now. Think about it, *bellissima*. It could be a fresh start. The beginning of our lives together.'

Seeing her startled expression, he quickly added, 'I know you'd be leaving a lot behind, but—'

'No!' He had misread her joy for shock – but this was perfect! 'Oh, Gio, it sounds wonderful!' Vivien fell into his arms. 'Yes, yes, take me, take me there now!'

'We're not visiting.' He made clear. 'It's to live… For a year, maybe longer.'

Elated, Vivien kissed him. This was the best wedding present she could ever have imagined. Finally, they would break away and start their future – far from Hollywood, far from the ghosts of her past, and, most crucially, far from Isabella.

'I said yes, didn't I?' she enthused, kissing him again. 'The house is ready?'

'It is,' laughed Gio, his features aglow like a boy at Christmas, gladdened at her reaction. Then, more serious: 'It's isolated, it's not what you're used to.'

'I don't care!'

'And you don't speak the language.'

'I'm learning!' Vivien bit her lip with pleasure. 'Oh, Gio, what a magnificent stroke of luck… And how generous of your uncle.'

'He was our mother's brother. After what happened to our family, he did all he could. He saved us, really, gave us sanctuary… He always vowed I would inherit.'

The 'us' bothered her, the 'our'. She ignored it. Nothing could ruin this moment. She and Gio were about to move into their own place. Their own home! Vivien had longed for it since they'd met: a roof she and Gio could share, a refuge that would spell years of happiness, that might one day hear the laughter of children…

'It sounds magical,' she said. 'I promise it will be the best decision we ever made.' This time their kiss was fervent, passion burning between them.

'Darling,' he said, grinning, 'you had something to say, too?'

Vivien considered it, the allegation on the tip of her tongue, but then she changed her mind. Gio was a good man, and what did it matter if his sister had done a spiteful thing, when they would soon be leaving her behind anyway? Vivien felt charity blossom in her heart. She would let Isabella get away with this one. After all, she herself was getting away with Isabella's brother – and with her uncle's house.

'It doesn't matter,' she said.

'Are you sure?'

'I'm sure.'

She squeezed his hand, her heart bursting with happiness.

'Good,' he said. 'In that case, I'll tell Isabella in the morning.'

Vivien blinked. She drew away. 'Excuse me?'

'Didn't I mention it?' said Gio. 'Isabella is coming with us.'

PART TWO

CHAPTER NINETEEN

Vivien, Italy, 1980

Their jet touched down in Florence in the early evening. Vivien had drunk so many Campari sodas that she felt woozy, only vaguely registering the burned sienna colour of the surrounding hills and the grey strip of runway as they approached.

'Home,' murmured Gio, next to her, and looped his fingers through hers.

Vivien returned his smile with a tight one of her own, and tried not to think about the damp patch flowering on her silk blouse, where Isabella had stood partway through the flight and spilled her drink. *Deliberate*, had been Vivien's first thought, seeing the way Isabella hung her head in mock shame and Gio, as always, stepped in to apologise on his sister's behalf. *You did that on purpose, you child.*

'It's good to be back, right?' Gio leaned across his wife to his sister, who was staring solemnly out of the window. Vivien heard the note of enquiry in his voice, of concern, for Isabella had not returned to Italy since they'd left their uncle's care. Once again, Vivien endeavoured to reignite her sympathy for the sister, but she struggled. How long could she hold her tongue? It had been impossible for her and Gio to have a honeymoon, even, without involving Isabella, and now she was joining them for the first phase of their brand new chapter, in their new home? It was ridiculous.

Isabella turned and gave a sad little nod. No wonder Gio treated her like a kicked puppy. Only Vivien saw through her act. Isabella was tough and calculating, and there wasn't room for both of them in this marriage.

Gio sat back, satisfied, as the wheels struck tarmac. Music boomed to life on the jet's speakers and Vivien unclipped her purse to apply coral lipstick. She was pleased with her likeness in the compact. She could have stepped straight out of a Duran Duran video, all peacock eye shadow and voluminous blonde hair. Vivien nurtured her difference from Isabella, who was more Kate Bush than Bonnie Tyler, and maximised her golden-girl Californian allure through glitzy jewellery and bold fashion statements. She wore these things like a shield, a reminder that she had been a bona fide movie star and in another league altogether from this shy, sinister sister; but other times, like now, they made her feel cheap and foolish. That look had only ever been a mask – it had been a mask at the Lalique and it had been a mask in Hollywood – and she feared she would forever be unable to peer beneath.

'You don't need to do that, sweetheart,' said Gio, with a little bat of his hand that made her feel silly and vain. Isabella wasn't putting on make-up, was she? She didn't need to. 'The paparazzi have been told to expect a different plane,' he said, 'at a different time. I wasn't risking any disturbances.' He shot a pointed look at Isabella.

Naturally. What wasn't about Isabella?

It hurt Vivien that he supposed her every effort was for someone else's benefit – in this case, for the cameras. What if she wanted to look nice, just for him?

She slicked the colour on anyway. Even if her shirt was ruined, her face didn't have to be. As the plane rumbled to its moorings, Gio saw her inspect the stain once more. 'It was an *accident*,' he reminded her, a little less gently than before.

Vivien longed to object, but she was scared to confront Gio. Scared of his disappointment, scared of his sadness, scared of exposing her disloyalty, scared of wounding him… And scared most of all that, if issued an ultimatum, there would be only one woman he would pick.

'I know,' she replied, giving him her loveliest smile.

*

They arrived at the Castillo Barbarossa at dusk. Gio's uncle's mansion crept out of the burgeoning twilight, amber glow cast across its giant facets and the scent of lemons heady in the air. Their car crunched up on the gravel drive and Vivien spotted two uniformed staff, a man and a woman, waiting for them at the door.

'What do you think?' Gio asked, kissing her cheek.

Vivien was stunned. She was accustomed to luxury back in America, but not of this ilk. This wasn't a palm trees and swimming pools kind of opulence; it was far more sophisticated, steeped in age-old class and in possession of an ancient elegance that all the hundred-dollar bills in La-La Land couldn't buy.

'It's beautiful,' she said truthfully. She couldn't believe that she was going to live here, that it would be hers and Gio's.

Gio helped Isabella out of the car first, and stood for a moment with his arm round his sister, looking up at the house. He whispered something in her ear. Vivien flinched, and opened the door to let herself out. She felt self-conscious in front of the man who came to take their luggage. Did he suppose Isabella was the wife?

'I am Salvatore, Signora Moretti,' he said, addressing her correctly – thank God. 'And this is Adalina.' The woman stepped forward, warm, friendly, her eyes bright with the promise of working for a movie star – that, or for Gio, who looked even more handsome, if that was possible, against his ancestral backdrop. In the style of the time, he wore a long dark coat with the collar turned up, his tousled hair a reckless vision and his single earring glinting in the tentative moonlight. Vivien's heart sang to see how content he looked, even with Isabella a blemish on the horizon. If only Gio's satisfaction could be something she alone could achieve. She feared it was not. There was only so much happiness she could give him.

Inside, the rooms unfolded like gloriously wrapped presents, a maze of endless corridors, exquisite wall hangings, antique *objets* and the kind of framed pictures that looked as if they belonged in Buckingham Palace. Salvatore and Adalina had lit all the spaces, so Gio and his new bride could choose their quarters at leisure. Vivien knew straight away the room they would have: the master at the front, overlooking the gardens and the fountain, from a window heavy with scarlet material.

'It's incredible, Gio,' she told him, as they stared at the view together, scarcely able at this hour to pick out the cypress trees beyond, and the stunning tiered gardens that tumbled down to the lawns. 'I love it. I absolutely love it.'

'And I absolutely love you,' he told her.

Vivien turned and beamed, finding his lips with hers.

Isabella stepped into the room. Gio broke off, steering his wife with one arm and greeting his sister with the other. Vivien disliked when he did this, stood between the two women as if each was as important to him as the other. She also disliked how, up close, she could smell Isabella's black hair, fragrant with a weirdly seductive scent that made her own gleaming bottles of Rive Gauche seem trite and sickly sweet.

Downstairs, a fire was blazing in the hall. Orange shadows danced and jumped across panelled walls, and she marvelled at the stone arch carved out of it.

'The ballroom, signora,' said Adalina, appearing at her side. 'Signor Dinapoli rarely used it, but it's a magnificent space.' Vivien left the others behind and stepped through, her delighted gaze taking in the corniced ceilings and polished parquet floor. She wondered about the uncle, Giacomo Dinapoli, and what sort of person he'd been – he was kind, presumably, to have taken in two orphans after his sister's death.

'Hey,' said Gio, in pursuit, 'this hasn't changed a bit!' Next to him, Isabella clung to his arm and relinquished a small smile. 'We used to play in here as kids,' Gio explained. 'What was it, Bella? The King and Queen of Everland?' He laughed. 'We hid from the grown-ups, made up our own fantasy world. Bella had the imagination, though, right?' He gave her an affectionate nudge. 'Always making up stories.'

Something didn't sit right in this memory. Had Isabella been able to speak, then? Had she saved her voice only for her brother? If this were the case, it unsettled Vivien that Gio hadn't told her. As if he wanted to keep it secret.

She suffocated her suspicions.

'Really?' said Vivien, just tetchily enough to warrant a flick of the eyes from Adalina. Vivien checked herself; she didn't want the maid drawing conclusions. Vivien was the mistress of this house, she owned it together with Gio, and she had to start behaving accordingly. Just because Isabella had been here before, and Isabella had the family tie, it didn't mean she could rule the roost. Vivien was the *wife*.

But Gio seemed oblivious to her mood. He spoke to Isabella in Italian, pointing to the windows, whose panes were wispy with cobwebs. Isabella made a light noise in her throat, the closest to a laugh that Vivien had heard.

All of a sudden, a wonderful idea assailed her.

'Let's have a party!' Vivien cried, clapping her hands.

It was the perfect way to celebrate Gio's homecoming. They would invite the notables of the region, set out a lavish banquet, dress in their finery, drink and dance long into the night. Vivien was gratified at Isabella's expression. It had to be Isabella's worst nightmare, being made to socialise with the people who had known her as a mute child, only to discover that she hadn't changed a bit. It was a shameful thought – but all Vivien had to do was remember the sister's spiteful hostility from the moment they had met, the cruelty of that wedding dress stunt, the constant sly glances and hateful stares, to be certain there was no love lost.

'We'll host it for Halloween,' enthused Vivien, who adored the seasonal celebration, largely because her father back in Claremont had denied her it. While other kids had carved pumpkins, fiery eyes flickering red in the night, and trailed the neighbourhood for trick or treats, Vivien had stayed shut up in her bedroom. *Devil worship*, Gilbert Lockhart had proclaimed. *It's no place for any daughter of mine.*

'Steady on, *bellissima*,' Gio said, smiling, 'we only just got here.'

'All the more reason.' Emboldened, Vivien went to embrace him. Isabella shrank from his side. 'It's been so long since the Barbarossa had guests – your uncle would have loved it. Look at this place! It's crying out for attention.'

With that, she steered her husband around the ballroom, spilling ideas as she went. This was one thing she had in spades over Isabella: the charm, the glamour and the wherewithal to plan. The sister could hide out all night, for all she cared.

CHAPTER TWENTY

Vivien ordered her costume from an elite tailor in London. The place on Pall Mall was a favourite of the day's power clique, boasting Goldie Hawn and Jamie Lee Curtis among its visiting clients. Within weeks, the order was ready.

Vivien couldn't wait for Gio to see it. He would be stunned. It was a second chance at her wedding gown, a white, ethereal number that wasn't strictly in keeping with the Halloween theme but that she could get away with nonetheless. She would be a fairy or a nymph, some water-dwelling siren that might once have been found adorning that old romantic fountain in front of the Barbarossa.

She was settling well into life in Europe. Twice she had travelled to Rome for lunch and shopping, and last month she had met an acquaintance in St Tropez for a brief stay on his yacht, sailing it as they had down to the old harbour at Portofino. Gio was bound up in work for much of the time, so when it was just she and Isabella in the mansion she found any excuse not to be there. Granted Isabella kept to herself, resigned to her quarters on the top floor, but somehow her very presence cast a gloom across the Barbarossa. Vivien wondered if the staff felt it, too. Vivien wished she could enjoy her young marriage in this beautiful country, but Isabella was the constant shadow at her heels. Isabella shot daggers whenever her brother's back was turned; she played the victim with Adalina and Salvatore, but when it was the two women alone, she didn't need words to convey her animosity. Vivien endeavoured, each morning extending the arm of reconciliation with a kind word or a polite enquiry that stole all her will and stamina, but always she was snubbed. She couldn't put her finger on it, but, day by day, minute by minute, Vivien sensed Isabella's aversion turning from hard grit into liquid form, an altogether more dangerous and insidious thing that could change shape, seep through cracks, infiltrate the tiniest slit until the body it occupied was filled to the brim. It became less of a passive notion and more of a threat – a threat too misty to pinpoint, and all the more unsettling for its obscurity.

Part of Vivien's desire to escape the Barbarossa was more to do with her fear of Isabella than it was any anxiety at being alone. Quite what she imagined Isabella would do, she wasn't sure, but behind that sheet of oil-black hair was a plotting mind that, she knew, would stop at nothing to secure Gio's devotion.

'Adalina, have the caterers confirmed for five o'clock tomorrow?'

Vivien swept into the staff kitchen and flicked her cigarette ash into the sink. Adalina, drying plates, gave nothing away at this audacious breach of etiquette; the Europeans she'd worked for would never have dreamed of venturing into their servants' domain. But she sensed that her new mistress wasn't necessarily as brash as she appeared – there was an insecure streak there, a little girl lost.

She nodded. '*Sí*, signora.'

'Good. And speaking of, what's for supper tonight?' Vivien fished in the pocket of her crushed-plum velvet pantsuit for another smoke. 'I want it to be ready for when my husband comes home.' She smiled. 'He'll believe I made it myself.'

'Chicken *cacciatore* with a white bean salad.'

Vivien lit the cigarette. 'I thought we were having lamb.'

'Signora Isabella changed it.' Adalina put forward the sheet of paper she set out at breakfast every morning, detailing a menu option for the day. Where Vivien had clearly ticked the red meat, another hand had scrawled through it.

Vivien blew out smoke. 'Right, yes.'

She concentrated on holding her temper, which railed like a rabid thing chained to a gatepost. She would speak to Gio. As lady of the house, she ought to have last word on every detail. It unnerved her that Isabella's preference had been upheld against her own, but she didn't, and couldn't, let on. 'Silly me, I forgot. I did ask Isabella to run down and change it. I decided chicken would be best.'

'Of course, signora.'

Vivien went to leave, before remembering her outfit for the party. 'Adalina, there will be a special delivery arriving in the morning. I need someone to take receipt of it and transport it to my room. Signor Moretti is not to see it.' A thrill coursed through her. Gio would deem her more enchanting than he had ever seen her.

'*Sí*, signora,' said Adalina. She continued drying the plates. 'I am to expect a conveyance for Signora Isabella as well. I will take care not to confuse the two.'

Vivien's smile was a rictus as she left the room.

*

When Gio returned from work the following evening, he was tetchy and distracted. Vivien rubbed his shoulders, encouraging him to relax.

'Bad day at the office?' she asked.

'It's all right for you,' he snapped back, 'coasting about here, planning parties, with nothing to—' Immediately, he retracted it. 'I'm sorry, *amore*. It's… It's nothing, really, just a long day.' He ran a hand over his face, features like the ocean after a storm, then kissed her. 'Don't listen to me, I don't know what I'm saying.'

Vivien was shocked at his temper – but she knew Gio was a passionate man, and his concern could emerge as anger. He cared too much; he had a lot on his mind.

'Is there anything I can do?' Vivien held him, squeezing tight as if to make sure he was real. She had endured a horrible dream the night before, of being back in LA, before him, existing from one day to another. On waking at dawn, she had slid alongside her husband, basking in his reassuring heat. She told herself it was unconnected to anything in the real world, just a nonsense borne out of his long hours and the change in their circumstances. She ignored the voice that informed her otherwise. That, weeks into Gio's mysterious project, he was as irascible and tightly wound as he'd ever been. *Work does that*, she reasoned, remembering the dizzy highs and crushing lows she had known in her career. *He'll come through it. Marriage is patience.*

'No, darling,' he answered. 'Just being you is enough.'

But there were shadows around her husband's eyes. Vivien had noticed them increasingly, the late finishes taking their toll. Gio was always vague with her about the nature of his project. '*It's boring,* bellissima, *just a lab full of white jackets bent over samples,*' he'd say. Vivien had asked for more, but he wouldn't be pushed.

'When are they turning up?' Gio loosened his tie. Vivien estimated this party was the last thing on earth he felt like hosting. She would play the consummate wife and compere, so he would need to do nothing at all. She checked the time.

'Eight o'clock.' That gave her two hours to get ready. The ballroom was looking fabulous, thanks to her creative efforts, the fires lit, the champagne chilling.

She waited until Gio was in the bathroom, the shower running, before venturing: 'I was rather taken aback about Isabella.'

'What about her?'

'Only that she wanted to come. She is attending tonight, isn't she?'

There was a sound of water drumming on tiles. 'As far as I know.'

Vivien chose her words. She knew, once spoken, they could not be retracted. 'A woman in her situation… I suppose I imagined she wouldn't.'

There was no response. Just the sound of the shower as it drenched the contours of his body, the change in pitch and rhythm as he moved beneath it.

'What I'm getting at,' said Vivien, 'is whether she might be improving?' That was code for: *Your sister's a game player. She doesn't need us. She doesn't need to be here. Let her go.* Who was to say Isabella had a problem at all; that she didn't do it all for attention, most of all her brother's?

'You think she should be locked upstairs for the evening?' he said.

'No! No, goodness, no.' Vivien got up from the bed. The last thing she wanted was to piss Gio off, especially right before they presented their love and union to their guests. 'Of course I want her to be with us.' *Lie, lie, lie.* 'I'm just getting used to her… behaviour, that's all. It goes without saying she should be involved.'

There was a short pause, before Gio called back, 'Aren't you getting ready?'

She knew her husband well enough to know that was the end of the exchange. Vivien retrieved her outfit from the bed and slipped into her dressing room. Venturing the subject of Isabella was a delicate and long-handed campaign, like chipping away at Mount Rushmore with a butter knife.

*

Vivien didn't need to be fluent in Italian to feel certain that she was admired.

As guests arrived, gleaming Ferraris pulling on to the

drive and spilling forth a host of glamorous women in marvellous dress-up, from vampires to mermaids and wolverines
to murderesses, the men on their arms filling the grand hall
with the most exquisite, expensive scents, Vivien stayed
glued to Gio's side as he accepted their compliments. She
knew she looked tremendous. The nymph creation was all
she had hoped for and more, offsetting her dramatic make-
up and impossibly long legs to a tee. She was the perfect
combination of European style and all-American goodness.
She had even instructed the seamstress to incorporate a
smattering of miniature diamonds into the neckline, which
glimmered and shimmered in the candlelight.

Next to her, Gio was irresistible as the Dark Count. His
long cape accentuated his height, and the uncanniness of his
one black eye, one green, lent him a gorgeous, sexy cruelty.
It had demanded all her restraint not to tear his costume off
the second she saw him and have him bite the life out of her.

'It's a pleasure to meet you,' she told guests, 'how lovely
of you to come... Yes, we're very happy, the best decision
we made... You knew Giacomo Dinapoli? How fascinat-
ing...' Vivien tried with the language, a deficiency she had
worried would play against her but in fact her efforts were
deemed charming.

'They adore you,' Gio told her in a quiet moment.

Vivien hadn't felt this content since they'd arrived in
Italy. The party was a raging success, with guests telling
them they should make it an annual occasion, and how
rewarding it was to see glory reinstated to the Barbarossa
after being so long unused.

'I can't thank you enough.' Gio touched the small of her back. 'I never would have thought of this. I don't deserve it – I know I don't. I've been neglectful to you lately. I've been away too much. And I might not say it every day, but I realise the set-up with my sister is unconventional, and that it's been hard for you.'

The triumph of the night, and the happy hum of alcohol, made her generous. 'It's you I love,' she said. 'And whatever comes with you. Don't mention it.'

When he told her he loved her back, she caught fire just as she had the first time. How silly it all was, she dressed up as a fairy and he as a bloodthirsty beast, desperate for each other and mad with adulation – but Gio was her destiny, her One. She watched him move across the room, and pictured them here in years to come with a family of their own, a girl and a boy running circles round their heels.

'We knew the children when they were small.'

Vivien heard a voice at her side. She turned to see a woman in her fifties, sipping Cinzano and speaking perfect English, with only a slight accent.

'You did?' Vivien smiled, wondered if she had lipstick on her teeth.

'It was so sad, the condition that brought them here, so young, so tragic…' The woman shook her head. 'But you know all this already.'

'Yes. It was terrible. Signor Dinapoli must have been a wonderful man.'

'He was generous. He helped Isabella enormously.' The

woman paused, as if about to disclose more, then took a long sip of her drink.

Then what the hell was Isabella like before? Vivien contemplated. As she nursed her umpteenth Dom Perignon, she reflected on the other factor that was making her evening so unreservedly pleasant: no Isabella. Perhaps the sister had had a last-minute attack of nerves, and that was the reason for her no-show. Everybody here seemed to understand and expect this, and so her name had scarcely been mentioned.

'You know the Barbarossa used to be a hospital?' volunteered the woman. 'A more accurate term these days would be "asylum" – for the sick in the head. Dinapoli wound the institution down. By then their methods were attracting criticism anyway, families opting for more conventional routes, psychiatrists, doctors, traditional medicine. I dare say some of their techniques were a little... extreme.'

Vivien scanned the room for Gio. He was talking with a man dressed as a werewolf and she had to resist the urge to laugh: it wasn't the moment.

'Rumour at the time was that Dinapoli tried these methods on the girl.'

Vivien looked at her sharply.

'Of course we can't be sure. But he became more and more of a recluse about it, to the point they rarely left the house. Some say he became obsessed.'

'With what?'

'Curing her. Isabella.'

Vivien imagined it. She couldn't ever picture being pinned to one place, the same walls for company, never venturing into the world. She would go crazy. All her life she had run from one thing to the next, afraid to settle – until now, that was.

'I'm unsure how much your husband knew,' the woman went on, 'or how he fitted in. No doubt you're more enlightened than I, just a nosy village gossip.' She nudged Vivien, so that a swish of champagne spilled over the lip of her glass. 'But I will tell you how nice it is to see Gio back here, and so well, with such a lovely wife.'

'Thank you.' Vivien swallowed.

'You're quite the star tonight. Everyone's saying so. Of course we'd heard of his achievements in America but still it seemed impossible to match that shy little boy with the man he is today. It's just a shame we haven't been able to meet…'

The woman stopped. Vivien watched her, before slowly following her gaze.

There, at the entrance to the ballroom, was a figure.

A black silhouette.

'Oh, my heavens…'

The woman's murmur was echoed around the room, as gasps and inhalations drifted up from the assembly like mist from a frozen lake. Admiration – *awe*, for that was the word that gnawed Vivien in that instant and for weeks after – soaked the crowd. Awe for the presence that had joined them, the wicked, beautiful queen.

Isabella was dressed in jet silk, head to toe, her outline as sharp as glass. Her hair had been curled and fell in waves and swathes like ink spilled on marble, a vision in drama and disaster. Her lips were blood red, her eyelashes intolerably long, and for once both eyes were visible, and with that clarity Vivien was struck by how utterly and defiantly stunning her sister-in-law was. *My sister-in-law.* How she envied her in that moment! Isabella's face was porcelain-pale, a sweep of deep purple on her lids, a mere brushstroke of blush on her cheekbones, precise as blades. Behind her, the fierce orange sunset could be seen through the window, staining the hills around Fiesole in shades of apricot. She appeared scarcely real, like a painting.

'She's beautiful,' whispered the woman. And clearly that sentiment was echoed throughout their company. Vivien stood back, long forgotten, as guests flocked to greet their new arrival. Isabella didn't need to speak to command attention, at first because her beauty did the talking, and then because Gio had gone to join them, his face lit with unfettered, childlike joy, the kind of joy Vivien herself had never been able to incite in him, and like the most natural thing in the world he was standing alongside Isabella, her mouthpiece, to field their enquiries and salutations.

Vivien was out in the cold. Nobody turned back to see the lone hostess in the centre of the dance floor. *Not even my damned husband.* Isabella smiled like an innocent flower, instead of the dreaded poison ivy Vivien knew her to be. She linked her brother's arm as if they were the married couple – and, really, Vivien conceded, it *was* their party. They had been the original pair to occupy this mansion, long before Vivien had a stake in it. They were the ones their guests had come to see.

She waited for Gio to look at her, to catch her eye, to

wonder, at least, where she was. But she was forgotten, cast aside like an old coat in favour of sequins.

But one person did catch her eye.

Isabella.

And that one look told her all she needed to know. Isabella had upstaged her deliberately. The sister had waited, bided her time, calculated her appearance to be the opposite of her rival's and all the more devastating for it – because her dusky gown dripped with sex and seduction where Vivien's own smacked of an uninitiated girl.

Isabella kept watching her, and Vivien dared herself not to look away.

Isabella's glare said it perfectly.

He'll never be yours. He'll always be mine. Whatever you try, however you try it, you're always going to lose. I'm his blood. You can't compete with that.

An idea occurred to Vivien, then.

Oh, you're wrong, Isabella. I can compete.

She knew what she had to do.

CHAPTER TWENTY-ONE

Italy, Summer 2016

It's a relief when Max asks to meet. The past week at the Barbarossa has been quiet, and all the more strange because of it, as if the thing I disturbed has retreated, but only to plot its resurgence. I am desperate to tell someone about the diary, the attic, about Salvatore and the image in the fountain, but nobody at home would understand and besides, whatever this is belongs here, in the hills and the gold summer light. Against London it seems absurd, which perhaps it is, but I'm not ready to relinquish it yet.

I had considered contacting Max myself, but after my insistence when we'd met that I wanted nothing to do with his investigation, I feel cautious.

He collects me at the foot of the drive.

'I remember coming here,' Max says, as I climb into his beaten-up Fiat. 'Lili never let me go past the gate.'

I wonder about Lili, the aunt. How close had she been to Vivien? I envy her that closeness. I feel as if one meeting with Vivien would answer so many questions, settle some faint query in my mind that would set off a chain reaction, see mysteries falling against each other like dominoes.

Was Lili like Max? I watch my companion as he steers us through the groves and out on to the heat-parched road, the windows down and the warm, fragrant breeze playing with his hair. I'd thought him handsome when we met in the café, but in daylight it's a true, real detail that appears more sharply in focus than it should, as if to remind me how it is to notice such a thing.

I haven't noticed it in anyone since him.

Since James.

'Are you OK?' Max asks. I watch his hand on the wheel, touching it lightly at the bottom, and am reminded of a night James drove us to the coast, on a whim, because I said I fancied fish and chips on the beach, so that was what we had.

'Yes,' I reply, quashing my memories. 'I've got a lot to tell you, that's all.'

*

I don't expect Max to take me to his home, but that's where we go. He lives in a modest apartment in the village, converted from an old monastery, so it's full of weird recesses and cool chambers whose walls are cold and moist to touch. It smells wonderful, like churches, and I like how he's furnished it with solid pieces that speak of ages past – 'Lili's belongings,' he explains, 'I couldn't get rid of it all...' – mixed with modern photography on the walls, black and white prints of Florence that turn out to be his. 'Just a hobby,' he downplays it, 'nothing special.'

I'm taking in his wall of books – mostly hardback history tomes, *The Road to Rome*; *Germany's War*; *Fall of the USSR*, things like that. 'Can I get you something to drink?' he asks. I notice that cleft in his chin again.

'Sure,' I say. 'Coffee would be great.'

We sit at the back, on a small patio surrounded by sun-scorched plants, and Max confesses that he's inadvertently killed every plant he's ever bought or been given. I find this funny, and when I laugh it feels uncomfortably like we're on a date. How I laughed at James's jokes, but more of a nervous laugh, more that I didn't know what else to do with myself besides laugh because he was my boss and this was off limits. With Max, it's an easy, natural laugh that comes from an honest place.

Bill would say this was a date. She was constantly has-sling me to get back in the mix, to 'put that idiot in perspec-tive'. *Is Max hot?* my friend had teased when I'd brought her up to speed. I'd reassured her it wasn't like that, it really wasn't, yet I knew that Bill would think he was hot, because… well, he *was*.

'So.' Max sits back. 'Tell me everything.'

I do. I tell him about my meeting with Salvatore in the Oval. I tell him about Vivien's outing to the doctor, and the pills that arrived previously; I tell him about the skel-eton key, exactly where he'd described it in the ballroom fireplace, and the opening of the attic and the discovery of the handwritten note. I tell him about Vivien's diary. For some reason I don't tell him about the spectre I saw in the fountain, partly because I'm not sure I did see something, and partly because it sounds so far-fetched as to negate the veracity of everything else I've said. In fact, I don't mention the fountain at all. The word doesn't pass my lips. It's forbidden.

'Did the diary mention Lili?' he asks.

I shake my head. 'I only saw that one entry.'

Max sits forward. 'We need to get hold of it again.'

'It's too risky. Honestly, Max, what Salvatore said scared me. This whole thing scares me. I feel like I'm going mad.'

'He's the mad one.'

'Is he?' I frown, remembering. 'Adalina warned me he'd lost his mind, but when she said it… it was as if she wanted me to disregard him. As if she was covering herself. She said he went crazy years ago. But even though he startled me, he seems like the most honest person I've met at the Barbarossa. Not that I've met many.'

'You still haven't seen Vivien?'

'I've glimpsed her. Saw her in the back of the car that day they went to the doctor's. I'm sure she's been watching when I've gone outside. And I'm pretty certain she's been up in that attic – I've heard her. But, no, I haven't met her.'

'That's odd.'

'Tell me about it. Even if I wanted to pass on Lili's message, I couldn't. Adalina's impossible to get past.' I think of another thing. I tell Max about the exchange I overheard when Vivien told her maid how I looked like someone.

'Who did they mean?'

'I have no idea. But that has to be connected, doesn't

it? The thing that drove Salvatore crazy, and your aunt's apology?'

Max lifts his shoulders. 'Maybe.'

I dig in my bag to produce the scrawl I found in the attic. *He'll never be yours. He'll always be mine.* I'd shared with Max its content, but nothing except the original can adequately conjure the sheer dementedness of it, that horrifying scratch.

'Wow,' he says.

'Who do you think wrote it?'

He blows air out of his mouth.

'It has to be the husband,' I jump in. 'Gio. It has to be about him, I mean.'

'*Sì.*' A beat.

'I feel like there's something you're not telling me.'

Max gives up on the coffee and goes to fetch something stronger. A bottle of grappa comes to the table, with two glasses. He fills them, takes his time.

'Lili used to talk about the sister,' he says. 'Isabella. What a misery she was making of Vivien. They were at each other's throats.'

'That would tie up with the diary entry.'

'It would. But what does it mean, that she had a thing for her own brother?'

I'm about to dismiss it, but don't. 'Did Lili say anything else?' I ask.

'I tried, but she only said Vivien was entitled to her privacy.'

'That figures, if they were close…' I'm thinking. Mostly

about the fountain and what Salvatore said, the woman who washed herself in it. Had he been talking about Isabella? Vivien? Even Lili? What did the water have to do with it?

We end up talking long into the night. It's ages since I got properly let-it-all-go drunk. The last time was with Bill, a few nights after Grace Calloway killed herself. I'd neither eaten nor slept since it happened, closeted in my room, afraid to get out of bed because that meant facing the world, and equally afraid to stay in it because that meant facing my demons. Eventually Bill hauled me out, produced a ton of vodka and we'd drunk it neat on ice cubes while I poured my heart out. Alcohol was the only thing that passed my lips that week. That was one sinister hangover.

But getting drunk with Max now – even in spite of the circumstances, it's fun. We move off topic, as if actually that was just a guise to bring me here, an excuse to see each other, and we talk about our lives, our histories, our fears and hopes. Max shares with me a funny story about an ex-girlfriend. I don't say anything about James. He tells me about his *mamma*, how he tried a while ago to get in touch with her but she didn't want to know. I tell him about mine, my dad and my sisters and what it was like growing up, and how I wish I remembered my mother better.

'I'm sorry,' he says.

'Don't be. It's fine. I've had long enough to get over it.'

My attempt at light-heartedness sounds empty.

'You can talk to me, you know,' says Max.

'Talk to you about what?'

'All the things you don't talk to anyone else about.'

'How would you know what I talk about when I'm not with you?' But I say it playfully, maybe to alleviate the serious ground we seem to have stumbled on to.

'Go on,' he encourages. 'I want to know a secret about Lucy Whittaker.'

I swallow. A secret…

I think about it. And then I say something I've never said to anyone.

I say how, after Mum died, I tried every day to make my father happy even though I didn't know how, and I just wanted to feel happy myself. I say how, on a bad week, Dad didn't get out of bed, and when anyone came to the door I pretended it was fine and he had just gone out to the shops. I say how Dad never talked to me about Mum, and I wished he would but I never pushed him because grief affected us in different ways. I say how, after my sisters went, it seemed impossible to leave because Dad needed me, so I took a local job, ploughing my earnings into the house and into paying the woman who came to play cards with Dad on the nights I was at work. I say how that woman gave me my life back, because, in time, a friendship grew between them and she moved in – and, in the same stroke, my old school friend Bill was looking for a flat share in London. I say how excited I was that my life was my own again… but that I always left a piece of me at home with Dad. I don't say what happened next. That I embarked on the most reckless of adventures because I had never known adventure before.

Max waits a long moment, before saying: 'It was nice of

you to care for your family.' He's searching my eyes, gently, curiously.

'Anyone would do it.'

Max makes a *Maybe* face.

'Aren't they worried about you?' he asks.

'Why would they be?'

There's that grin again – and, just like that, he's scooped us up and we're two friends, having a drink, and nothing is frightening or strange or sad.

'Beautiful, single girl out here on her own,' he says, 'she could get up to anything.' The grin holds for a moment, and then: 'You are single, right?'

I'm blushing at his description of me. 'Yeah,' I say into the glass.

'No one at home?' He refills me. 'There must be.'

'Why?'

'Just a feeling.'

'Well, your feeling's wrong. There's nobody.' It comes out harsher than I'd wanted, the last word catching. Where would I even begin, telling Max about James? I lost the words a long time ago, if indeed they ever existed.

'What about this Bill guy?'

I laugh and it's a nice release. 'Bill's a girl.'

'Ah. In that case, I like the sound of Bill.'

Somehow, we reach midnight. We make the appropriate noises about wrapping it up, but neither of us wants to, and, besides, we're both too smashed to drive. We reach one a.m.; one becomes two and two becomes three, and the sky outside is no longer pitch but giving way to lilac, a nascent dawn. Max makes up the couch and the next thing I know I'm awake, my head on a pillow and a blanket over me, the sun bursting through the windows and a headache like fire.

Thankfully, Max isn't awake. I check the time and it's still early; I can make it back to the Barbarossa and begin my day as normal. The thought of all I must do is, for a moment, more than I can take, and I consider being sick before dragging myself together and sinking a glass of water. I find a couple of painkillers in the bathroom and swill them down, then rub toothpaste on my gums. In the mirror, my reflection is frightful, my hair a nest and mascara smudged round my eyes. But there's a glint that saves it from being a completely lost cause. I had *fun* last night. Who cares if I've got the hangover to end all hangovers, or if I've got to grit my teeth and plod through the day when all I want is to collapse into sleep... I had *fun*.

I rearrange the sofa, leave a thank you note for Max, and grab my bag, before opening the door to the street. I can see the Barbarossa in the distance, and even though I don't know my way, I'm happy to amble a while and see where it takes me.

*

My good mood is still going strong when I arrive back at the castillo. Adalina is nowhere in evidence so I have a bowl of fruit, then take a shower and gather the cleaning equipment at the foot of the stairs. Remembering how my phone's been on silent, I quickly check it. The messages must have come in while I was in signal at Max's, only I was too wasted to notice. My mood falters.

The texts are from my dad. Three of the same; he never could work out how to use it. 'Why not just call somebody?' he'd say. And he'd tried that, too.

Four missed calls. I open the text.

I know something is wrong even before I read it.

Hi, darling. A young lady came by looking for you today, a journalist. Very determined. Is she a friend of yours? Told me to buy the papers in the morning. What did she mean?

CHAPTER TWENTY-TWO

Vivien, Italy, 1982

As the seasons passed and turned into a year, Vivien's plan to exile Isabella became less high-impact and more slow burn, whose hope fizzed to dust with every month that elapsed. The one sure-fire way she could think of to relegate her rival escaped her. The single way in which she could draw a line under her history rushed through her praying fingers like sand. Each time she had her period, she despaired. She and Gio made love at the right time, she was sure of it. What was the matter with her?

Many a tear had been shed on the lavatory seat. Vivien couldn't share her frustrations with Gio because Gio was none the wiser. Unbeknown to him, she had long stopped taking her contraceptive pill, emptying the tablets down the loo and tossing their packets in the garbage. They had discussed children in the past, she reasoned, and both wanted them, so where was the harm? Once Gio heard the news, a happy accident, he would be thrilled. So why was the news taking so long coming?

Vivien tried not to overthink the matter. Plenty of couples took at least twelve months to conceive, there was nothing unusual about it. But too often she spiralled into negative thoughts, obsessing about how it would feel to carry an unborn baby, to give birth to it, who it would look like, a girl or a boy; and, on dark nights, she would wonder if this was Gilbert Lockhart's curse, if what he had said all along was right – that she was sullied and sinful, and this was her punishment for rejecting his creed.

You don't deserve a baby. You never will. After what you did?

Was it Gilbert's voice, or her own? Because the voice was right: she didn't deserve it. She thought of her shameful actions at Boudoir Lalique, when she'd been a wide-eyed virgin too frightened to protest for fear of being chucked back out on the street. Back then she'd been terrified of falling pregnant, and willed her period each month, a sick dread growing in the pit of her stomach until she was saved by a bright red stain in her knickers. Now, she dreaded its arrival. It was a cruel irony.

Having spent most of her life in denial of family, Vivien's every waking hour was now preoccupied with it. A clean slate, a new unit: a wonderful, pure little person who had made none of her mistakes and knew none of her faults. She could be anyone in her child's eyes, the most perfect mother on earth. She longed to be that mother.

The mother she herself had never had.

'Pass the salt, would you, Bella?' Gio asked one night over the supper table. He signalled from the head of the table, and while his sister went to retrieve the shaker, Salvatore, after refilling their goblets, spared her the effort.

'*Prego*, signor,' he said, bringing it to Gio.

'*Grazie*, Salve.'

Vivien, drenched in the finery she always reserved for mealtimes, focused on her rabbit *pappardelle* and on avoiding Isabella's eye. It was customary for the trio to rotate their seats (Gio suggested it early on, for fear of his precious sister feeling left out), and tonight Vivien was on one arm of the absurdly long table, with brother and sister facing each other from opposite ends. It made an infant of her, dining with her parents. The finery was intended to counter that – and yet, it seemed, with each sun that rose Isabella became lovelier still. The chrysalis that had emerged on the night of the Halloween party had become a butterfly. Isabella now made an effort with her appearance that had been resolutely lacking in LA, her hair styled, her make-up applied, and a wardrobe advisor who sent delectably wrapped packages to the house.

'*Bellissima*, are you well?' asked Gio kindly. Had they been seated closer, he would have reached to take her hand. Vivien had a sudden longing for her beach house in Malibu, with the little breakfast bar at which they had eaten scrambled eggs.

'I'm fine.'

'You look pale.'

'It's nothing.'

He smiled. 'You know I have the weekend off?'

This was a first: Vivien couldn't remember the last time he had chosen home over the laboratory. What was so vital there? And why couldn't he share the details of his day when he returned, like a normal husband did? Gio claimed tiredness, batting off her enquiries like flies on a hot day. '*It's boring, amore, really,*' he said tersely, '*let's talk about something else.*' And then, lying awake at night, waiting for him to come to bed so she could seduce him and wonder if maybe, just maybe, this would be the time – both their bodies primed and the baby ready to be made – Vivien would surrender to paranoia, thinking she heard Gio talking in another room, talking with Isabella about the things he did, confiding in his sister where he couldn't in his wife.

'That's wonderful.' She returned his smile, chewing the pasta, beautifully *al dente* though on her tongue it felt rubbery as old boots. Saturday was Gio's birthday.

'I thought we could head into the countryside.' He drizzled oil on *ciabatta*. 'Take the car, some food, see where we end up? Just like we used to.'

Vivien remembered picnics on the beach. Making out in his convertible against the Pacific sunset. Those hazy, lazy days – they could still find that magic, couldn't they? Gio was looking directly at her. Instinctively, she knew his plans did not involve Isabella. For once, they would be alone. *Just like we used to be.*

'That sounds like bliss.' Vivien couldn't resist a glance in Isabella's direction, but the sister's expression was difficult to read. Suddenly, the pasta didn't taste so bad. The weekend unfolded ahead of her, full of possibility. She had resigned herself to fixing Gio a quick birthday breakfast before he headed off, but now they could let the hours melt by like sun on the skin, relishing each other's company like a true husband and wife. And who knew? The relaxation could do him good. Vivien had read about stress and exhaustion being accountable for difficulties in men... Perhaps this, at last, would be the weekend on which they would conceive.

Then there would be no alternative but for Isabella to be demoted. Gio's child, his blood, a blood richer and deeper than that which he shared with Isabella.

Gio's new family would be carved more clearly than ever, a baby for him to dote on, and his sister would be forced to take inferior standing. Vivien couldn't wait.

*

Adalina offered to prepare the hamper, but Vivien wished to pack it herself.

'Have we any lobster?' she asked the maid. The lunch was almost complete. A golden loaf of *focaccia*, scattered with oregano; a honeyed ham with his favourite piccalilli; sheets of *prosciutto* and salami dappled with fat; bright red tomatoes, plump with juice and plucked from the vine; a crumbling wedge of blue-veined *dolcelatte* with a crisp crop of pears; a carafe of locally produced wine, thick and sweet as a compote; and, naturally, a bottle of the Barbarossa's home-grown lemon press.

Adalina fetched the claws from the pan. 'It's an impressive spread, signora.'

'As was my intention, Adalina! Today will be wonderful. My husband has had a hard year, working every hour. He deserves a special day.'

Adalina helped her parcel the food in a white cloth, padding out the items that needed to stay cool with an ice pack. The women worked companionably, having become close enough over the months to share these small confidences about each other's private lives. Vivien liked Adalina's honesty. She liked her generosity. She liked that Adalina had a baby nephew whom she took care of at home, and while it required some effort for Vivien to look at pictures of the irresistible little guy with his brown hair and a dimple in his chin, feeling as she did the hollow cavity in her own belly, she put aside those selfish concerns and enjoyed their friendship.

'Salvatore is bringing the car round,' said the maid.

'Thank you, Adalina,' said Vivien.

'*Prego*, signora,' said the maid, with a smile, 'call me Lili.'

*

'Darling…' Gio caught her arm as she approached the waiting car. She had a brief moment to admire her reflection in the window – the flowing gypsy dress, the Jackie Onassis glasses and the glamorous headscarf – before it was all ruined.

'*Cara*, I'm sorry, but Isabella…' Vivien knew what was coming. 'She isn't herself today,' said Gio, 'I don't want to leave her. I can't.' His face was a picture of regret. So he *had* meant it to be the two of them, which was something, she supposed.

But to hell with Isabella!

'What's the matter with her?' she asked, biting her disappointment. If Isabella wasn't herself, that was surely a good thing for all of them.

Gio ran a hand over his jaw. Vivien hated that he should be distressed like this on his birthday, and once again resented his sister for causing him such pain.

'It's, um…' He cleared his throat. 'It happened around this time of year. My parents. It's a few days until the anniversary, in fact.'

'Why didn't you say something?' She touched his face.

'It wasn't worth it,' he said, kissing her hand, 'for me, in any case. But for Isabella, well, it's different. She isn't looking after herself. I can't remember the last time I saw her eat. I'm worried she's in the grip of a bad phase.'

Vivien was used to seeing the sister push food around her plate, but couldn't swear it wasn't controlled. The more weight Isabella lost, the more extremely her beauty seemed to shine; the wider her eyes and the fuller her lips.

'I think it's best if she comes with us today,' said Gio. 'I'm sorry, *amore*. I promise I'll make it up to you.'

It would be inelegant to object, for a number of reasons, so Vivien wore her best smile and kissed him deeply on the mouth. 'Of course,' she said.

Gio smiled and opened the car door, before setting back to collect Isabella.

*

As Gio's car navigated the winding lanes around Fiesole, Vivien could momentarily forget the brooding Isabella-shaped cloud on the back seat, and concentrate on the gorgeous countryside. Cypress trees like the ones she saw from her bedroom window spiked the amber hills. The air was warm and scented with citrus peel. They were spoiled for choice for a spot to enjoy their lunch, but Gio appeared set on a specific place he had visited as a boy, and, when they reached it, Vivien could see why.

'I wanted to show you this,' said Gio, as the car came to a stop beneath an olive tree laden with fruit. It was the site of an old shepherd's hut, reduced now to rubble but with the most incredible views Vivien had ever seen. Undulating hills panned far into the distance, a golden sheet beneath a pure blue sky. Next to her, Gio appeared like someone from a New Romantics power ballad, windswept and tortured.

'It's beautiful,' said Vivien, squeezing his hand. As she did so, their wedding rings touched. *I'm so glad you're mine*, she thought. *Everything will work out.*

The situation was marred slightly when Gio looped an arm round Isabella and spoke a brief burst of Italian into her ear. He pointed at a swing beyond the hut and his sister smiled. Clearly, they had been here before. Where hadn't Isabella been?

Vivien hauled the hamper from the boot of the car, and Gio helped her lay the blanket on the ground. Vivien tried not to imagine how flawless the scene would be were it not for Isabella, but there it was, and it was his day, so she swallowed it.

The food was exquisite and the wine made her woozy. Vivien and Gio chatted and kissed, lying back in the sun, while Isabella sat looking out at the horizon, her elbows across her knees, occasionally resisting the morsel of food Gio directed her way. 'Please eat,' he begged at one point. Isabella blanked him. Vivien could see him deciding whether or not to push it, and part of her wanted him to, to see how far his frustration would take him, but in the end he resolved to keep the peace.

As they came to the end of the wine, Vivien produced her gift: a gold watch, hideously expensive, of course, with a leather strap and embedded jewels. Gio had admired it on an early amble through Florence, and she had remembered.

He strapped it to his wrist. '*Bellissima*, this is too generous.'

'Not for you.'

'I love it. Thank you.' He embraced her. Had Isabella not been sitting there like a pimple on the mound, Vivien would have made love to him right here. It was the ideal spot for them to conceive. She imagined telling him weeks down the line.

It was your birthday, on the hillside…

Then it wouldn't be his and Isabella's place any more. It would be theirs.

At first, she didn't think Isabella was going to produce a present, but then she did. Gio took one look at it and kissed his sister's cheek. It made light of Vivien's present, which had required words, been belittled by them.

'What is it?' she asked, once their intimacy had passed.

Gio was choked, for it was a moment before he spoke. 'It's our parents. At the Barbarossa.'

He handed her the photograph. A smiling, fair-haired (she registered surprise at this) couple stood by the Barbarossa fountain with their arms round two children. Gio was impossibly good-looking as a boy, and, she conceded, Isabella wasn't far behind. She still had all that dark hair, skinny legs, and those solemn, vulnerable eyes. Gio was smiling but Isabella wasn't. She appeared full of malice even at that age.

'Is that your uncle?' Vivien managed, pointing to the man at his mother's side.

Gio nodded. Vivien noticed the distance between Signor Dinapoli and Isabella, both physically and emotionally, in the picture. Where Gio was clasping the man's hand, Isabella stood apart, an air of mistrust about her. Vivien thought of what the woman had told her at the party. What had happened between them at the castillo later on, after the children had arrived there under different circumstances?

Nevertheless it was a touching present, no doubt about it, and had succeeded in diminishing her own. The watch seemed frivolous in comparison.

'What a thoughtful gift,' Vivien said tightly. Gio's preoccupation with the photograph was clear. *Well done, Isabella. You win another one.*

But Isabella wasn't finished. As the trio packed up to leave, the sun fading over the mountains and the shadows lengthening between the trees, Isabella yielded an envelope from her coat pocket. Vivien thought she was about to hand

THE SILENT FOUNTAIN 213

it to Gio, but then, as Gio went ahead of them back to the car, instead she passed it to Vivien.

Vivien took it. Isabella set off after her brother, and Vivien, confused, hung back and peeled open the offering. Was it a reconciliatory gift? An apology? Later, she would curse herself for such saccharine thinking: she had always been prone to it. Isabella would never do such a thing. But at that moment she fell for the ruse, a part of her still yearning to be friends with Isabella in spite of everything. All that Isabella could be, the sister Vivien had longed for, an ally and confidante. To banish the eternal opposition that haunted her days at the mansion, oh, to make life easy.

What a fool she was.

Inside the envelope, something crackled. She withdrew it. One of her empty pill packets stared back at her. Written on the back were the words:

What's taking so long, Vivien?

CHAPTER TWENTY-THREE

Italy, Summer 2016

The next morning, I make my excuses to Adalina and catch the bus into town. I sit by the Arno and go online. Now it's happening, I feel oddly numb. It's almost a relief that it's finally out, no longer my privately nurtured sentence but a hanging by public demand. If I'm sent to the gallows, at least I go in good faith.

It's everything I feared. Headlines across the news sites holler my worst premonitions: SORDID AFFAIR THAT DROVE GRACE TO SUICIDE; MYSTERY LOVER HAS BLOOD ON HER HANDS; CALLOWAY COPPED OFF WITH SECRET MISTRESS; WHO IS THE WOMAN WHO MURDERED GRACE CALLOWAY?

I scan the articles, taking in phrases with speed and clarity, my focus absolute as I devour the information like a starved woman faced with a poisonous, seductive feast. It's like reading about someone I've never met, the names remote. *One of the UK's most renowned lawyers, James Calloway, who spearheaded the Freedom For Austin Avery campaign in 2011, lost his wife of nine years, TV personality Grace, earlier this year. Those who knew Grace were shocked at her suicide, and until now little has been certain about what drove the well-liked mother and popular chef to such measures. Today it emerged that Calloway's affair was the catalyst. Now people are asking: Who is this secret lover, and why hasn't she come forward?*

I absorb several variations on this, and it takes a while for it to sink in that none of them has my identity. When I've summoned the courage, I Google myself. No Lucy Whittakers, at least none connected to the case. The only link I recognise is to my old office contact at Calloway & Cooper. I try a few more variations – *Lucy Whittaker affair, Lucy Whittaker Grace Calloway, Lucy Whittaker suicide* – but nothing comes up. Relief smacks me in the face, but too quickly it is chased by fear.

The comments that accompany the items are vile. I know I shouldn't read them, Internet trolls letting loose behind the anonymity of their screens, but they suck me in like the last slurp of water down a plughole. *Who is this slut? No way can she get away with it. Whore. Bitch. Tramp. Husband-stealer. Home wrecker. Grace would still be alive if it weren't for her. How can she sleep? Doesn't she have a conscience? Cheating with a married man, one with kids as well. She deserves everything she gets. What a slag. Ugly cow. Find the bitch and bring her in.* On and on it goes. Those few dissenters, who argue it's impossible to blame only the woman and that James Calloway was the one who was actually married, are buried beneath the hate. I feel that hatred bury its way into me, ringing in my ears, making my face hot. The city continues about me, oblivious. The river runs on.

In a way, I wish my name were mentioned – get it all over at once, let the shame rain down. But this blank canvas is the perfect foil for all their judgements and verdicts. No face to remind them I am human, no name to make it real; instead, the woman who has killed Grace 'the nation's darling' Calloway is an empty space, my sole function to absorb every frustration and anxiety thrown my way. Without my name, I am defenceless. Do I wish to defend myself? Can I? Reading the accounts of what I've done, yes, it sounds awful. It doesn't sound at all like the emails I drafted to James in the library; it doesn't sound like the truth. And now the country has its chance to vent and loathe, stacking their sentiments against me so that when I am finally revealed – which I surely will be – they can spear the pig once and for all. It is only a matter of time. What appears a pardon is only a delay of the inevitable.

My phone jumps to life. It's Bill.

Are you OK? Call me. Been trying to reach you Xxx

I tap out a quick return message.

I'm fine. I'll ring in a bit. Don't worry.

I pause before sending, deciding to add a line about the visitor to my dad's house. Somebody out there *does* know my name, not to mention where I live. Dad won't be any the wiser (I hope) when he follows the woman's instructions and buys the morning papers. I wonder what he will make of the story. Will he abhor the nameless mistress as much as everyone else? My heart contracts because it's worse this way. It'll be worse when the truth emerges, his disbelief, his disappointment...

Oh, Lucy, my darling...

I ask Bill if anyone has come to the London flat. Her reply is instant.

> Was about to say no – then remembered this woman, seen her a few times now, hanging around on the street? Caught my eye because nearly every day. Could be same person? Xxx

Then:

> Don't mean to scare you. Probs unrelated. Love you Xxx

I read her message twice, thinking. I remember the anonymous female caller who spoke to Adalina at the Barbarossa. Then I turn my phone off and put it back in my pocket. It's like carrying a stone; a heavy reminder that sooner or later I will be compelled to walk into the water with it, and let it sink me down. For now, I stand and disappear into the crowds, just like anyone else, nobody important.

*

What I should do and what I end up doing are two separate things. I should call my dad and explain everything. I should come clean, and in doing so mitigate the flood. I should speak to Bill, to my sisters, to anyone else whom it will directly affect because once those people are reconciled, who cares what the rest of the world thinks. I should get in touch with James so that we can get our story straight (how mad that sounds, like accomplices in a robbery, as if there is any other version than the one we knew). I lack courage to do any of these things. Instead, I return to the Barbarossa and head straight to the Oval. As soon as I open the door to this sanctuary, my head clears. My mind becomes lucid and calm. I sit on the bench that must once have held Vivien and her husband. The wood is tight with secrets, hers and mine, and in that moment I desire only to be with her and to tell her what I've done. In return, she would tell me. We both loved a man. We both faced another woman and something happened that changed our lives. She would realise we had things in common, after all.

Adalina thinks I'm gone for the day. The estate is large enough to remain unseen and nobody will find me here. My invincibility feels powerful. The storm raging at home cannot touch the purple skies here. Those London offices buzzing with supposition and speculation are nonsense. I picture the newsrooms pecking on scraps like vultures over carrion: Who is she? Where is she? Where's our story?

The hunt is on. But as I listen to the birds in the Italian sky and the distant peal of a bell ringing out over sun-drenched hills, it seems, for the first time, less important than it did. James seems less important than he did. Not so long ago, I would have seized this as an opportunity to speak to him. Now, I'm not sure I want to.

What could he do for me anyway? I hear the exchange, plain as day.

Me: *Hi. It's been a while.*

Him: *You shouldn't call.*

We need to talk.

What about?

Don't be like this.

It's over, Lucy. I told you.

He would give me nothing more. What was there left to give?

There was a time when, in my imaginings, we would have been reunited. James would declare his love despite it all, say how he'd missed me and he wanted me back, and I would have believed every word. I would have believed, too, that nothing mattered except our love. No amount of backlash or criticism, no matter how we'd be ostracised, our love would protect and heal. Now, it's as if the fog has cleared. It will never be like that. There are too many people to consider, too much hurt and too many memories. Real life. The difficulty of a future, his kids, and the tragedy they would take a lifetime to get over. This perfect picture I've been carrying around, refusing to let go or to listen to Bill when she told me the truth, is a farce – a selfish fantasy that put James and me as the central players, when in fact it was never about us. It was about a mother and her children, and the devastation we caused.

He'll never be yours. He'll always be mine.

That's why I need to speak to Vivien.

It's almost as if she could have worn my clothes thirty years ago – another time, another woman, another heart broken. It's almost as if Grace Calloway could have written that note especially for me. As if she intended all along for me to find it.

*

That night, we have a power cut. They are common at the Barbarossa, apparently, and Adalina has a supply of candles ready in the store cupboard. She lights one and takes it to Vivien's room. I am left to sort through the butts of wax with a flashlight, until enough are aflame that I can see by their glow alone. Some look ancient, their wicks buried in wax, shapes molten and deformed, and the thought of them illuminating the castillo all these decades past gives our dark, silent night a pleasing kind of context.

The building appears changed in the soft, flickering light. Every noise is amplified, every crack and bump pronounced. Tree branches brush the windowpanes like fingers tapping to get in. I envisage the cold, pitch-black attic, and shiver.

I'm mounting the staircase when I hear him.

'I saw you in Vivien's room.'

The voice causes me such alarm that I gasp out loud. Salvatore is behind me on the stairs, his features lit orange and his expression jumping in the uncertain glow. All around, the shrouded portraits swell like oil in water; the faces behind them are with us, as real as us, for this is the space between light and dark where all other boundaries cease to exist. Salvatore's face is curious, not accusing.

'I was sent there,' I lie. 'I had to fetch something.'

'She's not who you think she is,' he says. 'Neither of them is.'

'What do you mean?'

'You should go. Go home. Go away. Before it's too late.'

'Tell me what you mean.'

'Can you hear it?' His voice drops to a whisper. 'I can, if I listen. *Shh* – listen. There. There it is. Can you hear it?'

And then I think I do. It's so faint, faint enough to be a trick of the wind or a quirk of the building, to fade in and away from my awareness… but it's there.

'Can you hear it?'

He's mad. Even Max thinks so. Don't listen to him.

But there it is again, clearer this time but still faded and feeble, obscured by the channels of the mansion but also by some greater distance beyond.

'That's the baby,' he says. 'The baby never left.'

I stumble back, and almost trip up the step behind me.

'Only she knows what happened,' he says. 'She made me stay because she was afraid I'd talk. That I'd tell everyone what happened. But they'd never believe me. *Salve's crazy*, that's what they say. You would be, too, if you'd seen what I had.'

He advances towards me. I turn to run, and the next part happens in pieces. The candle tips from my hand; I go to steady it and the flame catches hold of some piece of material, its tongue touching black and then racing to fiery red. It goes up in a *whoosh*. The sheet covering the portrait screams back at us, yellows and blues and all fierce colours of fury, until I begin to see the contours of the painted face behind it, and hear the racing thunder of Adalina's footsteps as she approaches like the wind.

CHAPTER TWENTY-FOUR

Vivien, Italy, 1984

Time passed, and Vivien had no choice but to tell Gio that she had been trying to get pregnant. No way was she letting Isabella get there first, make out in one of the poisonous notes she scribbled that Vivien was trying to entrap him. Gio might have been livid at the deception were it not for the tempering circumstances. Vivien was in tears. Without him knowing, they had been trying to conceive for over two years.

'Is it me?' was Gio's first question.

'I don't know. It might be me. I don't know.'

Vivien sat on their bed, the scene of their failure. Once, these sheets had been a tangle of passion and promise; now, they wafted disappointment like stale air.

'Should we see someone?' she asked helplessly.

'A doctor?' Gio frowned.

'Maybe. I mean, I want this…' That was an understatement. Vivien thought of nothing else. Each cycle, she convinced herself this might be it, spotted phantom clues where there were none, a brief tummy ache, headaches, dizziness, hot spells, only to visit the bathroom that night and find her dreams crushed.

'You want it too, don't you?' She looked up at him.

'Of course,' said Gio. 'But it's best we keep this to ourselves. It's a small community, I'd sooner people didn't know our business.'

'I'm not sure how much more disappointment I can take!' Vivien stood with arms folded, and went to the window. She looked down at the fountain, its stone contours blurring with the tears in her eyes; its fish splurging water was somehow a taunting symbol of abundant fertility, designed to belittle her. She had taken control of so much in her life, but this was something over which she had no jurisdiction. It was a lottery, a stupid fucking lottery where people like her parents could have children and treat them so badly that they ran away from home, and people like her and Gio could live in opulence and have love in their hearts and yet that joy remained perpetually beyond reach. Vivien could feel the weight of a baby in her arms. She coveted it so much it hurt.

Thou shalt not covet, Gilbert had preached from his pulpit.

Look at me now, Daddy, she thought. *I'm still a catastrophe.*

I'm still the Devil's child.

'It's been years for me, Gio. You've only just found out, but for me…'

'For you it's worse?'

Vivien couldn't blame the pinch of antagonism in her

husband's words. She had no right to pitch her frustration against his. It wasn't his fault he had been kept in the dark. 'No.' She turned, swiped the tears away. 'I'm sorry. I just know what a wonderful father you'd make and I want to be able to give that to you.'

'So do I. But, *bella*, there are things we could try…'

His term of endearment strangled her. The same name he called his sister.

'Like what?'

'I'll find out. We can solve this. We're strong enough.'

Vivien didn't know if she was. Her desire clouded everything. Every detail was sent to torment her. In the village, children played on the green, their dust-caked knees and tiny elbows and wrists like daggers in her back. She saw schools run out to play, children's books in the library, kids queueing for the bus while holding hands with their parents, and she knew she had to possess that bond. It was a closeness she'd never had with her own mother and father. She had to see if she had it in her; to prove that it hadn't been her with the problem, just like Gilbert always said it was. She was capable of love because she had found it with Gio. She wasn't the awful girl she had been led to believe, frozen out of God's heart because she hadn't obeyed her father.

'Viv…?' Gio put his hands on her shoulders. 'We are strong, aren't we?'

She glanced away, sniffed, said yes.

'I can't understand why you didn't tell me,' he said.

'I'm telling you now.'

'When you wanted to start trying, I mean. OK, it was a little earlier than we'd planned, but we could have adjusted our expectations...'

'Could we? What with your work—'

'To hell with work.' His face darkened and she didn't push it. Now wasn't the time. She needed to see the Gio she recognised, not the haunted, angry version she had come to associate with his job. He could be like two men – the noble, gentle one she loved, and the vicious, unpredictable one she... No, that was silly. She loved him all over. That was why they had to welcome a baby: they had so much love to give it.

'All right, then, what about Isabella?' Vivien was careful. Isabella's name was like the cap holding back a dam of water and it would be so easy to let the whole lot out. 'You were worried about her. And anyway, the situation's far from ideal.'

'What situation?' His voice took on a defensive edge.

'You, me, her – the three of us here.'

'I thought you were content with that. We've discussed it enough times.'

'I am,' she fibbed. 'But you must admit it's not an ideal scene to bring a child into. Isabella's a confusing person. It wouldn't be a normal upbringing.'

'And mine was?'

'This isn't about that.'

'And yours was?'

'That either.'

'It didn't stop you going ahead, though, did it? If you

were so concerned about bringing a child into this *situation*, you should have carried on using protection.'

She was stunned at his words, the malice in them, and at how quickly his temper caught light. The speed and potency of it made her afraid. She stepped back, not recognising the man in front of her. *She's getting to you*, she thought; *Isabella's turning you against me.* But now she had started, she found she couldn't stop. She pushed it further, mumbling her next words but fully intending him to hear them.

'I suppose I hoped she'd have left by now.'

'What did you say?'

'I said: *I hoped she'd have left by now*. It's been four years, Gio. She's with us all the time – I can't get away from her!'

'You knew about Isabella when you married me.'

'I didn't have a lot of choice in the matter, did I? And while we're on the subject, *that's* why I'm telling you now: because if I hadn't, Isabella would. She blackmailed me, Gio. She'd do anything to come between us.'

Gio snorted. 'Don't be absurd.'

'I'm not. She asked me what was taking so long. She wrote it down.'

'Let's see the evidence.'

'I threw it away. I panicked.'

'Right.'

'Why do you need to see evidence anyway?' she blazed. 'I'm your wife.'

'I suspect you misunderstood, that's all.'

'What is there to misunderstand? Isabella's hated me

from the start – and, believe me, she's enjoying every second of this. She walks around with her hand on her stomach, mocking me. My being barren is all her dreams come true.'

'This is lunacy.'

'Is it? What about the wedding dress, Gio?'

'Not this again.'

'Not what again?' The dam was gushing. 'I told you – *she did it*.'

'And I told you. I asked her and she didn't know a thing about it. Come on, it's not as if you didn't piss anyone else off in Hollywood. Most likely it was one of those actresses whose husbands you were screwing.'

It was like being slapped. Gio had never shown such spitefulness before. Vivien could taste her dismay. Why was he being like this?

'How dare you.'

'I'm sorry,' he said, turning from her, his shoulders tense. 'But you don't understand.'

'What don't I understand?'

There was a long pause. She feared he was about to say something irrevocable like: *Me. You don't understand me.* But he didn't. *I do understand you*, she wanted to scream. *But look at what she's doing to us! Look at who you've become!*

'It doesn't matter,' he said eventually, 'forget it.'

As if she could.

'Does the fact we're married count for nothing?' she whispered. 'That you're meant to be on my side, above all others? You should have written your own vows, Gio. You should have included your sister as a fucking caveat.'

He faced her. But instead of regret in his eyes, there was wrath.

'Can't you see it?' Vivien dared to tread further. She had passed the point of no return; there was no going back. 'She's constantly undermining me – at Halloween that first year, on your birthday, the way she steamrollers me with the staff…'

'How can a mute steamroller? You've lost your goddamn mind.'

'Isabella has her ways. She's cleverer than you know.'

But Vivien was in no doubt that Gio knew exactly how clever Isabella was – and then some. She was beleaguered by distrust, waking in the night to what she thought was a void where her husband should have lain, hearing whispers through the walls, a woman's laugh, talking, talking, Isabella talking, the two of them upstairs in her attic doing who knew what, only to surface from the trance and seem to find him on the other side of her sweat-drenched bed sheets, still there, always there.

Is he right? Am I losing it?

Gio was hitting back, but she couldn't hear a thing. She didn't want to hear. Every word he uttered was in support of his sister and she couldn't bear it any longer. She couldn't live like this. He had to decide.

'It's her or me, Gio. I mean it.'

The room plunged into silence. Gio's expression pierced her heart, their once simple, true love shattered by abominable Isabella. Immediately, she wanted to claw back her words. If she didn't have Gio, she had nothing.

All she had left was here. He was it. The Barbarossa was it.

'Don't do this, Vivien.'

Her mouth opened but no sound came out. He had given his answer.

She opened the door to their bedroom and fled downstairs, out on to the terrace, down the drive, and kept walking, anywhere, anywhere, but there.

*

All week, she stayed out of her husband's way. It wasn't difficult: Gio left at dawn and returned at dusk. A couple of times, he tried to approach her – but the wound was still raw. Unless he was about to say, *Bella means nothing to me, it's you I love, and if you want me to get rid of her, I will*, it could fix nothing. Even as she thought that, she knew how implausible it sounded. As if they were referencing a mistress.

She's his sister.

His sister.

The irony was that if Gio had said that, and meant it, she would have ceased to have a problem with Isabella, and, actually, there would be no need for Isabella to go. But Gio had never reassured her of his preference – that, in a disaster, it would be his wife he would save. Was it unreasonable of her to want that? She didn't know.

She only knew that it hurt.

Vivien left them to it. She let the siblings re-enter the make-believe world they had conjured here as children, let them dine alone at the grand table, let them wander the gardens together after dark, sitting on the old stone fountain, shoulder to shoulder.

What poison drops did Isabella leave in his ear?

Vivien spent her time in the staff quarters, veering between wild thoughts of returning to Hollywood and those of venturing to far-flung lands alone, taking a trip to India, or Egypt, all the while dreaming about Gio realising his mistake and missing her unbearably. Her dreams turned into elaborate fantasies of Isabella trying to make him happy and failing, or of the sister finally showing her true colours through some despicable act and Gio falling to his knees having been shown the light, regretting so terribly the words he had thrown Vivien's way. Then he would travel the earth in an attempt to track her down, and when he did she would tell him it was all right, that she had never stopped loving him, and now, at last, they could be man and wife...

Her thoughts came to nothing, as days passed and her fantasies failed to solidify. But the fantasies alone were almost enough. Vivien found that, inside her head, she could fabricate an alternate reality so real and convincing that there was little need for follow-through. She fantasised about hurting Isabella, or about Isabella being in need and begging for her forgiveness. She fantasised about being a person in this house who wasn't eternally left in the cold, looking in from the outside through a window frosted by the Morettis' indestructible bond.

Hadn't she always been like this? The one on the periphery, standing alone, wondering what it might feel like to be drawn into the fold... When Vivien had been young, for years she'd thought the expression was *lonely child*, not *only child*.

Adalina and Salvatore were perplexed by her behaviour but discreet enough not to pry. Once, Vivien would have been self-conscious at how her exile must look, but now, she didn't care. Salvatore was the epitome of courtesy, standing back to let her pass, addressing her formally at all times, and seeming not to notice when he came into the kitchen carrying kindling, only to find her sitting alone, staring into the fire. Adalina, meanwhile, prepared meals for the house and brought Vivien's to her separately, with no questions asked. On one occasion, seeing Vivien's meek smile of thanks as she set down the *melanzane parmigiana* she'd requested that morning, Adalina lingered at the door. 'Can I do anything else for you, signora?'

Vivien looked into the bowl. She could think of a million things that needed to be done, but none within Adalina's power. The aubergine turned her stomach.

'Oh, Lili...'

She couldn't be bothered keeping up the pretence any more. No, she wasn't fine. No, she wasn't OK. No, she wasn't just spending time away from the castillo because she found it draughty this time of year in some of the bigger rooms. For so much of her life, she had pretended a carefree disposition, as if by repeating one's wellness to oneself the invention might actually come true. She was tired of it. Since her argument with Gio, she was tired of everything. She woke in the morning in the Lilac Room, forgetting then remembering that Gio wasn't next to her, and she felt such bone-crushing tiredness in body as well as spirit, that it took every ounce she had just to get out of bed. Adalina's kind words brought it crashing down.

'I love him so much,' she told the maid. 'But I…' She thought how to say it then decided on the truth. 'But I *hate* her. I know what happened to her and I'm sorry for that but I can't pay for it with my marriage. She's made my life a misery since the moment she stepped into it. I've tried, Lili. You do believe me, don't you? I've tried. I know how important she is to Gio. But I can't do this any more – I can't!'

Adalina sat next to her. The maid had worked for many a mansion in which the secrets were as multiple and varied as the chambers themselves. It was true that all the money and standing in the world could not secure happiness. The lady of the house was a film star. She was also a human being.

'He feels the same about you,' she said kindly. 'We see a lot, Salve and I.'

'Then you'll have seen what a fool she's made of me!'

'You are no fool.'

'Aren't I?' Vivien swiped her tears. 'I should never have let her into our lives. I should have said no from the start. No, Gio, I can't do it. I can't share you with her!'

'Have you tried talking to your husband?'

'Yes.' Vivien sobbed. 'That's why I'm here. He can't bear to look at me after I made him choose. He chose her, of course.'

'He said that?'

Vivien gulped. 'He didn't need to.'

Adalina was quiet for a moment. 'May I speak frankly, signora?'

'That's all I want right now – the truth.'

'I think you need to realise the power you have in this house. You are Signor Moretti's wife. He chose you when he married you. You are the most important woman in his life and, if I might risk speaking out of turn, you should start behaving like it, instead of hiding here with us. In doing that, you are letting your rival win.'

Your rival…

'You agree, then?' Vivien turned to her. 'You agree she's out to get me? I'm not imagining it? Gio thinks I'm mad, that I'm making it up!'

'I think this is about you and your husband. Why make it about her?'

'Because she's got it in for me,' Vivien said bitterly. 'She'll do anything to tear Gio and me apart. She can't wait to see us fail.'

'Isn't that what you are showing her now?'

Vivien thought about it.

'Go to your husband,' counselled Adalina. 'If you have each other's love, the rest will follow. Your love has nothing to do with anyone else.'

Vivien looked again at her lunch. It no longer made her feel sick. She took a spoonful and it tasted slightly strange in her mouth, but not unpleasant.

'Better?' asked Adalina.

'I think so,' whispered Vivien, and she smiled at the maid.

*

Vivien returned to the castillo that night, having spent the afternoon in reflection. Adalina's words gave her confidence not just to reclaim her position as lady of the Barbarossa, but also the conviction that she had acquired a firm female ally who was prepared to stand in her corner. Adalina was the friend she'd always wanted: she was wise and generous, patient and intuitive. Vivien could let her guard down completely. She didn't find that easy to do, but with Lili, she could. Now, she had to reconcile with Gio. Kiss him, hold him, and tell him all she must.

An odd sensation overtook her as she was approaching the fountain. She stopped, put a hand on the stone to steady herself, and swallowed hard.

The fish with its open mouth stared back at her, choking silver. It had always bothered her that the water didn't quite run smooth from its fossilised pout, a slush and gurgle, as if the wretched creature had something caught in its throat. She felt dizzy, the ground tipping before righting itself. Bile rose in her chest then receded.

After a moment, it passed.

Instinctively, Vivien rested a hand on her stomach. The sun emerged from behind a drift of cloud and illuminated the water, making it sparkle.

She knew.

CHAPTER TWENTY-FIVE

Waiting for Gio to return to the castillo was excruciating. She tried to distract herself with tidying already immaculate spaces, writing letters or finally brushing the dirt off a set of paints he had given her last Christmas, and sketching a twist of roses from her bench in the Oval garden. Nothing worked. She was counting down the minutes.

At six p.m., earlier than usual, Vivien heard his car on the drive. She rushed downstairs to greet him, saw the glimmer of relief that crossed his face when he saw her, surprise that swiftly turned to pleasure. The old Gio; the one she fell for.

He forgives me. He loves me.

It was all she cared about. Even seeing Isabella emerge from the passenger side, when she'd thought the sister had been upstairs in her attic all day, couldn't dampen her spirits. Vivien ran into his open arms. Gio stroked her hair.

'I've missed you,' he murmured. 'So much.'

'I've missed you, too.' She looped her arms round his neck and kissed him. Over the roof of the car, Isabella's glare bored into her and she kissed him harder.

'I'm sorry,' Gio whispered into her shoulder.

'So am I.' Vivien caught Isabella's eye. 'But none of that matters now.'

As she led him inside, she asked, 'How was your day?' She wanted to keep things light, afraid that if she didn't, she would simply blurt her news. It had to be special, just the two of them. It took some effort to focus on Gio's reply, partly because it constituted his usual litany of non-specifics but also because she was reliving the moment earlier today when her whole world had changed. Already she was savouring it, as if it had happened years ago, a golden moment of nostalgia. She had relegated the tests to the back of the cabinet, having been faced with bad news too many times, and she'd had to check they were still in date. But it wasn't with the customary nerves that she set about the process – today she was calm, decided, focused, because in her heart she'd already been sure of the answer. A minute, maybe two, and there it was. An explosion of sheer happiness, the bubble of anxiety that had enveloped her these past weeks burst in a single flare. *I'm pregnant.*

The thought of the life growing inside her was as bizarre as it was magical. Apart from a niggling sickness that came and went, she felt just like herself. What had she expected? Some integral shift, perhaps, a moving of the earth's axis or a tilting of the stars, but it was all the more incredible for its normality. She imagined the cells multiplying into life, settling into their bed for the next nine months, a daughter or a son, the baby she had longed for. Her heart swelled with love and promised a prize she'd thought was beyond her. Hope blossomed inside her as certain as her child.

'... Bella came with me. I thought she could do with getting out of the house.'

Gio concluded his account, and the abruptness of this final statement regained Vivien's attention. She looked about her and Isabella was gone.

'Come with me,' she said, taking his hand. 'I have something for you.'

Once in the bedroom, Gio threw her on the sheets. 'Is this it?' His hands roamed her body, her breasts and her legs, the mistake and misery of their time apart renewing his appetite. '*Perdonami*, Viv, I'm sorry for what happened. I never want to upset you – it's the last thing I want. We're OK, aren't we?'

'We're better than OK.' She took his face and held it so she could see into his different-coloured eyes. 'Gio, do you know why I married you?'

'I like to think I do.'

'Then I don't need to say it. But what I will say is that I married you for better or worse, all of you, all that's important to you, including your family.'

Gio put his lips to hers. *I love this man so much*, she thought.

'And our family,' she whispered.

He pulled back. 'What did you say?'

'I said, we have a family now, too.' Vivien guided his fingers to her stomach.

His eyes widened, one black, one green – would their child have the same?

Vivien nodded, her joy brimming over, sheer, untempered

joy for the first time in years, and Gio kissed her again, this time with a refreshed, ravenous hunger that said so much more than words ever could. Everything was going to be fine.

*

The next morning, Gio woke her with breakfast in bed, a tray bursting with delights: sugary pastries, zesty orange juice, cappuccino and a single rose in a vase.

Vivien pushed herself up on the pillows and gave him a sleepy, grateful smile.

'I'm taking you for lunch, as well,' said Gio. 'Zeferelli's, just us.'

Zeferelli's was her favourite. 'That sounds wonderful.'

'Well, there's the both of you to feed now.' He set down the tray and kissed her lips. 'You've got to keep your strength up.'

The smell of the cappuccino made her queasy. 'I'll have Adalina bring up some tea instead,' said Gio, moving to go, but she stopped him.

'Let's enjoy this a moment longer,' said Vivien. And so he sat with her while she ate the pastries, and they talked about whether their child would be a boy or a girl, who it might look like, whether it would inherit Vivien's creativity or Gio's scientific mind, her blonde or his darkness, Gio's height or her petite frame.

'I can't wait to meet them.' Vivien beamed.

'Them?' Gio feigned alarm.

'It could be twins...' Vivien teased, and Gio started to tell a story about the identical twins he had been to school with, and the incredible bond between siblings.

'That reminds me,' he said, 'I told Bella. I hope you don't mind, but I thought, with things as they are, it might be best coming from me. And the thing is, Viv,' he lowered his voice, 'she's so happy for us. She told me she was pleased because she knew we'd been trying and how much of a strain that had been putting on you.'

Vivien's voice was tight. 'She said that?'

'I can show you – she wrote it down for me. I think this proves how the two of you can get along, don't you?' His optimism stung. 'I really think this whole situation has got out of hand. Bella wants to be your friend. In time, she'd like to be your sister. And she can't wait to become an aunt to this little one.'

An aunt. The idea of Isabella being in any way related to Vivien's child was horrendous. But what could she do? Isabella had her brother so tightly wound round her finger that he no longer knew which way was up. Vivien resolved to keep her lips sealed, determined not to let their conflict disrupt her happiness. She would simply have to accept that Isabella's place in her husband's life would never change. All she could do was ensure that her own place, and her child's, was ultimately more important. She could do that by embracing her role as doting wife and mother.

Vivien swallowed her misgivings. 'I can't wait for that, too.'

*

Isabella, it transpired, was determined to make herself useful. 'She wants you to know she's thinking of you,' said Gio, 'because she can't tell you herself.' Having spent most of her time at the Barbarossa in exile, Isabella was now set upon helping around the house, sweeping floors and cleaning bedrooms, all the jobs that were customarily Adalina's domain. Vivien watched the charade with some amusement, unsure what to make of it. She found herself enjoying the maid's quiet exasperation; Lili was far too professional to let on, but Vivien saw her annoyance grow by the day.

In the third month of the pregnancy, she and Gio went for a private scan. Despite the reassurance of her morning sickness, Vivien couldn't quite believe the wonder of her circumstances until she saw that tiny bean on the screen. Immediately, she fell in love with it. *Hello*, she thought, as she squeezed Gio's hand, *I know you*. The whole thing still felt like a fantastic dream from which she could at any second wake up. But no, there it was, in black and white, definite: their incredible baby.

Back at the castle, Gio kissed her goodbye: he was due at the lab at midday. 'You take care of us,' he said before he left, placing a hand on her belly. She had never felt so intimate with her husband, as if a sheltering force surrounded them.

'I will.'

'I mean it, *bellissima*. I wish I could stay home and look after you myself. Let Adalina and Isabella do the work. You have to rest, all right?'

The intensity of his concern was endearing – doubly so for making partners of the maid and the sister. Isabella had finally been demoted, and Vivien could at last assume her rightful role in his eyes, as one to be protected and revered.

Vivien was in such a good mood that she called hello to Isabella when she walked into the hall, peeling off her aubergine-leather gloves and dropping them on the telephone desk. It gratified her that Isabella was cleaning the floor, swishing her mop back and forth, the gentle *phish* and *whoosh* as she moved across the tiles, leaving a slick of slippery water in her wake. Adalina had been right – all she'd had to do was assert herself, and she had done so in the most effective way possible. Vivien was the woman of this great castle, its joint custodian, and her precious child would soon be heir. The pregnancy put her in an untouchable state. Isabella could only go so far in her demands. She had nothing against the imminence of her brother's offspring.

Isabella gave a gentle nod. She extended to Vivien a shy smile – at least it might have been a smile, or as close to one as Isabella could get.

'You don't need to do all this,' Vivien tried. 'That's what the staff are for.'

For a second, she thought the sister might speak. But no – just an echo of that strange half-smile, before Isabella resumed her task and continued towards the stairs.

Vivien swept up to her quarters to change. She hoped that Gio wouldn't be too late tonight as she was hoping to cook his favourite meal, with help from Lili for the chocolate tiramisu. Then they would fall asleep, safe in each other's cocoon.

So wrapped up was she in these thoughts that, on returning to the corridor and hurrying to meet the steps, she felt her foot meet something hard and round at the very top that, for a moment, seemed to support her weight before escaping from beneath her. There followed a brief, sliver-thin moment of panic, coupled with something like disbelief that this should happen now, on such an ordinary day, when she was doing nothing more unusual than wandering down to the kitchens while listening to the rain pattering on the windows, before Vivien tumbled forward, the stairs coming to meet her, and when her head hit the tiles she lost consciousness.

The last thing she saw was Isabella, halfway down, the dripping mop in her hand. Her black eyes gleamed, glittering and triumphant.

CHAPTER TWENTY-SIX

Italy, Summer 2016

Adalina finds me on the floor. I must have fallen backwards, back against the banister, and Salvatore has gone. Perhaps I passed out, because all I remember is the painting going up, bright, bright orange, and then this. Now. Adalina's scream…

'No!' she howls. '*No!*'

There is no getting past the flames. They are solid heat. *Get up*, I instruct myself, *move*. Then I'm staggering down the stairs, the fire like a wall behind me, threatening with each second to spread to the panels, the mahogany chest, devouring all in its path. Into the kitchen, where by the pale light of the moon I fill a basin with water, back up the stairs, into the fire and it fizzes, waning, so I do the same again. It doesn't sound like only Adalina screaming; it sounds like another woman, maybe two more, and a high, urgent, reedy cry that ricochets at angles across the vaulted ceiling. As I stumble with the water, I'm reminded of that Northern Line station and the cacophony of cries that followed me into fresh air, all those varied pitches and every one accusing.

The blaze at last extinguished, Adalina sinks against

the wall. Her skin is blackened and slick with soot, her hair untied from its usual severe bun. Her features wear an expression of such sadness that the anger I'm expecting is delayed for a while. For a moment, she reminds me of someone; just a glimmer of a suggestion and it's too hazy to pinpoint. A woman I saw once, someone I think I knew…

'Adalina…?'

My voice doesn't sound like my own. I go towards her.

'What have you done?' she rasps.

'I'm so sorry.' I'm in shock. 'It was an accident.'

She drops to the floor, and the victim of the crime. The portrait is scarcely recognisable as a person any more. The frame has melted and the canvas is smeared with black, curled up round the edges like hardened glue. One of the sitter's eyes remains, a green, piercing glint of light that shimmers out like a jewel on the ocean bed. That eye seems to watch me, and I place it immediately. It's the same man I saw when I first arrived at the Barbarossa, the man I believe to be Vivien's husband.

'As if it wasn't enough to lose him the first time,' Adalina whispers.

I don't know what to say. It was a stupid, stupid thing, and to repeat my apology only highlights this, and the woeful inadequacy of my defence.

'I was talking to Salvatore…' I begin.

Her head snaps up, mad-eyed. 'What did he say?'

'Nothing,' I backtrack, 'he… I don't listen to him anyway.'

'Good. He doesn't know what he's saying.'

The way she's speaking seems suddenly unfamiliar, like

it's a different person I'm talking to, somebody I've never met. It might be the gloom, silvery now with ash and despair. Water puddles on the step; the walls drip.

'He frightened me,' I say. 'The candle, I dropped it and…'

She's just staring at the portrait. At the face that once was.

The flames have caught the sheets covering the other likenesses and now I see glimpses of their models. One is Vivien, her movie star glamour unmistakeable. The other, still partly obscured by the cloth but with an insistent, passionate glare that demands to be addressed, is a darker woman. I put her at a similar age to Vivien, but her appearance couldn't be more different. Her hair is jet and her eyes are urgent, spitting a silent message. I connect her immediately with the man, with Gio, and seeing the three of them together like that, it becomes clear.

'I have to speak to Vivien,' I say. 'I'll explain this to her.'

'There is no explanation,' says Adalina flatly.

'I feel terrible.'

'Not as terrible as she will.' Adalina's voice cracks, before righting itself and coming back stronger. 'You will only make it worse. I will relay what happened.'

'I really think I ought to—'

'I don't.'

I suppose I am clutching at straws. Maybe if I had the opportunity to speak to Vivien, there would be a chance, however thin, however scarce, but still a chance that she would keep me on here. Coming from Adalina, this won't be the case. I might as well pack my bags now – and I deserve to. This portrait is more than the sum of its charred parts.

It's an irretrievable emblem of the life the woman upstairs once had.

Abruptly, the ancient chandelier sputters to life above our heads. It's like a spotlight on my disgrace, illuminating all the chaos this night has caused.

Adalina stands and lifts the portrait of the man. She handles it tenderly, securing it under one arm. It is heavy and I see her struggle but she won't accept my help. Weary, heavy-boned, she embarks on the stairs.

'Clean up,' she calls behind her. She is choked, the words dry. 'I don't want to see any evidence of this by the time you've finished.'

She doesn't wait for me to reply, but then I have nothing to say.

*

'There was a baby?'

Max brings me a mug of something warm to wrap my hands around. I'm shaking. I didn't know where else to come, just turned up on his doorstep, my words spilling out in random bursts. I'm too terrified of running into Vivien that I cannot stay at the Barbarossa. The next minute I'm terrified of meeting Adalina, having her serve me my notice – or, no, that's too kind, it would be instant dismissal.

'According to Salvatore,' I concede. 'But he was wild – I thought he was going to hurt me.'

'Why would he make up something like that?'

'I don't know.' The mug is trembling; I put it down. 'Max,

I don't know anything. The only thing I'm certain of is that they're going to get rid of me. What will I do then? Where will I go? I can't go home – I can't!'

Max sits opposite me, his soft brown eyes looking enquiringly into mine. He was in the middle of painting a wall when I arrived, his T-shirt splattered with white flecks. Even in my hectic state, I can appreciate the contrast the fabric makes with his arms, and the hard line of muscle beneath it. He's stockier than my usual type – if James can be called my type: yes, he was tall, but he was also in a completely different league to every guy I'd dated before and therefore it would be unfair to pit him against potential suitors. I catch myself. This time a month ago, I'd never have considered a future romance. I hadn't been capable of it.

'Why are you so mixed up about going back to England?' he asks.

'I'm not,' I say. 'I just need the money, that's all.'

'Don't your family want to see you?'

'They see enough of me.' Which is a complete lie – and, judging by the look on Max's face, he knows it. In an appalling slam, I remember the salacious reportage flooding through the UK news. Events at the Barbarossa have distanced me from it; the castillo isn't quite the real world. It's possible to forget.

Until I am banished, and I have to face it: my family, my friends... my life.

'What's going on, Lucy?'

He asks it so gently that, for a mad moment, I imagine telling him everything. But what I like about our friendship is, I admit, the woman he thinks I am. An English rose, pretty and pure, because that's the woman I would like to be.

'I can't tell you,' I say, looking at my hands.

'You can.' His gaze is serious. 'You really can.'

It comes as a relief when there is a knock at the door, and the moment is lost. Max doesn't move and I worry he's going to leave it, but then it comes again, more insistent this time. Reluctant, he stands. 'I'd better get that.'

When he leaves the room, I can exhale. I realise I've been holding my breath. The situation is impossible. I want to get to know Max better, I want to see him and spend time with him, but every time I do I am putting off the unavoidable. Sooner or later I will have to come clean about the person I really am, and then what? I'm tricking him, giving a false impression, and that makes a liar of me as well as a cheat.

I hear Max talking with his visitor. A woman's voice, and I can't make out what they're saying but then I don't need to, because he's back in the room.

'It's for you, Lucy,' he says.

The woman follows him in. She is young, brunette, attractive, and she smiles at me. 'Lucy Whittaker?' she enquires. She is English. My heart plummets.

'Alison Cooney,' she introduces herself. 'I'm a reporter with the *Onlooker*. I traced your whereabouts to the Castillo Barbarossa and followed you here today. I want to give you a chance to speak before somebody else does.'

CHAPTER TWENTY-SEVEN

Vivien, Italy, 1984

Vivien opened her eyes. She felt as if she had slept for a hundred years. Her head hurt, her teeth were sore. Her limbs ached and it took several moments to position herself back in her own body, the black cloud of memory clearing to daylight and with it the realisation of what she had been through. Her tongue bloated. She had to speak.

There was only one question.

'The baby…?' she said to no one, just a strip of bright lights. *Hospital.*

Then Gio appeared above her, his face a wreck of worry, and she thought, *It's you again*, just as it had been when they had first met.

'The baby,' she choked. 'Please, Gio, tell me the baby—'

'The baby's fine.' He touched her face. She was crying; tears of fear and relief soaked her cheeks. 'Viv, I thought you were dying. You're OK. The baby's OK.'

'I fell…' She tried to piece it together, stalled as once again the release of knowing her baby was well overwhelmed her. The slip, the stairs rushing up to meet her, the hard smack of the tiles against her skull before she'd passed out. Moving a hand to her tummy, she felt a reassuring squirm, and smiled. *Thank you*, she thought.

'You frightened me to death.' Gio's features pulled in and out of focus; he was trying to contain his emotions – and among them was anger, a stormy fury that tightened his brow. He must have found out what happened. He must know.

What did happen? Vivien touched it in her mind, that damnable, horrifying thing. Gio knew. He knew. But then—

'It was an accident,' he said, 'the wet floor. Isabella's mortified.'

Isabella...

Vivien clenched her fists on the sheets. Suddenly, she remembered seeing the sister's face on the staircase, a swift frame before the dark descended. The ghost of Isabella had been hovering in her memory since she'd come round, a shadowy, looming presence that left a bitter weight in the pit of her stomach.

'Is she here?' she whispered.

Gio frowned. 'She's at the Barbarossa.'

'She did it. She saw me fall.'

'Thank God she did,' he countered. 'Otherwise nobody would have found you.' There was that flash of anger again – only it wasn't for Isabella, it was for her. 'I told you to be careful,' he said harshly, torn between compassion and rage, as different as the colours of his eyes. 'Didn't I say that? You've got to be more responsible. There are two of you to look after now. I can't be there all the time.'

Vivien blinked. 'I am responsible,' she returned. 'This is

the most important thing that has ever happened to me.' How could he suggest that she was unable to take care of herself or the baby? That she would ever, ever deliberately put their child in danger? And she *had* been taking care, she had, until…

'If you'd been there,' she said, 'it wouldn't have happened.'

'No, because I'd have been looking out for you.'

'And you'd have seen Isabella.'

He watched her stoically. 'You need to be careful, Vivien.'

Oh, she was. She was taking care to remember.

'What time?' she said.

'What time what?'

'What time was I found?'

Gio was impatient. 'Salve called me at three.'

Vivien couldn't help her bitter smile. 'It wasn't then. I didn't fall, then. The accident happened right after you left for work.'

Gio knew where she was going. 'Come on, Viv—'

'You're telling me that Salvatore found me *hours* after I fell? How can that be possible, when Isabella was there? She was right there. I saw her.' She wanted to shake him: *how could he not see?* 'She made it happen and then she left me!'

Gio put a hand on her forehead. 'You're running a fever,' he said coolly, 'the doctors told me you might. There's bound to be some delirium.'

Delirium?

'You knocked your head, Vivien.'

'I know what happened.'

'It was an accident,' he said again.

Vivien had to bite her tongue to stop herself lashing out, cursing Isabella's wretched, devil-sent name, even though she knew no words could sufficiently convey the dreadful reality of her act. Was it possible? Was it? Was Isabella really so despicable as to want Vivien to lose her unborn child? Wicked as she believed Isabella to be, even she was appalled at the lengths the witch would go to.

'Vivien…?'

But she couldn't look at him. Isabella might be able to kid the rest, she might be able to kid her own brother, but she wasn't kidding Vivien.

'I'd like to be alone now,' she said, turning to the window.

Gio waited a while. 'I love you,' he said.

She watched a breeze move through the trees. He closed the door behind him.

*

In the weeks following her recovery, Vivien's body changed. She had always been so precious about it, honing it into shape for her work at Boudoir Lalique or making sure to snag the next movie role, but now that it was performing a function, an incredible miracle, she watched with astonishment as her curves grew and her edges softened.

Gio took care to bury their argument. He acted as if nothing had been said in that hospital room, no inference made, because for Vivien to accuse his sister of what she had was a point from which they could not come back. Instead, he lavished her with devotion, vowing that she wouldn't lift a finger, insisting on knowing where she was at all times – an unprecedented level of attention that, given the years since Isabella had entered their lives, she welcomed – and constantly bolstering her with compliments.

'You're sexy like this,' he told her, sneaking up behind her before he left for work to plant a kiss on the back of her neck. Vivien loved it; she felt just as she had when they'd first met. Since the drama of her fall, Gio had taken a step back from whatever assignment he was engaged in at the laboratory: Vivien was seeing more of him than ever. It finally felt as if their lives were settling; the baby was their anchor.

And she did feel sexy – sexier than Isabella, who, as Vivien blossomed and grew, seemed to fade, disappearing ever more into the gloom. Isabella spent much of her time now closeted up in her attic. Frequently she skipped meals, leaving Gio and Vivien to dine alone and feel like a properly married couple. When Vivien did see her, it gratified her to notice that the sister's beauty was diminishing. The sultry darkness that had rimmed her jet-black eyes was no longer seductive and appealing; instead it looked haunted and tired. Her high, sharp cheekbones appeared less cut glass and more tortured ghoul. Her once shiny hair, so glossy as to be the envy of every woman this side of Florence, was matt and dull. Vivien supposed that guilt did that to a person. *You know what you did*, she thought. But she never confronted Isabella. To do so would be to award the sister a satisfaction Vivien was unwilling to give. She sensed Isabella waiting for a showdown, the proof that her efforts had been gratified and that Vivien was crumbling as a result, but the showdown never came.

Gio seemed hardly to notice his sister's absence, which was the best part.

'Do you think Isabella's all right?' Vivien asked over Adalina's artichoke gnocchi one night, deliberately agitating the issue because it pleased her to appear the merciful wife. She wanted Gio to see her as the mature, enlightened, forgiving one, while Isabella became stranger and more reclusive by the day.

Gio scratched his chin. 'She's fine,' he said.

'I hope she isn't still upset after my… accident.'

'I'm sure she's not.'

'Good. Because I thought we were all past that.'

Gio disliked talking about his sister; he could rarely be drawn on the subject and would never elaborate, even when pressed. But, the way Vivien saw it, the more she tugged at that string, planting suggestion after suggestion, the more their tight knot of siblingship would start to unravel. She was carving her own niche in their relationship, hollowing it out and smoothing it down until it was a perfect fit.

The catch was that she herself was not past the so-called accident.

She would never be past it.

Each time she glimpsed Isabella's hateful glare, each time she felt the sister's sinister presence blowing on the leaves outside, scattering like wind on the stone fountain or drifting like fire-ash through the great hall, she felt more certain of what had happened. Isabella was a guilty would-be murderess. Not only had she sought to finish off Vivien, but her baby as well. It was a reprehensible act.

It was no wonder Gio couldn't bring himself to suspect her of it.

With any luck, Isabella's shame would keep her in solitary confinement forever, and out of their lives.

'Anyway, darling,' said Vivien, sipping her Montepulciano, 'tell me: what are our plans for the weekend?'

*

Their plans, it turned out, were meant to be a surprise – but come Friday evening, she could tell Gio was hiding some exciting reveal, his nervous energy and propensity for jumping from one topic to another was a giveaway.

'I've commissioned an artist to visit the house,' he told her. 'Now is as good a time as any,' he pulled her close, '*especially* now, to record our family.'

Vivien was delighted. 'What do you mean?'

'Portraits.' He kissed her. 'Shouldn't we document our residence at the Barbarossa? And when the *bambino* is born, he or she will have a space as well.'

Vivien was elated at this prospect. She had long admired the rarefied painting of Giacomo Dinapoli that adorned the ballroom, and throughout the castillo were littered many generations more, going right back to the eighteenth and nineteenth centuries: coiffed, seated women with their bejewelled hands resting in their laps; striking men draped in finery or out on hunts, and a particularly impressive one of a teenage girl lolling beneath an olive tree somewhere on the estate, her eyes dreamy and her flowing, ebony hair captured so wonderfully that it looked like liquid.

Soon, she would have a portrait all her own. She couldn't wait. It was one thing to live in the Barbarossa, and quite another to be initiated into its vaults. There was a timeless quality to it, permanence, meaning she would exist here long after the decades had passed. She would be sewn into the tapestry of its history. Vivien had never thought this important before, but now cherished the roots this place gave her.

'Gio, what a wonderful idea.'

'I was hoping you'd think so. I thought we'd hang them on the stairs.' He lowered his voice. 'I know that's a sensitive place for you, but...'

'No,' she interrupted, with a smile. 'It's ideal.'

On Saturday morning, Vivien enjoyed a peaceful few hours' sketching in the Oval, surrounded by birdsong and with the warm sun bathing her face. Her baby nudged and kicked as her pencil moved across the page. *One day I'll draw you*, she thought, and in that moment the world seemed utterly right and lovely in every way.

So content was Vivien that she hardly noticed the time. It was only when the chapel bell rung out for midday that she realised she was twenty minutes late for the portrait appointment. Gathering her things, she hurried up to the house.

Gio was out on the gravel, calling her name. She was

surprised at his countenance, wound like a spring, his face a mask of frantic concern.

'Vivien, thank God!' He rushed towards her. 'Where have you been?'

'In the garden,' she said, lifting her sketchbook. 'I thought I'd—'

'Do you know how worried I've been?' He gripped her roughly; it hurt. His eyes sparked danger, one black, one green, and she thought again how his temper rode that same knife edge: her loving husband one minute, a fervent stranger the next.

'I've been going out of my mind,' he went on. 'I've been looking all over for you. Adalina has, too. I thought something had happened to you!'

'I'm sorry. I – I should have told someone.'

'I thought you'd fallen again,' said Gio, shaking her. 'You might have passed out, knocked your head – I thought you were hurt or the baby was hurt.'

'But I was only—'

'You were only as thoughtless and careless as you were last time!'

Vivien was startled. She blinked through tears, the day's perfection shattered.

She didn't recognise him. Why was he being like this? Her fall was neither the result of thoughtlessness nor carelessness: it was the result of sabotage. Lethal sabotage.

'What do you think it's like for me?' Gio released her, turned away then turned back again. Vivien felt like a child being told off, a girl in church wearing a lily-white dress who kept getting the words wrong. 'I've got no control over what you do or where you go. I'm trying here, can't you see? I'm trying to look out for you.'

'I'm sorry,' she forced out for the second time. 'I didn't realise it was late. I'll be more careful in future.'

He shook his head at her. 'You don't get it, do you?'

Vivien swallowed. In her peripheral, she saw the portrait artist emerge at the door, then beat a hasty retreat inside when he saw his subjects arguing. What must they look like? The huge shadow of Gio in his long dark coat, bearing down on his pregnant wife – what right had he to speak to her like this? The attentiveness he had smothered her with since her fall became suffocating. Twenty minutes unaccounted for and he acted like it had been a week. Could she have no independence any longer?

'Do I have to spell it out for you?' he demanded. 'Are you really that stupid?'

Vivien was wounded. He had never thrown her lack of education at her and it was a cheap, lazy shot. *Stupid.* Yes, Gio had letters after his name, he was a doctor, for crying out loud, and she had left school at sixteen and prostituted herself – but what did he want her to say? *Of course, I'm a dumb, ridiculous blonde and you're fucking Einstein; how you stooped yourself to marry me I'll never know.*

'You're making a scene,' she said.

'I'm entitled to make any scene I like. This is my house and I'll behave as I please. I almost lost you that day, Vivien. I'm not losing another family – not like I did last time. I'm not going through that again. You're my future, you and this baby. You're everything to me. I love you. I can't lose two families. I can't.'

Vivien opened her mouth to speak, to apologise, to yell or to comfort him – she didn't know which because she didn't know to whom she was speaking. The man in front of her was at once someone she knew and someone she had never laid eyes on. The words she needed didn't come her way. Instead she pushed past him, tears flooding her eyes, and headed towards the castillo. Gio grabbed her wrist; she broke away, and it took every ounce of effort not to round on him and pound his chest with her fists – that, or fall into it and never let go.

*

The sitting got off to a strained start.

'Signora Moretti,' said the artist, who was young, bearded, handsome, 'it's a pleasure.' She shook his hand politely, determined to regain some dignity after the display they had put on outside. 'And may I say congratulations to the two of you,' he went on when Gio's dark form brooded in behind her. Vivien uncrossed her arms, aware how defensive she must look. The atmosphere crackled with tension.

'This way,' said Gio stiffly, as he led the man into the ballroom. The window overlooking the lawns would frame them; in the background, the fountain spewed liquid metal from the fish's open mouth. Vivien trailed after. She wished she could capture her earlier glow. Here they were, the two of them, together, no Isabella – she ought to be happy.

Indeed, Isabella hadn't been seen in days, not since Vivien had glimpsed her from her bedroom window, on the rim of the fountain, alone and staring at the sky. She gave her the creeps. Most days, Vivien relished the empty household – but sometimes, the horrid suspicion wormed its way beneath her skin that Isabella wasn't done yet. Her silence was preamble for a dreadful chorus.

Like the punchline of a horrid joke, the artist said:

'Are we waiting for one more?'

Vivien looked to Gio in confusion; Gio didn't take his eyes from the man.

'Yes,' he said. 'She'll be down in a moment.'

Oh, no, thought Vivien. *No, no, no.*

'Excellent,' said the man, as he set up his brushes and unpacked his easel. He loaded the first canvas on to the scaffold. 'We'll get started then.'

'Gio,' managed Vivien, in a strangled voice. 'May I have a word?'

Loath to incite another spectacle, Gio followed her into the hall.

'It's Isabella, isn't it,' spat Vivien. 'It's *her.*'

Gio's eyes gave nothing away. One black, one green: two distinct people. In that instant she could not be certain he wasn't punishing her; he wasn't playing with her just as Isabella did, taunting her, prodding her until she fell apart.

Then he delivered his crushing blow. 'It's her house, too, you know.'

Vivien was shaking. 'I don't understand.' But she did.

'My uncle left it to both of us.' Was he enjoying this?

Was this payback? 'Half this place belongs to Bella – it's hers by right. By birth.'

'I thought it was ours,' she said. 'Yours and mine. I thought it was ours.'

Vivien heard how petulant she sounded. It wasn't meant to come out like that, spoiled and entitled, she who had not earned the prestige of the castillo as Gio and Isabella had, she who was ultimately and inescapably the guest.

'You're making a scene,' he hit back, an echo of her earlier remonstration. Why was he mocking her? She searched for her husband but could not find him.

'You and Isabella own the Barbarossa together,' she whispered. 'Adalina and Salvatore work for you. Not for me. I'm just the extra one.'

'Come on,' he argued, his cool collectedness like fuel against the hot struck match of her passion, 'Bella hardly exercises her right. She keeps herself to herself. It's more than some women would do. You should consider yourself lucky—'

That was more than she could take. '*Lucky?*' she choked. 'Did you say *lucky*?'

Gio put his hands in his pockets.

'Lucky to share my world with the woman who's trying to ruin it? Lucky to share my husband? Lucky to escape with my baby's life after *she tried to kill us*?'

He didn't respond. He just looked at her, sadly. That look carved her inside out. It was worse than sadness – it was disappointment. Pity.

'I'm not lucky.' Vivien's ragged hiss was a thin attempt

to conceal their argument from the artist, who, on the other side of the door, would surely have heard everything. It was ruined. Ruined, ruined, ruined – and all by that bitch.

'The only reason Isabella's hiding out now is because she knows what she did,' Vivien said. 'She knows and I know. You're the only one who doesn't.'

Gio was quiet a moment, as if to make sure she had finished. Then he said:

'You're looking a bit peaky, Vivien.' He was totally cold. 'I'm not sure you're well enough to take part in this. Perhaps you ought to go upstairs and lie down.'

Vivien turned her back on him, blinded. 'Perhaps I ought,' she said.

CHAPTER TWENTY-EIGHT

Italy, Summer 2016

Alison watches me steadily. It must be only a matter of seconds, but it feels like an age. Max looks at me; I look at Alison. Nobody says anything.

Then Max breaks the silence. 'I should leave you two alone.'

'No!' I say quickly. 'I mean…' I can't meet his eye; I'm ashamed, fearful that one glance will reveal my story, expose my guilt. I'm not the person he thought I was. I only wish I were. 'We'll go somewhere else.'

It's a miracle I can speak. Max's curiosity follows me out of the room, Alison close behind, and when we reach the door, I turn briefly and he mouths:

'Are you all right?'

No, I want to cry. *Do you know what this is, Max? This is where it ends.*

My life here, my life at home: my life as I know it. My life as it might have been, or might still be. It's about to end. Alison holds the key and I am terrified of what it opens. I'm in the middle of an ocean, floundering, and the deep beneath me is a boundless drop, crashing towards my darkest confessions and imaginings.

Of course, I don't say this. Instead, I nod, every denial and rebuff just driving more of a wedge between us. I can never come back from this.

'Call me,' he murmurs, as Alison and I make our exit.

Out on the street, the world rushes past.

'OK, Lucy,' says Alison. 'Where would you feel most comfortable?'

*

Most comfortable… As if that were an attainable thing. In the end we sit in the gardens overlooking the river, holding cups of sweet, thick latte – Alison's shout.

'The coffee here is amazing,' she says, tipping a crinkly packet of sugar into the steaming liquid and blowing on it. She has a pretty top lip, and soft, long eyelashes. She doesn't look like someone to be afraid of. 'I shouldn't drink so much of it,' she goes on, as if we're two friends catching up in our lunch hour. 'If I drink it, I get wired… if I don't, the same. I need the caffeine, though. Long hours, you know?'

The incidental reference to her job plants me back in reality.

'What do you want?' I ask.

Alison sips her drink. 'I want your side of the story,' she says, 'like I said at your boyfriend's. This isn't about nailing you to the cross. I'm on your team.'

'He isn't my boyfriend.'

She raises an eyebrow. 'Forgive me for thinking you have a complicated love life.'

'And that's bullshit about being on my team. You want the story, just like everyone else. Pretending to like me doesn't make any difference.'

Alison puts her coffee on the arm of the bench and digs into her bag for her tablet. 'OK.' She looks at me. 'Do you know what the UK press are saying?'

'That James Calloway's mistress is a murdering bitch.'

'Something like that. You were lucky to escape with your name.'

'Which you're about to disclose – your editor must love you.'

'My editor doesn't know.'

I can't resist asking. 'How did you find out?'

'Natasha Fenwick is a friend of a friend. She told me everything.'

Of course. Natasha.

'Don't go thinking she's a snitch,' says Alison. 'She could have told any number of journalists and she didn't.'

'Just you.'

'Yeah.' Alison smiles. 'She knows she can trust me. And so can you.'

'Is that why you turned up at my dad's house, threatening him?'

Alison pauses. 'He was hardly threatened. But I am sorry about that. It wasn't me, in fact – it was my assistant. She shouldn't have spoken to him at all – she handled it badly. Believe me, we had words.'

I look away, the cup burning in my hand.

'Listen, Lucy, here's how it is. Your name is going to come out sooner or later. A couple of reporters I know are already sniffing it out. You and James kept it well hidden, I'll give you that much. He certainly hasn't been pressed on anything.'

My heart twinges. So he didn't drop me in it, after all.

'But they're getting close,' she tells me. 'And, depending on whose hands it ends up in, your world could be decimated. I'm talking a move abroad, a new start, the lot.' She looks about her. 'You had the right idea coming here.'

'What, then, makes you different?' My voice is cold. But despite myself, there is something about Alison I quite like. Maybe it's the fact that she's my age, clearly ambitious but innocent with it, as if she's playing at this callous writer act when in fact she can't believe the goldmine she's stumbled across.

'I'm not out to get you, Lucy. I want you to have a forum to speak. Clearly there is another side to this, right? Are you still in touch with him?'

I shake my head.

'That's probably best.' She nods. 'Ex-boyfriends are better off in the past.'

I don't know if this is a method to get me to talk more, or if we're sharing a twisted confidence. It's safest to assume the former.

'Was it love?' she asks.

I'm torn. I've kept this close for so long. Alison is a stranger.

But she's a kind stranger. I can see in her eyes that she's genuine, and I don't know what it is but I trust her to represent me fairly. Who knows what those rival publications are going to do with me once they smoke me out? There will certainly be violent reprisals, but if someone out there can speak for me, someone like Alison, won't it at least set the record straight, in some small corner?

I take a breath, and I tell her everything.

*

An hour later, we part company. I feel lighter. I should feel afraid, but I don't. Alison gives me a hug. 'You did the right thing talking to me,' she says.

'I hope so,' I reply.

It turns out Alison had a fling with a married man, a few years ago. 'I didn't know either,' she confided. 'And it wasn't as if I was even in love with him, which, believe me, is going to work in your favour when it comes to perceptions. Mine was just some stupid string of dates – it was exciting, and exciting because it was wrong. I grew up, I got wise, and I dumped him. He's an arsehole. Period.'

Clearly she was trying to get me to admit that James, too, was a bastard.

But I couldn't.

'You're not still hung up on him, are you?' she asked.

'Off the record?'

She nodded. I smiled. 'Nice try,' I said.

As I watch Alison head into her taxi, a glossy-haired

bomb about to return to England and detonate within a matter of hours, I feel… better. Calmer. As if getting it out isn't just catharsis, it's a realisation that I'm not a killer. I fell in love. That's all.

My phone springs to life. It's a message from Max:

Here if you need to talk. M

I push it back in my pocket. Determined to keep moving, I walk down to the river, winding lanes scented with jasmine and the easy bustle of tourists, who clutch cameras and gelato. From here, the view is beautiful. The Duomo appears lit by fire, a giant orb of golden sun: red, bronze, set against a cobalt-blue sky, the light fading now and twinkling spots flaring to life to mark the restaurants and bars. I'm not ready yet to return to the Barbarossa, and so cross the bridge and set out to my favourite spot in all of Florence: the steps by the Uffizi, that silver courtyard that thrums with violin strings and it is possible to hide in the back, out of sight, contained by shadows. This evening, it is a cauldron of low murmurs, as if to speak too loudly would disturb some unseen dignity, the weight of time and grace. A duo of musicians tunes up across the piazza. Strains vibrate in the air like dragonflies humming on a still pond.

A couple next to me holds hands and kisses. I sit with my knees together, leaning forward, my chin on my hand, and close my eyes. The music takes shape around me and the atmosphere swallows me up. I cherish my invisibility because I know it will not last. Nobody sees me. Nobody knows my name. Perhaps I can stay here. I need never return home. But then I think of my father and the women in his life who have left him, one by one, saying goodbye. I have already been here a month with scarce contact; I know I could never do that. My sisters have been able to stay away because they're afraid to face the broken picture, the place they came from that was shattered by tragedy. It's all too much of a reminder – me, Dad, the pictures of Mum on the mantelpiece. I've dealt with that; I'm armed. So I have to be there.

When I open my eyes again, my gaze is drawn straight to him.

I sit up. Wings batter inside my chest. *It can't be*.

He is only a figure. It is the back of him, leaning against the wall looking out at the square. But I would know that outline anywhere; the back of his head, so familiar, I know all its contours and how it feels to touch. My fingers tremble.

Somehow I stand. Somehow one foot lands in front of the other. Somehow I am moving across the piazza and with each step the vision becomes clearer and more certain, and at the same time more improbable.

I am close when he moves away, slipping into the crowd so to anyone else he would be one of the masses, but not to me. I am homed in on that head, moving between countless others that, in the twilight, are similar but altogether different. With each turn, dipping in and out of lit pockets, tantalising fragments of his face come into view, and the cloud of disbelief settles more firmly around my shoulders.

It can't be. But it is.

I cannot say his name. I could call it, I know I could call it and my tongue is ready to set it free but nothing comes. We reach the kerb. I walk a few paces behind. A car rushes past, but before it does he ducks across the street and disappears from sight. Frantically, I follow, searching every face, spinning in circles, but he is lost.

Then: 'Lucy?'

I turn. He's there. Stepped right out of my dream and into my world.

'I thought it was you,' he says.

CHAPTER TWENTY-NINE

Vivien, Italy, 1984

Just before Christmas, the portraits arrived at the Barbarossa.

'Why are there three?' Vivien asked quietly, putting a protective hand over her seven-month bump. 'I didn't sit. It should just be you and Isabella.'

Gio moved towards the packages. They were wrapped in crisp brown paper and tied securely with string. A large red stamp, in Italian, warned to handle with care. He checked the backs of all three, before moving the middle one to the front.

'This one's yours,' he said. 'It was Bella's idea.'

Vivien went towards it. Relations with her husband had all but broken down since the abandoned sitting; it hurt so much that there was still this wedge between them. This should be the best time of their lives, counting down to the arrival of their baby. But too much had been said, too much hurt exchanged. A chill touched the back of her neck at the mention of Isabella's name, but she neither had the courage nor energy to question it. Gio's intensity frightened her, both repellent and magnetic. She desired to run from it, but at the same time to lose herself in its ferocity, to have it protect her, to allow herself to be embraced by the sheer dark power of it.

'We were ready to have you sit at a later date.' He gestured for her to open the package. 'But Bella had a better idea. She produced a photograph of you. It was enough to work from. She was quite adamant we use this one.'

As Vivien's fingers plucked uncertainly at the packaging, it was clear to her that Gio viewed this gesture of Isabella's as an olive branch. That she, Isabella, was a more generous woman than Vivien, one whose innocence and goodness shone through in spite of the accusations thrown her way. Gio's tone plainly expected her to agree, to turn to him and say, 'Oh, Gio, isn't she just wonderful?'

She couldn't. Because she knew, even as she peeled away the paper, that Isabella would have the final laugh on this note, as well as on so many others.

'There,' said Gio, once all was revealed. 'What do you think?'

*

The picture defied words. Vivien stared at it dumbly.

'Just what the hell is that?' she whispered.

Gio came round to look at it with her. 'We thought—' He stopped. 'Oh.'

Vivien could think of more suitable words.

'This isn't what we agreed,' he said. 'Bella must have got confused. I thought we'd settled on the one I took of you after we arrived here.'

Vivien knew the one he meant. It was the one of her in front of the castillo, gazing into the camera. The one on the back of which he'd written, *V, 1981*.

Not this.

'I'm sorry, *cara*,' he said. 'This is a mistake.'

She was shaking. Of all the things Isabella could have done…

'I'll talk to her,' said Gio. 'She'll be so embarrassed. We'll get another one commissioned. We'll make this right.' He touched her arm, the first tenderness that had gone between them in weeks, and put his head to one side, assessing. 'Unless…'

'Unless what?'

'It's a beautiful likeness,' he ventured. 'You might want to keep it?'

Vivien whirled on him. 'Are you serious?'

'Viv, I know he hurt you. I know he was strict. So was my uncle. So are plenty of men from that generation. But he's dead now. He's gone. He isn't coming back.'

The lie she had told him so long ago still had the strength to wind her.

'I hate my father,' she said. 'I'll always hate him. I wish I'd killed him myself.'

Gio tried to talk her down. 'Now you're being dramatic.'

'Of course I am,' she blasted. 'Silly Vivien. Hysterical Vivien. Mad Vivien.'

'I'm not saying that.'

'You don't need to.'

She wished she could banish the tears from her eyes, but

still they came, hot and thick and threatening to fall. Of course her suffering at her father's hands would seem pale and limp in comparison with Isabella's. Vivien's childhood struggle was token when pitted against Isabella's, a petty grievance like so much else she complained about. Isabella won there, too. She won the Wrecked Childhood Award.

At least, through blurred vision, the horrendous portrait was dulled. For there, instead of the contemporary likeness Vivien had hoped for herself, the proud profile and blooming baby bump, was an image of herself as a girl, wearing the lily-white dress she had been marshalled into for church. Her hair was in pigtails and her eyes smothered a silent scream. Behind, looking on with proud satisfaction, stood the puppet master himself, Gilbert's hand clamped firm on to her shoulder.

Where had Isabella even got this photo?

'She's been through my things,' said Vivien, in disbelief. 'Isabella – she must have been into our room, found the box. I thought I'd hidden it—'

Gio put his hand on her arm. 'I gave Bella the box,' he said softly. 'I asked her to choose something from it. She meant well, Vivien. She really did.'

Vivien snatched her arm away. 'Do you know what else was in that box?' she hissed. 'I'll tell you, Gio. My *diary* from all those years ago – it would have told her everything she needed to know about my father. Things even you don't know. She knew this would hit me where it hurt and she was right.' A sob spilled out of her. 'She's evil, Gio, why can't you see it? Why can't you see what she's doing to me?'

She fled from the hall, tears stinging. And so it was that Gio's portrait was duly hung on the staircase alongside Isabella's, in which the sister looked more disarmingly beautiful than ever. They appeared as a couple – a gorgeous, raven-haired couple, the Barbarossa between them like a shared trophy.

It was months before Vivien, in a new pose but unable to hide the burgeoning dark in her eyes, joined them, wedged amid the siblings but forever the outsider.

*

It could be her imagination, but Vivien was sure it wasn't.

As Christmas approached and the hillsides froze, so there seemed to be a shift in Isabella. It was as if the portrait had given her conviction to claim what was hers. The unborn child was an unexpected inconvenience, but Isabella was still the sister. She still had Gio's love and she still possessed the wiles to work it in her favour.

Often, over the supper table, Isabella would move as if about to speak. Each time, Vivien tried to catch Gio's eye. *What's going on?* But her husband continued to slice his veal and talk about preparations for the New Year celebrations happening at the mansion of some friend of his, a count who lived in luxury up in the hills.

Isabella noticed her attention. Vivien swore she was playing with her. When Gio asked a question, Isabella eyed her with fierce determination, as if challenging her to answer before she did. It made Vivien's heart race and her palms sweat. The threat of Isabella's voice was akin to an inanimate object springing to life, some toy at the back of a closet jerking out of the gloom, limbs outstretched, *Boo!* What would the sister sound like? Was her voice deep, like her brother's; would it falter like a rusted car, or sing like a nightingale? What would she say? For all Vivien's words – useless, frivolous words that spilled out of her as free and bland as water – she could never equal the potency that Isabella's voice would have. Isabella's language would be rich as liquor, intoxicating and sweet. Years of silence had aged her voice like a fine wine or a precious gem. Each syllable she uttered would be liquid gold.

Vivien confided in Adalina.

'You believe Signora Isabella is no longer sick?' said the maid, as she checked the larder for their forthcoming Christmas feast. The question knew its answer and sought only to allow Vivien her tirade. It was how it worked between them – Lili fed the queries, while Vivien leaped on them, those little springboards that sent her frenzy flying. Vivien pondered how much Lili believed her. She had told the maid about the fall, her conviction that Isabella had caused it. But Adalina's professionalism hadn't allowed her to concur – it was, after all, a critical indictment. Instead she had listened, sympathised, and it was only after Vivien left the servants' quarters that she realised Adalina hadn't voiced her judgement either way. So the tone was set for all ensuing conversations about Isabella: Adalina allowed her to speak, but gave nothing away herself. Vivien could hardly blame her. Her own accusations were tremendous.

'Oh, she's still sick,' said Vivien darkly. 'She's always been sick.'

Adalina said nothing, just continued scrubbing potatoes. The sound was satisfying, coarsely determined, like nails attacking an itch.

'This mute act…' said Vivien. 'It suits her purpose, doesn't it?'

Adalina met Vivien's eye, but didn't stop scrubbing.

'She's to be exonerated from every damn thing,' Vivien rampaged on. 'Isabella can do whatever she likes without fear of reprisal. So long as she's without a voice, she's reminding everyone of the misfortune that befell her. She might as well be screaming it from the rooftops, for all the noise it makes.'

Through the window, Vivien saw Salvatore bringing the Christmas tree into the house. He had enlisted help from one of the gardeners, securing the ten-foot fir with ropes and carrying it over their shoulders. The pines shook and swayed.

'No one dares criticise Isabella, oh no. Poor thing can't talk back. She never has to justify any of it, does she? She never has to defend herself. Funny, isn't it, Lili – how defence looks like guilt. The more we protest our innocence, the less innocent we seem. Isabella doesn't have that problem. I, however, do.'

Adalina faced her. Vivien could see the maid weighing her options, not wishing to speak out. When she did, she chose her words carefully. 'If I can be so bold,' she said, 'but you and Signor Moretti are making a home here. It will be your child's home, and, I dare say, the home of your future. You must stand together.'

'Against her?'

Adalina glanced away.

'Gio won't listen to me,' said Vivien. 'He doesn't trust a word I say.'

'Then you will have to try again.'

Vivien sat while she watched the maid work. Adalina was right. Gio was the lynchpin: he alone could set her free. If only she had evidence that Isabella had sought to harm her and the baby – that would put an end to his naivety. She had to find proof. And if that meant drawing Isabella's wretched voice out of her, having Isabella trap herself by her own denials, then that was what she must do.

*

Christmas came and went in a burst of twinkling lights. The Barbarossa was always a spectacular venue, and never more so than at this time of year. Gold streamers looped between the arches, lanterns adorned the staircase and paper bells were strung high from the vaults. In the hall, the giant emerald tree was majestic. Glittering lights nestled in dark fronds; shiny glass baubles hung from a silver string. A swathe of tinsel glimmered on the high branches, and at the very top stood a dancing fairy, one knee poised behind her like a ballerina. Gathered on the floor were the Christmas boxes, brought in by Salvatore: exquisitely wrapped in thick crimson paper, green ribbons tied in elaborate bows, and totally empty. It reminded Vivien of Christmases she had read about as a child. A glowing fire, candlelight, the smell of mince pies baking in the oven. In spite of Gilbert Lockhart's religiousness, he hadn't believed in the 'commercialisation' of Christmas. Thus they had spent Christmas Day praying, and nothing else but. No presents, no Santa Claus, no staring out of the window on a blue-black Christmas Eve night, waiting for the jingle of the sleigh and the stamp of reindeer hooves. Christmas at the Barbarossa was magical. She couldn't wait for her own child to experience it, and to enjoy all that she had been denied.

On the first day of the New Year, Vivien came downstairs and ran straight into Isabella, who was slipping in from outside. Supposedly, the sister had been out yet again with Gio, at his work. What were they getting up to out there, and why was Isabella given special access when his wife was kept in the dark?

'Hello,' said Vivien. She stood at the Christmas tree, every inch the woman of the house. As ever, Isabella entered without a word. Vivien saw she wore new leather gloves, soft, fawn, and sprinkled with snow; she looked to the window and saw the white flurry spilling from the sky, tapping gently against the panes. Isabella took off her long coat, releasing her jet hair from the collar so it tumbled down her back.

'I said hello,' repeated Vivien.

Isabella watched her. Again, that shade of black mischief, as if Isabella held the cards to some devilishly clever trick, about which only Vivien had no clue.

'Where's Gio?' she asked.

Isabella gestured outside. So they had been together. The sister hung her coat on the stand and started towards the dining room, where their evening banquet had been set. Vivien noticed her slender hips and gliding sashay, and her confidence shook as she remembered her own softening thighs and non-existent waistline.

'Don't you walk away from me,' said Vivien.

Slowly, Isabella turned.

Her gimlet eyes met Vivien's. In that moment, Vivien was surer than ever. All those nights she had called herself crazy for thinking she heard Gio and his sister in conversation; all the times he had been out with her during the day; all the private stories between them, the connections that couldn't be just a one-way street.

She loathed those eyes.

'I suppose you thought it was funny,' said Vivien, battling to harness herself in the face of Isabella's control. 'Raking up my past like that. Gio thinks you made a mistake – but I know better. What did you expect he'd do? Did you expect him to actually *hang* that damn thing? You failed, Isabella. Against me, you'll always fail.'

Isabella raised an eyebrow. She didn't know what Vivien was talking about – or she did know, and she found it amusing. Like a cat with a mouse, she teased.

'And don't think for a second I don't know it was you who put me in hospital. You might hate me, Isabella, but do you hate your nephew, your niece, so much as to wish them dead? It makes you evil, Isabella, downright evil. Gio might not see it but I do. And, believe me, it's only a matter of time before I convince him.'

Isabella didn't move. Was that the trace of a smile on her lips?

'But then perhaps I won't need to,' Vivien went on. 'You'll convince him yourself because you can't keep this act up indefinitely. He'll see through you sooner or later. He'll know that you've been pretending this whole time.'

On cue, a car door slammed. She heard Gio's footsteps on the gravel.

'Go on, then,' Vivien goaded, unable to stand Isabella's silence any longer. 'Say something – I know you want to. I know you're desperate to. I know you want to tell me just how much you despise my being his wife, the mother to his child. Go on, then, Isabella!'

The door opened. Gio stepped inside.

Isabella looked at him, and he looked at Isabella.

'Shall we tell her, Gio?' Isabella said.

CHAPTER THIRTY

Italy, Summer 2016

'I thought it was you,' he says.

I can't believe it. It's him; he's here, right in front of me. I see it – but I can't believe it.

'James?'

Part of me expects him to deny it. He doesn't, of course.

'How did you know where to find me?' I'm amazed I sound as steady as I do.

'You're a hard girl to track down, that's for sure,' he says. I'm searching his face for a clue – affection, anger, apology… but nothing prepares me for what I find.

'In the end, I went to your flat. Spoke to Belinda, was it? Not easy with the paps camped outside my house, but, you know, I had to do it…'

He is hopeful. There it is: hope. The last thing I expected.

'What are you doing here?'

He blinks, grey eyes and sandy lashes, the features I fought to conjure so many nights on my own. I thought I would never see them again. James, my James, love of my life, my heart's obsession.

'Don't you know?' he answers quietly. The city seems to

fade around us, people occupied with useless bustle while he remains at the centre of it, untouchable, just as he had been at Calloway & Cooper: the big bad boss.

A ripple of old excitement courses through me: the ghost of forbidden lust.

'Can we go somewhere?' he says, after it becomes clear I don't know how to reply to his question. 'I know this must be a shock, a really big shock, and it is to me too, if I'm honest. I always want to be honest with you, Lucy...'

He scoops up my hand and we start walking. I don't know where we're going, just conscious of the feel of his palm against mine as he rushes me through the streets of Florence. It occurs to me that we could never do this at home. Only here are we unrecognisable; we're not criminals, we're not hated, just a couple, lovers, hand in hand, in the most romantic city in the world. James always promised we would come here. And he always promised we would sit by the Arno, which is where we go now.

The river is shimmering black when we get there, its grassy banks fallen into shadow. The bridge is glowing with light. In the sky, the first stars pinprick their sheet of dark. The violinists by the Uffizi fill the air with a classical timelessness, making this, now, us, seem somehow heroic.

'I'd rather be out here, wouldn't you?' says James, pulling me close. 'I spend too much time inside these days.'

When we sit, he touches my cheek with the backs of his fingers. It is achingly intimate, and the same thing he did when we first kissed, in his office late at night, when the rest of the company had gone home. I remember thinking then, as now:

Am I dreaming?

No, I am not. And I am not dreaming when his lips find mine, however briefly, and I receive his familiar scent, the lost treasure of his touch.

'I've missed that,' he says, pulling away.

I put my fingers to my lips. I'm full of the things I need to say, every thought and emotion that has passed through me these past weeks, and they pull me down so hard that none of them surface. I've missed it, too. I know that much.

'I don't understand,' I manage at last. 'I thought you never wanted to see me again. After what happened... And everything you're dealing with at home.'

'Are you joking?' He looks intensely into my eyes. He's lost weight, his cheekbones pronounced and his square jaw peppered with stubble. 'Lucy, I stayed away from you because I had to. Christ knows I still do, but I don't care, I can't help it any longer. If anything, this whole saga with the press has made me more determined than ever to pursue what I want. And I want you. I always have.'

They're the words I have yearned to hear. I should rejoice, hold him and never let go, safe in the knowledge that nothing can tear us apart.

'I don't blame you for running away,' he goes on. 'I'd be lying if I said I hadn't wanted to, as well. It would have been so much easier. But I had obligations, Grace's estate to manage...' It's the first time he has mentioned his wife. I scan his face for emotion, rage or sadness or both, and find none. I remember Dad after Mum died, how he went into himself and never let on how upset he was. Maybe James is the same. He says his wife's name as if he's referring to a household pet.

'How are your children?' I ask.

James flinches. 'Bearing up,' he says shortly. Then he softens. 'This isn't about them, Lucy, OK?' He takes my hand, turns it palm up and traces my lines with his fingertip – what he always used to do in bed while we swopped secrets, stories, sex. 'This is about us. I came out here to see you and I'm so glad I found you. I took a risk. I wanted to take a risk from day one but the stakes were too high.'

'I thought you hated me.'

'How could you think that? After everything, don't you trust me?'

There is a moment's pause before I say, 'Of course.'

'Then it can hardly be a surprise to see me.' He runs a hand through his golden hair. 'I've been on the cusp of phoning you so many times, sending a text, an email, whatever. I didn't even care if my phone might get bugged or someone was listening in. Did you hear the latest, the *Courier* hacking my line?' I shake my head. 'Anyway, I'm a careful man these days, put it that way. Unless it's something, some*one*, I'm serious about. I've been through hell without you. The funeral was a shambles, Grace would have hated it. The seafood puffs they served at the wake were like chalk.'

I stop him. 'You told me you were estranged.'

He frowns. 'What?'

'You and Grace: you told me you were nothing to each other. All that time we were together. Then I find out she was devoted to you, right to the end…'

I see him thinking. 'We'd agreed to separate months ago,' he says.

'That's not what she thought. According to the papers—'

It's James's turn to cut me off. 'According to the papers, what?' he says snappishly. 'Don't tell me you actually listen to a word they say?'

'No, it's just…'

'Just what?' There is impatience in his voice, in the way his features tense then relax. 'Come on, Lucy,' he says, his hand on my leg, 'you're not going to do this to me now, are you? I just want to be with you, no interrogation, no pressure. I get enough of that at home. I thought you'd be pleased to see me.'

'I am pleased to see you. I'm thrilled. I really am.'

'Good.' He kisses me, harder this time. His lips feel cold. I think of how it was before, and this is just the same – same face, same teeth, same hair, same scent of pinecones and sharp citrus shower gel.

'Is it terrible in London?' I ask, when we part.

James exhales. 'I won't lie to you,' he says, 'it's bad. But they don't have your name, right? And it's going to stay that way. Your friend told me no one in your circle knows. I paid Natasha Fenwick a visit, I always suspected she had an inkling.'

My mouth is dry. 'And…?'

'Even if she had, it's been knocked out of her now. I told

her she'd be fired from C & C quicker than I put in a sushi order if she so much as breathes a word.' He nods. 'That's why I was relieved you came to Italy – get you right away from the mess. Imagine if some hack gets a sniff. It'll be proven, then, won't it?'

I swallow. 'Isn't it already?'

James guffaws. 'God, no,' he says. 'My lawyers are working round the clock to discredit these ridiculous claims.' He pauses to shoot me a wink. I think of his wife in the ground and it makes me feel sick. 'According to my camp, it's slander, plain and simple. Grace was a troubled woman, she had demons unrelated to me – and that's true, by the way, she was a fruit loop from time to time.' He seizes my hand and kisses it. 'Once a suitable interval has passed, we can be together, Lucy. No one will think to link you with any of this. I came here to tell you that.'

A suitable interval…

I nod slowly. This is a lot to process.

'And to check,' he goes on, 'even though I know I don't need to: you haven't spoken to anyone about us, have you? No one except Belinda?'

I pull my hand away. He waits.

'No,' I say. 'No, I haven't.'

He watches me a second, as if trying to ascertain if I am lying. Then his features break into a grin. 'Good girl,' he says, 'I knew it. I'm sorry I had to ask.'

'Don't be.'

'It's just we've got to protect ourselves. There's too much on the line.'

'Yes.' Though I hear his 'we' as 'I', and his 'ourselves' as 'myself'.

'But not here, my darling.' James leaps up. 'Come on, I've got a hotel bed waiting for me and there's only one thing missing.' He pulls me to my feet and hoops his arms round my waist. The bird inside me tries to sing, and fails.

'Actually, I…' I begin. 'I'm expected somewhere.'

'You are?' He's perplexed. What does he think I've been doing out here all this time – just hanging around on street corners, waiting for my knight to arrive?

'Yes, I have a job, up in the hills. I work for a private estate.'

He smiles indulgently. 'I'm proud of you, Lucy. Always a doer.'

'I'm on duty tonight,' I fib. I have to get my head around everything; I have to be alone. A little voice tells me I should rush at the chance to go with James. Isn't this what I've been dreaming about? Another warns me to slow down. Wait. Just wait.

'Room for one more at this extravagant pile?' He kisses me again.

I draw back. 'They're strict,' I answer, hoping I appear disappointed. His expectant gaze compels me to say, 'But I could see you tomorrow?'

'I'm in town for a few days,' he says, 'so I guess that gives us time. Try to extend your curfew for tomorrow, then, yes?' He delivers this with the same authority he used at Calloway & Cooper. How my knees would tremble when he demanded his minutes, or his coffee from the Starbucks on the corner, whose order for soya milk and cinnamon foam I could never quite remember because I fancied him so much.

'Definitely,' I say, with more conviction than I feel. Too much has happened today, that's all. I know I will wake in the morning with nothing but ecstasy in my heart and the need to get down to see him. He came for me. He came.

*

Sleep evades me that night. Back at the Barbarossa, my mind spins in the dark, my dialogue with Alison, James's smile when he saw me, his touch, his lips, the bristle on his chin that I love so much, and, through it all, fast-fire glimpses of Max, that shot of limoncello he bought me when we first met, the clink of his glass against mine…

Even as I think, my story is being printed. I picture it travelling home with Alison in her smart leather bag, then on a computer screen in her apartment, cursor blinking as she chews her thumb, thinking of a headline; the words sent to her editor, the tick of approval, the let's-make-the-morning rush and then there it is in black and white, hundreds of thousands, millions of copies churning through machines, crisp papers set to hit the tables of countless breakfasting Britons, the frantic gossip on buses, trains, on texts – 'Did you see they finally caught that girl?' – and the ensuing explosion on social media. I wonder what my hashtag will be. When I looked online that day by the river, I found #RIPGrace and #CallowayAffair leading the trends. Now it will be #LucyFound or #BlameLucy. I don't know. Alison led me to believe she'd be kind, but what if? What if she paints me as a twisted fiend, hell-bent on wrecking a marriage and causing a mother to take her own life? However I appear, the truth is unequivocal: it came from my mouth. I admitted it all.

Dad. I burn with shame. And my sisters, unable to grasp how their gentle, predictable big sister could be capable of such an act... the very carelessness I never permitted in them. At the time, telling Alison everything seemed the only available route. Now, I'm realising the repercussions. This is going to hit me hard. I'll spend the rest of my life explaining.

You haven't spoken to anyone about us, have you?

I roll over in the dark, as if I can turn my back on thoughts of James.

It doesn't help. There he is, in front of me, his optimistic smile and trusting eyes, and the subtle note of menace in his voice, which felt familiar because it was how he had always spoken to me. I hadn't noticed that before. Always this quiet suggestion of what my answer should be; the response that would please him was the one that I gave. Just like today. I lied. Why hadn't I felt able to tell him the truth?

I wish I could go back and unpick it. Tomorrow, I'll see him, and I'll set it all straight. But I know there won't be a tomorrow. James will wake up to a call from someone at home, his lawyer, or his best friend Grant who I never liked, and that will be it. I'll never have a chance to see him again. In and out of my life, just like that.

The thought arrives with a hot bright flash of relief, which is swiftly eclipsed by sadness. James said he wanted to be with me. Every word I'd hoped he'd ever utter had been spoken. *I want you. I always have.* In my stupidity I had thrown it away.

*

I must eventually drift off to sleep, because I am woken by a whisper.

Lucy...

It's still dark. A thin band of moonlight creeps through the curtains. I check the time: 3:12 a.m. I listen hard, my heart pumping, waiting to hear it again. I'm not afraid, just alert, and I know it is the same voice I heard in the ballroom on my first day. The room feels cold, and saturated with thick, cloying menace.

Seconds – minutes? – pass, and the quiet is absolute. I look down at my body lying beneath the crisp white sheet, and for an instant it doesn't look like mine; it could be the body of any woman, slender and still, the outline of a body in a morgue.

It begins with the slightest movement, so faint as to be missed with a blink.

The sheet twitches, a small sharp tug at the foot, as if being administered by someone out of sight, concealed at the end of the bed. I gasp, draw my legs up, and it is a quirk of the night, I'm sure, but it takes a moment for the contour of the body to catch up with the movement, as if we are divided by seconds, an original and an echo.

I go to scream but cannot make a sound. I'm paralysed,

pinned to the sheets, transfixed by the site of the movement and waiting for the next pull, that little jerk, mischievous almost, fascinated by and afraid of it in equal measure. In the dusk I search, terrified, for a hand or a head, some shape to this invisible company.

There is none. I wait and I wait, and it does not happen again.

I get out of bed, the floorboards coarse and cold beneath my feet. Gingerly, I take a few steps, my wide eyes drawn into the pitch, searching and frightened of that search. It's freezing. The skin on my arms is riddled with goosebumps; a chill trickles down the back of my neck, my legs, puddling round my feet. It shouldn't be this cold.

Am I dreaming? My nerves are spiked with the certainty that anything could happen; I'm in a zone where normal rules fly out of the window and all that's left is infinite, fearsome possibility. There is no safety net here. Whatever is with me cannot be escaped; I can run, I can leave this room, but it will still be with me. The air seems to pulse, pregnant with an urgent warning: a shout that drowns in silence.

Tap, tap, tap.

There is a knock at my bedroom door. My hand shakes as I reach to open it, white fingers trembling in the black like some shiver of life fifty fathoms beneath the sea. *Don't come again* is all I can think. *Please don't. Please don't.*

I open the door. Darkness surrounds me, and at my feet is an object.

It is Vivien Lockhart's diary.

CHAPTER THIRTY-ONE

Vivien, Italy, 1985

'Shall we tell her, Gio?' Isabella said.

Vivien looked between them, too stunned to speak. Isabella's voice sailed into silence, throbbing there like a living thing. The subsequent moment of absolute quiet lasted so long that Vivien wondered if she had imagined it.

One look at Isabella told her she had not. The sister wore a smirk – no, more subtle than that, something Gio would never see – and licked her lips as if polishing a weapon that had laid unused in a chest for years, slowly gathering dust.

'Tell me what?' Vivien whispered. She both desired and feared hearing Isabella's voice again. It was a higher register than she had imagined, softer, more lilting, more like a girl's half her age, as if through lack of use it had preserved its infancy, like a gleaming set of silver cutlery kept pristine in a drawer.

'Gio…?' Vivien turned to her husband but he didn't speak. From his expression, eyes lowered, that telltale dagger of shame, she knew that Isabella's voice wasn't a revelation to him. Vivien had been right. They had been talking.

'Bella,' he said at last, with a swift movement of his

head, 'could you leave us alone?' Isabella watched him in a horrible instant of conspiracy, before retreating.

Tell me what?

A thousand terrors occurred to Vivien at lightning speed, then dissolved just as quick. She kept her eyes on her husband.

Protect this moment, she thought. *Everything is about to change.*

*

He took her into the drawing room so that she could sit down. Funny how that was the precursor to every rash of bad news ever uttered. *Are you sitting down?*

'I guess you need an explanation,' Gio said.

For the first time, Vivien disliked her husband. She had railed against him before, countless times – but she had never actually despised him. Why wasn't he kneeling in front of her, taking her hands, pleading with her to understand whatever odious truth he was steadying himself to reveal? Why was he staring at the floor?

'How long has it been going on?' She wasn't sure what 'it' was; it sounded like a goddamn affair, though that was absurd. 'How long has she been talking?'

His gaze flickered. Was he going to lie? The eyes settled. No, he wasn't.

'A year after we came here,' he said. 'Give or take.'

Vivien swallowed. All that time... Five years... It was worse than an affair. If Gio had come home and told her he had met someone else, one of the diamond-drenched socialites who attended the Barbarossa soirees, the knife would have twisted less deep. All the time they had been here, sitting in silence at the supper table, Vivien's queries fumbling into the familiar abyss of quiet, Gio pretending while all the while Isabella's muteness had been for Vivien's benefit alone, was a blade-sharp betrayal. She could not process it.

'*Give or take*?' she echoed.

'I can explain,' he said. 'It's complicated.'

'It seems simple to me, Gio,' she said, utterly frozen. 'You've been lying to me for half a decade. You've been having secret conversations with your sister, making a fool of me, laughing at my expense—'

'No,' he objected, 'it was never like that.'

'No? Not even when you were whispering in corridors, hiding away upstairs? What's the big secret, Gio? What's this about? Tell me now or I walk, and I take your child with me. I mean it. I can't be with someone capable of this.'

Gio ran a hand through his wild black hair. How she loved his hands. How his hands had broken her heart, and every other part of her.

'We thought it was safer this way.' Quickly he clarified, 'Not Bella and me – it wasn't our decision. It was work. They told me not to. Not until we were sure.'

'I'm not following, Gio,' she said. 'You'll have to be clear.'

Outside, rain began drumming against the windows. The room collapsed in darkness. Gio looked tired. Not sleepless-nights tired, but bone tired, as if tiredness had been chasing him for years and he had only just surrendered and let it claim him.

'I came to Italy to continue my uncle's work,' he said. 'What Dinapoli was engaged in was… controversial, to say the least. I had to sign a confidentiality agreement, and, I'm sorry, *bellissima*, but that included you.'

'But not your sister.'

He paused. 'I'm getting to that part.'

'I suggest you hurry.'

The rain grew heavier. The lamps in the drawing room flickered before righting themselves. Gio's expression was strained as he chose his words.

'Bella was – is – key to our trials,' he said cautiously. 'We're learning so much through her, work my uncle was never able to complete. When they asked me to come back, I was torn. I didn't want to dig up the past and neither would Bella. But when I spoke to her about it, she wrote to me vowing that she had to face what happened, and so she was willing to give it a try. How could I ignore that? It was an opportunity for closure on my parents' tragedy, the chance to recover the sister I lost. I owed it to her. It was my fault she ended up like this. If I'd gone that day…' He shook his head. 'Viv, I was excited – to get to work on something important, after so long stitching up cuts in an ER. What Dinapoli did was revolutionary, he was—'

'Hang on,' said Vivien. Her mind strove to grasp it. She kept thinking of her husband consulting over the move with Isabella. Had he consulted his wife? No. From the start, he'd hidden the truth, brought her here under false pretences.

'What work?' she asked. She couldn't think of the number of times she had enquired after his employment, how he spent his days, her questions deflected like light bouncing off mirrors. It was secret, and that was the end of that.

A secret to everyone except Isabella…

A muscle twitched by Gio's green eye.

There's nowhere to hide now, darling.

'When we lived here as teenagers,' he confessed, 'Dinapoli sought to treat Isabella. To cure her, recover her voice. Each day he would spend hours with her, upstairs, in the attic where she sleeps now.'

'He didn't succeed,' said Vivien.

'His methods grew dark,' divulged Gio. 'His colleagues say he lost his way towards the end. He became obsessed. Isabella was a private torture – he was desperate to hear her speak before we left for America… but she didn't.'

'Didn't or wouldn't.'

'Couldn't. Not then.'

'But now she can. Just like that.'

'Not just like that, no.'

'That's what it looks like. Strange how I'd think that, isn't it, Gio? Yesterday she was quiet as a stone and today, the first day of the fucking year, she's talking? Only it wasn't like that for you. You knew. You knew and you didn't tell me.'

'I was sworn to secrecy. I'm sorry. I wanted to.' His eyes brimmed with feeling and she believed him, even though she tried not to. It was easier not to.

'What methods?' she demanded.

'Sorry?'

'Dinapoli. What methods was he using? What is this about?'

Gio ran a hand over his tired face; it pained him to talk about it. Pained him to discuss anything that hurt Isabella, precious Isabella...

'Shock treatment,' he said. 'Chemically induced seizures. Hysteria therapy.'

It brought to mind Victorian asylums; poor women strapped to beds and having the brains torn out of them. Vivien remembered that the Barbarossa had once been a hospital. She grappled between pity and fury.

'He was so kind to us as children,' said Gio. 'But his work took over – he became insane. Isabella told me what she'd been subjected to. She trusted our uncle and so did I. We were wrong. But before Dinapoli lost his mind, he set out the groundwork for her recovery – groundwork my team and I have toiled on. His theory was that the water Bella took on that day our parents drowned damaged her throat, so that it wasn't just a psychological but a physiological cure we were looking for. All the therapy in the world wasn't going to get us anywhere – we needed to examine Bella's lung tissue, her raised voice box, and work towards training her up, like a singer with a contamination. We were sceptical at first, but there's something in it, Viv. This could mean big things for patients like Bella. If it's a true thing we can fix, just think of the places my studies could take me, the treatments we can uncover...'

He trailed off at her expression.

'You lied to me,' she said.

'It's been a journey. Bella was the only patient who agreed to these tests – the same tests Dinapoli set up when he was alive – and it's through them that we've had this breakthrough. But until the success rate is proven, it carries too much risk.'

'I'm not asking you to shout it from the rooftops, Gio. I'm asking you to tell your *wife*. I don't know, maybe I think that kind of honesty's important in marriage.'

'It is. That's why it's been so hard for me.'

'For you?' She snorted. 'Enlighten me. I'd love to know what's been so difficult.'

'Seeing Bella in pain,' he said, without skipping a beat; Vivien wished she hadn't asked. 'These trials are invasive: cameras down the oesophagus, medicines and side effects – not to mention dragging up all those memories. If she hadn't stressed again and again how she wanted to do it, I'd never have let her. The lab wanted us both back, but they never thought Bella would agree. I didn't, either. But months on and look where we are... It *worked*. She's back. My sister.' Gio's face lit up, then dimmed again as he met Vivien's unsatisfied one. 'Do you think I didn't want to tell you?' he murmured. 'It took everything I had for me not to. It was impossible.'

'Not quite impossible.'

'Come on, Vivien, please. Can't you see the bigger picture? Bella's *talking*.'

'So now she can tell me to my face how much she despises me.'

He stood back, a quick, controlled movement to let her

know she had overstepped the mark. 'I know you can't abide my sister,' he said. 'I know you've never tried. But can't you find it in you to celebrate this news?'

'Who did she speak to first?' said Vivien.

'What?'

'At the trials – when she finally spoke, to whom did she direct it?'

He blinked. 'I was there,' he said. 'So were a couple of others.'

'How convenient.'

'Excuse me?'

'Of course it would be you. *You* cured her. She won't credit any of those other professionals who helped her – you do realise that, don't you? *You* saved her.'

'I'm not following.'

'Are you really this gullible, Gio?' Never mind over-stepping the mark – Vivien was about to dive over it and sprint to the finish. 'Isabella will do anything to drive a stake between us – she'll have loved every moment of this secrecy between the pair of you. I bet she encouraged you to keep it from me, and I bet she relished dropping her bombshell just now, causing us this fight, making me feel like the leftovers from your feast for two. That's all she's ever wanted and now she's got it. Who helped her get there? *You.* Isabella has taken advantage of you since day one – of your guilt at the accident, knowing it can secure her anything she likes, and the thing she covets most in the world is exclusive rights to her brother. Making out like a helpless maiden rescued by her hero: from this day on *you'll* be the one who gave her a second chance at life. How do you know she hasn't been able to speak all along? That this wasn't an elaborate ruse to pin you to her side for evermore? Can't you see? At every turn, she has twisted this situation to her advantage. All those years in America, holding you hostage, suffocating your relationships, keeping you prisoner to regret. Then here, playing the victim through your work. And now, well, now she's champion. Queen Isabella. I'll wager you think she's marvellous, am I right? The most extraordinary woman you've ever met?' Her hands shook. 'More extraordinary than *me*?'

Gio's mouth was parted.

'Well? Say something!' Vivien was about to burst into tears. Isabella had her in a corner. This kind of meltdown was exactly what the sister would have anticipated and here was Vivien, handing it to her on a plate. She hated herself and she hated Isabella, and she wasn't sure in that instant who she hated more.

'After everything I gave up for you,' she stormed on. 'I gave up my career, my fame—'

'You loathed all that.'

'Excuse me?'

'You loathed Hollywood. Don't pretend that you didn't. You wrecked your life there, some might say deliberately. You've always been on self-destruct, Vivien.'

'Maybe I did loathe it. But do you know what? I loathe this more.'

'I think you need time to calm down.'

He didn't sound like himself – harder, colder, as if she

were calling to him across windswept mountains, an unfea-
sible distance between them now that she had spoken her
heart. He would never understand where she was coming
from. He was on Isabella's side. He always had been. Vivien
felt her baby kick inside her and she had to stop herself
from shaking her husband until he hurt and screaming in
his face that *they* were his future, she and his unborn child,
not Isabella, never Isabella.

'Perhaps I need time full stop,' she said, and left him
standing alone.

*

Winter turned to spring, and Vivien's bump bloomed as
fast and fruitful as the cherry blossom that grew on the
trees in the Oval, ready to drop and carpet the grass. The
atmosphere at the castillo sagged and sighed in sympathy,
with Vivien doing all she could to avoid the dreaded sister,
and only just coming to terms with her forgiveness of Gio.
As the weeks passed, she saw she had no choice. Where
would she go, and how? What would she say to her child
in a year, five years, ten, about why she had left his or her
father? *He helped your mute aunt to speak again.* Hardly
the crime of the century – and while Vivien knew the layers
of his deceit ran deeper and more complex than that, those
bare bones remained, gleaming amid the rubble.

She was uncomfortable in the late stages of her pregnancy,
struggling to sleep and ungainly as she pushed herself out of
chairs and puffed up the stairs, stopping to catch her breath.

Meanwhile, Isabella glided through the Barbarossa like a weightless water nymph, showcasing her svelte contours with the lightest of gossamer dresses, a wisp of dandelion dancing on the wind. In contrast, Vivien felt like a whale.

She had been convinced that Isabella would goad her at every turn with her newfound voice, unable to resist delivering that long-preserved venom whenever she could. Surprisingly, she didn't, and Vivien was disconcerted. Where Vivien chattered with neither focus nor direction to Gio or Adalina, Isabella remained in dignified silence, able to restrain her throat after so long unused, and so, when she did speak, she still had the power to command her listeners into a sort of hypnosis.

Vivien couldn't stand it. The quieter and statelier Isabella appeared, the more Vivien gabbled and spouted, angry at herself but unable to stop.

'I thought you had expected this,' said Adalina one day, as she weeded the front porch. Vivien stood next to her, wishing she could smoke a cigarette.

'Yes,' she said tightly, convinced that she herself spoke like a crone.

Of course she had expected it. She had long been certain of Isabella's game, and it was a slow and patient one indeed. In finding her voice, Isabella might have relinquished her mystery. Not so. She continued to leave with Gio twice a week for the lab. She would ensure that she gave them just enough to needle their interest; to make them believe in their progress but not yet be satisfied by it. It was fake, all of it.

She tried to soothe her nerves. With every door handle

that turned or step that echoed, she was convinced that
Isabella was at her back. She lived in mesmerised fear of
hearing the sister's voice, which words would cast her blow.
Never before had she been so afraid of language. *Sticks
and stones...* But words *could* hurt her, and hurt her horribly. Words were free, they didn't need a licence and they
attacked with deadly discretion, able to pounce at any time
and slay her with their force.

Shall we tell her, Gio?

Vivien would never forget the sister's arch satisfaction.
How she had savoured every note, every syllable; the sheer
pleasure she had taken in dispensing this shock. *Shall we
let her in on our secret? Can she be a member of our club,
can she* really?

She had to stay calm for the sake of her baby. Her doctor
had warned her against high blood pressure, and Vivien's
was creeping up by the day. She longed for Gio's touch, his
affection and his kiss. But he kept those things from her.

What did she expect? He was civil to her – occasionally
even warm, and would put an arm round her shoulders
or touch her stomach and in an instant she felt secure and
loved. But, most of the time, he shut her out. After all, he
had tried to let her in and she had refused; she couldn't
pretend to like Isabella, not even for him. So he left in the
week earlier than ever, and returned as late as he could. In
his eyes, she saw a wounded animal. She had hurt him, not
just through her hatred of his sister but through her rejection
of everything he had laboured for since their move to Italy.
Her rejection of his past, his family, and the trauma they

had suffered. Vivien saw all this, understood that this was what he was feeling, but she couldn't change her stance.

If she could apologise, there might be a way back. But the word sat on her tongue as squat and immovable as Isabella's vocabulary for the last two decades.

Adalina stopped what she was doing. She did so abruptly and with purpose, so that Vivien was pulled from her thoughts and compelled to meet the maid's eye. What Adalina said next required a great force of will: Vivien could see it rising in her.

'I expected it, too,' said the maid.

Vivien heard her own heart beating. She waited.

'I expected Isabella to speak.'

Conviction held her in thrall. Vivien didn't dare interrupt, for fear she would halt Lili in her tracks. She sensed the maid had more to say – and, boy, was she right.

'I can no longer ignore my conscience ,' said Adalina in a fierce whisper. 'The day you fell down the stairs… When Signora Isabella came to alert us, Salve and me, it wasn't right. Her appearance. The way she told us. She looked energised, happy, more alive than I'd seen her. It wasn't normal. She was excited, there was light in her eyes: she could scarcely write her note, her hands were shaking with adrenalin.'

Vivien's mouth was dry. 'You believe me,' she said thickly, 'don't you?'

Adalina nodded. It felt criminal, this exchange – scandalous and wrong and deliciously gratifying. Vivien hadn't imagined it. Isabella was a killer.

'I pretended I hadn't noticed,' said Adalina. 'I told myself I was wrong… but I knew that I wasn't. Isabella wasn't a woman in despair, she wasn't frightened, she wasn't any of the things she should have been. She was *pleased*. Triumphant. Delighted. Oh, signora – I believe she wishes to destroy you!'

Vivien reached to touch the wall behind her: she had to hold on to something.

'Lili – you must tell Gio—'

'No!' Adalina had never spoken with such force. 'I will not.'

'But don't you see? This is the only way! Gio trusts you—'

'I would do so much for you, signora, but I will not do that.'

'Why?'

'As you said before, we have no evidence – only our word. If Signor does not believe you, he will certainly not believe me. He will think you convinced me.'

Vivien could see it now, the accusations flying. Though she hated to admit it, Lili was right. Gio would charge her with poisoning the maid against Isabella. He would tell her she had lost her mind once and for all. Who knew – perhaps his precious associates at the lab would take an interest in *her*, then, for a change?

But this proved it. This proved that the sister was a malevolent force. It wasn't just Vivien – she wasn't crazy, she wasn't all the things Gio said she was. Lili saw it too.

'Lili,' she said, gripping the maid, 'we have to do something. We have to act.'

'Signora, please, you must keep calm.' But Vivien couldn't. She felt the fever escalating, thoughts and plans chasing each other towards infinite horizon. Something in her shifted, a leap off a cliff. At first she thought it was relief, but then—

'Signora? Signora, look at me. You're not well. You've gone pale.'

Vivien realised she was dizzy. She sank to the step.

'I, uh…'

'Signora?' Adalina dropped to Vivien's side.

Vivien clutched her stomach. A tide of pain rose and fell, her insides clenched by some awesome fist. The baby was coming. Black spots dazzled her eyes.

Don't panic.

'It's time,' she groaned. 'Get Signor Moretti. Quick!'

CHAPTER THIRTY-TWO

Italy, Summer 2016

Vivien remembers it as if it were yesterday: the tightening sensation in her abdomen, the pressure and the promise. Her baby on its way, all those months of waiting and finally here they are, about to meet. The fear and excitement, and, at the heart of it, the certainty that everything will be OK. Her body can do this. It was made to do it.

She hears the girl finish up for the day, the final wheeze of the vacuum cleaner followed by a series of closed cupboards. The girl is so young, so optimistic, with the most interesting part of her life still ahead of her. How must that feel? One day, she might experience the joy that comes from having a child: from keeping, nurturing and loving a child, with no one to wreck it or blow it away. A girl like her has never known what it is to lose – not to misplace or squander, but to lose, absolutely and irretrievably, to have something snatched away like a ghost in the night, what should have been hers forever. The thing Vivien has lost is solid still in her arms, an invisible weight she recalls as precisely as if she were carrying a basket, right in this moment, and looking down at the bundle within. His cheeks, so red, and his little pink nose...

Time heals all wounds, except this one. She thinks of him every day, every minute. Over the years the pain has dulled, but perhaps it is worse for that. She used to be able to feel it; it used to *hurt*. Now it nags and sighs, a ceaseless ache. Like her child, her pain is preserved, a fossil in a jar: an insect suspended in amber.

Downstairs, a door opens and shuts. Vivien goes to the window. Light is seeping out of the day and the sky is a brushstroke of orange, white crests chasing each other on a blue sea. She hears the girl's footsteps, watches her walk past the fountain and keep on walking, until she vanishes down the drive out of sight. Oh, to walk out of here, to be able to leave. The fountain looks back, that horrid unseeing eye, its lens stagnant and its belly full. *Bulldoze it*, Adalina has told her. *Get rid of it. Why do you want it staring you in the face every day?* She cannot. It's all she has left.

It's why she cannot let it run dry. Each week, the containers are filled and the water poured into the stone. Adalina used to question it, but she doesn't any more.

A knock at her bedroom: 'Signora, your pills?'

Vivien blinks: the maid's voice is a whisper on the wind. She turns.

Adalina sweeps in and sets out the stall, just as she has for years. Admittedly, there are more these days, bottle after bottle after bottle. Vivien watches her shake the tablets out and count them on her palm, before setting them straight on the wooden side table, a perfect concoction. On cue,

Vivien starts to cough. *Damn!* The cough is bad, hacking and dry, like ants swarming in an unreachable part of her throat. Always when Adalina is here, prompting the maid to fuss and fret. 'I'm fine,' Vivien croaks, which only makes it worse, and she has to turn her back to cough into a ball of tissue, and when she pulls it away from her mouth she sees those tiny specks of blood. Quickly, she stuffs the tissue into the pocket of her robe. 'I'm fine.'

'Do you need anything else, signora?'

Adalina's expectant face, always so ready to please, reminds her of the nurses that day at the hospital. They had been kind to her, ushering her into a private room and she had gripped the midwives' hands as she gave birth to her baby; it was possible to excavate their soothing assurances from the deep pool of memory, as comforting to her now as a mother's hand across a fevered brow. She hadn't wanted Gio with her – a man's place was outside. She doesn't know if he ever forgave her for that. He thought her reasons were personal: their fight had banished him in the cold. Had he been right? It had been a buried punishment, muffled beneath a preference that need never be justified. *You denied me the birth of my son.* Or so he said.

'No, thank you,' says Vivien.

Then, sensing Adalina slipping away from her, she asks: 'Where is the girl going?'

Adalina's voice reaches her from afar. 'Lucy? Into town, I expect.'

Vivien sits on the bed. 'She knows.'

There is a pause. Adalina has heard this before, many times.

'She cannot possibly.'

'Can't she?' Vivien looks at her. The maid flickers for a moment in her vision, like a cracked reel of film, as if she's not really there. 'I sense her fascination.'

'You cannot blame her. She is young. Impressionable.'

'She is finding out about me. About… us.'

Adalina is confused. 'How can she be? Signora, we're careful…'

'Are we? What if she suspects us?'

There is no reply. Vivien swallows, closes her eyes. All she hears is silence. She concentrates. 'I want you to investigate her,' she says.

'I'm sorry?' says Adalina.

'I want to know everything: where she came from, why, what she left behind. I want the whole story, from start to finish. I can't be powerless.'

Adalina considers her next move.

'This isn't about…' she falters, 'her resemblance to…?'

Vivien waits. 'Go on,' she challenges, 'say her name.'

Adalina can't. 'Signora, I think it's best if we—'

'*I* think it's best if we find out all there is. I don't trust her.'

You don't trust anyone. That was what the maid wanted to say; Vivien could hear it in the air as surely as if it had been on her lips. Can Adalina blame her? A moment passes where it looks as if she might go in for another disagreement. Then:

'Very well, signora.'

'Report back to me in the morning. I hope I'm proved wrong, but, Adalina, we should prepare ourselves to lose another one.'

Adalina wears a resigned expression. She has anticipated this. Next month they will hire another, the same the month after that. An endless merry-go-round of hopeful young things who are doomed from the start. But Lucy is worse; she looks like Isabella. Next, Vivien will ask for a photograph to accompany the application.

If her illness spares her that long...

'May I leave you now, signora?'

Vivien turns back to the wall.

'Yes,' she says tightly. 'You have work to do.'

Alone, she rests a hand on her stomach, empty and longing.

I'll protect you this time, she thinks. *No one is taking you, ever again.*

CHAPTER THIRTY-THREE

I'm due to meet Max at midday. He's waiting on a terrace by the Duomo, drinking espresso and smoking a cigarette. I didn't know he smoked.

'Hey,' he says when he sees me. 'What's up?'

His manner is aloof but I expected no less. He's messaged me a few times since Alison but I've stalled on every reply, unsure how to play it. Either I lie about the whole thing, deny James's existence because it's easier, or I open the whole basket of snakes and let Max into the most disgraceful event of my life. Only twenty-four hours have passed since Alison's visit but it feels like an eternity.

'Thanks for meeting,' I say, pulling out a chair. A waiter comes to take my order. I ask for a Coke, though I don't really like it: I can't think of anything else.

'You look tired,' he says.

'I was up most of last night.'

He waits. He doesn't need to express his interest, his need to know: it's there all over his face. It's a kind face, open and intelligent. Not the shadows I am used to.

'I've got Vivien's diary,' I say. It isn't what he wants to hear and his features drop with disappointment. But this is our business; this is what brought us together in the first place, Max's desire to solve the Barbarossa mystery and my agreeing to help. Nothing about my personal life has the slightest bearing on that.

'Really.'

'It was weird. Someone put it outside my door in the middle of the night.' In saying it, another thing occurs to me. 'I keep waking at the same time each morning: twelve minutes past three. I see it on the clock. That's when the diary showed up.'

Max can't conceal his interest, though he's trying.

'Who put it there?'

'It has to be Adalina. It's hardly going to be Vivien herself – and Salvatore would never get access. Besides, I haven't seen him since the portrait fire.'

I pause.

'There is another person who could have given me the diary,' I venture.

Max lifts an eyebrow.

'This is going to sound mad,' I say, 'but it's true. It's the latest in a series of strange things that have happened to me at the Barbarossa. I thought I'd heard it before... seen things, you know, but it wasn't until last night that I knew for sure.'

Max doesn't follow. 'Knew what?'

'It's haunted.'

He sits back. I'm aware this could discredit me entirely, but I know what happened in that bed. I was there. Someone – some*thing* – else was, too.

'You're talking about a ghost?'

Max's voice carries the quirk of humour; he isn't taking me seriously. Nonetheless I tell him about the sheet being pulled. He asks if I was drowsy, imagining things, all the doubts I anticipate. I wasn't, I didn't; I'm sure of what I felt.

'Lucy, this is...'

'Mad, I told you. But I swear it. Isabella's dead, right? This "tragedy" they talk about. But she's still there – she's still at the Barbarossa. She's been trying to get through to me, and now I know why. Don't look at me like that, Max. I'm not crazy.'

'No, but you do have a lot on your mind.'

'What would you know about what's on my mind?'

'Not much,' he says, 'since you won't tell me.'

Well, I walked into that one. 'That's completely irrelevant,' I say.

'Is it? Lucy, you're right, I haven't a clue what's going on with you, but the way you've been acting lately, that woman showing up, all this secrecy... I mean, I thought we were friends? All I'm saying is that it would be understandable if you were letting it get on top of you. All this stuff bottled up, whatever it is.'

'I'm not bottling anything up.'

'No?'

'No. And that has nothing to do with this.' I'm angry. 'You asked for my help, Max – you asked me to join you because you needed to know. Here I am about to share a goldmine and instead you're fixated on my private life?'

'I'm pointing out that all this rubbish about spooks and hauntings… well, it might be because you don't want to think about your own problems.'

I'm stunned. 'How dare you,' I say.

'I want to be a friend to you, that's all.'

I swallow hard. At least he's made my decision easy.

I fish in my bag and bring out the diary. 'I haven't read it,' I say, sliding it across the table to him. 'And I'm not going to.'

He frowns, not understanding. But I know this is the right thing. It's the only thing. I told Max at the start that this wasn't for me – I had enough on my plate. And now I know for sure that I'm in too deep. I'm scared. Whatever I felt, whatever this is, it's telling me to go: it doesn't want me at the Barbarossa.

Max's expression shifts. 'You're leaving,' he says flatly.

I nod.

'When?'

'My train leaves first thing in the morning.'

His features close, letting me know I'm shut out. He finishes his espresso and takes his time repositioning the cup on its saucer. There's an uncomfortable pause.

'We're so close,' he says at last. 'The truth's in that diary – you know that, right?'

I nod. The truth is what I'm afraid of. I look at the diary, just as I had until dawn, my fingers itching to lift its cover but my racing heart telling me not to.

'I'm not sure I want to know the truth,' I say. 'I'm done with truths.'

Max watches me for a moment, as if working out if he

can change my mind. He must decide that he can't, because then he says:

'Is it something to do with him?'

I'm confused. 'Who?'

'The guy over there.' Max nods over my shoulder. 'He's been watching us this whole time. Someone you know?'

*

I walk briskly, but I sense he's behind me. I pretended I didn't know him on the terrace. I wasn't prepared to give Max the satisfaction of seeing me run into his arms.

'Lucy—'

He has called my name a few times; this last is firmer, aggressive, like it was the last time we spoke before I left Calloway & Cooper. He grabs my arm; I act startled, stop, turn, and arrange my features into pleased surprise.

'Didn't you hear me? I've been following you for ages.'

'James, hi. Sorry… I'm in a hurry.'

'Where to?' There is a grey cloud in his eyes, warning of a storm. I used to adore how his eyes gave him away, so passionate and fervent.

'Back to work,' I lie. He knows it.

'Who was that?'

'Who?'

'That man you were talking to. Don't tell me you've moved on already?'

I'm shocked by his tone. It's a side I've never seen before, sniping, mean, derogatory. I half expect him to call me a tramp or a slut, all those names the internet threw at me. My heart drops. The papers. It's today. James will know. His lawyers will have called him first thing.

'Of course not,' I say quietly. 'He's a colleague.'

James snorts. 'At the *private estate*?'

'Yes.' It's only half an invention. It occurs to me that I shouldn't have to lie about Max at all – I've nothing to hide. But the way James is confronting me makes me want to hide things. It makes me want to hide, full stop. I swear he never used to be like this. All he ever did was tell me how much he cared for me, walked hand in hand with me on deserted night streets, made love to me in that flat he used in Vauxhall. I don't recognise this version. Out of context, away from his powerhouse in London, he seems more ordinary. He's wearing the same clothes as yesterday.

'Were you with him last night?'

This isn't a conversation I want to have in the middle of a piazza.

'James, do we have to—'

'Yes, I'd say we have to.'

I'm about to deny it when a thought surfaces. Why would he be so hung up on Max if he'd already heard about my story hitting the stands? Surely, then, he'd have greater matters on his mind. Is it possible James hasn't been informed? It's lunchtime here, tourists trickling into cobbled trattoria for pizza and sorbet; at home, the whirlwind will only just have hit. I picture his advisors in crisis meetings. *How do we break this to him? What's the least debilitating transmission we can come up with?*

Hesitantly, I say, 'There's nothing going on. I spent last night alone.'

Abruptly, his features lighten. There he is, the James I know.

'I'm sorry,' he says. 'You understand, don't you? It's such a difficult time. You're the only thing that's making me see clearly.'

'I understand.'

'I don't know what I'd do if I lost you.'

'You won't.' My mouth is dry.

'Good.' He smiles and takes my hand. 'You'd never let me down, would you, Lucy? You're on my side, our secret is our secret?'

I nod. The deeper in, the quicker the sand; it's too late to get out now.

*

He insists we eat. I have no appetite and the linguine he orders for me sticks like cement to the roof of my mouth. He talks as if we've never been apart – about how beautiful the city is (how I must remind him to take me to Venice, to Rome, to Verona) and how it's so special to be here with me. It's more special than when he was with Grace. I wish he wouldn't talk about her, and I don't know if that makes me a coward or him a cretin. Once again, I think of his children. Where are they?

Every time his phone beeps, which is often, I feel the ground slip out from under me. 'Football scores,' he says, or, 'Bloody bank.' The ground reappears.

When my own goes with a missive from Alison, telling me that the story has been delayed to tomorrow's press, I relax a little. My execution postponed a day longer. I know I should come right out and say what I've done, that I did it in good faith and what was I supposed to think, I hadn't heard from him in months. I know I should be able to do this, to be truthful, if our love is what I believe it to be, if it's what he promises it is. But I can't. Every part of me tells me not to.

'So how long are you staying?' James asks, spearing a spiral of *fusilli*.

I open my mouth to tell him, but then I stop. I don't want him to know. Come the morning, come Alison's reveal, I want to be as far away as possible, somewhere he can't find me. *Tell him now or you'll blow it. You could have a future with James, all you ever wanted – Lucy Calloway, by his side forever. Tell him now or it's over.*

'A while, I expect,' I mumble. 'How about you?'

'Tomorrow,' he says, throwing back red wine. 'I don't want to, darling, but my team are clamouring for my return. Seeing you has been like a shot in the arm.'

A lethal injection, more like. The guillotine hovers. *Tomorrow.*

CHAPTER THIRTY-FOUR

Vivien, Italy, 1985

They named the boy Alfonso, Alfie for short. Vivien considered him the most perfect person she had ever laid eyes on. She fell in love instantly with his skin and his smell, his wide blue eyes that were older and wiser than their days, and the softness of his gently downed head as it rested against her shoulder. Her son. Her wonder.

For a while, Alfie's arrival smoothed the path towards Gio. Both were too enamoured with their baby to remember their fight, the birth a punctuation mark more decisive than any they could have contrived. It put all else in perspective. They had made this child together: with his lovely dark hair and glacial eyes, he was a flawless mixture of them both. Vivien had always thought that most babies looked a bit shrivelled, like sultanas wrapped in muslin, yet it was an unspoken duty to coo over how sweet and immaculate they were. In Alfie's case, every word was true.

'Look at him,' she would whisper, just to herself, as she stood rocking him in the deep of night, tired beyond reason but with reserves of energy she never knew she possessed. That was love, she decided: the unquestioning instinct to put another before oneself. She had never done it before – if she were truthful, not even with Gio.

Here was someone who needed her, really needed her, and the focus she gave to caring for Alfie eclipsed all she had done before. It all seemed meaningless now.

She kissed Alfie's head and sang him a lullaby:

'*Do you know where the pear tree grows?*
Up on the hill, by the old corn mill…'

She couldn't remember where she had heard the rhyme, the tune trickling back to her after years. A nanny, perhaps, one of the crinkly-faced black women whom Gilbert employed; he would never say hello to them in the market, but he would let them clean the dirt off his boots. *Love thy neighbour.* Another lesson unheeded.

Gazing down at her newborn son's face, Vivien was filled with indignation. How her parents had palmed her off on the help, her mother hiding behind closed doors, afraid to meet her husband's eye, too timid to reach out and touch her only daughter. For so long, she had considered Millicent Lockhart a victim. Now, fired by an unconditional commitment to her own offspring, Vivien wondered if Millicent hadn't been as much to blame as her father. How had she got to duck out? How was it OK for her to keep quiet, put up with the beatings and the threats, and, in not saying anything, to say: *This is fine. Keep doing it. I've no complaints.* Millicent had been the adult and Vivien the defenceless child. She held Alfie now to her chest, listened to his gentle breath. Her protection of him was a force field. Millicent had lacked that spirit.

Alfie's eyes were closed, his tiny chest rising and falling. 'Is he asleep?'

Gio appeared at the door, his handsome face exhausted but happy. They talked about their son like a couple in the first throes of love, in hushed, reverential tones, tender with each other as they were with the baby. *Are we still in love?* Vivien wondered. She adored Gio as much as she ever had, but she feared that the words they had spoken and the anger they'd exchanged was a path with no return. Too many times, she had shown her jealous, rageful self. She wanted to appear wonderful to him, as wonderful as Isabella, but she could never compete with the walking miracle that was his sister. Even after childbirth, after bearing him a son and all the astonishment that contained, she still could not occupy the place that his sister did. Gio could pretend, he could spend the rest of his life pretending, but Vivien knew it was an act. He had lied since they came to Italy. He had put Isabella first.

'Yes,' she answered, holding Alfie out so his father could take him. Seeing Gio cradle their son was magical. She drank in moments like this, thinking, *These are the pictures I'll remember.* Quite when she would remember them, she never got round to settling. When she was old, grey, lost? When she was dying?

'Isn't he perfect?' she murmured. Gio nodded. She wished he would say something like, *As perfect as you*, which he might have once upon a time, and even in that instant of contentment she felt the familiar stab of envy. Alfie looked nothing like Isabella, except, perhaps, for a trace around the chin. Was Gio looking for his sister? Had he hoped to find more of her, of his parents, in his son?

'Have you seen Bella this morning?'

His question was so aptly timed that it made her flinch. 'No,' she said.

Gio frowned. 'She hasn't been out of her room in a couple of days. Adalina hasn't seen her for meals. I think Alfie's arrival has unnerved her.'

Vivien gritted her teeth. She was amazed at her husband's perseverance. He was all too conscious of the hostilities, how Vivien couldn't bear the sound of the sister's name and how the very existence of Isabella had nearly broken them so many times – but still he persisted. Perhaps he sensed that if he ceased to mention or care for Isabella then Vivien would consider it as good as a death. So he revived his sister every day, breathed life into her name, massaged her heart until he could hear it thumping; he reminded Vivien that she was still a real part of their lives, and one he was not, under any circumstances, even his wife's misery, willing to relinquish.

It took a monumental effort to say, 'I'm sure she's fine. It's an adjustment for all of us.'

He put an arm round her, the other holding their son close. 'Hmm,' he said, 'perhaps you're right.' *We're stronger now*, thought Vivien. *You can't get us.*

'It's just I worry,' he went on. 'Now we have our family, I'm concerned she feels… out in the cold. We have to make sure she's included.'

How could we not? Vivien considered sourly. It was on the tip of her tongue, as it was every minute of every day, to blurt Adalina's solidarity – that the maid knew of Isabella's sinfulness, that the precious baby in their arms wouldn't even be here if Isabella had had her way. But she knew it would be the final insult to tear them apart.

'Would you check on her, *bellissima*?' Gio asked. 'It's just I'm already running late at the lab…' In his eyes, she saw uncertainty and hope. The hope never waned in Gio that his wife and his sister would find reconciliation.

'Of course,' she said, taking back her baby.

*

Later that day, when the Barbarossa was quiet, Vivien left Alfie napping with Adalina while she ventured upstairs to the attic. It was months since she had come this way, the ascent too much on her heavy stomach and aching knees, and she had never set foot inside Isabella's room. It was always locked. The only reason she had for coming was to admire the view from the uppermost windows, all across the surrounding Tuscan hillsides, gold in summer and mauve in winter, and the endless skies above.

Gio hadn't specifically told her that she could use the skeleton key, but he might as well have done. How else was she going to get access to his sister's quarters? Even though Isabella's voice had been unleashed, she still barely treated Vivien to it, and if Vivien were to knock on the door and enquire after Isabella's welfare, there was a good chance she would be ignored. So, this was the only way. If Gio wanted to know how his sister was, Vivien would tell him.

'Are you sure about this, signora?' Adalina asked. On pain of death would the maid part with the skeleton key. Vivien could see her desire to consult with the master of the house, but the women's friendship overrode it, as so often women's friendships did. Besides, since their confidence, Gio was a third party, excluded by his ignorance.

'Trust me, Lili,' said Vivien. 'I'm sure.'

Now, she inserted the key in the lock and gently turned. It rotated smooth as butter, and as Vivien pushed the door she prepared herself for what she might find: Isabella in bed, the sheets pulled up over her dark, dark hair, in the slump of a mighty depression; or upright by the window, immaculately dressed; or sitting at her desk, engrossed in study. Any one of these was plausible. Vivien didn't know her at all.

But what she discovered was none of these. Isabella was nowhere. Gone.

Vivien stepped inside. It was draughty, the window open a crack. She went to close it, and, once she had, the silence and stillness surrounding her was total.

The walls held an eerie sensation, as if Isabella were about to emerge from thin air, or her voice whisper at Vivien's shoulder, the mesmerising tone that had captured her husband's fascination and his colleagues'. She felt she was being observed, and when she turned to the room there appeared a flash of black on the bed, like a wave of jet silk rippling across the covers then vanishing.

Vivien gasped, before catching her breath and telling herself not to be so easily rattled. She'd had three hours' broken sleep last night, par for the course these days, and couldn't trust what she was seeing. *Get a grip. This is your chance.*

Chance at what? To find something on Isabella, something conclusive that would settle their score once and for all; that would prove to Vivien as much as anyone else that she wasn't imagining Isabella's vitriol, and that their rivalry ran as hot and fast and sure as the blood in her veins.

She began by going through Isabella's clothes. There weren't many of them here, just a few black dresses, and the same went for the furniture in the room. It was sparse, just a bed, a wardrobe, a chest of drawers and a side table with a lamp on it. Isabella left no clues: she was the eternal enigma. Vivien checked the pockets of her gowns, rifled through a purse on the mantelpiece, and found nothing but a handful of lira and some postage stamps. Who was she writing to?

Oh, to uncover a diary like the one she kept herself! It struck her that she was just as infatuated with Isabella as her husband was, the sheer mystery of her, the refusal to reveal anything, and opening a journal would be like delving into an instruction manual, sating her like a long cool drink. Just as Vivien was giving up, as a last attempt she lifted the sister's pillow and what she saw surprised her. It was a pair of ticket stubs to Francesco Rosi's *Carmen*. Vivien drew them out. They were dated a couple of years ago, the seats together, the stubs torn imperfectly at their perforations as if done in a hurry. She remembered her own longing to see the film at the time, hinting to Gio to take her, but he was always too busy with work. Who had Isabella gone with? Vivien swallowed her dismay. She turned the tickets over.

On their reverse, the same mantra was repeated:

I want him I want him I want him I want him I want him I want him

Her hands trembled. The attic swelled and shook. In a far reach of the castillo, she heard her son's cry ring out and quickly she pocketed the stubs and left the room, her heart and throat burning all the way to take him in her arms.

*

'We have to get rid of her.'

Vivien took a drag on her cigarette and blew a plume of smoke out of the window and into the night, where it curled on the purple for a moment before dispersing. She could hear her ragged breath, ragged still after hours away from that place. *The attic*. It chilled her to the core. The starkness of Isabella's confession, proof if ever there were any that she coveted Vivien's husband. That she was *obsessed*.

'Signora, I would urge you to speak to Signor Moretti.'

'What's he going to do?' Vivien whirled on Adalina. 'You know it's as good as useless. He won't accept it. She's a *danger* to us, do you understand?'

'Perhaps the note was not about him.'

Vivien laughed, a high, harsh sound. 'Of course it was. Who else was it about? She wants my husband, Lili, her own *brother*. She's wrong in the head. She's sick.'

'We must talk to her.'

'No. She'll deny it, deny everything... We have to be more cunning than that. We have to get her away from this place, away from us, once and for all.'

She could see Adalina panicking. Vivien bet Lili wished she'd never said anything, never told Vivien what she suspected – because there was no reclaiming that. It was a mark in the sand that the tide could never wash. Every day, Vivien saw the maid fight her loyalty to Gio, torn between her ingrained urge to serve the master and the nagging reminder of her better judgement.

'What are you going to do?' Adalina whispered, afraid of her response.

'I don't know yet,' said Vivien, grinding her smoke out on the sill, where it left a chalky mark. Her eyes fixed on the flourishing night, the stone fountain with its still water, a liquid, unseeing pupil, at the centre of which that grotesque fish blurted its guts from dawn until dusk. 'But believe me, I'll think of something.'

CHAPTER THIRTY-FIVE

Italy, Summer 2016

Morning comes. I've hardly slept, fitful imaginings keeping me up past two, three, all hours of the night. I think I hear that cry again, long and lean, a child's cry or a baby's cry, but I no longer know what is real and what is not. When my alarm sounds at seven, I go to the bathroom and am sick. Blood throbs in my temples and behind my eyeballs. My stomach contracts, empty.

It's happened. I know it without needing to be told.

I shower, dress and pack my bags. Downstairs, Adalina offers me breakfast but I say no. I am being cowardly, taking the easy way out, but I don't care. I've walked the hard way for too long, and I have enough confrontations ahead of me.

'I need to go out this morning,' I say, hoping she won't notice the dark rings round my eyes or the rasp in my voice. My bags are ready to be swept down just as soon as they leave for Vivien's doctor's appointment. 'Would that be OK?'

Adalina eyes me suspiciously. 'As long as you're back by midday.'

'I will be.'

'You're not planning on meeting Max Conti, are you?'

The question floors me, as does the sound of his name. What does she know about Max? Momentarily I consider denying all knowledge of him, then realise how false that will sound. I haven't the energy to deceive. 'No,' I say. 'Why?'

'He isn't a good influence.'

'I've only met him a few times.' I remember our last encounter with an ache of regret, and I pinch out my feelings. I'll never see him again. 'We're barely friends.'

I turn to leave when Adalina's cough stops me. It sounds dreadful.

'Are you all right?' The maid is red in the face and I rush to collect a glass of water, which she accepts, her hands shaking. Gradually, the hacking subsides and she draws the back of her wrist across her mouth, reassembling her dignity.

She makes a movement for me to go, and I'm grateful because her weakness has granted me acquittal, a swift exit where she might otherwise have tripped me up.

*

I take a shortcut across the lemon groves, instead of the main road. There's a chance of Vivien and Adalina coming past in the car and I don't want to risk them seeing me. It's clear I'm making an escape. Such is the distraction of my hollow stomach and my aching head that I haven't time to dwell on what it means to abandon the Barbarossa. It's been my safe haven these past weeks, by turns a sanctuary and a welcome diversion. It was the place where I started to let go of James, and to realise that life existed without him. A pity that came too late…

My phone jolts in my pocket, once, twice, three times, four. I was prepared for this. There's another, and another, messages flooding in from Alison, my sisters and my dad, from Bill, from my colleagues at Calloway & Cooper, from James, no doubt, call upon call unanswered. I had thought about switching it off but what would be the point? The truth is out. It's there in black and white. There's no taking back what has already been done and I will have to face the music; I will have to survive.

I stop by the wall to the road, shrug off my rucksack and sit with my back against it, unscrewing a bottle of water. I'm reminded of my first walk here all that time ago – how long it seems, how much has changed. I'm different now, stronger.

Taking my phone from my pocket, I bring up the messages. Contrary to what I've envisaged ever since Grace Calloway's death, they don't go into searing detail about how awful I am. There are no random numbers of people I knew long ago, telling me they always knew I'd wind up like this. The ones from my family read:

Lucy? Please phone home.

Big sister, I need to speak to you.

Luce, what is going on? Are you all right?

The ones from Bill are more to the point:

You probably know but the shit's hit. Call me. Xxx

I've twenty or more missed calls. There's an email from Alison attaching the article and thanking me for my time. She hopes this 'clears things up', and when I read the item I understand why. She has been true to her word, recounting the story of James's and my love affair with sincerity and truth. I actually don't sound that bad, less like the murdering harlot the public were ready to slay and more like a girl who fell in love. I wince at a couple of junctures where James is painted badly. '*He made me believe I was everything,*' I'm printed as saying. I guess I did say that. '*And then he left me with nothing. His marriage was never in crisis, it was all a lie.*'

Alison has wholeheartedly taken my side; if anything she's leaped to my defence more than was necessary. I feel oddly grateful to her, to have found this clear, clean outlet where all others were dirt-stained. But James…

Six of my missed calls are from him. It's not so much the number as the intervals the calls came in, mere seconds apart, as if he fell to a burst of pure fury.

It's only a distant part of myself that is troubled by this. I'm afraid of his rage but I'm not saddened by it. If ever a blade could be driven into the heart of our relationship, this is it. There is no turnaround; he'll never speak to me again. I observe this as if it doesn't quite involve me, as if I can understand the remorse it provokes but cannot feel it. I think I stopped feeling it the day he arrived in Florence.

My screen dances to life once more. It's a local number and I assume it to be James trying from an anonymous landline. Or else it's Max.

Max.

Is it possible he's found out? I'm sure of what I would have done in his position... I'd have Googled me. Until today, he would have drawn a blank. This morning, he'd have stumbled across a jackpot. Shame washes through me and tears spring to my eyes, which I swipe away. Why should Max be the one to elicit this response? James didn't, my family didn't, so I'm not letting him.

The number rings off. I wait for it to leave a voicemail but it doesn't.

All at once, my attention is diverted to a sound from the road: an approaching engine. Keeping low to the wall, I peer over and spy Vivien's car. Staying out of sight, I wait for it to pass. It's moving slowly, and when it comes near I see why. Adalina is at the wheel, coughing violently. I hear her through the open window.

As the vehicle passes, it slows almost to a stop. I'm about to forsake my hiding place and run to her aid when something pulls me up short. There is no Vivien in the back – at least, not from my vantage point. I move to get a better look, emboldened by Adalina's preoccupation. Still, I see no one. Even if Vivien were lying down, I'd spot her from here. I try to think what happened. Was Vivien unable to leave the house today? Has the doctor's appointment been cancelled? In any case, it looks as if it's Adalina who should be the one seeing the doctor, not Vivien.

I linger in a bizarre moment of uncertainty as to what to do next, wholly visible to anyone who cared to notice.

Finally, the car moves on and out of sight. I look after it, torn in all directions, and then decide what it is I must do.

*

Before leaving Florence, I buy a postcard from the train station and sit at a trattoria to write it. The postcard is standard, innocuous, a tourist shot of the Duomo.

Vivien

Max's aunt says she is sorry. You will know what that means.

I'm sorry, too, that I have to leave. I wish you the best for the future.

Lucy

There's more I want to say, but I'm not sure what – or how.

I scribble the Barbarossa's address, affix a stamp and post it into the nearest box, before rushing down the platform to catch my train.

CHAPTER THIRTY-SIX

Vivien, Italy, 1986

The next months passed in a fog of sleepless nights, first smiles and burbling laughter. Having a baby was hard work. Adalina was on hand to help but Vivien wanted to take the lion's share herself. She had to prove she was good at this; that, for the first time since discovering she could act, she had an aptitude, a knack, an instinct. She was determined that Alfie would grow up feeling secure and loved, and each time he cried or didn't cry, ate too much or ate too little, she worried that she was harming him.

'You are doing wonderfully, signora,' Adalina told her. If only her husband were as reassuring. Producing a child had shone a spotlight on their collapsed marriage, with every blip and crease magnified once initial elation gave way to ordinary life. These days they snapped too readily at each other, engaged in a perpetual and pointless contest as to who was the more tired, who did more for Alfie, who should be working harder and who wasn't working enough. Vivien had seen it happen to other couples and had always vowed it would never become her. *I don't want us to be like this*, she thought, even as she was screaming at Gio for not heating the baby's milk properly, or for leaving him to cry a moment too long. Gio was equally to blame. He came home exhausted and tetchy, leaving her and Alfie with the dregs of his mood. Of course it didn't help that Vivien felt he was spending his days with his mistress. Gio was more reluctant than ever to tell her about his time away, and the less he told her, the less she wanted to know, and the more their discussions became solely about Alfie and the practicalities and logistics of taking care of him.

The gulf between them grew. Vivien's birthday passed with little note. Gone were the days when Gio would bring her breakfast with a dozen red roses. This year, before rushing out of the door, he managed a card and a promise of a getaway, though he didn't say when or where. She didn't want to challenge him – he'd tell her she was overthinking it, and that they simply had less time to focus on themselves since the baby came along. It was all about Alfie now; she came second.

Third, if she counted Isabella.

Though it was a distant memory, the shock of the message she'd found in the attic still had the power to stun her. *I want him.* She saw it in dreams, chased it in nightmares. She would find herself totally preoccupied with the baby, then in a rare quiet moment she would stop, and the sister and all her secrets seemed to bear down on Vivien, circling over her head like the heavy flap of a dark bird's wings.

Adalina urged her to wait. 'Let time pass, signora, I beg you…' Vivien was unmovable, determined to act, until: 'If not for your marriage then for your baby.'

That was what did it. Alfie. If Vivien let her preoccupation with Isabella steal the very first part of her baby's life, steal her attention and her devotion, steal time away from tending his needs and his cries, then Isabella had triumphed there too.

As the weeks wore on, Adalina led her to hope that Gio would step up: as he watched his son grow, so his sister would be put in the shade. But it didn't happen. Their dynamic was as insufferable as ever. Vivien began to suspect that Adalina had merely been buying time for herself, seeking to slip away from a situation before she became embroiled in it. *Too late*, thought Vivien. *You're part of this.*

Often, it was close to irresistible to tell Gio what she had found, the defaced ticket stubs calling to her from where she'd concealed them in a drawer: *I want him, I want him, I want him.* But she knew what he would say, how he would twist it to his sister's favour. He had taken Isabella to *Carmen* as a thank you; the note she'd scrawled on the back couldn't possibly reference him, it would be another suitor, perhaps a colleague of his; Isabella had always been sentimental about possessions, which was why she'd kept the memento – as a child she had filled a memory box, another quirk of hers, one of the many peculiarities that made her magnificent…

Vivien could not abide a single utterance more in defence of Isabella. And so it was one more thing she kept from Gio, a lie piled on a lie piled on a lie. It made no difference. Through their fights, she had discredited herself. Nothing

she said, even if she swore it on her life, would resonate
sufficiently for him to take against her.

*

Come the autumn, an opportunity presented itself. Vivien
had pondered how this would emerge – the opening she
needed – because surely it would. One night, after Vivien
had bathed Alfie and put him to bed, Gio returned to the
Barbarossa with a shock announcement. He had to leave
Tuscany for three weeks on a placement.

'I'm sorry,' he said, 'I know it's bad timing... but I can't
get out of it. It'll pass quickly, you'll see. I'll be back before
you know it.'

'Is Isabella going?'

He shook his head.

Good, she thought. *Isabella will be here – with me.*

Gio was up early the next morning to pack. A car was
collecting him at midday. Vivien prepared Alfie in his cor-
duroys and little sailor shirt to say goodbye, and as they
hugged at the door she felt a nascent glow at the knowledge
that, unbeknownst to Gio, by the time he returned home
everything would be different.

When the door closed behind him, Vivien turned to see
Isabella at the foot of the stairs. The sister had emerged from
her confinement, as she often did, looking immaculate, like
a mermaid from the tangle of the deep. Her eyes roamed
Vivien's generous, shapeless smock, a far cry from her own
tailored silhouette.

To hell with you, Vivien thought. *I've got a beautiful baby to show for it.*

'Can I hold him?' Isabella put her arms out. She didn't look at Vivien when she asked the question, just at Alfie, who gazed back at her with a dizzy, silly smile.

If the sister so much as thought that Vivien would allow her within touching distance of Alfie, she was sorely mistaken. Vivien had seen how Isabella looked at the boy, regarding him with scarcely controlled hunger that at times bordered on outright starvation. Vivien had been protective since the birth, refusing to permit Isabella access, and it was only when she was taking a bath, or catching up on her sleep, that Isabella, via Gio, could spend time with him. Vivien knew that Isabella would never put a foot wrong while Gio was present, she wouldn't dare, and Vivien had made her husband promise never to let their son out of his sight. Now, she felt the customary jolt of satisfaction that she finally possessed something that the other woman didn't. Isabella would never have that bond with Gio. She would never be his partner in the fullest sense.

Vivien tightened her hold on her son. She turned and walked away.

'It looks like it's just you and me now, Vivien,' came Isabella's voice from behind her, beautiful and deadly both at once. 'Just you and me and your baby.'

*

The trick was to make it appear as if Isabella had made this decision herself; that there was nothing left for her here, not now Gio and Vivien had their family. This was her only way out: the world had never welcomed her; she could no longer find happiness in any corner of it. Gio would be devastated, naturally, but he would come to realise that it had been inevitable. Isabella had always been destined for such an end.

Vivien settled on a day, forty-eight hours after Gio's departure. Long enough for there to be some safe distance between the Barbarossa and her husband, but not so long as to feel Isabella's claws sinking too deep into her back. 'Shall I take him?' Isabella would offer from the doorway, her black eyes gleaming. 'Give him to me,' she would encourage, when Vivien was attempting to fasten her coat one-handed. Vivien saw the way the sister's face lit up at the sight of Alfie. *You can covet my husband*, she thought, *but you will never come close to my son*. If Gio were here, he would tell her to be generous, let Isabella play the role of doting aunt. And she'd play it well, in front of him. Only Vivien knew the risk she would be taking. It was why the time for action had arrived.

She scoured her conscience, looking to rake up any vestige of sympathy for Isabella, but she found none. Each time she passed that portrait in the hall, Isabella as the queen of the castle, her hatred and resentment refreshed. Leave it much longer and the sister would destroy Vivien's marriage for good. She could not let that happen. As she cradled her baby and kissed the soft hair above his ears, determined to give him all she herself had missed out on, she knew she could not let that happen.

When the morning came, she was up at dawn. Miraculously, Alfie slept on, so Vivien tied her robe and padded downstairs. The house was quiet. Tentative daylight bathed the floor in milky glow. On the staircase, the gloom-shrouded portraits glared back at her – Gio, her accuser; Isabella, her assailant; and herself, a last-minute bolt-on, an arbitrary extra, here as in real life. In the dark, their features seemed to twist and morph, real and not real, half alive, half dead.

Calmly, she went to prepare the tincture. Adalina had hinted at the quantity just sufficiently to give Vivien what she needed, but the maid's conscience hadn't allowed her to become a real, working part of it. '*My nephew,*' she appealed to Vivien. '*If we were to be caught… I'm sorry, signora, I can't. You are on your own.*'

As the day's first sun stretched its fingers through the shutters of the gallery, Vivien perfected her mixture with care. Beyond the window, the mottled stone fountain emerged from its long dark night. It seemed to glare at her with fixed abomination, as if she had wronged it in a former life, as if it was waiting to pounce.

She would pounce first.

Vivien concluded her work; her hands were steady as a surgeon's. It felt good to regain her power. Back to the woman she used to be, a survivor, not a victim.

Two things happened as she emerged into the hall, the concoction concealed in her dressing robe. The first was the sound of her baby's cry, howling from a far chamber. The second was the shock of the great door ringing. It was early for visitors. Who should be dropping by at this antisocial hour? She went to answer it.

She saw him, but it took a moment for her brain to catch up.

You.

Standing on the doorstep, his cap in hand, was Gilbert Lockhart.

'Hello, Vivien,' he said. 'Surprise.'

CHAPTER THIRTY-SEVEN

Italy, Summer 2016

The platform is packed with travellers, shouts in Italian darting between them like colourful birds, and I hurry through the fray towards my carriage. I'm about to board the train when something catches my foot; I trip, put my hands out and the ground slams into my palms. It hurts; my wrist throbs where it took the impact. My bag falls from my shoulder. A scatter of change rolls away from me.

'*Stai bene?*' asks a passing guy, stopping to help. 'Are you all right?'

'*Sí, grazie,*' I reply, dusting myself off. Faces peer down at me from the carriage windows. We gather the coins; I thank him, shove them in my pocket.

He steps on to the train ahead of me and I'm about to follow.

But then I stop.

I stop and stare. And stare.

There is a face I know. Only… it can't be.

Looking right at me, third row back, cream skin, wide green eyes; the glass between us rendering her complexion misty, like a drift of cloud on a photograph.

Her name is on my lips: that most trusted of names, the first name, the simplest, most natural name of all, but there is a sob in my throat and no sound comes out. I'm hot then I'm cold. I trust then I don't trust. It can't be. It's not.

Mum.

It's just someone who looks like her.

The woman opens her mouth and her features are kind, full of love, just like I remember. She says something, one word, and I understand it immediately.

The photograph fades, reappears. I want to run to her. My feet won't move.

'Are you boarding?' asks the guard in Italian.

I blink. Shake my head. He blows his whistle. The train moves off.

*

My legs barely carry me back to the concourse. The world around me ceases to be real, the sky turned on its head. I am living in the negative: the dark side of the moon.

'Lucy!'

My name takes a while to reach me, as if it doesn't belong to me, a paper tag I unlooped from my ankle. Then I turn, the world shifting, settling. It's Max.

He's rushing through the crowds, up the steps, takes my arm when he reaches me then drops it. His face is hard to read, confusion, relief, hope. I fight to focus.

It can't have been her. It can't.

It was.

'Lucy, thank God I made it,' he says. 'You can't go.'

I nod. My lips are dry. 'I know. She told me not to. She told me to stay.'

He catches his breath. 'Who? Vivien?'

She was real, she was there – so brief, like the bright gold flash of a firework before it dissolves into night. 'No. Nothing. No one. It doesn't matter.'

'Well, this does,' says Max. 'I read Vivien's diary, Lucy. It's…' He runs a hand through his hair. 'I couldn't let you leave. I have to talk to you. It's urgent.'

An announcement rings out for the last departure to Rome.

Max touches my arm. 'Are you OK? You look like you've seen a ghost.'

At last, I meet his eye. 'I need fresh air,' I say.

*

Out on the street, crowds swarm around our little island. It strikes me for a moment how we must appear, like lovers about to be parted, or else reunited.

I shiver. I can no longer trust what I'm seeing, what is real and what is not.

Stay.

Have I lost my mind, or have I found it?

I look at Max. *Stay.*

Vivien. The Barbarossa. It isn't over yet.

Stay.

'I thought it was time to go home,' I say to Max, slowly,

carefully. 'I'm guessing you know the story.' He doesn't need to answer. He'll have found out.

'I have people to explain things to.' I think of Dad, my family and friends. It sounds dismissive, as if Max, my friend in Italy, doesn't warrant an explanation; the others are more important. Well, of course they are. 'I came to Italy to escape something that happened to me. I thought I was the one who made it happen, that it was my fault… but now I know it wasn't just me.'

Max waits a beat. 'Was he the guy you left with the other day?'

I remember James watching us on the terrace. 'Yes.'

'Do you love him?'

I can see from Max's expression that it matters. I guess the reportage didn't make it clear either way. Alison was careful not to paint me as a bitter ex-mistress still desperately pining for a lover she couldn't have; equally, it was evident how much I'd adored him, even after Grace committed suicide. I have to think about my answer, and the fact I do tells me what I need to know. I shake my head. 'I did,' I say.

Max puts his hands in his pockets. It's hot, the sky above us huge and blue. A nearby busker plays Bob Marley. 'What changed your mind?' he asks.

I hesitate, consider telling him, and then decide that it's mine, just mine.

'Too much here,' I answer, 'making me want to stick around.'

Max gives the trace of a smile, looks down, and nicks the

cleft in his chin. My heart skips. I don't know why. I don't know where we go from here.

Before I can find out, my phone buzzes with a call from Bill.

'I should take this,' I say. Max frowns (wondering if it's James? I don't reassure him that it isn't) and draws a cigarette out of his pocket, leaning against the sun-soaked wall to smoke. I realise he isn't going to let me out of his sight.

I pick up. 'Hey.'

'Hey, yourself,' says Bill. It's good to hear her voice, and that nothing in the way she speaks to me has changed. 'What time do you get in?'

'Here's the thing. I'm not coming back any more.'

'What?'

'I mean, I am, eventually. Soon. But something came up.'

'Newsflash, Luce – something came up here, too.'

'I know. But maybe it's best if I postpone. Wait for things to cool down.'

'It's because James is there, isn't it?'

'Sorry?'

'Don't tell me you're hooking up with him again, Lucy, please—'

'I'm not.'

There's quiet on the line and I wonder if we've been cut off. Then Bill says:

'I didn't want to say this on the phone, but since you're not coming back…'

'What is it?'

'You can't trust him, Lucy. I mean it.'

Annoyance flashes through me. This is so far from my intentions right now that I resent Bill's lack of understanding, and lack of belief in me.

'He didn't come to Florence to win you back,' she goes on, 'whatever he's told you. He's issued a reply online.' She waits a beat. 'Basically it counters everything you've said – everything that was in Alison Cooney's reveal. He maintains he tried to tell you no, but you wouldn't accept it. He says you seduced him, stalked him, turned him against his wife. How he never really loved you. And how…'

'How what?' My voice is strained.

'How you threatened his kids if he called it off with you.'

'*What?*'

'That's right. He's not holding back, Lucy. He wants to make you suffer.'

'No kidding.' I'm numb, stumbling to keep up.

'There's more. He was with Natasha – the whole time he was with you.'

'Natasha Fenwick?'

But it couldn't be anyone else. Of course… Natasha.

'He's painting himself as the casualty here,' says Bill. 'Said you made him despair about his marriage, convinced him Grace was playing around behind his back, flirting with her co-stars, coming home late at night… How you got him drinking, even taking drugs to help blot it out, and he started seeing other women because you tortured him emotionally. I mean, it's all bollocks, clearly the most ludicrous bollocks I've ever heard, but it's out there, Lucy – and it's your word against his.'

I'm stunned, and turn my back on Max so he can't see. I knew that James would be furious at my unleashing my version of events, but this is taking it to extremes. To go so far as to soil his dead wife's name – what kind of man is he?

And Natasha? I should have known. She always hated me: now I know why.

But why tell me all that bullshit when he got here, about how he wanted me back? He'd made me feel like the only girl on earth, like it was him and me against the world. All that time he was probably saying the exact same thing to Natasha.

'I reckon he only came out to Florence to get you on side,' says Bill. 'He feared something like this would happen and he wanted to keep you quiet.'

I swallow. Bill's right. Tears spring to my eyes but they're not born of sadness. They're tears of frustration and anger, at James but mostly at myself. If I had taken a single moment to assess how he'd treated me, the heartbreaking silence since Grace's death, I might have realised that he'd always be a player. He would always put his own interests before mine. How blind I've been. How blind and stupid.

'Luce, are you still there?'

'Yes.'

'I think you should come home. The fact you're not here makes it look worse.'

'Makes what look worse?'

'Everything James is saying. You should be here to defend yourself.'

'I don't need to. I know the truth.'

'But others don't.'

My patience snaps. 'Do you know what, Bill? I've given up caring what other people think. Why should I? They can draw whatever conclusions they want.'

'But what about the people who matter?'

'They should know me better than to believe any of that.'

Bill pauses; it's probably just to think about her next comment, but I read her silence as some refutation of this fact and before I know it I'm shouting:

'It would be nice if you could support my decision to stay. Don't you think I've had enough criticism, and I might just want a friend to talk to?'

This isn't strictly fair. Bill has been nothing but a dear friend to me. But my upset has a momentum of its own, and all the things I ought to direct at James, I direct at her. It stings that she was right all along about him and this proves it. Even though her disclosure isn't an 'I told you so,' that's how it feels.

'That isn't fair,' she says coolly.

'Is any of this fair on me?'

'I spoke to your dad today. Should I call him back, tell him you're not coming any more? I'm sick of dealing with things here, Lucy. I do have a life of my own, you know. And then you yell at me for taking the time to give you a wake-up call?'

A tear leaks out of my eye and plops down my cheek. I hang up, knowing as I do that it's a horribly spineless thing to do. I wait for a second with the phone in my hand, half wishing and half fearing that she'll ring back, but of course she doesn't. I wouldn't. I've been a complete bitch, after all she's done for me.

I sense Max at my back, and am embarrassed by my outburst.

'Come with me,' he says, taking my hand.

CHAPTER THIRTY-EIGHT

Vivien, Italy, 1986

For a moment, she couldn't speak. Then she went to close the door.

Gilbert pushed against it. 'Vivien, my child – let me in.'

She drove her whole weight into the effort. Her mind raced, tripping over itself, too much and too fast, how had this happened, how had he found her?

'Vivien! Please, my lamb, a chance is all I ask—'

She'd forgotten how strong he was. Even now, in his fifties, he possessed brute strength: the power of an iron will, of determination, of never losing, of keeping her down. Vivien could support his resistance no longer. In the distance, Alfie's cries reached fever pitch. She heard Adalina's footsteps hurry across the hall upstairs.

Gilbert Lockhart stood before her. He was like a ghost, not least because she had figured him for dead: her bastard father.

This can't be happening. It's a dream.

Nightmare upon nightmare crashed in on her, dark memories heaped one on top of another.

'What are you doing here?' she rasped.

Gilbert stood before her, his hands by his sides, palms up in a gesture of reconciliation. For the first time she took in his appearance, haggard lines etched across his face, thinning hair, a disappointed droop to the mouth. What had happened since she'd left? What had become of him after her mother died? His clothes were thin and poor, his shoes battered. '*You always get a measure of a guy by what he wears on his feet,*' Mickey had used to say at Boudoir Lalique. You could tell a drunk, a pauper, a pervert. Gilbert Lockhart's shoes had seen better days – as had the threadbare bag in which, it seemed, were contained all his worldly belongings.

What had happened to the Lord's providence?

'God showed me the path back to you,' he answered simply. 'Vivien, my darling – it's been so long. I had to see you. I had to see my daughter. I prayed for this, years I've prayed, and finally my prayers were answered. God decided the time was right – his Great Plan permitted me this clemency. I have to meet my grandson.'

Shock paralysed her. The thought of her father going anywhere near Alfie was anathema. At any moment, she expected to wake in bed, embroiled in sweat-soaked sheets, having imagined the whole thing. The gentle rattle of Isabella's potion in her pocket reminded her that this was real: horribly, inescapably real.

'Stay back,' she said. 'Don't come any closer.'

But he wouldn't be deterred. In her father's zealous, manic eyes she saw how ready he was to climb the mountain to absolution, and nothing she could say would dissuade him. This was more than his heart's desire: it was a holy mission.

'We had our problems,' Gilbert went on, 'I accept that – but I've changed, Vivien. Have faith in me as I have faith in God's mercy.' He seized her hand, his own clammy with moisture and excitement. 'He granted me wisdom to know my sins and beg forgiveness for them, and I will spend the rest of my days begging forgiveness from you. I want to be a father to you, Vivien, and a grandfather to your boy.'

'Never.' She snatched her hand away.

Did he expect her to cave that easily? To say: *All is forgiven, Daddy, all it ever took was a few words, and then I'd forget about the beatings and the torture.*

'The Lord advised me to prepare for this. He told me you would fight.'

'I'm amazed at His insight,' she said acidly.

'Let me come in. Let me talk to you. Twenty minutes – that's all I ask.'

He put his hands together in prayer, gazing skyward like a martyred saint: bully, aggressor, tyrant of her childhood… *the man who's supposed to be dead.*

Panic surged as she recalled her lie to Gio. It was too long and too deep to ever recover from. Telling him she was an orphan when he'd suffered the real thing, and so terribly. Imagine if her husband were here! She couldn't think it – it was too dreadful. She had to evict Gilbert before anybody saw. Before anyone found out.

'Turn around,' she said, 'go back to America, find

whatever hole you crawled out of and crawl right back into it again. I don't want to see you. I never will.'

'Your mother—!' he appealed, as she was shutting the door.

The mention of Millicent pulled her up short; she hated her mother for her weakness but there would always be a bond between them, of casualty if nothing else. She felt guilty about having missed her mother's funeral, drinking her way through the news like a coward. She waited for Gilbert's poison words, the Biblical blathering he'd spouted from the pulpit, chilling her to the core while forcing her to listen.

'Millicent wanted this...' Gilbert implored her. 'When she went, she begged me to find you. She said it was her only hope, and how sorry she was that things turned out as they did.' That part Vivien could believe: her poor mother had never been happy, and in running from home Vivien had stolen any modicum of joy life still had to offer. 'And now you have a son,' said Gilbert. 'We have a right to see him – if not for me then for your mother. She loved you. She missed you, right to the end.'

A hot swell rose in Vivien's chest and she fought it down. He would not see her cry: she had given him too many tears back in Claremont.

'Please,' he ventured, 'let me in. Just for a short while. Let me show you how I've changed. Let me realise your mother's wish. Let me make it up to you – and, if you still want me to leave, I promise to do so and never to bother you again.'

Vivien checked behind her. The house was quiet. She

could take him to the library, hear him out in private then send him on his way. Otherwise, she feared his return. It was not a risk she could afford to take. She stepped back to let him in.

*

No sooner had Vivien decided how she would play it – keep him standing, so as not to imply he would be getting any longer than the allocated time; make no offer of a drink or any other extension of hospitality; fold her arms and listen stoically, while letting his words skim off her like flies – than the worst happened.

Isabella. Oh, that wretched Isabella.

'I thought I heard a guest,' she sang, sweeping into the library as unexpectedly as a gust of bitter wind on a spring day, shooting Gilbert her sweetest smile while laying down a glittering tray of coffee and macaroons. 'What a treat!' She extended an alabaster hand, fingers delicate as a robber bride's. 'I am Isabella Moretti.'

Vivien fought to keep control. A million ideas occurred to her at once – how she could get out of this, say he was someone else; anything but admit he was—

'Vivien's father,' he practically fell on Isabella's beauty, 'Gilbert Lockhart.'

There was a split second where Isabella, untouchable, unfathomable Isabella, was flummoxed. Then a sharp delight crossed her features. 'How thrilling,' she said.

'I expect Vivien told you all about me,' he spouted, like a

gushing tap. 'We haven't been in touch in a while. I've been searching for her for years.'

Isabella's face was a picture of amazement. 'I'm sorry,' she said, laughing lightly. 'I seem shocked. It's just… you look so similar.'

'That's what they used to say back in South Carolina!'

'Is that right.'

'Seeing her name in lights, you can imagine how proud I was. How proud I am.'

'Indeed.'

At last, Isabella met her eye. Through clouds of fury and disappointment, Vivien made herself meet it: that dark, satisfied glint. This was it, her final exposure. Isabella would tell her brother everything. Isabella had succeeded. It was over.

Screw you, Daddy, she thought dementedly. *You've done it again.*

She waited for Isabella to give her away. *That's a funny thing*, she'd say to Gilbert, relishing every second. *Vivien told us you were dead.* But Isabella didn't.

Instead, she said:

'Well, you will sit a while and have coffee with us, won't you?'

'He was just leaving,' mumbled Vivien. 'He's not staying.'

'What a shame,' said Isabella.

'I could stay…?' suggested Gilbert, as Isabella offered the tray of delicacies. He removed one and popped the whole thing in his mouth, which was obscene, somehow, eyeing Vivien as he did with a host of silent victories.

*

Vivien knew that Isabella was multi-faceted, but even she was impressed at the dazzling persona that now charmed Gilbert Lockhart like a snake winding through grass. It made her rage that Gio never saw this dual performance of hers: quiet and reserved around him, ever the wounded; and then like this, brimming with poise and conviction, a different woman entirely. Which was the real Isabella?

I want him. That was the real one.

To Vivien's disgust, Gilbert stumbled his words, while Isabella hung off every one, and he, like every deluded man before him, imagined this temptress found his old bones attractive and wanted to be close to him. Perhaps a life spent in God's service had addled Gilbert's brain, made him think he was a gift to women; his ego hadn't suffered the years. Meanwhile Vivien looked on, dismayed, trapped between how the hell she was going to get her father as far away from here as possible before Gio returned, and desperate to come up with a way to stop Isabella disclosing the truth.

'What did you think of Vivien's career?' asked Isabella over supper, her chin on her hand as she awaited Gilbert's answer with rapt attention. She wore a clinging jade gown, her hair in sleek waves. *Are you trying to seduce every man in my life?* Vivien was astounded, yet at the same time completely unsurprised. She understood how Isabella's mind worked. Vivien had been unable to impress her father. These days she couldn't care less, but once upon a time, when she'd been young, of course she had yearned for his approval.

Isabella wanted to show how easily she could amaze, with a laugh or a flash of her eyes. She was better than Vivien, in all ways, to all men.

'Well...' Gilbert was lightly sweating; Vivien was sickened. 'Obviously it was a surprise. I discouraged her from pursuing her ambitions in Hollywood...'

Discouraged? That was one word for it.

'But then, when she did well, I realised I myself had been responsible for it.'

Vivien's mouth fell open. Oh, she *had* to see where this one was going.

'You see, I encouraged her through religion during her childhood. She came to see how vital God is in guiding us through life and in trusting in Him, and that if we have the courage to ask for what we want, He will deliver. Isn't that right, Vivien?'

The two of them turned on her. In Isabella's eyes was a shimmer of mischief. Vivien thought of all the occasions where she had appealed to Gilbert's God and heard nothing in response. *Please stop my daddy hurting me.* No reply.

'I made my own way,' she said tightly.

'Which was precisely the Lord's doing,' continued Gilbert, as if they were in accord. 'Vivien's success was in His plan for her. I merely facilitated it. God has been a shining light in our family for generations, a beacon in times of despair.'

Isabella was nodding. 'I completely agree,' she said softly, liquid eyes darting to her lap; even Vivien thought her gorgeous in that moment. 'I believe that God saved my life. I nearly drowned as a child. My parents died and I was left to die with them. But someone saved me.' *Sure did*, thought Vivien, *the coastguards.*

'No,' gasped Gilbert, reaching out. 'You poor child.'

Incredibly, Isabella went on to recount the events of that day. Vivien had never heard the sister speak of them before, but there was a disingenuous note to her delivery, as if this were a mere fiction she had narrated many times before, and in its retelling she had become distant from it, as if it had happened to somebody else.

Salvatore refilled their glasses, his face dutifully neutral. Adalina stood in the doorway; Vivien couldn't bear to look at her. What must the maid think of her? A liar, a hypocrite, but never an orphan – after all the insults she had thrown at Isabella!

She should have been honest with her friend.

I should have been honest with Gio.

'How inspiring…' Gilbert was fascinated.

'I try to take inspiration from it.'

'And you've only recently regained your voice?'

'All thanks to my brother.' Isabella sipped red wine and surveyed Vivien over the rim of her glass. 'He truly is a wonderful man.'

Gilbert seemed to remember that Vivien was with them, and regarded her in a slightly perplexed way, as if having to remind himself that this brilliant Gio Moretti, who had such a captivating sister as Isabella, had chosen his plain little daughter as a wife. Perhaps he saw himself in a similar way, having stooped or compromised in his marriage to Millicent, when in reality he'd been destined for more.

'And my daughter is a lucky woman,' simpered Gilbert, 'to have such a sister-in-law as you. I look forward to meeting the man himself!'

'Gio's away,' said Vivien quickly.

'Yes, but he'll be back soon,' crooned Isabella.

'It would be all right if I waited for him, wouldn't it?' said Gilbert.

'No,' said Vivien. 'He's not home until the end of the month.'

'Why not?' Isabella countered. She had the courtesy, at least, to react to the barbed glare Vivien shot her way and go on to add, 'It's hardly as if there isn't room!'

'It's too much with a small baby,' said Vivien, throttled by fear.

'I'm sure I can entertain your father,' said Isabella. 'Oh, come to think of it, you must see this, Gilbert. Vivien hasn't shown you the painting already, has she?'

'What painting?' Gilbert nearly tripped over himself in his efforts to stand from the chair and follow her. Before Vivien could object, he had trailed Isabella into the hall like a simpering puppy. Vivien went after them, at first confused and then not needing to hear her father's gleeful cry to know what had happened. For there, on the staircase, was the monstrous portrait Vivien had rejected – the one Isabella had orchestrated after her fight with Gio, the one of her as a girl, the lily-white dress and the pigtails, her father at her shoulder. Isabella must have mounted it this afternoon, removing the re-commissioned one, so that it sat dwarfed next to the Morettis, excruciating and evil and every bad thing she could summon. That irrepressible *witch*!

Vivien had asked Gio to destroy it. Clearly, he had gone against her wishes.

'You included me!' Gilbert was jubilant, rushing to stand in front of it like somebody embarrassing at a museum.

'It was Isabella's idea,' Vivien said sourly. It was meant to pack a punch from her side, but instead it just made Isabella's star glow brighter.

'I should have known,' said Gilbert, and Isabella smiled warmly at him.

'Adalina,' Isabella directed, 'could you make up the Lilac Room? I want Vivien's father to be as comfortable as possible while he stays with us. He's travelled a long way.' She smiled at Vivien. 'And it's such an unexpected pleasure to see him.'

*

That night, Vivien didn't sleep. The baby was one thing; her delirium was another. She kept being jolted from the cusp of oblivion, the dread knowledge that her father was under the same roof like a knife to the stomach. She longed to speak to Gio but could not bring herself to ring him or answer his calls: she hadn't a clue what she would say. Her confession sat like a toad on her tongue, threatening to leap out at any moment. If she came clean, it would cement her insanity as far as he was concerned. Essentially she had fabricated a childhood, made Gio fall in love with her under false pretences, having believed she shared with him this most poisoned chalice. There was no way out: every word speared her to the cross. Nothing she ever uttered again would hold any value. Vivien tossed and turned and tortured herself with images from the past. She heard whispers in the walls, echoes of Isabella's laugh that couldn't be real but tricked her as they ducked and swooped through the vaults.

Gio's side of the bed was empty and cold. In the crib next to her, Alfie's gentle breath was undisturbed. She hated that Gilbert's blood was in him, her lying, grasping father, who was no doubt here for a piece of the pie. He had fallen on hard times, that much was clear. Isabella and her golden welcome spelled the end to his troubles. Well, if he thought he could get his hands on Vivien's son he was mistaken.

She would administer Isabella's poison in the morning. She would not fail. There would be no deviation. Vivien could talk Salvatore and Lili into keeping quiet about their unexpected guest – it was Isabella's silence she had to secure. With the sister's untimely death and the house in turmoil, Gilbert would be made to leave. His reappearance would never have happened. Her lie would be safe.

Unable to rest, Vivien got up and washed her hands and face, just as she had done as a girl, as if Gilbert's taint was dirt she could scrub off.

As she was preparing to return to bed, she spotted someone outside on the drive. In between the cypress trees, by the stone fountain, stood a figure in white.

Isabella.

Was the sister sleepwalking? She drifted between light

and shade like a spectre, as silver and fluid as water. In moments the figure was real; in others a phantom, something Vivien could blink away. Vivien watched as the vision trailed a hand through the still, sapphire pond surrounding that mottled fish, and then Isabella, or a version of Isabella, did something despicable: she raised her head and looked directly at Vivien. Vivien gasped and stumbled back from the window, unable to tear her eyes from the vile sight. She focused and refocused, losing Isabella then catching her, and Isabella's horrid, beautiful features contorted into a smile.

Throwing on her robe, Vivien fled into the hall and down the stairs, determined to catch her nemesis. She ran through the chill and flung open the door, spat out on to the porch where she abruptly came up short.

The fountain sat steady and motionless, a smooth pale ring like a socket in a skull. The cypress trees were alone. The night weighed heavy and quiet, the kind of quiet so contained and entire that to break it would be unthinkable. Vivien had the impression that she was standing in a painting, the only living, breathing thing, her surroundings existing only to situate her, and she could imagine the frame hanging in a gallery, passers-by commenting on the shocked expression on her face, that lonely woman in the doorway of a great house, smothered in darkness.

Her feet carried her to the rim of the fountain. When she peered into it, she half expected, half *desired*, to see Isabella's face looking back. But all she saw was her own reflection, delicate as mist, and the swollen hulk of that atrocious fish.

She leaned closer. Water sputtered from the fish's gullet,

that not-quite easy passage. Rust, most likely: the build-up of an age. Her hand reached to touch its pout, cold and slippery, and before she could question what she was doing, her fingers crept into its mouth, stemming the flow so it sprayed and licked around her fist, soaking her night sleeve. She explored that smooth cavity, deeper and further, tighter in…

There.

Her fingers clasped around it, hard edges gripped. Slowly, she drew it out. The fish spouted freely, its blockage released, the steady gush of liquid like a new pulse.

What terrible secret have you been hiding?

Moonlight coated the discovery, a cool, patient spotlight.

CHAPTER THIRTY-NINE

Italy, Summer 2016

We go back to Max's place. I let him steer me, hail the taxi, too dazed to object. Max seems determined to lift my spirits, fixing me a drink and setting me up on his patio that overlooks the river. I am grateful that he doesn't ask about my conversation.

'Are you feeling OK?' It's the only reference he makes.

I nod. He accepts it. 'So,' he sits opposite me, the sun behind him so his face is in shadow, dark and intense, 'Vivien's diary.'

I'm grateful that we are back on neutral ground. But one look at his troubled expression reveals that what he's about to tell me isn't going to be easy.

'Much of it we already knew.' He breathes out. 'How Vivien felt about the Barbarossa, about Gio, about his sister… It's pretty intense.'

'I can imagine.'

'Then we get to the end. And Isabella.'

'What about her?'

The sun moves behind a cloud, drenching us in shade.

'She was involved with Dinapoli,' says Max. 'The uncle.'

'*What?*'

'Vivien talks at length about it. Her husband never knew. She's pleased she's got something on her – you know, something he has no idea about.'

I sit forward. 'Was it consensual? With Dinapoli?'

Max shakes his head.

'Oh, my God. That's awful. Poor Isabella.'

'Vivien didn't think so. Her hate is clear right up to the last entry. She can't see Isabella as a victim. She decides she must have seduced Dinapoli just like she tried to seduce Vivien's father.' He fills me in on Gilbert Lockhart's shock arrival at the house. I'm amazed. 'Then the diary ends,' says Max, 'suddenly. I think some of the pages are missing. I'm not surprised… given the other thing.'

'There's more?'

Max pauses. 'Vivien and Lili: they were planning a trap for Isabella.'

'A trap?'

'To get rid of her.'

I shake my head. 'Come on, Max – this is your aunt we're talking about.'

'Yes, and Lili could be very determined once she set her mind to something.'

I don't believe it. I tell him so.

'Read it for yourself,' he says, producing the diary. 'Lucy, this goes deeper than either of us was prepared for. Isabella was damaged, we both know that, but this was serious. Gio Moretti had no idea what was going on up in that attic. Isabella was subjected to Dinapoli's crazy experiments and it seems to me he took liberties with retrieving more than her voice. She was a child – fourteen, fifteen? All that time he must have spent alone with her, in the name of work, unquestioned. He was in love with her. For Vivien, it was the prize she'd been waiting for. Her chance at revenge.'

Reluctant, I take the journal. It burns in my hand with a red-hot warning. I open it. Vivien's writing is scrawled across the pages, increasingly fraught.

'This is what it's all been about,' says Max. 'My aunt's apology.'

I recall the postcard I sent to Vivien. Will she have read it? Will it make sense to her? I turn Max's idea over as the manic pages spill through my hands, screaming capitals, raging underlines, floods of spilled ink like the guts of an insect: Isabella, Giacomo Dinapoli… a horrid secret rotting at the core of the Barbarossa. The 'tragedy' at the castillo: those '*events that took place last winter*'.

'Go on,' I encourage.

'Vivien knew about the abuse – but instead of feeling sorry for Isabella, she continues to despise her. Isabella's done too much, her actions too unforgivable. There's no going back, as far as Vivien's concerned. So what does she do?' He rubs his chin. 'She knows a sensation like this would kill her husband's reputation for good. She'd do anything for Gio and that includes silencing his sister. Isabella's too much of a risk. She secured Lili's help and they finished her off.'

This is getting more far-fetched by the minute. He sounds like a soap opera.

But Max is grave. 'Think about it,' he says. 'She's solving

two problems in one: getting rid of her adversary and protecting her husband and son. She talked at length about her upset at Isabella being involved in Gio's work. Imagine if a scandal on this scale got out. *Giovanni Moretti continuing the work of his abusive uncle…*'

'I think we're getting a bit ahead of ourselves—'

'Are we?' He leans forward. 'Lucy, I'm convinced. This is what happened. This is where it comes to a head and this is where the diary ends.'

'It doesn't mean she…' I trail off. Max watches me.

'It's impossible,' I say, standing, and he stands too.

'Is it? Finally, she had a reason to hang this on – what Vivien really wanted to do. When Gio found out about her crime, he ran. He couldn't look at her. Couldn't touch her. Couldn't stand to breathe the same air as her.'

'And you're accusing your aunt of this as well?'

Max's face sets. 'It hasn't been an easy conclusion.'

'So this was her apology.' I bite my lip. 'This was it.'

'Perhaps Lili talked Vivien into it. Persuaded her it was the only route. When she died, the way she gripped my hand… it was so *important*, Lucy; she *had* to have her message heard. Because what happened between them was drastic.'

Those pieces are swimming together more definitely now, the link between them solidifying, joining parts together, pooling and multiplying and merging.

'Haven't you ever done anything impulsive?' Max asks. He takes a step towards me so our faces are inches apart.

There's an energy coming off him, a wild energy I haven't met before. My skin prickles in proximity to it.

'You know I have,' I say.

'Maybe they knew they shouldn't,' says Max. 'It was dangerous and wrong. But they did it anyway because the way they saw it, the risk was worth it.'

His eyes flicker across my mouth, in the single most promising and exciting moment of my life. And then he kisses me.

CHAPTER FORTY

Vivien, Italy, 1986

It was a box, small, the kind of box that might contain an engagement ring. Its environment had rotted what once might have been leather, faded gold stitching around its edge, and an indentation, which, when pressed, should spring its lid. Vivien tried, and when it failed she tore at the object, scratched it, knowing it had to open.

At once, it did.

To her alarm, the box did contain a ring. It was tarnished almost beyond recognition, like a shipwreck left for centuries at the bottom of the sea. A faint sparkle shone through despite its condition, a glimmer of hope and resilience that was somehow heartbreaking: a lone, enduring twinkle in a long night. Vivien went to slip it on to her finger but it was too small. She replaced it in its box and hurried inside.

Back in her room, she worked fast. Vivien shone a light on her find, drying it carefully, lovingly, and when she caught sight of a further detail beneath the rust, she scraped and scoured obsessively for an hour or more, losing track of time, the work so precise that a headache yawned behind her desperate eyes. Finally, it was revealed.

An inscription, only just legible, appeared on the inside:

TO MY ONLY LOVE, ISABELLA – YOURS, ALWAYS,
GIACOMO

Vivien stared at it, as if in the study of those eight words they might reveal more of themselves. For, as they were, they made no sense.

Isabella… her uncle…

It couldn't be.

There was an imperfection at the bottom of the ring box, invisible unless one was searching for it. The cushioned panel had been taken out and then sewn back on, not quite square with its contours, the stitching just detectible.

Vivien picked it loose; it came apart easily. Beneath was a folded piece of card. It had survived well, cocooned in its shell. She read inside:

To whoever finds this, please help me. He does not love me. He hurts me. He wants me against my will. What he is doing is wrong. Find me. Save me. I beg you.

CHAPTER FORTY-ONE

Italy, Summer 2016

I'm scared to go back to the Barbarossa, but I must. I must tell Vivien that she's safe, that we're not going to tell the police about her crime. We're not going to tell anyone what happened on a winter's night all those years ago, and this is where it ends. Maybe, if she knows that, she can stop fearing and fighting every day of her life. She can stop torturing herself. She can emerge from her confines, from the Barbarossa and back into the world. She might find pleasure in small places. She hasn't got long. The trips to the doctor, the pills Adalina hid from me, prove it… She'll be gone soon.

Max takes a lock of my hair and tucks it behind my ear.

'What's on your mind?' he murmurs.

I turn to him in bed. We kiss, the smell of him like lemons in the heat.

'Isabella…' I say. 'I keep playing out what happened to her. Vivien and your aunt must have been so full of regret. It's why Vivien's shut herself away, why she's too ashamed to be seen. I bet Isabella never left either of them.'

Max continues to stroke my hair. He wears a faraway look.

It's my turn to ask what he is thinking.

'I still find it weird,' he says, 'that Vivien would employ someone with the same name as my aunt. I thought it was strange before, but now... Now we know what they did, you'd think she'd want to forget, not be reminded of it every day.'

I push myself up on one elbow. 'What are you talking about?'

Max rubs his earlobe with his thumb. 'I never thought it worth mentioning,' he says. 'Adalina was my aunt's name. Everyone called her Lili – she was only ever known as Lili. In fact, for years, I thought that was the only name she had. But then I found out it was short for Adalina. Don't you think it's odd that Vivien has another maid now called the same? I mean, it's not as if it's a common name.'

I'm surprised at this discovery.

'Yeah,' I say. 'That is strange.'

'They were obviously so close. I'd have thought it would be too painful.'

'Perhaps that's why. She wanted to replace her?'

Max isn't convinced, but says, 'Nothing that woman does could amaze me any more.'

I chew my lip. 'Do you think Gio Moretti is still alive?'

Max narrows his eyes at me. 'We got the truth, Lucy. We can stop now.'

'I know. I just... There's something missing.'

I can't help thinking about Vivien. Alone in a house full of memories, ailing towards her inevitable death, her husband long gone and her son...

'What happened to the son?' I turn to Max.

He lifts his shoulders. 'Gio probably took him.'

I frown. 'Yeah,' I say, thinking of the boy, dark curls and blue eyes, and then letting him go as quickly as I caught him. 'Probably.'

*

I wake early the next morning, knowing what I must do.

I creep out of bed and phone my father before I can talk myself out of it.

'Dad?'

'Lucy!' One word: so full of feeling and hope. He's never sounded like this – not even when Mum died. It hits me how unfair I've been. Running into wilderness when all along there was this pair of arms behind me, waiting to bring me home.

'I don't know where to begin,' he chokes out. 'Are you OK? Where are you?'

'I'm still in Italy.'

There's a pause, too much to communicate. 'Why didn't you tell me?' he says at last. 'I thought you could tell me anything.'

Why had I never considered that this would be my father's reaction? All I'd expected was disappointment and disapproval, when he just wanted to be there. He wasn't interested in punishing me or telling me off, and if I'd had any sense I might have entertained this possibility. After all, I had been there for him when nobody else was. Those years we'd shared were irreplaceable; of course he was never going to turn me away. A hot sob threatens to break free.

'I'm sorry, Dad.'

'All that you've been through, my darling... all on your own.'

'I had Bill.' There was that sob again.

'I'll kill that man if I ever see him,' says Dad. The thought almost makes me laugh, the idea of James and my father at deadlock. They couldn't be more different: Dad, gentle, patient, interested, truthful; and James, well, none of the above.

'I was too ashamed to talk to you about it,' I explain. 'The affair was one thing, but then what happened with Grace...' Even now, I don't feel I have rights to speak her name; I don't deserve to. 'It's like I got myself in too far and I didn't know how to get out again. I'm sorry I stopped calling. Every time we spoke it felt as if I was lying to you, because there was this huge part of my life I kept secret.'

'Did you tell your sisters?'

'No.'

'Not even Tilda?' It's interesting that Dad says this. I always thought that exciting, adventurous Tilda was so far removed from my own nature. But now I see that my father doesn't agree. He has known our similarities since we were girls, and the course my life has taken over the past year proves it.

'Is she back from Barbados?' I ask.

'Obviously not, then,' says Dad. 'Yes, she's been back a while. All three of them have. Well, not permanently, of course, they've got their own lives. Mary and I are enjoying seeing more of them, though. It's nice. Mary cooks a Sunday roast, and most weeks we get at least one of them over. It's since you went away, my sweetheart. Everyone's been so worried, all the messages we've sent and the times we've tried to call. It's brought us together, if nothing else. We love you, Lucy.'

Bill used to tell me that I made things hard for myself. Put a situation in a bad light to make it easier when life went wrong. These people, my family, had never been against me. Any one of them would have supported me, but instead I chose to go it alone. And look how far that had got me, hiding out in another country, and all I yearned for in that instant was to go home and sit around the table for one of Mary's Sunday lunches and listen to them all chatter on about their lives.

'When are you coming home?' Dad asks.

'Soon.'

'When?'

'I can't say right now. But trust me, Dad… Just trust me.'

'I do trust you.'

'Does everyone hate me?' I ask after a moment.

'Everyone? No. We miss you and love you.'

'I mean… You know what I mean.'

My dad takes a second to reply. 'I don't mind what everyone thinks. They don't know you. *I* know you. You're *my* daughter. And I know for a fact that you are a wise, good, kind-hearted thing, and the rest of it matters not a jot.'

*

Immediately after I get off the phone, I go to the window and look out at the hillside. There it is: the Barbarossa. It's like another universe. Max embraces me from behind, kisses my neck. Warmth spreads up from my toes, right to my fingertips, cradling my heart. It's too soon to wonder, too soon to hope. I'm here with Max and I'm happy.

'Spend today with me,' he says, 'before you go back.'

I agree, and Max makes me breakfast, which I eat sitting on his terrace wearing one of his old T-shirts. Afterwards we stroll into the Italian sunshine and the world is renewed, the air crisp and fresh as if I'm stepping into it for the first time. The sun seems brighter, the sky more blue, the voices around me like singing.

We see Florence as I have never seen it before. It's different as a couple, the possibilities multiply, a secret door closed to my single self, of tables for two and shared bowls of pasta, of strolling round museums hand in hand, of licking ice cream on church steps, relaxed in companionable quiet. A city rediscovered, glittering gold.

In future, I will look back at that day as the perfect moment before everything changed. For, by the time Max and I return to his apartment, the sun fading in the pink-streaked sky and the first tentative stars beginning to prick their canopy, we could never have anticipated the revelation that awaited us there.

CHAPTER FORTY-TWO

It would be easy for Vivien Lockhart to close her eyes and never open them again.

She is tired, a tiredness close to death. Her bones are weary, her limbs heavy enough to sink to the bottom of the ocean, her mind thick and cobwebbed...

Adalina enters with her medication. The bottles are lined up on her table, and suddenly Adalina isn't there any more. Vivien blinks, concentrates hard. Yes, there she is; there's the maid, smiling at her, younger today than she has been in a while.

Vivien reaches for her, touches the other woman's arm before her fingertips trip into thin air.

Gone again.

'Adalina...' she whispers. 'Lili.' Nothing. Nobody.

Perhaps the maid will come back later. Perhaps she was never here in the first place. Vivien sighs and rolls over, reaching for her pills. One, two, three, down with water, their hard plastic shells lodging momentarily in her throat before she swallows.

Alfie...

Her son's name swoops into her head.

Don't leave me. Come with me. I'm waiting.

He would catch her. They would be together again.

Vivien rings the bell at the side of her bed, and listens for Adalina's footsteps. She hears none, just the sound of birdsong outside her window, that forbidden world she has not stepped into in decades. And then occasionally she will experience a flash of being in a car, driving or being driven, and the Duomo coming into view like a half-marble left on a beach, glinting in the light. She will see the roads and the lemon groves, and it feels a bit like her old life, in America, playing a part and reading a script, and feeling that rich and intoxicating sense of stepping into another person's shoes, forgetting herself and who she was, embracing another woman for a day.

Adalina isn't coming.

Next to the bell, her fingers touch the card. *Max's aunt says she is sorry. You will know what that means.* Vivien knows. And so, clearly, does the girl.

Vivien lets a thin rasp escape her lips. Finally, it's out, the secret she has kept buried all this time. Guilt? Perhaps. Sorrow? Most definitely. But at the root of it just an immense, hollow sadness, a sadness that has crippled her all these years and now prepares to finish her off. The pills are a temporary measure; she has always known that, and welcomed it, because what does this life still hold for her?

If only she could explain it to him. If she could see her husband one more time and tell him she was sorry; that if it weren't for her selfishness, they might still be living here as a family. Alfie and Gio, her boys, the loves of her life.

Disappeared, just like the rest.

The smell of smoke brings her back to the present, a subtle burn emerging through an open window. She remembers a dropped match, a hungry flame, a bright glow... but she cannot place it. Salvatore must be having a bonfire. It's all he is good for these days, the old habits. She supposes they all are, both are, whatever.

Vivien sits up in bed. The movement steals every ounce of her energy.

The girl knows. She *knows*.

Carefully, Vivien lowers her legs from the bed. She can do it, one last push. She has to. Pulling on her coat, she gathers her strength. It's time.

CHAPTER FORTY-THREE

Vivien, Italy, 1986

'This is it, Lili, *look*.' The next morning, Vivien thrust the box in front of Adalina. 'The ring, the note – they were together: Isabella and her uncle!'

It had taken every ounce of will not to wake the maid in the middle of the night, show her the discovery and share it. She had turned it round and round in the dark, attempting to fathom the impossible truth. Isabella would have been a teenager when they had lived in this house, Giacomo Dinapoli three times her age. Images shot through her mind of Isabella flirting with Gilbert – did the sister possess a weakness for older men? Had she been involved with Dinapoli the whole time? Was this a secret she had kept at all costs from Gio? Vivien soared at the possibility. At last, something Gio didn't know. Surely, he didn't know. He thought he knew everything about his precious, flawless, guileless Isabella... only he didn't know this.

It was a payoff beyond measure – a treasure she could never have hoped for.

But now, instead of the gratifying response she had

expected from Adalina, the maid put a hand over the ring box and looked directly at Vivien.

'What are you going to do?' she asked.

Vivien blinked. 'What do you mean, what am I going to do? You know full well what I'm going to do. And it's perfect now – don't you see? This is as good as a suicide note – we don't even have to forge anything!'

Adalina shook her head. 'There is no "we", signora.'

'Fine, fine, whatever.' She waved a hand. 'It's a gift. It's a get-out.'

Adalina was quiet.

'Lili,' said Vivien, 'I'm sorry I lied about my father. I should have been truthful with you but I hope you can understand why I wasn't.'

'Of course I understand,' said Adalina.

'Then what's the matter?'

The maid released her hold on the ring box, pushing it gently across the counter so that it sat between them, lonely and small.

'Please don't go through with it,' she said.

The wind was snatched from Vivien's sails. 'Excuse me?'

'You cannot. It's wrong. It's evil. It's murder.'

Vivien gritted her teeth. 'I've explained this to you, Lili. I thought you were on my side. It's her or me. Never doubt that. You know what you saw – you know she tried to kill me. She tried to kill *my unborn child*. She made it clear then that whoever acts first wins. This time, it has to be me. I cannot risk my son's life or my own.'

Adalina chose her words carefully.

'I wonder if this changes things,' she said.

'Changes what?' Vivien said sharply.

'Isabella was a victim.' Adalina gestured to the box. 'Giacomo Dinapoli was a man of extremes: he had a fearsome temper and an obsessive insanity. I cannot imagine what he put her through.'

'Then it runs in the family.'

'Please, signora, consider it.'

'I am considering it!' Vivien stormed. 'Isabella has to go – and if you're too weak to help me then I'll manage on my own.'

'How are you going to explain it to your husband?'

'I won't have to. The note says it all.'

'To be faced with her suicide will destroy him.'

'He will still have me.'

'She's his sister,' Adalina countered. 'And if he ever found out, he would leave you. He would take Alfie with him. You would never see either of them again.'

Vivien stumbled, momentarily floored. She thought of Gio's tears, his heartache. No. She had to be strong. *This is for both of us.*

'Gio doesn't know Isabella like I do. He's in denial.'

'What about your father being alive? What will Signor Moretti say when he finds out about that?'

'It's her or me, Lili,' said Vivien viciously. 'And as long as it's her then Gio need never know a thing. She's the only one who'd give me away.'

Adalina lifted her chin. Brave fear brimmed in her eyes. 'Is she?'

Vivien blinked. 'You wouldn't dare,' she said.

'I would and I will,' said Adalina, her voice quaking, 'if you refuse to back down. You cannot harm Signora Isabella. It is an unforgivable route and I'm sorry that I entertained it even for a moment. I demand that you abandon it this instant.'

Vivien laughed. 'You cannot demand anything of me.'

'It will only lead to disaster.'

'What would you know about disaster? Isabella Moretti is a walking disaster and I cannot allow her to threaten me any longer. Or you, for that matter!'

'Will you murder me as well?'

Vivien gripped the side of the counter. 'You betray me, Lili. I thought you were my friend.'

'I am your friend and this is my way of protecting you. What happened on the stairs... the fall... It was a long time ago. Is it possible that she's changed?'

Vivien couldn't believe her ears. 'She's got you fooled, too, has she?'

'That girl has suffered,' said the maid, 'more terribly than we know. She's a victim. She was Dinapoli's prey. Don't make her yours, too. You must forsake this reckless plan. You alone should be the one to tell your husband about Gilbert, not me and not Salve and certainly not Isabella. You cannot run any more. This is where it ends. Here. Now. In deciding you forgive.'

'I will never forgive what she's done.'

'You'll never forgive yourself if you go through with it.'

'At least I'll be alive to consider it!'

'Do you really think she would hurt Alfie? She loves that boy.'

'Ha! She wouldn't know love for anyone but Gio if it hit her in the face.'

'She adores your son. I've seen her with him – so gentle, so patient.'

'Lili, you've lost your mind.'

'I haven't. It's you who is not thinking clearly.'

Vivien's mouth dried, her arguments like bullets firing into nothing. She felt her ammunition running low, grasping for a refill and finding none. This was meant to be the beginning of the end for Isabella, the perfect storm. What was happening?

'Isabella has more in common with you than you realise,' Adalina said, as she prepared to deliver the last blast in her arsenal. 'You've both been terrorised by men. You've both been crushed. You've both been hurt and beaten and damaged. You've both done things to survive and you've both got scars to prove it. What happened to solidarity? To compassion? Read that note again, Vivien.' She held up Isabella's plea. *Help me. Save me. I beg you.* 'Read it and tell me you feel nothing. That you've never wished for the same. Isabella must have been a similar age to you, when you ran away from home. A despairing girl, fighting for her life – just like you. I wonder whether she hid from him, as you hid from your father. I wonder whether she barricaded her door. I wonder whether she wept at his feet and begged him silently to stop. I wonder whether she dreamed of escaping, but never found the resources to do it.'

Vivien was stunned. For the first time since her discovery in the fish's mouth – since Gilbert's arrival, truthfully – she stopped. She stopped thinking at a thousand miles an hour, plots forming and shifting and growing and changing, never once pausing to measure what it meant, or what had developed. Astonished at the potency of Adalina's spirit, a potency she would never have attributed to the mild-mannered maid, a leak started to appear, a fissure in her resolve, a crack that melted and spread.

But I hate her. I hate her.

Vivien's shoulders sagged. The battle seeped out of her.

'Oh, Lili.' She brought her hand to her face. 'I'm tired of fighting.'

The maid came round to hold her shoulders, and when Vivien started to weep she held her close. 'It's all right, signora…' She rubbed her back. 'It will be all right.'

'Will it?'

Adalina pulled back. She forced Vivien to look at her.

'Do you trust me?' she said.

Vivien nodded.

'Then give it to me.'

Vivien hesitated, but knew she would. She reached into her robe and collected the toxic vial. She handed it to Adalina, who closed it in her fist.

'This is the right thing,' said Adalina. 'No harm will come to you. I swear it.'

*

Vivien paced between the walls of the Oval. Conversations whirled in her head – with Lili, with Gilbert, the many fights she'd had with Gio. *Gio*. She pictured kissing him in their early days, his wild hair and his soft mouth – how would she account for her father? How could she defend her invention? She could see no way out – no way that he would ever be able to trust her again. Yes, Isabella had ruined so much of their love – but Vivien herself had sabotaged it right from the start. Right from when she told him that her parents were dead. When Gio had later confided his loss, she should have come clean. She'd had so many opportunities to do the right thing and she had failed. Why did she always fail? Why did everything she touched rot and die?

The leaves whispered. *She's done it now. Silly girl. Stupid girl.*

The thought of Gilbert inside the Barbarossa chilled her. At breakfast that morning he had torn into croissants, sloshed out juice, slathered butter on toast. She could not stand to look at him, hating him more with every second.

Desperately, she implored the sky.

So you're the God that brought him back to me, are you? How could you? How could you do this to me? Clouds drifted. The sky returned her gaze, blankly.

At first, the voice seemed to come out of the blue. Then she turned, startled.

'I'll say it was me.'

Isabella was standing at the entrance to the garden, beneath a delicate golden arbour. Her hair was braided prettily around her crown, like *The Lady of Shalott*; she wore no make-up. She appeared young, adolescent, almost innocent. Almost.

'What did you say?' Vivien's voice shook.

The sister repeated: 'I'll tell Gio it was me. It was my fault.'

Vivien stepped back, frightened. She didn't know what Isabella was talking about. All she knew was that she was vulnerable, here alone, a sitting target.

'I'll say I convinced you to keep him secret,' Isabella said. Her expression gave little away. Her almond eyes were black. 'I'll say that you were ready to tell Gio that your father was alive – it was just a lie you told because you loved him – but I persuaded you otherwise. I told you it would hurt him. You wanted to give the truth but I was the one who stopped you.'

The women stood opposite each other, tentative as wolves.

'Why would you do that?' said Vivien hollowly.

Isabella was the first to move. She went to one of the benches and sat.

'Because I'm sorry,' she said, hands clasped in her lap.

Vivien's own hands were unsteady. Had she heard right?

'I know what I've done to your life,' Isabella said. 'It's been deliberate, I admit. I was jealous. I have been from the beginning. I hate how much my brother loves you. He loves you more than he loves me and I couldn't – I can't – bear it.'

Vivien tried to slow her rival's words, welcome each one as the sweet, sweet victory it was. How she had longed to hear Isabella confess! How she had longed to hear her grovel! Could it be happening? Was Isabella really sitting before her, ashamed, regretful, desperate to make amends? She couldn't believe it.

'He always loved me most,' said Isabella, 'and it was the only love I knew. Until you, Vivien, there were women, but I always knew he put me first. But when you came along, he didn't love me in the same way any more. I came second. And why shouldn't I? I'm only his sister. But if I didn't have him, I didn't have anything.'

Vivien wanted her to say it all again. Say it when Gio was here.

'I know about you and Dinapoli,' Vivien said, on impulse.

Isabella's eyes snapped up.

'I found the ring box.'

Isabella was silent, as she had been so many times. Vivien questioned if that whole mute saga had been a ruse, a convenience to avoid interaction with strangers, Isabella's way of coping with what had befallen her under Giacomo Dinapoli's reign. Vivien knew all too well how a man could pinch out every shred of light and hope.

'I don't know what you're talking about,' said Isabella, but there wasn't any conviction in it. It was a token denial, an obligatory pretence. Empty.

'I know what your uncle did to you,' said Vivien, and she was surprised at her own soft tone, the sympathy that emerged despite her better judgement.

Isabella glanced away. The beautiful victim.

'You don't have to pretend any more,' said Vivien. And when Isabella met her eye this time, it was a new Isabella.

The guard was down; the insolence, the resentment, the mist of antipathy evaporated, and with amazement and no small degree of gladness Vivien realised that Gio, too, had been deceived. Gio had no clue about this part of her life. Isabella faked with him as much as with everyone else.

Vivien was the only person who had her true confidence. And Isabella, in turn, had hers. Isabella, who knew about the secret she had kept from Gio – moreover, the reasons she'd done it – and was prepared to stand with her shoulder to shoulder.

It didn't seem real.

'Will you tell my brother about Giacomo?' Isabella choked.

Vivien set her jaw. 'Will you tell him about Gilbert?'

Isabella shook her head.

'No, then,' said Vivien. 'I won't.'

Seconds passed where the women assessed one another.

Then, as if they had been friends their whole lives instead of enemies, Isabella told her story. She told Vivien about the boat on which her mother and father had died. She told about being sent to the Barbarossa to live under Giacomo Dinapoli's care. She told about how Gio was the only sane thing in her life during those years, and how she had protected the purity and clarity of that love by refusing to confide in him when their uncle's attacks started happening. Vivien heard how, beneath the guise of finding Isabella a cure, Dinapoli had instead spent his days grooming his niece into slavery. All those hours in which Gio had imagined them to be working on restoring his sister's voice, Dinapoli had been up in that attic silencing her. Oh, he had silenced her. He had silenced her with his hand, with his fist, with parts of his body that Vivien didn't need to be told about. He had silenced her for years and years beyond his welcome death, for Isabella had never felt able to speak about it until now. She had never felt able to speak at all. Silence became her only power.

'He loved me,' Isabella said, 'in his way. He imagined that it was real between us. He thought that I wanted him… but I didn't. And I decided that I deserved it. He told me I deserved it. It was my punishment for letting my parents die.'

Vivien went to object, but Isabella got there first.

'I know. Gio didn't let them die, either – it wasn't his fault. I've tried to tell him, but he won't listen. Then I'm guilty for making him feel as if he can't leave. And the worst part is that he can't,' Isabella searched her face, 'because I couldn't cope, Vivien, I couldn't. There it is, the awful truth: I would fall apart. And I fought for my brother in the only way I knew – by trying to remind him of what we meant to each other, us against the world, like it had been for so long. I didn't think of you. I didn't care, pulling stunts like wrecking your wedding dress, which I know was mean and I'd say sorry until next year if I thought it would make a difference, and all the times I tried to upstage you with the staff and at those parties, it was pathetic. I didn't think of him either, of what was good for him and what made him happy – I thought only of myself. Because what makes him happy is *you*, Vivien. You always have. I can't compete with that. You're his wife. He chose you. He never chose me: I was a given.'

Vivien swallowed the ball of wire in her chest.

'Did you try to hurt me,' she asked, 'that day on the stairs?'

All else was spite, emotionally but not physically harmful. This was the one thing she could not move past – not until it was answered.

'I think so,' said Isabella thickly. 'I'd remembered the ring box that morning, remembered that note I'd scribbled the night he first raped me. I'd got rid of it years ago, stuffing it as far down that ugly fish's throat as I could, but it didn't drown the pain and it didn't make me forget. I went mad. I didn't think about the consequences – all I knew was that Gio was about to have a family with you and then I'd be frozen out completely. I'm sorry, Vivien. I don't deserve your pardon, but I'm hoping for your tolerance. It was a treacherous move born of loneliness, and I've regretted it ever since. I've wanted to apologise so many times but I've never known how, and everything I've said or done comes out wrong, when I only mean to make amends.'

'You left me there for hours,' said Vivien, 'at the bottom of the stairs.'

Isabella shook her head. 'I didn't. As soon as you fell, I realised what I'd done and I couldn't bear it. I ran to Salvatore right away and he tried to get hold of Gio but Gio was in meetings and that was the reason for the delay.'

It wasn't possible…

Was it?

Vivien battled her judgement. What if Gio had been right? What if Isabella had meant well by commissioning that portrait, and had simply judged it wrong? What if her welcoming Gilbert now was an attempt at reconciliation, not antipathy? What if the glares and scowls had been shame, misread by Vivien's fixation?

In a gesture that would have been unthinkable a year ago, Isabella took Vivien's hand. It was only a second before she released it, unable to help her impulse towards intimacy but ultimately unable to sustain it. Was Isabella telling the truth? Could she be a more complicated antagonist than the one-dimensional threat Vivien had taken her for? Yes, Gio had vowed that his sister was broken – but he didn't know the half of it. Their parents' deaths were so removed from Vivien's personal experience; the episode was too grotesque, too alien, and as a result became something better suited to a fictional drama, the kind of soap opera Millicent might have watched at the wives' houses in Claremont because Gilbert hadn't permitted a television. But the idea that Isabella had been cajoled, abused, whichever word one called it, by a man in a position of power, chimed horrifyingly true. A swift shot of empathy towards Isabella, her most hated adversary, wound its way beneath her skin.

'Please believe me, Vivien,' said Isabella. 'Now I know Alfie, I would never, ever put him in danger. I love him. I would never harm him.'

'And me?' said Vivien. 'Would you harm me?'

Isabella shook her head. 'Those days are over. It's you and me now, Vivien. We're sisters.'

CHAPTER FORTY-FOUR

Vivien, Italy, 1987

The seasons passed and there was movement in the earth. The tides shifted, the axis tilted, and the sands that Vivien had been standing on these past years dissolved beneath her feet. For weeks she treaded water in that open sky, with a mixture of apprehension and excitement, before at last she discovered her wings.

Following her conversation with Isabella, everything changed – more significantly than Vivien could have dreamed. The Barbarossa, for the first time, became a family home. After Gio returned from his trip, he was a different man. No, that wasn't right: he was the same man, the man Vivien had met in a long-ago hospital suite, the man she had first fallen in love with. He took news of Gilbert courageously, listening as the women delivered their explanation, through shock then confusion then comprehension. 'He was as good as gone to her anyway,' said Isabella faithfully. 'She only tried to do what was right.' Vivien suspected Gio's amnesty stemmed more from the newfound truce between his wife and sister than any pardon he was prepared to give: he had yearned for it, and it put all else in the shade. She should never have lied, but Isabella should never, by her account, have discouraged a confession. Gio didn't know which to blame, if indeed he should blame either.

'What happened,' asked Gio, amazed at the women's reconciliation, 'for you to change your mind?' Vivien told him that she and Isabella had called a ceasefire, simply that it was time 'to let bygones be bygones'. Gio didn't question it further. As far as he was concerned, females were cryptic creatures and their alliances could form and dissolve on the slightest wind. It had happened, and that was what mattered.

Vivien was thrilled at the change in her husband. She realised what a strain her abhorrence of Isabella had put on their marriage, and saw now that it wasn't so much Isabella herself that had been the sticking point as it was Vivien's reaction to her. *Why did I let her torment me?* Vivien pondered. *She's just a person – after all, just a person.* Each time Vivien looked at her sister-in-law, she felt a stab of rage towards Giacomo Dinapoli. She wished she could rain down her hatred upon him, representing as he did every man who had taken advantage of an innocent woman. Her bond with Isabella was separate to Gio; they were both privy to electrifying truths that he would never know about. Maybe this was and always had been key.

When Vivien thought how close she had come to…

No. Hate had driven her mad, had almost driven her to that most wanton, despicable act… Thank goodness Adalina had talked her out of it.

Alfie turned two, and blossomed by the day. He blurted

funny nonsense whenever Vivien was around, holding his fat arms out for a hug, and, at night, as she held him, she asked herself if she had ever seen anything so perfect and beautiful in her life. He was her eternal wonder. Now that she had made peace with Isabella, she began to allow Alfie to go to his aunt. It was a slow process and Isabella was careful not to take liberties, but once Alfie had spent an hour, then two, then three, then a whole afternoon, in her company, it was clear he worshipped her. Isabella was tender with him; she treated him as fondly as she would her own. Vivien looked on with astonishment and pleasure. The old Isabella seemed entirely vanished – that harsh, cold version so at odds with the warmth of her new incarnation. Gio volunteered that Alfie could soften anyone, and Vivien was inclined to agree.

But the most fundamental change was in Gilbert. That, in a way, was the biggest surprise of all. Vivien hadn't intended for her father to stay – she would never have envisaged given all eternity that they would find resolution. Even now, a year after he had first rung on her door, Vivien would find herself looking in the mirror and shaking her head at the bizarre nature of it all. To think how far she'd come. She had moved from having no one to having them all – a husband, a sister, a father. Family, friendship and trust: that exotic, elusive triumvirate she had spent all her life pursuing.

By the time Gio came back from his trip, father and daughter had already set out on the path to reconciliation. Vivien's U-turn with Isabella made her believe in the impossible, that people could be misunderstood – or, failing that, could change. Adalina confirmed what a reformed man Gilbert seemed, and encouraged her to see past the religious fervour to the regretful heart beneath. At first Vivien reviled him, and wrestled her revulsion. 'I'm not like I used to be,' Gilbert said, over and over, and she replied, 'Words mean nothing, I've heard too many lies from you.' She battled his act, because surely it was an act, a game designed to trip her into taking him back. Vivien wasn't ready, so she watched, she waited, and she expected him to fail.

He didn't. With each sun that rose and fell, Gilbert continued to toil, clawing his way back into her favour with tireless love and devotion that her mind told her to repel but her soul found hard to resist. He transpired to be an attentive grandfather to Alfie, spending time with him, playing with him, gentle and kind, and it wounded Vivien in a painful, deeply buried place – a place that still desired, in spite of the years, to be a child cared for and fussed over by her father. She loathed what he had done, but she still craved his affection and his approval, and wished they could go back to Claremont and do it differently. Seeing that love lavished on Alfie was impossible to dismiss. Seeing how happy her son was with him, the way his little face lit up the moment Gilbert came into the room, promising to read him a story, to help him build a tower, to take him to plant his vegetable seeds, slowly, drop by drop, a chamber at a time, her heart began to thaw. This was a side to her father that she had never seen. 'I wasn't like this, then,' he explained. 'God has shown me a better way. I wasn't fair to you or Millicent – but God forgives, and in time I've forgiven myself.'

After a cool reception, Gio, too, fell under her father's spell. He watched Gilbert's devotion to Alfie – the only grandparent the boy would have – and how every minute of the day he was attempting to make peace with his daughter. 'You can't fault his resolve,' said Gio. 'He's found his second chance and he's taking it.'

That was the clincher – if her husband accepted him, surely Vivien could learn to. She had never considered pardoning her father. But seeing him with Alfie, her past and future tied together, offered her a rebirth she knew would come around only once. After years of hurt, this was her chance to make things right. She would never forget the wounds he had inflicted on her and the injustices she had suffered at his hands, but perhaps she could move past them, if not for herself then for her baby.

As the weeks and months rolled on, Vivien's resistance wore her out. She felt she was swimming against a tide so strong and inevitable that eventually it would engulf her, and to go with it would carry her to the pleasure island on which everyone else seemed to have washed up. Revelation followed revelation and her astonishment grew, until the day arrived that she left the house for a city visit and on impulse she hugged her father goodbye. She hadn't even done that when she was a girl.

'Darling,' said Gilbert, his eyes pricked by tears. 'You won't regret this.'

For a while, the five of them existed in comfortable kinship, and whenever Vivien took a step back and analysed it all as the queerest of outcomes, she saw how good it was for her son: Isabella, his loving aunt; and Gilbert, his caring grandfather. It was so much better for him to have people around, and what was more to have parents who were no longer adversaries. As Vivien released her paranoia, or rather it released her, she started to cherish every moment of the day. 'We feel like us,' Gio said to her, as they strolled through the gardens at dusk. 'We feel like us again, Viv.'

She should have known it was too good to be true. That life didn't work that way – it wasn't a romance, it wasn't one of her movies, it wasn't happy ever after.

Hadn't she learned as much? Hadn't she learned anything?

For, as winter drew in, draping the Barbarossa in freezing mists and thick black shadows, a menace descended. Vivien felt the chill approach like a living thing, the cypress trees outside her window dipped in white, like paintbrushes obscured in water. She woke on edge several mornings in a row, having dreamed she was being chased through an emerald forest, but when she turned there was nobody there, just an echo of her persecutor, like a footprint washed away by the tide.

*

On the day it happened, Gio's voice woke her. He had taken Alfie downstairs to enable her to lie in, and now her eyes snapped open with the sound of his shout.

As ever, when her baby was out of the room, Vivien leaped to action, dashing down in her nightdress. 'What is it?' she demanded, when she met him in the hall. 'Where's Alfie? What is it – is he OK?'

She could already see that he was, nestled in Gio's arms. But Gio wore an expression of dread, his face ashen. 'It's Gilbert,' he said. 'He's gone.'

Vivien's mouth went dry.

'What do you mean, he's gone?'

'He's left. With everything.'

Vivien reached out to hold on to something, but there was only empty space. A series of images rushed through her mind: of Gilbert with Alfie, of the embrace she'd given him that day she left, of his smile and his promises, his kindness…

Of the way he'd clasped her hand when he arrived.

Too hard. Too tight. *Vivien, my child – let me in.*

She already knew. How could she not? All along, that latent suspicion that never quite went away. That little worm-head that burrowed into her conscience and asked: *Is this really happening? Shouldn't you know better than this?*

'He's taken the contents of the safe,' said Gio. His eyes flashed, one green, one black. Alfie began to cry. 'All that money, Viv, it's gone with him.'

Vivien ought to be shocked, or at least appear shocked; she owed her husband that. But now the outcome was here, in all its grisly, depressing predictability, she could not feign surprise. She remembered her father's shoes when he had turned up on the doorstep. Of course he had robbed them. He had inveigled his way into their lives and hearts and taken full advantage of their trust. The safe had contained all of Gio's savings through his work; everything they had set aside for Alfie's future; Gio's mother's pearls, and his father's wristwatch. It was sentiment as well as fortune.

'Gio, I...'

'It's all gone.'

'I'll find him.'

'How?' Gio spat his words. 'That twisted, evil *bastard*! I'll kill him, I'll—'

Vivien took the baby while Gio reassembled himself. The hallway spun, that godforsaken portrait of her father dancing in her vision. How could she have been so senseless? She should never have believed his lies, never! She should have trusted her instincts and turned him away, bolting the door behind him. Her weakness had failed her, her readiness, her *need* to trust. Gilbert's treachery was wicked, as impossible as it was inescapable. 'How could he?' she forced out. 'Gio, I'm sorry. I'm so sorry.'

Gio had his palms on the wall, his head hung between his arms.

'How did he unlock it?' he rasped. 'How did he get the code?'

Vivien went to say that she did not know. Then a fleeting idea occurred to her, just a glimmer of a shadow of one, an idea she might once have had but she'd learned better since then. Duly, she quashed it. 'I've no idea,' she said.

'He must have known to look inside the portrait.' Gio turned to her. 'I move the code every six months. Its latest place was sewn into the back of your picture.'

How ironic: the image of Vivien and her father together.

'Does anyone else know where you hid it?' she asked.

A flicker crossed Gio's features – or had she imagined it? 'No,' he said.

He sank down the wall and put his head in his hands. 'Viv, we've lost so much. Everything was in there: our savings, our *life*.'

She could scarcely fathom it. 'I was a fool,' she said.

'It was Alfie's,' Gio said emptily. 'All of it was for Alfie.'

'Then we'll make more for Alfie,' she spluttered. 'Gio, there are ways.' Already she was grasping at unlikely straws – she'd go back to Hollywood, she'd find work there, they couldn't have forgotten about her completely; there'd be a way in...

In the hall, they held each other, Vivien and Gio and their baby in between. Tears flowed and hands held. At least they had each other.

From the shadows, Isabella saw it all. She watched for a while, interested, like somebody studying ants in a jar, before she turned and disappeared into the dark.

CHAPTER FORTY-FIVE

Italy, Summer 2016

We stop at the market on the way back to Max's to pick up spaghetti, wine and seafood – apparently he's going to make me the best *marinara* I've ever tasted. The moonlit streets carry us along. I'm so content that passages of time go unchecked – the walk from the river back into the city, the stroll hand in hand that we take across the piazza – as if I am being transported from one instant to the next, so wrapped up in conversation and the warm glow of our union that the real world ceases to exist.

I guess I'm still in this frame of mind when we first see her, so it takes a moment to rationalise that she's not a stranger loitering on a street corner; she is known to us, more, she is waiting for us. She is dressed heavily, a long dark coat with a collar, so that it's difficult to see her face clearly. Yet, I would know it anywhere.

'It's Adalina,' I say. The bubble containing our day is pricked.

'Are you sure?' Max stops. 'It looks like…'

'It's definitely her. I'll handle it.' Max goes to take my

hand but I'm too quick. I'm done with running. I'll deal with this head-on, I have nothing to hide.

'Adalina,' I say, 'what are you doing here?'

Adalina's eyes regard me warily from the shadows. She spies Max and takes a step back into the gloom, not wanting to be seen. Who can blame her? Max and his family have a past with that house – a serious, murderous past. Adalina and Vivien aren't yet aware of our intentions to exclude the police. For all they know, we could already have informed them, armed guards marching their way to the castillo.

'I must speak to you,' Adalina says. 'It's urgent.'

'If it's about my resignation, I won't reconsider.'

Adalina meets my eye. 'I wouldn't expect you to.' Her gaze keeps flitting to Max, as if she's worried that he will see her.

I get straight to the point. 'Vivien's secret is safe with us,' I say gently. Her eyes dart to mine, but I cannot read what they contain. Is it fear, gratitude? It's sadness: definitely sadness. 'We're not going to tell anyone. Who are we to judge what happened all those years ago? We weren't there. We didn't know Isabella.'

'Isabella died.' It is as if Adalina hasn't spoken her name in decades – maybe she hasn't. The name chokes out like a rusted key spat from a lock.

'We know,' I say.

As Adalina opens her mouth to continue, I fill in the blanks for her.

'We know what Vivien did. We know that she...' I can't

say the word, 'made her disappear. It was the fountain, wasn't it? That was where she drowned her.'

Adalina blinks, frowns, blinks again. 'No,' she says. 'That isn't right.'

I've thought of it so many times – two women carrying a drugged bundle wrapped in a sheet, one at the head and one at the feet, the moon high and wide in a black sky, their breath emerging in the cold air in gusts of white steam – that it's been accepted as fact. These aren't images I've fabricated: they're really what happened.

'It isn't?'

Adalina shakes her head. She takes my arm and tries to move me away.

'I need your help,' she says. 'I will tell you everything in return for your help.'

I think of her mistress back at the Barbarossa, slowly dying.

'Is it Vivien?' I ask.

Adalina throws one last glance at Max.

'It's always Vivien,' she says.

CHAPTER FORTY-SIX

Vivien, Italy, 1988

In the year following Gilbert Lockhart's departure, Isabella was kinder to them than ever. She was there for Vivien to talk to, nodding gently and listening as Vivien raged about the man who had done her wrong; generously she covered any practical aspects of the daily running of the house whenever Lili was indisposed; selflessly she offered to contribute what paltry sum she had saved in an account, which of course they refused; and willingly she cared for Alfie while Vivien sought to make inroads in her career, which was the only way she could fathom of earning back the funds they had lost. Vivien romanticised about reigniting her fame, of being a star again, of winning back what they had lost ten times over so that when Gilbert came calling for more she would hold a loaded pistol to his head and gleefully fire the trigger.

It wasn't going to be easy, however. Dandy Michaels was in retirement and wouldn't give her the time of day. 'The industry's moved on, Viv,' he told her over a bad line. 'I don't see a place for you any more. It's big tits and big hair these days.' *I can do big tits and big hair*, she thought. *I can do anything.* She hung up from Dandy and immediately got on the phone to a host of other talent agents, most of whom were too young to remember how bright her star had once burned. 'Ah, Vivien Lockhart, right…' some assistant would singsong, promising that their senior would ring back.

'Don't be disheartened,' encouraged Isabella, helping her to unearth her old contacts, calling distant sun-drenched offices and leaving messages that somehow, unlike Vivien's, managed to sound intriguing rather than begging. Vivien couldn't eradicate that note of begging from her own voice. She was desperate, and it showed.

Occasionally she bought a batch of imported celebrity magazines – a torture and a luxury – from a newsagent's in the city, to check up on her circus of Hollywood acquaintances. When she'd first left, Vivien had figured in a snapshot here, a rumour there, but over time that had gradually dwindled to obscurity. Last month, one article described her as a 'forgotten face', a label that had stayed with her, niggling at her when she least expected it, getting ready for bed at night or walking alone in the gardens during the day. By the time she left LA, she had convinced herself she hated it, she was over it… but to be a *forgotten face*? Was that all her efforts amounted to?

The grit with which Vivien attacked this revival project was reminiscent of her early days, powering through her struggle with Jonny Laing and all that followed. It struck her that only her father could light this fire within her, the flames of indignation, the *need* to triumph, and never fall victim to him again.

But where was Gilbert?

The authorities brought up nothing. What little money Vivien had left she gambled on a private detective, to no avail. He was the best in the business but Gilbert had left no trace. 'In all my thirty years doing this job,' said her guy, 'I've never come across an absconder like this.' Had Gilbert changed his name? Vivien queried. Had surgery, altered his appearance? She was only half being serious but the detective nodded. 'Undoubtedly,' he replied. 'And that isn't normally a problem. But I'm searching for any ends here and I'm coming up short. I'm sorry.' To his credit, he returned her money. If only he could have returned her sonofabitch father.

Gio stroked her hair in bed. 'We'll get through this,' he told her, kissing her, and, as she lay with him, their baby in his little bed next door, she felt her rage momentarily subside because at least she had them, her family, and all the riches in the world couldn't buy Gilbert that. He was the poorest man she knew.

*

If Vivien had told her former self that one day she would like Isabella, be *thankful* for her, she would have laughed herself out of town. As it was, the sister was a support not just to Vivien but also to Gio, taking care of matters discreetly and without needing to be praised, oiling the cogs of their marriage and enabling them to work to their best capacity as parents. Tempers were fraught and moods were unpredictable. Isabella acted as a necessary mediator and Vivien was grateful. She thought back to the day Adalina had changed her mind, dismantling Vivien's emotion and forcing her to see Isabella as the casualty she was. If she hadn't, Isabella wouldn't be here at all.

It was dreadful to remember how close she had got to that wicked act. If Adalina hadn't been so strong in her persuasion, Isabella would be in the ground.

Just one thing niggled Vivien. She had never asked Isabella about the note she had found: *I want him*. Upon mentioning it to Lili, the maid had shrugged and said, 'A man at Signor Moretti's work?' It had occurred to her before: Isabella was lonely; it was probable that she had fallen for someone during her trips with Gio and the feeling was unrequited. The note was odd, yes, but Isabella was the first to admit that her behaviour had hardly been normal. To bring it up would only embarrass her further.

Especially after the conversation Vivien had shared with Gio a week before:

'Do you think Isabella will ever have kids? She's so good with Alfie.'

Gio had been reading the paper. He glanced up briefly, paused, seemed to think twice about what he was readying to say, then answered: 'She can't.'

'She can't?'

'No. We don't know why. She was told when she was twenty. She's unable.'

Vivien's mouth parted in surprise. Gio's firm tone signalled that he did not wish to discuss it, and that was fortunate because she'd been on the cusp of blurting something out about Dinapoli – because that was it, surely? The awful things Dinapoli had done to Isabella had left her barren. As if his abuse hadn't been enough!

Once more, sympathy flooded through her. So much made sense about Isabella now. She had been dealt more blows than anyone could take.

It also went some of the way to explaining the strange possessions Vivien had stumbled across in Isabella's bedroom. On Friday morning, she had gone up to the attic to ask if Isabella might watch Alfie for an hour while she went to the bank and begged another loan. Isabella wasn't there, but the door was ajar, and through it Vivien spied a collection of toys: a rocking horse, a carousel and a cotton army of soldiers. Of course, she had been playing up here with Alfie. Perhaps she had procured the toys without Vivien knowing – Vivien certainly hadn't seen her son with them before. Or maybe Isabella had them already, because who knew what went through the mind of a woman who had been ruined like that? Vivien was in no position to judge.

In the weeks and months to come, in the long and lonely years until her death, Vivien would gaze back on these flags as the universe's red warning. They weren't even subtle hints; they were full-on alarms. How could she have missed them?

I want him.

Him. But not a man at all…

A boy. A child.

If she had followed just one of them up, she might have

been able to prevent the horror. But perhaps she hadn't wanted to see what was right in front of her.

Perhaps, after trusting and being betrayed by her father, she could not endure it again. Perhaps she could not acknowledge any more drama, and guarded her family from it with everything she had – even ignorance. Perhaps she was afraid.

Then again it took guts to remember the events leading up to that night, and she had done that enough times, so she couldn't be a coward. She had to be strong.

If only…

How she would come to hate those two words. How they would come to define her every waking thought, and every sleeping terror. If only she had protected her mistrust of that woman. If only she had nurtured it and let it grow. If only she had ignored Adalina and seen her plan through. If only she had refused to believe the deceits – or believe them but not let them touch her, because making somebody the victim did not make that person immune from becoming the perpetrator.

And then the incidentals: if only she had gone away with Alfie that night (but who was to say it wouldn't have happened the next night, or the night after?); if only she had taken her baby into her bed; if only she had held him in her arms and kissed his sweet head over and over, just one more time, oh, she would give her life just to kiss him one more time. In her blackest hours, if only he hadn't been born – for then the wild weed of her pain could have been annihilated at its root.

CHAPTER FORTY-SEVEN

The hour came. A Sunday. Vivien went to bed early, shortly after her son. She fell asleep instantly and it seemed only a second before she was woken again, scrambling to consult the time, midnight, and in the fever of having been roused from a deep yet unaccountably troubled sleep, patting the sheets beside her for the baby she must have fallen asleep with and buried beneath the covers – a frequent trick of the mind.

What had woken her? A shout. A man's shout. It came again.

She didn't recognise it. Awful. Not that she didn't recognise the person making it – Salvatore, who else? – but the bite of terror that accompanied it she had never heard before. She couldn't decipher what he was saying, just this urgent pitch, horribly, horribly urgent, fearful, a man who has shed all protocol, and in Salvatore's case that was unheard of, all etiquette, to show the whites of his bones, the skeleton of his fright. It was an animal cry, a wolf in the mountains. *Danger, danger!*

She knew before she knew. The instant her feet hit that floor and she started running, she knew. She didn't even have to go into his bedroom to see his empty cot, or his open door: she knew. A sound emerged from her as she flew down the stairs and into the night, black night shuddering through her, or she through it, and it came from a place so grim and yawning that it seemed to carry all her blood and breath along with it, and she supposed that everyone had this place inside them but it was only a few, only a damned few, who ever got to discover it was there.

The fountain. Salve. The body in his arms, wetly asleep, a dripping boy, his ankles crossed, and she ran for him, calling his name, but he couldn't hear her.

CHAPTER FORTY-EIGHT

Italy, Summer 2016

I expect us to return to the Barbarossa, but we don't. Instead Adalina takes me to an old church on the Piazza Maria, a modest peach and white building, set in its own courtyard. Inside, it's cool and empty, the pews deserted. A crucifixion hangs at the altar, Christ's feet crossed and nailed, his head bowed. Prayer candles flicker.

'I often come,' says Adalina, 'to pray for them.'

We sit together. It's cold. I want to be back in Max's apartment, curled up on his sofa, watching him cook. Adalina appears older in this light, not quite herself. She doesn't look well. Against the backdrop of the Barbarossa, she exudes a certain authority, but here she looks tired and ill, more like how I imagine Vivien.

'Pray for whom?' I ask. It's as good a place to start as any.

'My son,' she says. She looks hopefully at me, as if she's waiting for me to grasp something so that she doesn't have to say it. 'And Isabella.'

'Adalina, what happened to Isabella?'

'She killed herself. Vivien didn't kill her.'

'Max's aunt…?'

Adalina shakes her head. 'No. Never. Lili wasn't like that. She was a gentle woman – a best friend. The only true friend the Barbarossa had.'

'Why?' Isabella: bright, vibrant, damaged, hopeless. 'Why did she do it?'

'You were right about the fountain,' says Adalina. 'Isabella weighed herself down and stepped into it, and she waited…' Adalina's features flicker in the light, focused as if trying to conjure the finest detail in her memory, as if that might answer the myriad questions to which she was yet to find adequate response. 'She must have been so patient, just letting the breath run out of her. She must have wanted to die *so much*, to have that will… to override every signal in her body telling her to surface.'

I close my eyes. 'It was in the middle of the night, wasn't it?'

I don't need to open them to know that I'm right. Twelve minutes past three in the morning. All those times I awoke at the Barbarossa, unsure what had roused me. The figure in white by the fountain… The phantom in my bedroom… The noises in the attic…

'Salvatore found her,' Adalina goes on. 'It was the final trauma. He was never the same after that.'

I cannot look at her. Instead, I watch the crucifix. I am not religious and yet in moments of crisis and uncertainty, there is comfort in this presence, constant and true, in reassurance that sinners have come and gone and all is judged at the final hour.

'But Vivien kept him on?'

'He was too unreliable to let go. And, I suppose... she felt sorry for him.'

That was it, then. That was the 'accident' that the papers had cited. That was why Gio had run from his marriage. It all made sense now. Isabella was more broken than anyone could have anticipated. Nothing could have stopped her – the Morettis' deaths, the abuse at Dinapoli's hands, her brother leaving her behind...

But that's not all.

'What did Max's aunt have to apologise for?'

Adalina exhales. She clasps her hands together in her lap, old hands, fragile hands, but the nails are perfect, glamorous even, long and shaped and pearlescent. I have never noticed before. They do not look like the hands of a maid.

'She didn't, really,' she says. 'It wasn't her fault.'

'What wasn't?' I wait. 'Adalina...?'

At last, she meets my eye.

'Isabella killed herself because she could not live any longer. She could not live with her guilt. It ate her up and so she had to follow him into that watery grave.'

I try to join the dots. 'Her father?' I think of his drowning, her mother too. 'She had to follow her parents?'

Adalina shakes her head as if to say, *I wish that were it. I wish that were true.*

She speaks in a whisper. 'Isabella had to follow Alfonso.'

Alfie. Vivien's son. A horrid sensation gathers in the pit of my stomach.

'She drowned him.'

Those three words, emerging from Adalina's lips, sound

like another language. There is such pain in them, such awful, irrepressible pain, the kind of pain that lasts a lifetime and beyond, the kind of pain that can never be dulled, never be dimmed; it exists in its own black sphere beyond the realm of our comprehension.

'She took him from his bed and she drowned him. He was three years old.' Adalina sobs, one harsh sob, alive with grief, then a series of silent ones that shake her whole body. 'Such was her hatred for our family. You'd think she would have spared him for Gio's sake alone, but no. That innocent boy, my world, my love – that poor, innocent child at the beginning of his precious life… Oh, Alfie, darling Alfie…'

The dots join. The picture is revealed.

I take Vivien's hand.

'He was your son, wasn't he?' I say.

She squeezes my fingers; there is no need for words. Adalina never existed – at least not in the here and now. She existed once, as Max's aunt and Vivien's maid, and when she died Vivien sought to replace her. She couldn't be alone: she had lost too many people. Her son was gone. Her husband was gone. There was no one left.

'I was lonely,' Vivien whispers, picking up my train of thought. 'But neither could I abide anyone at the house. I couldn't bear the thought of stepping out into the world, let alone allowing it in. I was so lonely, and I…' She lifts her shoulders. 'I invented her. I acted her. I brought her back to life. Pathetic, isn't it.'

I try to work out what it is. In another context it would be troubling, insane even, but, sitting here next to her, listening to her account of her poor son's death, all I can feel for Vivien is sympathy and understanding. No wonder she had let go of her mind, when she had been made to let go of everything else. She had been fraught and confused and ultimately it was easier to play a role because then she didn't have to be herself. She didn't have to answer to anyone, least of all me, or any of the other help she'd been compelled to hire because she couldn't cope on her own.

I trip back over the times I saw the women leave the house – or, rather, the times I saw the person I believed to be Adalina leave the house. I never saw Vivien. I assumed she was hidden in the backs of cars, behind closed doors, that arch voice that interviewed me over the phone and when I arrived, assuming her to be the renowned recluse I'd heard about and whom I honestly had no expectation of meeting. But there had never been a hidden Vivien: she'd been in front of me the whole time.

Why hadn't I seen it? Now I know, I can pick out the echoes – the line of the cheekbones, the curve of the mouth, but, truly, there is so little in common between the woman before me and the starlet the world knew that anyone could have been fooled. Age, yes, but more than that: anguish. The years have changed Vivien wholly.

'Lili's been so real to me at times,' Vivien goes on. 'I've dreamed her – entire conversations with her, I don't know if they've happened or if I've made them up.'

'What did she do wrong?' I ask softly.

It was painful for her to remember.

'Lili talked me out of it,' Vivien says. 'I was all ready.

I was this close to removing Isabella from our lives, but at the last moment she stopped me. She told me it would destroy my husband. That I should have empathy for that siren because we had both been victims.' Vivien's shoulders tense against the memory. 'But I should have made her the victim,' she spits, 'before she got to my son. I told Lili what she was capable of. I told her it was Isabella or us – but did she listen? No. She looked me straight in the eye and asked me to trust her. She swore to me that we would be safe.'

There it is, the gleaming truth. 'If Max's aunt hadn't stopped you,' I say, 'Isabella wouldn't have been alive to kill Alfie.'

Vivien nods. 'But I never blamed Lili,' she whispers. 'How could I? It was Isabella – the evil belonged to her, no one else. From the moment I met her, I knew she meant me harm, but even I never suspected the lengths she was willing to go to. For the most part, it was a petty rivalry, vying to be the woman in my husband's life. She took it to a new place. She made me suffer more than any living soul should have to suffer.' Vivien grips my arm. 'The death of a child,' she says, 'is suffering beyond imagination. They say that time heals but it doesn't. I miss my baby every day.'

'Isabella regretted it.'

'Apparently. I only regret that she did away with herself before I could do it for her. After Alfie, she ran. The police were out looking for her but she disappeared into thin air. A week later, we woke to the body – or, rather, Salvatore woke us. She'd drowned herself in the place where she drowned him. She couldn't even leave me that, his burial ground – she couldn't even leave that pure. Forever that fountain is his and forever it is hers. She claimed him in the end, just as she'd always wanted.'

A thousand questions spring to my throat. None emerges.

'Do you know the worst part?' says Vivien. 'She made me trust her. In that final year, she became my friend. I actually felt *sorry* for her – can you believe that? I defended her, I felt compassion for her, I forgave her all that she had done against me. The night she took him, I went to bed early. I'll never forget her standing by the door, how she turned back into the room and held up a hand and said, "Good night."' Vivien swallows. 'All these years, I've looked for a clue in that. Something in the way she said it, some warning I might have missed and that could have made a difference. If I'd just taken Alfie into bed with me. If I'd just locked the door…'

Vivien's head bows. A tear drops on to her lap.

'You managed to keep it so quiet,' I venture. I want to touch her, put a hand on her, but I have the sense that such contact, such tenderness, might break her, like pressing a fingertip to a soap bubble only to make it vanish.

'Gio ensured it,' she says. 'We couldn't have people knowing how it happened. Of course, they found out that we'd lost him – both him and her in the same month. But over my dead body were they finding out how. I think somebody did – there was a report at the time that we fought to suppress.'

So Vivien became the woman she is today. Having stifled that giant event in her life, the obvious thing was to stifle the rest of it. She was the one who'd planted her diary by my door that night, at 3:12 a.m., the moment Isabella had perished. She'd *wanted* the truth to come out, and for me to be the one to find it.

'I never believed in God,' says Vivien. The change of tack makes me release the long breath I've been holding. 'My father was terrible and he turned me against it. But then I found out that it was only the god he'd been worshipping that didn't exist. Other ones did. I found another one. It's a god inside me, most of the time.' She nods to the crucifix. 'Not this one. Well, a version of this one, but it's not one I share. I don't come to church to be with other people. My church is wherever I am. It's in my soul and in my memories of my son. Only my god and I know that.'

She coughs. It begins mildly but quickly escalates, until she is doubled over, hacking into a handkerchief. Now I do rub her back and her spine feels thin and frail. All that time, the woman I supposed to be Adalina had been collecting the pills herself. I'd pictured her taking them upstairs to Vivien, counting them out, pressing her to swallow them with a beaker of water. All along it had been her. Her illness.

'I'm dying,' she says. The handkerchief comes away and I see an angry flash of blood. 'It will be soon. That's why I need to ask something of you.' New energy fires up her eyes. 'There you have it, my story, Lucy: you wanted it and there it is. Do what you like with it. After I'm gone, I won't care.'

I move to object: there is no possibility that I would ever exploit her story. Aside from a basic decency I would never compromise, I have had it done to me. I know what it's like to be on the receiving end of malicious gossip, and gossip they would. The world would salivate over her tragedy, when at the core of it was a broken woman who had lost her most sacred thing.

But she stops me. 'In exchange I ask for your help.'

'Of course.'

She licks dry lips. 'My husband,' she says. 'I don't know where he is. He left the Barbarossa right after Isabella's suicide. Losing Alfie was one thing. He refused to accept that Isabella had done it, even when they did the autopsy and confirmed her involvement…' She trails off; I decide not to ask. 'Then when she died it came crashing in… the double catastrophe he had suffered. We should have supported each other, but these things tear you apart, as individuals as well as husband and wife. Each of us mourned in our own way, shut off from the other. Gio's feelings about Isabella were different to mine, of course. I abominated her. I remember trying to think of any word stronger than that, some word that could pinpoint just how I detested her, but there wasn't any strong enough. Until I felt my fingers close around her throat, I would never know peace. He condemned her act, but he didn't condemn her. Not enough. He didn't admit that if he'd listened to me, it might have saved Alfie's life.'

I imagine what they were like when they first met, so in love, and the currents of deep affection that had character-ised their marriage. In another life, one free from Isabella, from the baggage of both their pasts, it might have been different. It might have been perfect. I can see that Vivien knows this, too.

'I must find him before I go,' she says, looking once more at me. She doesn't need to say where she is going. 'I have had to accept that all else is lost to me, but I know two things with certainty.' A beat. 'I know that my son is waiting for me. And I know that I must see Giovanni's face one more time before I die.'

'Is he still in Italy?'

'I don't know where he is. I haven't heard from him since that day he left in 1989. He could be dead... but I have to try. Or, you do. Please, Lucy. You're the only hope I have. Please, help me. Help me to find my husband.'

CHAPTER FORTY-NINE

She leaves me clutching a piece of paper. On it, she has written the address of her new residence: a retreat on Lake Como in the north of the country. It's a sanctuary for the sick, she tells me, where she can receive all the care she needs.

Vivien is not returning to the Barbarossa – the castillo is gone to her now. She will have said her goodbyes and deserted her demons. I watch her melt into the crowds until they swallow her up, and it must have taken such bravery to venture here, away from her quarantine and out into the world. She appears small, a glimpse of the woman she was. I think about her life, the loss and heartache, the glamour and grief, and it's all I can do not to run after her. What for? What can I do?

I realise there is much I want to say to her, so many words, about how the Barbarossa saved me; how her mystery drew me out of myself and back into the universe; and how if it weren't for her allowing me into her life, I might never have recovered my own. Our situations are leagues apart, but at the same time we are not so different. We both loved a man, we both faced another woman, and we both confronted a death that changed everything. But my story? It's a picture book compared with the saga of Vivien Lockhart. I only wish it hadn't ended so sadly for her. I glance down at the piece of paper. I am possessed by the need to achieve her request. I have to find Gio Moretti before it's too late – and I haven't got long.

Max calls. There is too much to go into over the phone, so I arrange to meet him later. I consider how I am going to begin telling him everything, starting with the truth about Vivien's identity, the invention of Adalina... and ending with the death of her son. All this time I've been obsessing over my own predicament, regretting and resenting and waiting for life to start back up again, but I haven't had a clue about what it is to really struggle. To hell with James Calloway and his selfish agenda. To hell with anyone in England who passes judgement on my actions, when they cannot begin to comprehend the reality. Vivien has proven that the only people who matter are those at the centre of the storm: they know the facts. The rest falls away.

*

I sit outside the church for some time, working out my next move. Giovanni Moretti hasn't been seen or heard from in decades; the last Vivien knew of him was of his retreating back as it abandoned the Barbarossa, a single bag slung over his shoulder.

'The sun was setting behind him,' Vivien told me as she departed. 'I always thought he was sent to me as an angel, and never more so than in that moment...'

I'm distracted from my thoughts by the sudden, screeching sound of a siren.

It slices across the silence so abruptly that I startle, and am drawn out through the church courtyard and on to the street. The scene that greets me is one of chaos. Crowds push and shove, gathering towards something visible from the bridge.

'What's going on?' I ask the man next to me, in Italian.

'There's a blaze over the hill,' he tells me, and as he does I turn and see the smoke rising in a plume in the distance. 'They're saying it's the Castillo Barbarossa.'

*

Before I know it, I'm sprinting; the acrid smell of burning fills my nostrils, the grey jet of ash and hope rising high on the hill. I don't realise how good my Italian has become until I'm bartering with a guy at the side of the road to loan me his Vespa. In minutes I'm thrusting cash into his hand and mounting the bike.

Emergency vehicles have clogged up the streets and the traffic is a non-starter, so I duck into a shortcut and loop through the backstreets, frustrated that I can't go faster, willing the roads to disappear beneath my wheels and the cobbles to give way to the hillsides that have become home. *Home*. The word stirs me, because surely the Barbarossa is anything but – that strange, remote, intimidating castle I stumbled upon all those weeks before. And yet, I race for it as I would for my father's house, the house where I grew up, the house where my mum died. It matters to me.

As the streets narrow to lanes and the lanes climb, people are stopping to watch the horizon; the blare of sirens draws everything taut. Smoke spreads, filling the blue sky with churning grey, and it's more than the expulsion of powder and dust; it's a living thing, a shape that swells with love and hate and death and disorder.

I pass a woman relaying events into her phone, a group of boys filming the action. The Barbarossa is an institution here, as much a part of the Fiesole hills as the lemon groves and the tiny churches with their cool-to-touch frescoes and gentle bell chimes that ring out in the morning. As I draw nearer and hook up with the original road, the scent is stronger and the engine wails are louder, interspersed now with human voices and shouted directions, the rescue team working together.

Rescue. Is Vivien there? No, she's gone. A thought crosses my mind, a thought about Vivien and the fire and how it started, but the sirens drown it.

At last, I reach the wall of the castillo, and now I can see the house – or what is left of it. Giant orange flames leap from window to window in the upper vaults; fire dances and spits; clouds of soot billow from every wound. I ditch the bike and dash for the gate, unable in any case to manoeuvre past the raft of trucks gathered there, hoses spraying, ladders mounted, futile attempts at harnessing pandemonium. The Barbarossa flares and glows, like a scream held for years in the throat.

'Signora, you're not allowed past here,' says one of the *carabinieri*.

'I live here.'

'Your name?'

'Lucy Whittaker – I'm a friend of Vivien Lockhart.'

'Where is Vivien?'

I open my mouth to tell him where she's headed, the scribbled details hidden in my pocket, but I stop. 'She's not here,' I say, and his expression relaxes.

'You're certain?'

I nod. There is no doubt in my mind, and, seeing the Barbarossa alive and aglow, violent and frantic, I know that my thought about Vivien and the fire was right. She was never coming back. There would be nowhere to come back to.

'What happened?' I ask, though I know.

The officer nods to the blazing roof. 'The attic,' he says. 'Someone dropped a match up there. Whoever did this meant to: they wanted it destroyed. Likely a local trouble-maker, we've had reports in the area. Unfortunately places like this attract attention – sometimes the wrong kind. It's terrible, to do this to a family home.' The hot glare dances in his eyes. 'All those memories gone up in smoke.'

All those memories…

They were precisely why she had done it.

The man is called back to action, and I'm left to watch history turn to dust. Until I am drawn to a figure I recognise, crouching by the wall on a bag of his belongings.

Salvatore. I go to him.

'She left,' he says, not taking his eyes from the fire.

'Yes.'

'Did she do it?'

'I think so.'

His expression is unreadable, his tone without feeling. 'It's all gone. I said it would. I said you should get out before it took you too.'

'Where will you go, Salve?'

He waits a moment, then shows me something I have never seen before: his smile. No, not quite a smile, a remnant of one – what his smile might once have been.

'Anywhere,' he tells me. 'Anywhere but here.'

'You're free,' I say. 'It's over.'

He lifts his head, and when our gazes lock this time it is with understanding. In that instant, Salvatore knows that I know. I know what he saw, what he found, and how it ruined him. And I glimpse in him his release from the house, from Vivien Lockhart, a shade of the man he used to be, the Barbarossa lessening its grip bit by bit until it lets him go. He appears younger, as young as he was before it happened.

A deafening clap severs our exchange. I turn back to the castle in time to see a portion of the façade crumble away. It does so with a casual slip, as smooth and deadly as the break of an avalanche. As if in slow motion, the tranche of rock falls to the ground, scattering the crowd of fighters beneath. Then, with an almighty boom, it crashes into stone, into a silent, twisted fish, its mouth open and empty to the sky.

It takes a second for me to process what has been struck. Then, with the spray of water bursting into the air, I realise.

'It's over,' repeats Salvatore. 'It's over.'

CHAPTER FIFTY

Five months later

At last, I'm ready. I'm going home.

As I queue to check in at Pisa airport, I only wish I had better news. But I know I tried my best. I said as much in my letter to Vivien.

Please know that I searched for him tirelessly… There was nothing I didn't try, no avenue I didn't explore… Over the past few months I have scoured the country from top to tail, followed a lead into France, down into Spain, even, at one point, chasing up contacts in America. The closest I got was with the wife of an ex-colleague of Gio's, who said she had last seen him running a boat-hire venture for holidaymakers in St Barts. But by the time I reached it, the venture had folded and elusive Gio had moved on again. The contact thought he might have changed his surname, but she couldn't remember to what – his grandmother's maiden name, perhaps? Cue a refreshed search, beginning with the census detailing his grandmother as a Bastianelli, but there were no Giovanni Bastianellis to be found anywhere across the globe…

The search went cold.

If there was anything else I could do, I would, I wrote in my letter. Before sending it, I called the Lake Como retreat to ask after Vivien's wellbeing – if I'm honest, to ask if she was alive. She was, but part of me feared my sending of the note would snuff out any remaining candle she still held. Knowing of my search for Gio and the anticipation of his return would be what kept her going. But I had drawn it out long enough. I owed her honesty. And I could not delay my own life any further.

I, too, am sad to leave him behind: this man I've never met.

I shared this with Vivien in my message – I guess it was my way of showing her that I cared, and of telling her goodbye. In finding out so much about Giovanni Moretti, his early life and the loss of his beloved parents, his career and move to the States, his subsequent return to Italy and, of course, the greatest love affair of his life, with Vivien, I feel I know him. And, in knowing him, I am confident in how he felt about her, a sense cemented by the many past acquaintances I interviewed. Gio had been devoted to Vivien from the start. Any considerations he had held for Isabella over the years were held purely through a sense of sibling duty and regret.

As I hand my passport to the check-in desk, I hope this will bring Vivien some small comfort in her final days, knowing that her memories of their love were true and lasting. For what else does she have? How I would have treasured the chance to bring him to her, to see her face light up after so many years in the shade.

I gaze up at the Departures board: London, Heathrow, in two hours from now. My time in Italy seems not only to have brought me to another country but also to another time, and to leave it feels strange, like surfacing from a dream.

There's a wince in my chest when I think of Max.

What is he doing now? Where is he? Who is he with? That last one hurts, but I have no right. I told him months ago, before I left in search of Gio, that I wouldn't be back. Part of it was the complication of having a companion, especially one whom I knew would prove a diversion; and part of it was some small voice in my heart telling me that this was scarred ground, and did I really want another person treading on it so soon? Self-preservation, whatever you call it. It was the right choice. The last thing I need is another complicated relationship. It was fun while I was here, a distraction brought about through our connection to the Barbarossa – but once I'm home, it will fade to insignificance just as that house will. It's for the best.

'Why do you have to go?' I will never forget how Max searched my eyes, right before I went. 'She lied to us. She's been lying all this time. Why her?'

I tried to explain it – how the death of that boy Alfie played on a loop in my mind; the tragedy of Isabella right after him; the demolition of the fountain when the Barbarossa burned down. Max said it was done with – I should move on. But I couldn't. In this quest for Vivien, I had found my own shot at redemption.

It occurs to me that thinking of Max shouldn't sting

after all this time. I've been gone from him longer than I knew him. And yet… Time doesn't always have the answers. Spending ten years with someone doesn't mean it's any better than in spending ten days – it's just different. But still that part of me holds strong. It's too soon. James hurt me and I haven't yet healed. Max isn't the answer.

Besides, I ponder as I meander through Departures, blindly scoping magazines and souvenirs – including a postcard of a slice of Fiesole that details the Barbarossa, like a weathered jewel on the hillside – we are from two separate worlds. Even I've become distanced from my life in London; imagine how it would be for him. No, Max belongs here, in Italy, in my adventure with the Barbarossa. He belongs in my past.

*

We land fifteen minutes ahead of schedule. I drank on the plane and my head feels warm. It counters the sharp grey edges of an England I've forgotten, somehow more real and immediate than Italy – but not, I am pleased to report, as real and immediate as when I left. The last time I was here had been in a state of fear and distress.

Now, I feel calm. Or is that the wine?

Heads that might have turned months, even weeks, ago, do not. Newspaper stands that once screamed my name have moved on to other more pressing reports. The world does not revolve around me. It never did. Yes, I got some hate, and yes, people held a mild interest in me for a while

– but God knows there are stories that warrant greater attention than mine.

I must look changed, too. My hair is shorter; the worry took its toll and I'm slimmer than I've ever been. My skin is a deep brown. My wardrobe is different.

As I pass through Arrivals, I'm so caught up in a renewed sense of purpose, and in the many people I need to make amends with, starting with one person in particular, that at first I don't hear my name being called. Then it comes again.

'Lucy?'

I turn. It's Bill. She's holding a bunch of slightly sad-looking carnations.

'Your dad told me your flight,' she says.

It's so long since I've seen her. Months since I've spoken to her – our fight was the last time. I drop my bag and hug her. The flowers are squashed between us.

'I'm sorry,' I say.

'I'm sorry, too,' she says, and we stay like that for a long time, just hugging.

*

Back at my dad's house in the Cotswolds, the weeks slowly pass. It's a nice slowness, a welcome one that eases me back into my former life. I spend my days walking the dog, curled up with a book, dunking digestive biscuits into proper tea. I know I am hiding from the world, that sooner or later I'll have to step back into it, but for now this is a necessary recuperation, a shedding of the old skin in preparation to become someone new. With each hour, Italy recedes in my memory, its outlines shimmering, its colours fading, and some nights I wake at that dead hour, three a.m., and question if it ever happened at all. The Barbarossa could be on another planet for how distant it seems now. I cannot believe it is gone. It will always be alive inside me, the gardens, the Lilac Room, the portraits, the attic, the fountain...

My dad makes me tell him everything about Vivien and the house. I don't plan to, it's complicated, but one look in his eyes and I can never lie to him again. I've always seen him as this frail old man in need of being taken care of, when actually he is a strong and brave person who has survived against the odds. I know another of those.

He listens as I relay it all, winding up with Vivien's deception and my promise to her that I would find Gio Moretti. And in searching for that man during my time away, instead I discovered myself. My future. Things I had thought were lost.

'This man of yours,' he pushes softly, 'Max. Why not give him a chance?'

I shake my head. 'It's not happening, Dad. Let's not talk about it.'

My sisters say the same, and it's weird to hear them give me advice when all our lives it's been the other way round. But I know what I'm doing. I admit that my sisters have pursued paths that I have always, on some level, envied – I was jealous of them escaping our village and forging their journeys; I resented that I had enabled their glittering worlds and in turn my own became drab and unexciting – but Italy is a place they will never know like I do. They will never see the Barbarossa, catch its scent of old leather and stone, touch the dovecote in the Oval, or walk between the lemon groves, boughs heavy with fruit, to get down to the city at night. This is mine.

For once, I'm not the one stuck at home. With only the lightest account of my time there, Helen's rich engagement suddenly doesn't seem so appealing, nor does Sophie's glamorous catwalk, nor do Tilda's runaway jaunts with her surfer boyfriend. At last, I have something to say, and I'm more than their stand-in, second-rate mother. I have a story that none of them will ever know. It's my secret. And I see it in their eyes: that their sister finally set out on her own, away from them, to independence she had forgotten. More than that, they witness the way my dad looks at me because he and I have a bond that they missed out on. Now, I see them grasping at ways to help him – 'I'll make the coffee, Dad,' 'Let me give you a hand with that,' 'No, Dad, you put your feet up,' – when he doesn't need help any more.

I think about what Dad said about me being a good person. 'Just like your mum,' he tells me one night, kissing my cheek before I go up to bed.

I think of the woman on the train that day in Italy, and I go to sleep smiling.

*

Bill is on at me about going back to London. She's since left our old flat but there's a new place in Shoreditch that she's keen on, sharing with a couple of guys. I feel as if I'm letting her down by not being suitably excited about this – the men as well as the place – but I can't help it. I don't want to return to the city. I've been trying to figure out what I do want to do, but it's not being a PA and it's not commuting in on the tube every day. Dad suggests I retrain in a skill I feel passionate about. I search online and come across an ad for an apprenticeship restoring an old English Heritage property in Cambridge. It seems far-fetched at first, but I keep the window open, and every day I open my tablet and it's there, blinking back at me, waiting.

It's on one of these days when I'm meandering idly that I decide to Google Vivien. I don't expect anything new to come up, but then I see a name I recognise:

RUNAWAY CULT LEADER FOUND. Gilbert Lockhart, father to one-time actress Vivien, was picked up by police on Sunday morning outside an all-day bar in Houston, Texas, and taken in for questioning. Octogenarian Mr Lockhart has evaded authorities since his disappearance from his daughter's Italian home in 1988, having stolen the family's assets, a fortune thought to be, in modern currency, in excess of twenty million Euros. Mr Lockhart claims to no longer be in possession of the money, having funnelled his wealth into the notorious Sixth Gate cult. The now-defunct sect hit headlines in 2003 for the Blakestown Massacre, resulting in the mass suicide of fourteen people, and has long been associated with fanaticism and religious radicalisation. Ms Lockhart has been informed of the development.

I read the item twice then immediately search for more details. Other sites report the same. So Gilbert Lockhart finally lost his mind, if he had ever had possession of it in the first place. And for all his lies and violence and betrayals, he wound up an old, staggering drunk on a sidewalk, bankrupt and destitute. I wonder if he has anything else to show for his years, or whether his self-destruction is it.

My mind buzzes with the information, but one thing sticks:

Vivien is alive.

CHAPTER FIFTY-ONE

We're all together for that Sunday lunch Dad promised. Mary fusses around us, nervous with my sisters and especially with me, because this was our house with our mother and we're not used to feeling like guests. But I don't mind. I like it. I like to be one of them, not the parent. We've all moved on. We're all moving forward.

It's chaos. Helen and her betrothed are bickering about the cost of their wedding venue, while Sophie keeps disappearing into the kitchen to take a call with her agent. Tilda refuses alcohol and looks peaky and I wonder if she might be pregnant, but nobody else seems to notice and of course I don't raise it.

Somehow, Mary manages to get us all to sit down just after one.

'Tell us about James again, Lucy, please!' says Helen, passing the potatoes to our dad. 'This is a great story,' she nudges her fiancé, 'you've got to hear it.'

Embarrassed, I wave her down.

'Go *on*!' encourages Sophie. Once upon a time, I would never have commanded the attention of this congregation, always the one who was batted off with her ultimatums about homework or administration of curfews.

'It was nothing, really,' I say. 'I bumped into him last week.'

'*Such* a bastard,' mutters Tilda.

Sophie smiles. 'Have you heard this, Dad?'

Dad nods. He tops up my wine. 'She handled it beautifully.'

'What did you say to him?' asks Mary.

'I hope you told him exactly what you thought of him,' says Tilda.

The thing was, I hadn't planned to. It hadn't been important.

It hadn't occurred to me to feel ill will towards James – I had spent so long obsessing over him that, when the time came for real anger, I think my mind was too exhausted with him to bother. Ultimately, his behaviour hadn't surprised me. And I'd had so much else occupying my thoughts, more important stuff, that he'd kind of faded to insignificance. Even so, seeing my family's anticipation, I can't help but take some small pleasure in recounting the details once more. After all, the opportunity had presented itself perfectly and out of the blue – how could I have resisted?

So I tell them how I'd been visiting Bill in London, and how one day I'd taken myself off shopping down Carnaby Street. This is something I thought I'd never do again – just amble about the city, as free and easy as the next person. But it turned out to be true, what they said: something about today's news being tomorrow's chip paper. Almost a year on from Grace Calloway's death, people had forgotten me. My name might raise a few eyebrows, but my face, well, that had hardly ever been in the news, and even if it had my changed appearance extinguished any trace. My scandal had been eclipsed by the next unfortunate fodder, over whom the public could wield their righteousness: some race row on *Big Brother*, the latest *Strictly* affair or a footballer caught cheating with his brother's wife. I still feel deep remorse about what happened. Often, I check to see how the children are doing. To James's credit, he is devoting more time to them these days, and by design or coincidence gets pictured playing with them in the park, or taking them off to Dubai to swim with dolphins in a six-star retreat. The cynical part of me suspects it is a deliberate PR move, painting him as this martyred single dad, but I hope he has genuinely changed – in that respect, at least. He hasn't changed as far as women are concerned.

I recount how I'd slipped into a café and then, bam, there he was. He was sitting with a brunette. Even though her back was to me, I knew that it was Natasha Fenwick: the sharp line of the bare neck, and her precise, swinging ponytail. They were laughing, and there was a note in that laugh that dismayed me utterly, the disrespect, the selfishness, and before I knew it I was stalking to their table.

He had a coffee, and she had a spaghetti Bolognese. It struck me as odd that she should be eating when he wasn't, and something other than a lettuce leaf. Almost as if somebody on my side had painted this picture and added in the detail, a tempting anomaly, whispering at my shoulder, *Go on, do it, you know you want to do it...*

I saw him double take, through appreciation before recognition. He thought I was some hot woman about to ask for his number, never mind that he was sitting with his girlfriend, and his willingness to dismiss that fact entirely only proved to me for the final time what a cheap shit I had once adored. But when he made the connection, oh, that was satisfying: total face-drop, mouth hanging open as if he'd been slapped. Perhaps he thought he was about to be. I thought about it too.

'Hello, James,' I said. Natasha's shoulders curled. I saw her thinking, *Please don't make a scene.* I thought: *Bad luck. You wrote this farce and now the curtain's up.* To his credit, James said hello back. He didn't pretend not to know me. Maybe he saw in my eyes that I wasn't the same person he had taken advantage of.

It felt like a long time that I was standing there, and that the rest of the café was transfixed. In reality, it can't have been more than a few seconds and nobody else cared. Regardless, I picked up Natasha's plate of pasta and emptied it over James's head. Tendrils of spaghetti dripped down the sides of his face, brown meat in his hair and an audible squelch as a pat of it landed in his YSL-suited lap. I took my time emptying the bowl, shaking out the last clinging slime of tomato before replacing it on the table. Natasha gasped, a little cry of appalled surprise that wasn't quite brave enough to be anything else, anything louder – anything that might challenge me because she, too, sensed that I could not be challenged.

James took it, his face grey and unmoved. I expect he had wondered how this episode would play out, when the past finally caught up with him. I don't know, he might have preferred public humiliation to the chilling alternative of a heart to heart.

There were a million things I could have said and they all rushed up at once. Natasha was too incidental to bother with: she could have been one of a hundred women and I felt sorry for her. But James… Yes, I wanted to tell him how he had made me feel, how horribly he had treated me and what a lying cheat he had been from the start, and all this was on my tongue and I could taste every word and then I swallowed it. I thought: *I'm done with being angry. I'm tired of feeling hate.* And if I'd believed he would listen or that it would have changed anything for the better, maybe, but I didn't believe it. James would never understand what he had done. He was doing it all over again, with Natasha. He didn't care about me. He never had.

So I turned on my heel and left, the door swinging shut behind me.

'Go, Lucy!' Helen enthuses now.

'It's quite a story,' agrees Mary, with a smile. I drink more wine. It gives me a glow to remember it: the dignity I took away with me; the mess I left behind.

For the rest of the meal, I'm content to listen to my sisters' conversation, getting slowly light-headed and relaxed. It's a surprise, therefore, when the doorbell rings. Nobody is expecting a visitor. Since I'm closest, I go.

'Who is it?' Tilda calls, before I've opened the door.

At first, when I do, I'm not sure of the answer – and even if I were I'm not confident I can speak. But I do know this person, from a dream I once had, a lemon-scented dream, except he's older, much older, with one black eye and one green.

CHAPTER FIFTY-TWO

Italy, Winter 2016

The lake is grey-blue and shining. Its surface changes as clouds pass, dipping it in ink one second and throwing cool light on it the next. It is the kind of lake one could look at every day, and still discover something new. There is a timeless quality; its mirror reflected long before this life began, and will reflect long after it ends.

Vivien's rest home is nestled in the valley. I've seen pictures online but nothing prepares me for the serenity of the place. The structure is Alpine-looking, with wooden balconies and a long, sloping roof, and out front is a collection of reclining loungers. All around, the gravity of rolling hills cushions and protects.

We step into Reception, but the desk is empty. There is a notice board tacked with fliers: timetables for afternoon trips, tea and cake in the garden, a menu for that evening's supper. It's a far cry from the wild, ruthless glamour of the Barbarossa, but Vivien won't see it that way. She will enjoy the orderliness, the compact quiet, and most of all how every floor and wall is anonymous to her: no secrets or shadows.

I tap the bell. Gio Moretti steps up beside me. In his

sixties, he remains a strikingly handsome man, and those eyes are something else.

'Are you ready?' I ask.

He turns to me, black and green, like dark sea crashing against an emerald shore. 'I've waited this many years,' he says. There is passion in his eyes that I once saw in my fantasies as a girl, imagining what true love looked like. There it is. Gio has it. 'I don't mind waiting a little longer.'

On the wall, the clock spits seconds. *Tick, tick, tick…*

My hands are shaking, so I put them in my pockets. I can't believe he's next to me. I can't believe I've brought him back to her.

I was amazed when Gio turned up at my father's door. I'd been difficult to find, he told me. Me? What about him? It transpired that he had been searching for me the entire time I had been searching for him – and so, of course, had never stayed put, moving from place to place, just as I was, each of us seeking out the other.

He had read about the Barbarossa burning down. My name came up, as it had in a few articles published at the time. 'I had to find out who you were,' he told me that day at Dad's. It was clear I had worked at the castle, and had a friendship with Maximo Conti, whose aunt he had employed. 'It didn't take much,' he said. 'You knew more than you should. And I hoped you'd know where Vivien was.'

Ever since Gio materialised, all through our shared accounts, our painful revelations, the decision to come out here, every moment of the flight from London, I've been able to think about only one thing: Vivien's face when she sees him again.

Will she cry? Will she laugh? Will she run to him? It's so right to picture them holding each other, together. Looking at Gio, I can see he's anticipating the same. 'My arms have felt empty for too long,' he told me, over one of our many cups of coffee, Dad bringing refills and hovering by the door, pretending not to listen.

During our confidences, I swung between trust and caution.

Why hadn't he tried to contact his wife before? He had, he pledged, in the early days. But then… Too many vicious words had passed between them, toxic accusations that could never be retracted. Vivien wrote to him soon after he walked out – who could blame her? Gio certainly didn't – telling him they had reached the end and she could never see him again. Isabella was his fault: Vivien had warned him from the start. 'I should have kept trying,' Gio disclosed. 'But Vivien was waking me up to everything I already knew and didn't want to face. I'd always known that Isabella was ruined – but I never opened my eyes and saw how much. There wasn't a way back for her. She'd gone too far down the road to destruction, alone, mapping out her vengeance. I just never thought she would hurt me. Taking Alfie from us… Never mind Vivien longing to kill her, I'd kill her myself.' He'd shaken his head. 'There was always a part of Isabella I couldn't get to, as much as I tried – and I ignored it because it frightened me. Alfie was our world. We loved him so much…'

On the counter, there is a leather-bound Visitor Book. Gio lifts the cover; his long fingers turn the pages delicately, respectfully. There is a column for entrants to record who they have come to see. Vivien's name is absent.

Has she wished for company, or has she preferred life without it?

Please, help me. Help me to find my husband.

I did find him, Vivien, I think. *I found him. He's here. Look.*

I ring the bell again.

It was a relief, for me, to be able to share Vivien's desire: that she was as set on their reunion as he was. Gio's reaction to her present state had been hard to read. He seemed to accept news of her illness with stoicism, as if he had thought such a thing inevitable. When I shared her deception over Adalina, he'd nodded, and said:

'It's a long time to be alone.'

I am about to call out, impatient now, when we catch sight of a frail woman at the end of the corridor. Gio moves before I do. I am not sure what I see: a flash of white-blonde hair, brittle shoulders, before she turns a corner and disappears.

'There she is.'

I don't know if he says it, or I do. But then we're through the doors and following, Gio up front, and my knees feel wobbly and my heart is thumping.

What will Gio see when he looks at her? Will she be the woman he married or the woman he lost? Will she be the film star or the grieving mother? Will she be the wife he fought with, or the one he made love with? Will she be the girl who screamed at him, or the victim weeping over their son's body? Watching Gio rush ahead, it strikes me how much guilt this man has carried. His quarantine has been self-imposed, a shame borne of his inability to see Isabella for the creature she really was.

But none of that matters now. Not now they're going to be together again.

A shout rings out from behind us.

'Signor!' a nurse calls. 'You can't go through there!'

Gio pushes through a second set of doors and we round a bend. Several things happen at once. First there is the woman with the white-blonde hair, easing herself into a chair in the courtyard, and, now we see her face, she is not Vivien at all. Then there is an open suite right there next to us, and on the wall a tablet reading VIVIEN LOCKHART. And when we look inside, we cannot understand what we see.

The room is empty and the bed is stripped.

Silence.

The sheets are covered in winter sunlight. I see dust mites drifting through a shaft of warmth. Somewhere in the distance, a long way away, a dog barks.

'Are you looking for Signora Lockhart?'

I turn to the nurse. She's supposed to be mad, and I wish she were. I wish I saw anger instead of concern. I wait for Gio to speak. He doesn't.

'We're looking for Vivien,' I say, and the words are leaden in my mouth.

'I'm very sorry,' the nurse says. 'Vivien died this morning.'

The room throbs, once, hard. Its edges dissolve, reassemble.

This morning we were boarding our flight. This morning we were nearly here.

She can't be! I want to shout. *She's here! You're lying!*

But I know she's not. I'm afraid to look at Gio, but he doesn't make me.

Instead, he walks to Vivien's bed. He runs a hand across those sun-kissed sheets and he bows his head. He murmurs something in Italian that I can't hear.

'I'll leave you alone,' says the nurse gently. 'Vivien is in the chapel if you'd like to say goodbye. I'd be happy to show you where.'

She leaves us. I don't know whether I should go too, let Gio be alone, but before I can decide he turns to me. I expect to read all sorts of emotions in his face, mirrors of my own a hundred times over – frustration at not having got here sooner, anger at the injustice of death, despair at how it has cheated us of our ending.

I read none of these things.

All I can see when I look at Gio Moretti is peace.

'She's with him now,' he says.

My voice is a whisper. 'But what about you?'

Gio smiles. 'I won't lose her again,' he says, and passes his hand through the golden sunbeam, alive, shimmering, glimmering, light. 'She's everywhere.'

I close my eyes. I see Vivien walking away from the Barbarossa. I see the fire behind her, the ghosts dissolved. I see her start to run.

'We were too late,' I say.

He shakes his head.

'No, we weren't. This was Vivien's time. She was ready.'

*

We step out into the cold. Gio and the nurse go ahead. The chapel is down by the water, a modest building on the lip of the lake. It's hard to imagine her there.

I stop. This is his, now. Theirs.

'Thank you, Lucy,' Gio says. 'For bringing us back together.'

I want to say something meaningful, but my heart is heavy and I'm afraid I will cry. I nod, take his hand, and he squeezes life back into mine before letting it go.

I watch him walk across the lawn towards her, the gentle slope in the grass. There is a quiet ripple where the lake comes into shore, blue, clear, quiet. I feel cold, and wrap my coat tighter around me.

'Hey...'

Max slips an arm round my shoulder and draws me close.

We stand together as the distance between Gio and Vivien gets narrower, Gio taking his time, not hurrying, for they have time now, whatever time is left.

Max kisses my hair and I lean into him, closing my eyes, safe.

'You did the right thing,' he says.

And, as I watch Gio open the door to the chapel, pausing

briefly before he vanishes inside, I know that I did. I did the right thing for Vivien, and for Gio.

I did the right thing for me.

My mum knew it, when I didn't. When I was ready to run, she told me to stay. She knew I wasn't finished with the Barbarossa yet – and it wasn't finished with me. I was meant to find this secret and the secret turned into a key, and the key would be the opening to the rest of my life. She knew that our worlds, Vivien's and mine, had yet to discover their meeting point – and this was it. This day, this hour, this place.

I set Vivien Lockhart free, and she did the same for me. One fate balanced against the other, a future in exchange for a past.

I turn to Max and kiss him, the deepest kiss I've ever given, deep with desire and intent and every good thing I will never let slip away.

'What was that for?' He laughs, stroking my cheek.

'We're alive,' I say.

'We are.' He smiles. 'So come on.'

I take his hand and we walk back to the car, and he warms my fingers in his, shooting me that sideways smile that I love. 'Buy you an ice cream?' he says.

'It's freezing!'

'Limoncello, then.' He hugs me as we walk. 'Warm you up a bit.'

As we drive away from the lake, I know in my heart that Vivien wasn't alone when she died. She was with him. Her son. She saw his face, and he saw hers.

They were together.

There is wonder in this, I think, as we thread between soft green hills and out towards the road. There is wonder in Max's hand as it rests on my knee. There is wonder in the sky, and the earth, and the burst of birdsong as bright and clear as an open window on a February morning. There is wonder in knowing that Vivien has found her peace – and that the end of her story might just be where mine begins.

EPILOGUE

It was always the same dream, and she moved into it for the last time just like any other. A bright light, gathering pace from a sheet of dark. A lucid thought, a picture more real than any she could fathom in waking hours. She stepped towards the light, arms open, weak, and she knew it was a trick, but suddenly there she was, blissful, forgetting, her lips on his forehead, his soft skin and his smell, inside the deepest parts of her, never gone, never dimmed, a candle shimmering against absolute black.

Come with me.

I've been waiting.

She thinks: *I've been waiting too.*

The water, still and cool and silver and quiet. Inviting.

Come with me...

It feels sublime to hold him, her son, her boy; for the first time he is real, the weight of him in her arms, living, bright, that wriggle of energy as he goes to break free and show her the way. She takes his hand and follows him into the glow.

ACKNOWLEDGEMENTS

Thank you to Clio Cornish, my exceptional editor, whose understanding of this story and ideas to make it better have been invaluable. To the whole team at HQ, especially Lisa Milton, Nick Bates, Louise McGrory and Jennifer Porter. To Lesley Jones for her sensitive copyedit. Also to Tory Lyne-Pirkis at Midas PR for being the best in the business – and the most fun too!

To Madeleine Milburn, Thérèse Coen and Hayley Steed, who work so passionately and brilliantly for my books.

To Mum, Dad, Toria and Mark for enabling me to write with a baby.

And to little Charlotte. I love you more than I can say.

HQ
One Place. Many Stories

The home of bold, innovative
and empowering publishing.

Follow us online

 @HQStories

 @HQStories

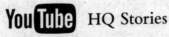 HQStories

HQ Stories

 HQMusic

Bound by blood.
Separated by scandal.

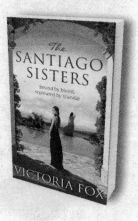

Twins Calida and Terisita Santiago have never known a
world without each other… until Terisita is wrenched
from their Argentinian home to be adopted by world-
famous actress Simone Geddes.

Now, while Terisita is provided with all that money can
buy, Calida must fight her way to the top – her only
chance of reuniting with her twin.

But no-one could have predicted the explosive events
which finally bring the Santiago sisters into the
spotlight together…

The eagerly awaited debut novel from the much-loved winner of *The Great British Bake Off*

The four Amir sisters are the only young Muslims in the quaint English village of Wyvernage.

On the outside, despite not quite fitting in with their neighbours, the Amirs are happy. But on the inside, each sister is secretly struggling.

Yet when family tragedy strikes, it brings the Amir sisters closer together and forces them to learn more about life, love, faith and each other than they ever thought possible.

One Place. Many Stories

In Nazi-occupied Holland, seventeen-year-old
Noa snatches a baby from a train bound for the
concentration camps, fleeing with him into
the snowy wilderness surrounding the train tracks.

Passing through the woods is a German circus,
led by the infamous Herr Neuroff. They agree to take
in Noa and the baby, on one condition: to earn her
keep, Noa must master the flying trapeze – under
the tutorage of mysterious aerialist, Astrid.

Soaring high above the crowds, Noa and Astrid
must learn to trust one another…or plummet.
But with the threat of war closing in, loyalty
can become the most dangerous trait of all.

One Place. Many Stories

'Have you met them yet, the new couple?'

When Gav and Lou move into the house next door,
Sara spends days plucking up courage to say hello.
The neighbours are glamorous, chaotic and just
a little eccentric. They make the rest of
Sara's street seem dull by comparison.

When the hand of friendship is extended, Sara is
delighted and flattered — and the more time Sara
spends with Gav and Lou, the more she longs to make
changes in her own life. But those changes will come
at a price. Soon Gav and Lou will be asking things
they've no right to ask of their neighbours, with
shattering consequences for all of them…

One Place. Many Stories